the Elf-King's Roses

Diane Duane

ASPECT®

WARNER BOOKS

An AOL Time Warner Company

WARNER BOOKS EDITION

Copyright © 2002 by Diane Duane

Cover design by Shasti O'Leary Soudant / Don Puckey
Cover illustration by Don Maitz
Book design by Giorgetta Bell McRee

Aspect® name and logo are registered trademarks of Warner Books, Inc.

Warner Books, Inc.
1271 Avenue of the Americas
New York, NY 10020

Visit our Web site at www.twbookmark.com.

An AOL Time Warner Company

Printed in the United States of America

First Printing: November 2002

10 9 8 7 6 5 4 3 2 1

ATTENTION: SCHOOLS AND CORPORATIONS
WARNER books are available at quantity discounts with bulk purchase for educational, business, or sales promotional use. For information, please write to: SPECIAL SALES DEPARTMENT, WARNER BOOKS, 1271 AVENUE OF THE AMERICAS, NEW YORK, N.Y. 10020

WAR AGAINST THE ELF-KING

"Lee!" Gelert barked, and threw himself from the rock spine, straight at Lee and the Elf-King. They tumbled over the stones, Gelert coming down on top of them; and blaster fire from the silent craft that had come down on them blew the top of the spire to chips and stinging splinters. Lee reached out to grab the Elf-King's arm, pulling him after her, but something held her still. He was looking at the Craft as it swung around for another pass, simply looking at it—

Every part of Lee prickled intolerably, her eyes burned—and lightning came streaking down out of the tattered sky to strike the craft full on. Deafened, blinded, she was thrown back; it was some moments before her eyes cleared enough of the afterimage of the lightning to show her surroundings again.

"Nasty," Lee said softly. "Were you expecting a coup d'etat?"

"For a century or so now," the Elf-King said.

more . . .

"Duane handles every aspect of her work with care and expertise."
—*West Coast Review of Books*

"Duane has a rare gift for weaving a tale."
—*Midwest Review of Books*

"Duane is a compelling master-storyteller."
—*Transit*

Books by Diane Duane

The Book of Night With Moon

To Visit the Queeen

For Don Maass,
the first one into the garden

The going from a world we know
to one a wonder still
is like the child's adversity
whose vista is a hill;

Behind the hill is sorcery
and everything unknown,
but will the secret compensate
for climbing it alone?

—Emily Dickinson: #1603

Stealing
the Elf-King's
Roses

Commodities Week

Last week's confirmation by the Nobel high-energy research team at CERN's Erqumitsuliaq (Greenland) Quadruple Array Survey Collider of the existence of a sixth alternate Earth has had widespread effects on the worlds' commodities markets, especially due to the continuing uncertainty as to how soon trade could be permitted with the new world (dubbed "Terra" by the Nobel team).

The team director, Dr. Birgitta Helgasdottir of the University of Mainz, confirmed at a press conference Thursday that the new world has not yet produced the MacIlwain worldgating breakthrough. Speculation continues to run high as to whether the growing current economic crisis will cause the veto powers to push the UN&ME into allowing an exception to the "technological parity" ruling, and inviting "Terra" into the Five-Geneva Pact. However, there has been early concern in the marketplace about the economic status of the new world, and its inevitable effects on otherwordly marketplaces.

"We haven't had a chance as yet to study the situation in depth," says Professor Ron Kialeha, Nobel team economist and senior lecturer in intercontinual economics at Queens' College,

(CONTINUED ON PAGE C-2)

(CONTINUED FROM PAGE C-2)

Cambridge. "But initial findings are encouraging. This world's economy is presently in the late stages of recovery from a mini-recession, in line with early predictions based on the 'interworld mirroring' principle, and on 'Terra's' present alignment with Huichtilopochtli and Xaihon. Additionally, the new Earth's conventions for handling monetary float and currency exchange conform closely to our norms, even though 'Terra's' economy involves an unusually complex grouping of national sovereignties. They've evolved unique solutions to their version of the multiple-currency problem, including several artificial exchange rate mechanisms which seem to have stood them in good stead during the process of 'decession.' If 'Terra' were to be invited to join the Pact, we don't feel its admission would present any problem even distantly approaching the magnitude of what the UN&ME had to deal with when Midgarth entered. However, the question may soon become moot, since there are presently not just one, but *four* MacIlwains studying high-energy physics or doing postgraduate physics work at key 'Terran' universities— an unmistakable sign that one of them is about to replicate parallel breakthroughs by other physicists with similar names in the other known universes. We don't know which of them is the breakthrough physicist yet—but even if we don't immediately open trade with 'Terra,' indications are that they could well be coming after *us* within three to five years."

Action on the world commodities market over the last week seems to indicate that both buyers and sellers broadly agree with this assessment. Fairy gold, always a reliable indicator of moods among the worldgating industries, ended the week on the Comex with December contracts at $2825 an ounce, only slightly below the all-time 1967 high caused by the discovery of Xaihon. Trading at London and Chicago Mercantile lagged slightly behind this figure, apparently owing to a decrease in the number of Alfen brokers offering end-of-year contracts. However, according to Martin Zermühle, fairy gold specialist at Shearson, Hamill's Zürich commodities trading bureau, this hedging can be expected to taper off over the next few weeks as interest among the supranational corporations becomes more aggressive in view of the prospect of the profits inevitably awaiting them in a new, unexplored economy.

Elsewhere, nervousness about intra-EU support for genetically engineered crop cultivars in the wake of disagreements at the Copenhagen summit caused October soybean contracts to plunge on the Neue Market, with other losses

(CONTINUED ON PAGE C-3)

One

"All rise for the right honorable Charles Redpath, magistrate," said the bailiff, "acting in and for the City and County of Los Angeles, in proceedings designated DL-5745-27 and to be enacted this day, April 27, 2004, in the City and County Circuit Court, session nine hundred and forty-five. Let all who desire Justice draw near, and Justice shall be done them."

Lee was still always amazed that the last sentence of the "blurb" didn't cause a rush for the doors. Nevertheless, everyone stayed where they were, and they all stood up, and in a flurry of black silk robes over that brown tweed suit, here came Charles out of his chambers and up the steps to the bench—a brisk, florid little dark-haired man, running slightly to stoutness now, with a short bristly mustache that could make him look extremely stern until he forgot himself and smiled. But he rarely forgot himself in the courtroom, and when he did, people were usually sorry afterward that they had tried to provoke the smile in the first place, or expected it to indicate humor. Lee kept her face very straight, and noticed that beside her, Gelert was for once not wagging his tail.

"Please be seated," Charles said, and in a rustle everyone

sat down. The court was a little fuller than usual today, for this was sentencing, and the case had attracted some attention in the papers: more than usual, since Mr. Redpath had excused the cameras last week, citing only the traditional stricture (as was his right) that "the camera looks, but Justice sees." Now the magistrate shuffled through his paperwork and unlimbered his laptop, waiting a moment for the pertinent documents to display themselves. "All right," he said, "this is the continuation of Ellay City docket 88-38715-4548, the People versus Lawrence J. Blair. . . ." He looked up from the papers, glanced around the courtroom. "We'll resume as from our recess of last Friday," he said, "assuming no one has anything strictly procedural to add. Mr. Hess?"

"Nothing, Your Honor," said Alan: very prudently, Lee thought, since he had pretty much exhausted Mr. Redpath's patience last week with procedural interferences of various kinds, all apparently directed toward one purpose: stalling.

"Ms. Enfield? *Madra* Gelert?"

"Nothing, Your Honor," Lee said, and Gelert shook his head.

"Very well. Summations may commence," Mr. Redpath said. "Prosecution?"

Lee stood up, shrugging her own silks into place over the new light blue dress. As always on a summation and sentencing morning, she was nervous for no good reason, and her chain of office felt like it was askew, and twice as heavy as it really was. She knew she looked all right, knew that she looked polished and professional enough, knew what the jury and Charles Redpath and all the newsies were seeing: a woman of medium height and medium build, face with all the features in the usual order, figure not terrible for her age, and nice hair, for the new shorter cut and the blond streaking worked well. Yet she felt haggard, unprepared, clammy, tired from having stayed up late preparing, and unready for what she knew was about to happen.

"Ladies and gentlemen of the jury, Your Honor, and Justice here present—" she said. And all that preparation cut in and started to make her feel better, as it usually did. "You've heard the evidence which my colleague has presented to you. The defendant stands before you now accused of a chain of frauds which have finally caught up with him— several of them directly connected, as we have proven, to the one for which he has been brought before you in this proceeding. . . ."

Lawrence Blair was a promoter who put together concert packages for various popular and rock musicians, some famous, some just getting started and rather vulnerable, financially at least. Five years or so ago a concert involving several large bands appeared to have been badly undersold by the "packaging" company handling ticket sales. There had been allegations of ineptitude on the part of the packaging company, a couple of civil suits filed, later dropped when Blair entered into a gentleman's agreement with the debtors and promised to repay them their losses.

His debtors accepted the arrangement and settled back to wait a reasonable time to be paid what they were owed, and Blair went on to organize other gigs, some successful, some not. Some of his creditor "clients" got paid, and most did not. "Mr. Blair's defense," Lee said to the jury, "would like you to believe that the people who didn't get paid on time, or at all, were merely the victims of accidents: lost payments, misunderstandings with the bank, unavoidable cashflow difficulties. But we've shown that the cause of these nonpayments was Mr. Blair's own redirection of the funds owed these people into other projects destined to make him more money."

She reminded the jury of dates and names, while in the

background hearing Gel lie down on his pad, the links of his chain sounding softly against each other—not the normal gold a human practitioner might wear, but fairy gold—low-carat, but still an extravagance hidden in plain sight. Gel loved such extravagances, and not being caught at them. But that was typical of how he preferred to operate, letting Lee do the "front work" while he stepped softly around in the background, fading into it where necessary.

He had nothing to do this morning except observe the verdict; all his work had been done with his usual skill in the discovery stage of the case. Lee thought sometimes that part of his success at eliciting testimony lay in the continuing fascination of many humans with the *madrín*. They hadn't been common in Lee's universe until twenty years or so ago, and there were lots of people who were charmed by the sound of a melliflous voice and courteous conversation coming out of what appeared to be a frizzy-coated white wolfhound the size of a small horse. If the big goofy-looking grin Gelert could produce while conducting an interview put people off their guard, Lee didn't mind. And if the lolling tongue and dingbat expression, or the way he twitched those big shell-pink ears around, made other people discount or entirely forget Gelert's expertise, Lee didn't mind that either . . . and she knew her partner, one of the first products of UCLA's doctorate program in litigative mantics, enjoyed taking advantage of the misapprehension. She threw a glance over her shoulder at him as she wound up her closing statement. Gelert opened those huge jaws in a gigantic, silent stage yawn, exhibiting entirely too many fangs: a private signal of profound confidence and a desire to cut to the chase.

"Joel Delaney's case brings us up to the present," said Lee, coming to a stand now at the foreman's end of the jury box. "Out of forty performers whom Mr. Blair has engaged to perform over the last three years, only ten have been paid in full: five have received partial payments, well short of what was promised: and the rest, still unpaid, have pooled a significant amount of funds in order to bring this case into the civil courts, so that Justice might be given a chance to operate where other agencies have failed. We ask you to look with us at the defendant and open the way for Justice to enter here; to see the truth of the matter, find him guilty as charged, and to participate in sentencing should the verdict so require."

Lee nodded to the foreman and to the other jurors, turned and went to sit down. In a few moments Alan was on his feet, and had begun addressing the jury with his usual smoothness. Right now he was making the whole case sound like a series of coincidences, complicated by incompetent accountants, accidents, and badly drawn-up contracts. He went on to make everything Lee had said sound either foolish or mischievous, and finally said, "We ask you to look with us at the defendant, opening the way for Justice; to see the truth of the matter and to find him innocent."

He sat down.

"Thank you," said Mr. Redpath, and tapped at his laptop's keyboard briefly. He looked over at the jurors' box. "Before we proceed, do any of you ladies or gentlemen require a recess at this time?"

The foreman, a small round woman with long wavy blond hair, looked down the length of the box at her fellow jurors. Heads were shaken. "No, Your Honor," she said after a moment.

"Very well." Mr. Redpath glanced at the bailiff. "Secure the room," he said.

The bailiff nodded, went over to confirm the time with the clerk of the court: the clerk reached under her desk to touch the button that locked the doors. Mr. Redpath folded down his laptop's screen, then folded his hands in front of him. There was a spate of the usual brief shuffling and last-chance-to-cough coughing. Then things got very still.

The prosaic courtroom—the slightly dusty windows through which the afternoon's sunlight was beginning to pour, the pale golden birch paneling of the walls, the terrazzo floor and the acoustic ceiling, now started to take on a strange, sharp-edged quality, as if another kind of light were starting to suffuse the place, different from the hot sunlight, harsher, clearer. A different view of human affairs began to superimpose itself over the merely human one, as the Other without whom no court was fully functional began to manifest.

Once such manifestations had taken much more work. In ancient Greece, men had compelled Justice's presence by sheer weight of numbers. As technique improved, the Romans and Byzantines managed it with tribunals of fifty, and medieval Europe with only "twelve good men and true." In this country, most jurisdictions kept the jury as a check on the judiciary process. But you really needed only two or three properly trained people, these days—the two advocates, and the magistrate who maintained the structure which compelled the Power's attention. Once you had Justice's attention, everything else happened very quickly indeed.

That sense of the Other's presence deepened. Mr. Redpath just gazed down at his folded hands as the presence increased in the room, as everything became subtly more visible. Redpath wasn't one of those jurists who went in for voiced invocations or flamboyant gestures; he simply made room in the courtroom for Justice, and it arrived, without fuss, focused and fully empowered. Such matter-of-fact competence would probably push him into the Court of Appeal eventually, maybe even the State Supreme Court. But right now Lee was glad he was here, since with that matter-of-fact quality came the certainty of control. Justice might be a good thing, but if improperly mediated, a cardinal Virtue could get out of hand and affect everyone in a court-room, not just those in whose cause it had been invoked.

The silence around Lee was no longer something that needed to be enforced. People felt it looking at them. Like small creatures caught suddenly under the regard of some-thing with sharp eyes and sharp claws, people tended to hold still and try not to attract its notice. Yet soon enough that ad-ditional effect set in, the sense of the stately presence of an ancient and deserved grandeur, something intangible yet powerful and splendid; possibly what people spoke of when they mentioned "the majesty of the law." The bailiff, the court clerk, the security guards minding the doors, all stood up when they felt it. Others stood as well, some in a hurry, some more slowly. Finally, only Charles, already standing for Justice in his person, remained seated.

Lee looked into the "well," the empty space between the bench and the counsels' tables, and Saw edges—that two-edged sword with which the Power manifesting here was so often pictured, immaterial but multiplied many times over, a tangle or nest of potential enforcement, like so much barbed wire. Mr. Redpath swallowed once, a strained motion, and looked up. "Let the defendant come forward and be judged," he said.

Lawrence Blair came out from behind the defense table, exchanged a suddenly nervous glance with Alan Hess, and stepped out into the well. He stood there with a most neutral expression, one which for Lee didn't hide his feelings at all. Finally, this late in the proceeding, he had had the sense to become afraid.

Lee let her gaze rest on Lawrence Blair and concentrated on letting Justice here present see so clearly through her that others wouldn't be able to help seeing as well. Across the aisle, Alan Hess was doing the same. And leaning against them like sunlight made solid, heavy and intent, the Power looked at Blair.

Lee looked at the defendant, and waited, letting the Sight work, concentrating on keeping her own thoughts quiet and making of herself a transparent conduit through which Justice could gaze unimpeded. Trained and inured to the Regard as she was, it hurt somewhat. Lee was better than usual at bearing the discomfort, partly because she did so much work in the forensic side of Seeing—perceiving the truth about things. But things hurt less to look at than people, and Lee stood there and shook as the pain increased.

Standing there in the well, among swords of light that he could not see but was beginning to feel, Blair started to tremble too . . . and inside him, the Balance shook itself loose and wavered between rise and fall. In it lay his soul, and Justice's other tool, the sense of true right or wrong, even more powerful than the mind to work its will on the harboring body.

And the Balance began to sink. Lee Saw in Blair the swathing concealment of self-delusive good intention (. . . *I'll pay them as soon as I have it . . .*) and expediency (. . . *I really need the funds more for this new project, they can wait a little longer . . .*) and calculation (. . . *If I don't pay this guy, he's powerful enough to make trouble down the line . . .*). And from long ago, from sometime buried in his past, the image: his mother's words, when she first caught him stealing. "You little w—"

Even now he tried not to hear the word, to see the image. But Lee saw it as Justice, looking through her, did. She felt the Balance inside Blair shift with a groan—the soul admitting itself, in the unavoidable hot glare of Justice's regard, to have been found wanting, and weighing the scales hard down.

The first sound came from someone on the jury, the kind of angry gasp a man might make when he's cut himself. Then came another, someone wishing they could deny what they saw, and unable to. If only one juror failed to see what both the prosecution and Justice saw, the judgment would not take.

One last soft moan came from the jury box. Lee didn't see who it was, but she felt the mind behind the moan make the verdict unanimous. The Power in the room with them struck through her and Alan like lightning; and the nest of unseen swords rose up, surrounded Blair, and sliced him through.

Blair didn't have a throat for long enough to finish his scream—not a human throat, anyway. The "containment area" in the well, defined by the two-meter-wide, dull red square outline of forcefield on the floor, activated with the administration of the sentence. And in the middle of the square, crouching, stunned, was a weasel. It was a very large weasel, for though Justice might affect the soul in a body, and that body's shape, it had no effect on mass. Clenching its claws against the floor, staring around at its counsel, at Lee, at the magistrate and the jury, the weasel began to make a small, terrible rough sound in its throat, over and over, like a whispered screech.

The pressure of the Regard was gone, vanished like a dream or a nightmare. A lot of people sat down, shocked, but more kept standing, to see better. Lee and Alan both staggered, released, and made their way back to their tables.

Mr. Redpath looked down over his desk at the containment area. "Guilty as charged," said Mr. Redpath. "Defendant will retain this semblance during the pleasure of inward and outward Justice, here manifested. Upon the end of sentence, the court will be informed whether the defendant desires the optional restitutory stage. Otherwise, here and until the end of sentence, Justice is served."

The courtroom was very quiet now, that initial rustle of shock and horror having died away. Lee was still blinking hard and trying to get her normal, unaugmented vision back. *Boy,* she thought, *some of the sketch artists in here are going to have a field day with* this *verdict.*

"Your Honor," said Blair's counsel, "we desire to lodge an appeal at once, on the grounds that the sentence is excessively severe."

Mr. Redpath looked down again into the containment area, where the weasel was now trying to sit up on its haunches, and failing. It came down hard on its forefeet again, staring at the long delicate claws and breathing fast. "I so allow. See the court clerk for scheduling. However, Mr. Hess," said Mr. Redpath, looking down at him rather dryly, "I think the verdict's severity is secondary to your client having perjured himself. You may want to take advice from your client's family to discover whether they really want to proceed."

"Yes, Your Honor," said Hess, looking glum.

"Then I declare this proceeding to be complete, and I adjourn it *sine die,*" Mr. Redpath said, and banged his gavel on the desk. "Open the doors; and thank you, ladies and gentlemen." He got up and headed for his chamber, shrugging his gown back into kilter as he went.

"Please clear the court for the next proceeding," the bailiff shouted, and people started to file out. In the middle of the courtroom, a uniformed security officer arrived with a large wheeled protective carrier, and there followed an unfortunately humorous interlude while the court security staff tried to get the weasel, presently flinging itself against the walls of the containment area, into the carrier and out of the court.

Lee had been bracing herself against their table. Now Gelert came up beside her and put his cold nose against her neck.

"Stop that," she said, and pushed his snout away, not half as hard as she would have under less casual circumstances, or if she'd had the strength. She wobbled.

"You need the retiring room?" he said privately, implant to implant.

Lee shook her head, still trying to get her breath back. She would pay the price tonight, in sleep, when the reaction set in and her dreams reflected that inexorable gaze concentrating, not on Blair, but on her. Tomorrow, abashed and sore with yet another reminder of her own many failings, she'd ache all over and not be good for much. But the price was worth paying.

From the other side of the aisle came the shuffle and snap of paperwork and a laptop being put away. She glanced over at Hess, stood up straight as her breathing got back to normal, and reflected that at least she wasn't the only one here who looked completely wrecked. Alan was pale under his tan, and the resultant color made him look very unwell. But "Nice one, Lee," said Hess to her, polite as always, despite the circumstances.

Lee nodded to him. "Thanks, Al. Look, you did good work, too . . . Good luck with the appeal."

He nodded back, went out. "Give me five minutes for the ladies' room," Lee said to Gelert.

It was closer to ten, for Lee's mascara was nowhere near as waterproof as the manufacturer claimed. But the repairs would suffice for the waiting cameras. She slipped out of her silks with a sigh of relief, took off her chain, folded the silks around it, and stowed everything in her briefcase.

Shortly Lee was out in the echoing glass-and-terrazzo main hall again, where Gelert awaited her, and together they went out through the glass doors into the blinding light of a ferocious afternoon, the temperature now pushing above a hundred. The Santa Ana wind was up, blowing so fiercely that the palm trees around New Parker Plaza were bending in the force of it, and the feather-duster tops hissed and rattled, each individual frond glinting as if wet in the harsh bright sun. Dust flew everywhere. Lee winced a little at the light but could do nothing about it for the moment; for here were the newsies already, two cameras and a few print people, waiting on the courthouse steps to take a statement from them.

"Good afternoon, folks," Gelert said amiably, sitting down on the top step. Lee, pausing beside him, sneezed. "Afternoon, all," she said. "Please forgive me, it's the dust . . ."

"Do you have a prepared statement?" said one of the waiting reporters, not one of the familiar ones. Lee thought she was possibly from *Variety* or the *Reporter.*

"No," Lee said. "We thought we'd just ad-lib today."

Gelert sneezed too. "Sorry," he said. "Can everybody hear me okay? My implant's speaker's been acting up lately when the volume's turned up out in the open."

"No problem," said the *Variety* reporter, and the others shook their heads.

"Right," said a third reporter, a little, casually dressed man with dimples and a deceptively innocent face. "Ms. Enfield, this has been the sixth high-profile case your firm has been assigned to in the last four months. How do you answer the charge that the DA's Office is showing favoritism to you because of your former relationship with—"

"If it *was* a charge," Lee said, interrupting him and doing her best to keep her smile casual, "I'd suggest that the person making it should look at the results in the cases involved. Our firm appears to produce results, as this is our fifth 'win' out of those six cases. If we're 'favorites' with the DA's Office at the moment, it seems we're favorites with Justice as well . . . and there's no way to buy or influence *that*. Unless you've found one?" She gave the reporter what she hoped would pass for an amused look.

"The Ellay District Attorney's Office assigns cases to the pool of qualified prosecuting teams on an availability basis," Gelert said, "as you can confirm by checking the court calendar. Our last five cases have been assigned us because in each case we'd just finished another proceeding, and were available. The luck of the draw. But it helps to know what to *do* with luck."

A mutter as some of the reporters paused to take notes. "What message would you send to Mr. Blair's wife and children?" said another.

"That Mr. Blair, like every other defendant," Lee said, "has himself chosen the form of his punishment. And that we, like his family, look forward to the day when the Justice living inside him, as it lives inside everyone, decides that he's served his sentence and can go free. He, and Justice, will work that out for themselves."

Another mutter from the reporters. "The case is going to appeal," said another one.

"That's right," Gelert said. "And we wish the defendant well. However, we feel that this time out, Justice has prevailed. But then it always does."

"Dr. Gelert," said another reporter, a small trim woman with long blond hair tied back, "what's your reaction to the statement made by one of your people recently that direct judicial intervention is a 'blunt instrument' in this time of increased understanding of criminal motivation?"

Gelert dropped that big fringed jaw and showed many

more of his teeth than Lee thought strictly necessary. " 'Cruel and unusual punishment' again?" Gelert said. "How can Justice's own self be cruel? And if it's unusual, that's *our* fault, not Its. 'Hers,' if you prefer to see Justice that way; lots of humans do. My people, too, actually." A gust of wind blew a great swirl of dust across the entrance of the court-house, Lee sneezed, and so did several of the reporters. Gelert shook himself all over, and his chain rang softly. "My people," Gelert added, "have no crime. No murder, no assault, no theft, nothing of the kind. Certainly no fraud. It colors some of our opinions about the judicial system here. Me, I'll wait until Councillor Dynef's been mugged for his ear-rings some night, coming home from the movies in West-wood. After he's needed to go through the courts himself, we'll see how 'blunt' he thinks the Hoodwinked Lady's sword is."

There was some chuckling at that. "Anything else, ladies and gentlemen?" Lee said. "We've got places to be."

Heads were shaken. "Thanks, then," Lee said, and she and Gelert turned away. The reporters went off down the stairs.

Lee sneezed again. "Places to be," Gelert said softly. "What a fibber you are."

"Huh." Lee paused to open her briefcase and rummage around in it for her sunglasses. "They keep asking about that," she muttered. "Why can't they just let it drop?"

"What? The DA's Office? Because they're newsies, as a result of their moms putting scandal in their baby bottles instead of milk. Because it's obvious, and some of them are only good at obvious."

Lee sighed. "Yeah, but all they have to do is check the facts to find out—"

"Lee, if it was facts they were after, they wouldn't be on the courthouse steps. They would have been inside. That guy from the *Times,* he's just after evidence to support his pet theory. When he can't find any, he'll stop bothering us."

She found the sunglasses, then put them on and made a face. "Yeah, okay, you're right," she said. "It's just this wind getting to me, I guess. . . ."

"So come on, let's get out of it," Gelert said. "Let's go eat. I've got a table booked."

"Absolutely. Where?"

"Perdu."

She blinked at him. "What, New York? For *lunch?* We're late for that already. And anyway, nobody could get a booking at that place on the same day they call!"

"I reserved it a week ago. And not lunch. Dinner. If we get our tails up to the port instead of standing here chewing over the dry bones, we'll be just in time for seven-thirty."

"How did you— Gel," Lee said, "sometimes I think you're holding out on me. You're a forward clairvoyant, and you've never bothered to register."

"Too much paperwork," Gelert said, as they headed for the Metro. "And all clairvoyants get a squint. I refuse to ruin my youthful good looks."

"Then again, maybe you're just delusional," Lee said. "You think you're a millionaire, all of a sudden, to drop the price of a transcontinental jump for a dinner?"

"We deserve it," Gelert said, and grinned with all those teeth. "Besides, I dumped a bunch of Oklahoma munis over the weekend and scored thirty percent on the deal. If I keep the money, it'll only burn a hole in my pocket."

"*What* pocket?!"

"Pedant. Come on, or they'll give away our table."

Two hours later, when Lee glanced up from her fondue and suddenly noticed the King of all the Elves sitting across the room, perusing the wine list, it came as a surprise, but not a huge one—an amusing end to a long day. After all, Le Chalet Perdu was (very quietly) one of the best restaurants in Manhattan. Given the Elf-king's reputation, and the restaurant's, sooner or later someone was bound to have brought the two together in an attempt to impress each with the other. And here the Elf-king sat, in a dark blazer and tie and charcoal twills, surrounded by calm-voiced men in Cardin or Botany double-breasted suits—men wearing their mature assurance, or their smoldering youthful cleverness, as if they were weapons. Lee looked away after a first glance, much amused by their talk of wines and entrées. To someone with her training, the lighthearted conversation across the room had a distinct sound of nervous saber rattling. She turned her attention back to her meal.

"Gel," she said, holding out his fondue fork to him, "you smell anything interesting?"

Gelert nipped the cheese-dipped bread cube off the fork, chewed, swallowed, and paused long enough to put his tongue out and lick an escaped blob of Emmenthaler off his whiskers. "Too much nutmeg," he said, "not enough kirsch."

"In *Konni's* fondue? Hardly. Something else."

Gelert's nose twitched. "Elves."

"Huh-uh. Elf. *The* Elf. Laurin."

Her partner's pink ears went straight up. "Really. Thought he was supposed to be in The Hague for that conference."

"Maybe he's on his way," Lee said. She speared a chunk of bread for herself, dunked it, waved it in the air, munched. "There isn't too much nutmeg, either."

"I was kidding, Lee." Gelert paused and ducked his head to lap at his bowl of Perrier. "Who else is he with?"

"I don't recognize any of them. Not that I'd have reason to. We could ask Konni."

"Right." Gelert busied himself with finishing his drink. Lee took the opportunity to steal another glance at the table by the far wall. Le Chalet was a small place, done in cream-pale stucco and warmly, brightly lit, so that there was no trouble seeing. The slim, dark man in the elegantly under-stated jacket and tie put the wine list aside with a gesture that would have been much too graceful, if not for the thoughtless strength inherent in it. Then, all courtesy and attention, he settled down to listen to one of his dinner companions' remarks about business.

Yet there was something else going on over there. Lee dipped another cube of bread, watching it. The three other well-dressed men, for all their apparent casualness, looked stiff and strained. Their ease was artificial, applied. And the quiet-eyed man who listened to them, though physically alert and erect enough, at the same time seemed inwardly to be *lounging*—watching their nervousness from a carefully maintained distance, aloof and ever so faintly amused. It was a look that Lee had seen before in Elves. *Hell,* she thought, *everybody's seen it. It's one of the ways you tell an Elf in the first place.* But in this Elf, *the* Elf, the effect was both more subtle and more concentrated. Lee looked away and speared more bread.

Gelert lifted his head from his drink, and within a few seconds—neither too quickly nor too slowly—Konrad Egli made his way over to their banquette table. Herr Egli was a great, gray, craggy block of a man, like a small Alp; forty years the master of this house and long past being ruffled by anything, even the presence of the absolute master of an entire otherworld. Mortal kings and princesses, and rock stars and politicos and chairmen of the board, all the lesser sorts of royalty, had been dining in his restaurant for years. He treated them all with the same benevolent, ruthless hospitality that he bestowed on first-timers just in off the street, and nothing any of them said or did ever seemed to catch him off guard. Now Herr Egli leaned down beside Gelert—not too far: even sitting on the floor, Gelert was tall enough to have to look slightly downward at Lee—and nodded at the empty Waterford bowl. "Another one, *madra?*"

"Please."

"Konni," Lee said, keeping her voice low, "does he come here often?" She nodded at the far side of the room, where jocund voices were rising in discreet merriment at some carefully witty remark.

Herr Egli shook his head. "A few times a year. Always business dinners, or lunches." He glanced over his shoulder for a second, then added with a smile and a fatherly scowl, "His guests—they never seem to finish what they order."

Lee smiled wryly. Herr Egli took his role of patron seriously, and was not above scolding his favorite customers in friendly fashion if they seemed to need it. "You notice," she said in mock-daughterly respect, "that I ate all my spinach."

"Good girl. Another glass of wine?"

"Yes, Konni, thank you."

He picked up her wineglass and Gelert's bowl and carried them away to the bar; then, at the thump the inner front door made when the outer door was opened, turned to greet an arriving guest. Lee dunked another chunk of bread for Gelert and offered it to him. He accepted it with eyes half-closed, a sybarite's lazy look, and thumped his tail gently on the wine-colored carpet as he chewed. "I'm glad we came," he said. "Even if you think you can't afford it."

"Excuse me," Lee said, "*you're* paying for this one, you said."

Gelert grinned, exhibiting many sharp white fangs. "But Lee, my portfolio—"

"—needs a forklift to pick it up. I'd ask you how you do it, except I'd be afraid we'd have the Securities and Exchange Commission after us about ten minutes later. And anyway, you're right, we *do* deserve it. We worked our butts off on that case. Here at least we can have dinner without the people from the local TV stations shoving cameras in our faces. So I will ever so gracefully, just this once, let you pay."

Gelert was still grinning. "Oh, well . . . it was worth a try."

Herr Egli came back with their drinks. "Konni," Lee said, "the great white pig here has, I would say 'single-handedly' if he had hands, finished off the fondue—"

"She starves me all day," Gelert said, dropping his ears down flat and attempting to look piteous. "Eating out's my only chance at sustenance. And look what I wind up with. Bread and water."

"How you suffer," Lee said. "Konni, how about dessert?"

"Fine. What would you like?"

"Chocolate fondue," said Gelert.

"Gel, no. You'll get it in your fur again. . . ."

The argument ran its predictable course, and Herr Egli went off to have them brought coffee, and to arrange for the chocolate fondue. Lee held out the next-to-last bit of bread and cheese to Gelert, looking over his shoulder as Konni paused by that one table across the room, checking on the guests seated there. One of them, the host of the Elf-King's party, was ordering, looking back and forth from Herr Egli to the trim blond woman in Swiss bodice and skirt who was actually taking the order. The Elf-king sat back in his chair, his malt-brown eyes shifting from one member of the party to another, lingering on them, unreadable. It was the typical

Alfen gaze—that cool, easy regard, rooted in the kind of
calm for which only an immortal had leisure. . . .

Lee became aware that she was staring. Nonetheless she
prolonged the examination just a bit, fascinated by the man's
remoteness, his mild amusement, his too-perfect handsomeness. Her own fascination embarrassed and puzzled her a
bit; though she delighted in good looks in men, gawking was
hardly her style. *Still,* she thought, almost defiantly—and
whom was she defying?—*just a little exercise of curiosity
on my own time* . . . And then her embarrassment escalated,
for those brown eyes were suddenly staring right back at her,
a considering look: interested, and ever so slightly disturbed.

Still Lee wouldn't immediately look away, though she
did start to blush at being caught staring at a celebrity like
some tourist just in from the edgeworlds. There was something latent beneath that look of his, something rising like
blood under skin, and it made her curious. Her Sight worried
at it, fraying away at the edges of it, unraveling the seeming
that overlay the truth. A few moments more and she would
know the hidden thought, the answer to what was puzzling
her—

The still, dark man wouldn't look away, and Lee's embarrassment finally got the better of her. She broke gaze,
glanced away for something else to look at, anything, and
took glad refuge in the arrival of the waitress with the coffee. *Rude,* Lee thought, annoyed with herself. *And dumb.
What if I'd gone judicial?* Though that was unlikely. Both
by training and intention Lee was enough of a professional
not to look at other human beings in the normal course of
daily life in the same way she looked at plaintiffs or the accused in the courtroom. Yet it was impossible ever to turn
the Sight completely off, and insights did slip through . . .
Oh, come on, she thought, annoyed at her own attempt to

rationalize it. *Eavesdropping at a perfect stranger like that . . . and this one, in particular. What's the* matter *with me?—*

But when Lee looked up again, the Elf-king had turned his attention back to his dinner companions as if nothing had happened, and business went on uninterrupted on the other side of the room. Dessert arrived, and Gelert *did* get chocolate in his fur, and Herr Egli scolded him good-naturedly and sent to the kitchen for hot towels and club soda. Only much later, over the remains of the coffee and snifters of Grand Marnier, while the check was being reckoned up, did Gelert lean toward Lee, and say, "What was *that* about?" He flicked one ear backward, in the direction of the Elf-King's table.

"I don't know," Lee said. "Curiosity." And the first part of that was truer than the second. She snitched a final puff of toasted meringue off the dessert plate, ignoring Gelert's indignant growl. "Come on, better dig out your plastic, or we'll have nothing left to catch but the red-eye."

And he did, and they did, so that an hour or so later the two of them stepped from late evening at Kennedy to summer sunset at Los Angeles Intercontinual—a late-lingering volcano sunset that lowered red-hot over the Santa Susanas and turned Lake Val San Fernando to a sea of blood, flat and thick-looking under the breathless, baking air. They caught choppers for home in opposite directions—Lee, as soon as she'd recovered from the inevitable tummy-flutter that gating caused her, heading eastward to the park-and-fly and her house in Pasadena; Gelert heading west to his mate and pups and their condo in a *madrín* co-op at Malibu. Neither of them thought much of that dinner at Le Chalet in the days that followed.

But that night, as the late news came on, Lee thought about it for some time. "A fatal 'gangland'-style shooting late tonight in the Wilshire District," said the eleven o'clock anchor; and the camera cut from the studio to a remote of a murky scene lit in pink-yellow streetlights and the flashing reds and blues of ambulances and police black-and-whites. The on-scene newsman babbled on about names and circumstances and unclear motives. But what froze Lee in horror, blocking words away, was the quick shot of the slim, well-muscled form, all the Alfen elegance and strength gone out of it now, lying sprawled facedown on the pavement. Lee made a face. It was sweeps week, and all the stations' news coverage had become unusually sensational of late. But as they maneuvered the body onto the stretcher, she still couldn't look away from the handsome, cool, clean-chiseled face, pale and smudged with street grime, still beautiful in death. She did look away when the hastily tucked drape slipped just enough askew in the moving to show the wet pink-and-white gleam of ribs splintered by a shotgun blast to the back.

In the morning and in days to follow, Lee would read the conjectures in the *Ellay Times* about successful or unsuccessful attempts by the Mob to get one of the local Alfen to "play ball" in some unspecified racket. But right now Lee found herself thinking about the expression being slowly frozen by rigor into the dead Elf's face, and how very similar it was to the way the Elf-king had looked at his poor dinner companions. That aloof, gentle immortal's gaze; fearless, calmly certain, invulnerable to the petty machinations of those who knew far better than the Alfen how to die. . . .

Lee breathed out and settled back to wait for the weather report.

TWO

The next morning was like most mornings the day after a court appearance: filled with paperwork and dogged by a lingering hungover feeling that didn't even have associated with it the guilty satisfaction of a previous night spent partying. Additionally, also as usual, the overhang wasn't evenly distributed. When Lee got into the office, she found that Gel had been there for an hour before her even though she'd come in early.

Mass looked up from behind his plain dark desk inside their office's little reception area as Lee pushed open the frosted glass door that said REH'MECHREN AND ENFIELD, LLP: LANTHANOMANCERS AT LAW. Massimo Alighieri had been with Lee and Gelert since a year after they started their practice, and had not changed even a hair's worth in all that time. He still looked like a kid just out of grad school, lean, dark-haired, with huge dark eyes, a great aquiline nose, and a shock of untameable black hair that gave him the look of either a crazed composer or a mad scientist, depending on the time of day and the state of his blood sugar. Now, as Lee came in, he gave her a look that suggested the blood sugar was presently a problem. "Any messages?" Lee said.

"DA's Office," Mass growled.

Lee flushed. "Oh no. Not—"

"Yup," Mass said. "But I think it was business. He didn't look embarrassed."

"Hmm," Lee said, and went on past, through the joint sitting area and into her office. It was spare enough, Lee having decided long ago to use the sheer size of the space to make whatever statements needed to be made to impress or reassure a client. Dark brown rug, the desk a six-foot-by-four-foot slab of goldstone with a tall-backed black leather chair behind it, and behind that, the commwall, Lee's only self-indulgence—floor-to-ceiling, a considerable expense considering the height of the ceilings in this building. She opened up one of the storage cabinets faired into the wall, chucked her briefcase into it, and stood there brooding for a moment, wondering how long she could put off making the call.

The wall opposite the commwall depaqued, and Gelert strolled in from his own office in front of a blast of noise. His office was as luxurious as Lee's in its own way, including a matching commwall, but Gelert's taste ran more to what Lee liked to annoy him by calling bric-a-brac—ten pedestals' worth of ancient art, everything from Earth Minoan sculpture to Xainese iridium-glazed porcelain six thousand years old. The other indulgence was the sound system, which (along with its necessary soundproofing) had actually been more expensive than the commwall, and which now was thundering something symphonic: literally thundering. "What is that?" Lee shouted.

Gelert sat down, and the sound diminished to a whisper. "Hovhannes," he said. " 'Atmospherics.' "

"Sounds like rain."

"That's the next movement. Mass tell you who called?"

"Yes. Why couldn't you have taken it, if you were in?"

"What," Gelert said, "and deny you a chance for personal growth?"

"Personal spite, you mean," Lee said. "That's about all I feel up for this morning. All right, fine, let's get it over with. *Mass?*"

"You don't need to shout, I heard you. . . ."

The commwall in Lee's office lit up in blue with the seal of the Ellay County DA's Office—the un-Hoodwinked Lady, seated on the curule seat with scales and sword, and under it all, the single word HOLDING. "I bet his secretary answers," Gelert said.

"Be nice if that happened," Lee said. "Somehow I doubt it will."

And she was right, for abruptly, there was Matt, looking, for him, unusually wrung out. Lee's heart seized a little at the sight of him, a reaction that she suspected it was going to take her entirely too long to learn to control. Furious though she might be with him, heartsore and bruised though Lee might be, he looked no less handsome to her than he had the month before, and the urge to reach out and hold him and comfort him jumped right up in her as if the breakup had never happened. The reaction was infuriating, and unbearable, and she was just going to have to deal with it. "I got your message," Lee said.

Matt sat back in his chair and ran his hands through his hair, a gesture that succeeded no more at calming it down than it ever had. "You did a nice job on the Blair thing," he said.

"Thanks," said Lee and Gelert more or less in unison.

"We have a little problem," said Matt.

"The day you don't," Gelert said, "is the day we all go on the dole, so all I can say is, How nice. Details?"

"We had an Elf murdered last night," Matt said, and made it sound as if the murder had been pointed specifically at him. But that was one of the reasons he'd moved up in the DA's Office so fast: he took everything personally, and worked as if every murder or assault had happened in his own living room—with intelligence, and an odd uncalculating animus that confused and annoyed some of his coworkers.

"Dil'Sorren," Lee said, remembering the late news. Gelert cocked an eye at her, said nothing.

"Sorden," said Matt.

"A shooting. Messy," Lee said to Gelert. She glanced back at Matt. "Wilshire District, wasn't it?"

"That's right. We're still in the early stages—"

"Eight hours on?" Gelert said. "I should think so."

Matt bent his most furious frown on Gelert, though Lee thought he should have known it was wasted. *He's been up all night,* she thought. *Why would that happen on a murder this fresh?* "We've been getting some grief from dil'Sorden's employers," he said. "They're not satisfied with our progress."

"After eight hours?" Lee said. "Are they nuts? You'd be lucky to have even beginning forensics done by then."

"You shouldn't even let them into the office so soon," Gelert said.

Matt looked even more furious. "We can't keep them out. They're ExTel."

Lee and Gelert exchanged another look. "Oh really," Lee said. "Not our friend Mr. Hagen?"

"The very same," said Matt, "and he's set a fire under Renselaar, which is the reason for this call."

Jim Renselaar was the DA, and up for reappointment this year, which had turned him into something of a firebreather in service to the Mayor's Office . . . not that anyone was fooled by this: they knew Big Jim had his eye on the mayoral chain himself. *And Renselaar can't afford to ignore the support which a locally based multinational like ExTel could lend to his campaign someday,* Lee thought. *Not to mention his campaign chest.*

"The boss wants you two to come in and do psycho-forensics on dil'Sorden," Matt said. "He knows you're sweet with Hagen after that last job you did for ExTel, and you're in a good spot with the press right now. And batting hot, four for four . . . so he expects you to produce."

"Themis does seem to have been on our side these last couple of months," Gelert said, "but we can't make any guarantees as regards Lady Luck . . . which Big Jim knows. I suspect he's got our good relationship with Hagen more on his mind. We're going to be, shall we say, his asbestos seat cushion."

"*Just* forensics?" Lee said, perhaps more sharply than she intended. "Not litigation?"

"That we'll negotiate later."

"Not the slightest chance, Matt," Lee said. "We sort that out *now*. No *way* we do the tough spadework on this case and then hand it off to a lit team that's going to blow all our disclosure work, or plea-bargain it off for a quick small win."

"Lee, you know what they're going to say—"

"All too damn well," Lee said. "Because they were saying it on the courthouse steps, and they're not going to stop saying it no matter how we participate in this case. The only thing that matters now is that we find out just who left that poor Elf with his insides blown out last night, and why. If we discover, we prosecute. The press won't give a damn after you've leaked the salient details to them and made your boss look good. We get a kill, because you know we're just about the best you've got right now. You get good PR. We get a fee commensurate with the work we *really* did, instead of some split-fee bargain-basement deal with one of the DA's superannuated cronies. Maybe even a leg up into the Upper Bar next year: at least, another rung on the ladder. And everybody's happy. Including, we desperately hope, the soul of that poor bastard, avenged by the event; and Justice Herself, for being served. That being the reason we're all here, or so I'm told."

Matt looked at her—Lee counted the seconds off: she knew about how long he liked to hold one of these "penetrating looks"—and then made a sour half-smile. "You put your case subtly, as ever," he said.

"She speaks for me," Gelert said, "so don't get personal. Say the word, Matt, and we're on it. We'll get on the horn to Hagen and get him off your boss's case."

Matt sighed. "Go," he said. "The crime scene team wants to see you soonest. Call Parker Center, get the address, get down there and deal with them. Blessington's handling it."

And they were left staring at the blue screen again. Gelert gave Lee one of those big toothy grins. "What a social animal he is," he said. "I see why you ditched him."

His irony was showing only slightly less than it might have been. "Would it had only been so," Lee muttered, and got up, staring at the commwall as it dissolved back to her default view. "What's Hagen's problem, I wonder? He's usually been fairly mellow when we've worked with him."

"Maybe he doesn't have an asbestos seat cushion," Gelert said. "Let's call him and find out. Mass?"

"You don't have to shout. Got his assistant on the line now."

"ETA?"

"He's playing the talking-to-someone-more-important-right-now game, the little *cucaracha*. Five minutes, because he knows his boss really wants to hear from you."

"Gee, what would he do if this was a matter of life and death?" Lee said softly, and bent backward a little with her hands in the small of her back, trying to work out a kink. Her sleep had not done her much good last night.

"How'd you know about the murder?" Gelert said.

"The same way you would have, if you weren't snoring within minutes of getting home last night, or playing with the pups before breakfast," Lee said.

"Guilty and guilty," Gelert said. "If I didn't save the broadcast news and the papers for when I got to work, what else would I do in the office all day? But now I won't bother. Why prejudice myself with some yellow journalist's take on whatever minuscule evidence there was at that point?"

He lay down on his cushion and sagged back, yawned. "So do we play this as usual?"

"We may as well start that way," Lee said. "We'll sniff the scene together, anyway. But after that you'd better see what you can do with prediscovery."

"You always do this to me when Alfen are involved," Gelert said. "I hate it."

"You're better at data search than I am," Lee said. "It's not my fault you take every opportunity to rub my nose in your competence. And with those people's data protection laws, any tricks you've got, we're going to need."

Gelert looked briefly glum. "Mass?" Lee said.

"Two minutes, Lee."

"Not that. Cut a copy of the usual discovery-and-litigation agreement and sim it over to Matt's office before he thinks of a way to weasel out of the commitment."

"There before you, boss-lady. You're slipping."

Lee smiled slightly. "Heads up, he's on," Mass said.

The commwall went bright with the view into Charl Hagen's office. This could have been mistaken for a view of the outdoors, for Hagen was fairly "old management" in what was now the biggest of the telecomms multiuniversals, and Lee remembered her astonishment at discovering that the witness she had been dispatched to interview had not only a forest in his office, but a trout stream. Right now sun was pouring through the rooftop glass of the conservatory side of Hagen's office, and the man himself was coming around from behind the desk. "Lee. Gelert. Thanks for calling."

"No problem at all," Lee said, looking Hagen over non-judicially for a second as he sat on the front of his desk. It had been six months now since the end of the Xainacom antitrust trials, and Hagen looked a little less harried, had put on a little weight—though it didn't show that much on his big-boned six-foot-two. He was well turned out as always, in a fashionable one-piece suit that nonetheless betrayed its off-the-rack origins and its wearer's too-busy-for-fittings attitude, looking as if someone had applied it to Hagen with a shovel. The dark shaggy hair and the little, close-set, thoughtful eyes in the man's blunt face always made Lee wonder if Hagen had any Midgarthr blood in him, and whether the human seeming might be a courtesy-covering over something more basic, a formal suit allowed to fall away for short periods when the Moon was right.

"It's been a little while," Hagen said. "You two been all right?"

"Busy," Gelert said.

Hagen grinned, and again Lee saw bear, and had to put the image aside. "Here, too," Hagen said.

Lee nodded. At the end of a legal case lasting years, Xainacom had been forced into a massive corporate divestiture in the Earth universe. The truth was that the defeat for the company was a minor one—the market in Earth's universe being nothing like the size of those in Xainese home space, spread across thousands of planets—and when the appeals process was exhausted, the "home office" hadn't considered the affair worth going to war over. Xainacom

Earth had been fractured into a number of still-huge communications- and media-related companies, and those of its competitors who had spent vast sums of money assisting with the prosecution were now circling the staggering survivors with an eye to either absorption or destruction. Of all the competitors, ExTel was by far the biggest, and it was wasting no time assuring itself of the best pickings among the divestitures. Lee could believe that Hagen, as the company's CEO for extracontinual affairs, had been a lot more than "busy."

"We got a call from Matt Carathen just now," Lee said. "He suggested that you had asked for our services."

"That's right. Omren dil'Sorden is one of my local people. I don't have time for some anonymous flunky at Parker to fiddle around with it and maybe get a result, maybe not— I want this thing cleaned up *before* it gets high-profile enough to make the company's PR people have to start spinning God knows what to the national press. We have enough going on around here at the moment. So right now, I need Parker's best, and right now, that looks like you."

Lee smiled gently at the flattery, while thinking that "cleaned up" was a strange way to put it, but she supposed she could see his point. "What was dil'Sorden's position, exactly?" she said.

"R&D," Hagen said. "He was working on network development, especially intercontinually gatewayed links— you'll have to check his personnel records for the details, the technologies he was working on were still pretty theoretical. They could have been very important, though, and I want whoever did this identified and locked up."

"Do you have any suspicions?" Gelert said.

The irony in his tone caught Hagen just short enough to make him laugh. "You mean Xainacom?" he said. "I doubt they'd be so obvious. No, they're being good enough losers . . . insofar as they've actually lost anything but face. It's the other companies hereabouts I'd wonder about. We're the biggest target left standing, and if you check dil'Sorden's intelligence file, you'll see references to a couple of failed head-hunts in the last few months—ConAmalgam and Vmax, I think. There might have been people working there who thought the man better off dead than alive and happy to be working for us, though I wish I didn't find it so easy to believe."

"Well, if the evidence suggests anything of the sort, we'll certainly have our minds open to the possibility," Lee said.

Gelert stretched a little on his pad. "There's one thing I'd like to clear up," he said. "That ExTel's impending acquisition of Maermen GmbH, which was Xainacom Europe until about five weeks ago, doesn't have anything to do with your urgency about this murder investigation."

Hagen said nothing for an entire second, smiling all the while like a still image. "Nothing whatsoever," he said. "The markets are always full of rumors, Gelert; if half of them were worth half what they were supposed to be, we'd all be rich."

"Of course," Gelert said.

"Mr. Hagen," Lee said, working on how to phrase this. "ExTel employs enough Alfen across its facilities that you know better than most what kind of problems a party can run into when looking for even very basic personal information about them, at least from sources in Alfheim."

Hagen's expression went sour. "Tell me about it."

"Naturally you'll be passing on your corporate profile on dil'Sorden to us. But we may need to call on you during the course of this investigation for information that might be . . . more difficult to access."

Hagen looked uncomfortable, and held that still-image look again for a moment or two. In shadowy blue, a line of stick-and-curl Palmerrand characters ran across the bottom of Lee's field of vision, transcribing the words Gelert was subvocalizing right now: *Let's see how high he blows.*

"I take your meaning," Hagen said. "If it comes to that, we'll talk. Meanwhile, I'll see to it that his personnel file is on your desk in a few minutes."

"That's fine," Lee said. "Thanks for the assistance. We'll be in touch."

She waved the link dead, then looked over at Gelert.

"Did you think he was going to say 'no' right then?" Gelert said. "Because I did."

"I was wondering, myself," Lee said. "And in the unsubtlety stakes, *you're* certainly batting strong today. What was that business about Maermen?"

"He tried to blow it off as a rumor," Gelert said, and grinned. "Not that he thought I bought it, either. He knows my sources are better than that. Lee, Hagen's boss, the president of ExTel, is on a rampage right now! After eleven years of frustration, he's finally got the biggest shopping cart in the world, given him by the UN & ME itself, and he's running up and down the aisles grabbing every available chunk of Xainacom that's got '50% OFF!' marked on it. So the word has gone down the line to his minions . . . especially Hagen. His cash liquidity is stretched to the limit, and he does not want anything in the news right now, *anything,* that could make his company look even slightly bad and impair his credit rating. Especially not a murder."

Lee got up and stretched again, then started kneading at her back. "Why especially?"

"It's too personal. Portfolio managers and stock analysts are timid creatures." Gelert smiled, showing teeth. "Show them a cloud no bigger than a man's hand, and they see a thunderstorm and dump all their wheat futures. Show them blood and they faint, then sell everything short when they come to. The publicity surrounding a high-profile murder can start all kinds of paranoia working in the people who do the valuation on your company's stock, and if there's anything Hagen's boss doesn't need right this minute, it's a slump in his share price. The asset managers will be praying for a quick fix or a *crime passionelle*." Gelert got up from his pad and stretched fore and aft. "And you know what *you* should be looking for? A new mattress."

Lee stopped rubbing her back. "Fatherhood is turning you into a real pain," she said. "Let me go change into my flats, and we'll go sniff us a murder."

The black-and-whites were dotted around the intersection of Eighteenth and Melrose when they got there, the yellow tapes in place stretched between palm tree and parking meter and mailbox and antiram stanchion, screaming PO-LICE! DO NOT CROSS! in various major languages of Earth and the Worlds. The street itself was absolutely typical of this part of Ellay—blacktop four cars wide, patched halfheartedly a couple of years ago and shimmering in Mondrian gray/black/gray down the length of it toward Santa Monica Boulevard; short green curbside lawn already going brown, in places, in this too-arid spring; wide white sidewalks, half the slabs cracked; bungalow houses in white stucco with red or brown tile roofs, ornamental palms and cacti bristling here and there, interspersed with poinsettia trailing splashes of dilapidated red; doorways gated and locked against the thugs from the next neighborhood over. Over everything the hot blue sky arched, the white sun in it standing lunchtime-high, and the erstwhile inhabitants of the black-and-whites stood around in the meager shadow of the royal palms nearest the corner and tried to look as if they were doing something. Near them, half across a driveway, was a white tarp, and under that, a blue one.

Lee and Gelert had left their company hov parked on Wilshire. They walked around the corner and saw it all laid out for them, and as they did, one of the shapes standing in shadow looked up and saw them: the only one of the people standing there likely to get much good of the shadow, being nearly as skinny as a palm tree himself. Jim Blessington came stalking along toward them in the sun, head down, shoulders bent as if the light had weight, the blue LAPD coverall glancing the sunlight back from rank patches and the rolled-back hood. Only as he got close did he look up. "Mz. Enfield," he said.

"Mr. Blessington," Lee said. "How's the family?"

"Doing well, thank you. Marta turned three last week."

"I can't believe it," Lee said. "It seems like about half an hour ago that we flew Michelle over to Cedars. The boys all right?"

"As good as they can be with the Birthday Girl ruling the roost." Blessington grinned a little, then nodded at Gelert: Gel tilted his head, flipped his ears forward. It was all the greeting they ever exchanged. Jim worked professionally enough with *madrín* but found it hard to socialize with them, and only his tremendous skill as a detective, and his "kill rate," had kept this from becoming a firing offense.

"So what have we got, Jim?" Lee said, as they walked toward the tarp.

"We're hoping you'll tell us. Body's at LACC right now. As far as we can tell, the guy came around the corner from Melrose, walked down toward his car. Someone waited for him . . ." Jim made a "blooey" gesture with his hands. "Left the scene. On foot, we think . . . but your reading, we hope, will confirm."

"We'll see."

Gelert paused. "Blessington," he said, "you know that this is some damn political thing from Upstairs. We're not needed here."

"Damn well I know it," Jim muttered. "Nice you know it, too."

"Wanted to make sure you knew we knew it."

"Always said you were a gentleman," Jim said, "as houn' dogs go."

Lee took no official notice of any of this. "Jim," she said, "any sign of the murder weapon as yet? It would do us the most good."

"We're conducting a house-to-house. Don't think we're going to find it here, though. I'm betting it's fifty miles away in a dry wash somewhere, or a lot farther off than that. Meanwhile, we've already been all over this area for physical-forensics purposes: you don't have to worry about fouling anything."

The three of them paused by the spread-out tarp. The other uniforms, two men and a woman, nodded to Lee and Gelert as they paused by the tarp. "The samples have gone down to Parker?" Lee said.

"Yeah. You want me to move people back?" Blessington said.

Gelert gave him a very straight-faced look. "What are we, a kindergarten class? We can tell your people from the perps just fine. Maybe they want to get back in the shade, though. No reason for them to boil their brains."

"Huh," said Blessington, one of the seemingly null noises he made that Lee had learned to translate as approval. He waved a hand casually at them and headed back to the palm trees.

Lee stood there over the tarp for a moment, Gelert beside her, and closed her eyes. *Madam, we're on Your business now,* she thought, as she executed the series of tiny jaw-clenches and neck movements that brought her implant online and started it recording. *Be in what we see, for the innocent's sake . . .*

She waited a few seconds for the "aura" that came with the onset of judicial sight: a blurring around the edges, not quite a rainbowing as of visible light but a sense of multiple possibilities. Lee leaned over and pulled the tarp away.

The bloodstain had sunk deep into the cracked white cement of the sidewalk, running down the cracks and the joins between the slabs. Lee blinked, her eyes watering at the strength of the impression of what had happened here, still so recent. The body lay there already, drowning out everything else. *No,* she thought. *Earlier.*

The vision resisted her, lying there with limbs splayed, its chest shot away, seeping. Death in any given spot always impressed itself powerfully on the matter there, making it hard to perceive any life sharing the same spot in time and space: and it was life that Lee needed to see now. She did not turn her eyes away from the body, but held her gaze steady, waiting for the shift. Slowly it came, but not before she'd had to spend a good long while looking at the chiseled, classic beauty of Omren dil'Sorden's face. It had been much easier, last night, seeing it in just a glimpse, on the news, before she knew his name.

Lee held her pity in check, waited. It was not pity she needed now, but paraperception, and slowly it came. The body was no longer lying in front of her, but falling to the ground past her left shoulder. Through the silvery mist of uncertainties implied by the movement of the air molecules between her and the murdered man, Lee felt the wind and concussion of the second shotgun blast as it hit dil'Sorden. A second, faded perception overlaid her first: the last tattering impressions leaking from dil'Sorden's sensorium as he fell. Lee took note of the perception, but didn't expect much from it. Hydrostatic shock, nerve damage and blood loss, let alone the overriding disbelief and horror at what was happening, had left dil'Sorden's own view of his last moments nothing much more than a terrible dark blur, with a long wet jagged bloom of brightness laid across it at the very end, the remnant of a last glimpse of the nearby streetlight as he went down.

Slowly, because the moment resisted quick movement and was likely to be denatured by it, Lee turned a little, looked over her shoulder. The fall was in process again, from a slightly earlier point in time. There were only so many of these reversals she could induce without draining that "site" or point of view dry: she had to see as much as possible in each of them. Here was the first shotgun blast, from a little farther down the sidewalk. Lee looked at the shape holding the gun, but from this "angle" could only see clearly what dil'Sorden had seen clearly; and that was little. Eyes, then the barrel of the gun. The shape itself was far more uncertain, a dark blur. Still, not a tall man: he barely came up to dil'Sorden's shoulder. Stocky, perhaps a hundred kilograms, a head that looked almost rectangular. *Turn a little,* she willed him, but from this angle there was no profile, or not enough, the features all lost in darkness and blur.

The emotional context was starting to force its way through the merely physical. This was inevitable, but Lee resisted it for the moment and concentrated on seeing. What she saw was no longer a fall, but a run, the tall slender blur running around the corner, away from the light of Melrose, garish through the Heisenberg blur. The second shape, the stocky man, running after, bringing up the sawed-off shotgun. Lee watched as they ran toward her, seeing the first blast again, and saw dil'Sorden's arms fling up as if in surprise as he stumbled; but before the second blast, she turned away from the fall she knew was already beginning, and saw the second shape come around the corner.

But not all the way around. Close to the wall he stopped, watched, a shadow. He was in sharper focus than the others, the uncertainties about him less, though still present. Tall, taller even than dil'Sorden; a slender man, erect, very still. After a moment he slipped back around the corner, out of sight.

Lee knelt there and considered going after him. That had its dangers: pull too much energy out of the forensic "field" of the area right now and it could be exhausted for further investigation later. *I have enough to go on with as a start,* she thought: *after we've pulled his profile and coordinated with physical forensics, I can have another run.*

She closed her eyes, let the state of investigative vision lapse, and looked around her again, closing down the recording her implant was making and adding her digital "signature" to it as it closed. The sealed record would feed itself wirelessly into the city judicial-data system as soon as she got near a transponder: it might be doing so now if there was a 'sponder in one of the black-and-whites, which seemed likely. Blessington was standing not too far away: as Lee replaced the tarp and got up, brushing herself off, he walked over.

"One triggerman," she said. "Human. A hundred seventy centimeters or so, stocky, very square-built, say a hundred kilos. Wearing a business suit of some kind, to judge from the color and the contour of the artifact."

"Good, that's good," Blessington said.

"But look for someone else, too," Lee said. "Alfen. Tall, say two hundred ten centimeters. Thin. Not muscular. Another business-suit type, but more elegantly cut."

"Aren't they all," Blessington said rather sourly.

Lee smiled slightly. "Maybe just a witness," she said,

"but somehow I don't think so. I'd see if physical forensics finds any trace of his involvement on the body . . . fibers or whatever. They might give us a lead that would be useful."

"That's confirmed already," Blessington said. "The guys at Parker have picked up some of that. And Gelert smelled him straight off."

Lee nodded, followed Blessington's glance. Gelert was about halfway down the block, walking very slowly, stiff-legged, bristling, while the uniformed cops watched him with idle curiosity. Lee smiled very slightly as she watched him stalk along. Her paraperceptual cues came in visual form when she was working, but Gel's, predictably, came as scent. Gelert's people were the greatest trackers in the worlds; at the core of their nature as a species was the understanding that what they hunted, eventually they found. The hunting could take all kinds of forms, quarry variously concrete or abstract; all over the Worlds, *madrín* were researchers and scientists, consultants and advisers. But finally it all came down to noses, one way or another, a situation Gelert often complained about as seeming awfully undignified in someone with a doctorate. Yet nothing could have moved him to give up this particular form of the talent, and the hot fierce look in Gel's eyes after he had been working on a crime scene always made it plain to Lee that this particular style of discovery was what he lived for.

"What's he after now? Did he say?"

Blessington shrugged. "He growled. I couldn't understand him."

Lee raised her eyebrows. "He tends to drop into dialect when he's distracted." Gelert had put his nose down to the sidewalk, and his pace was speeding up: he was nearly to the end of the block.

"Lee, you want us to keep this end of the scene locked down for a while?" Blessington said.

"It's a good idea. I need to talk to the people at Parker and have a look at the victim's profile and recent history before I come back for another look."

"Okay. Bensen, Echevarria," Blessington called over to two of his people as Gelert turned left around the house on the corner lot and vanished from sight, "better go with the gentleman and keep people out of his way while he's working." The two uniforms nodded to their boss and headed off after Gelert at a dogtrot.

"You know this neighborhood at all?" Lee said to Blessington.

He gave her an amused look. "I lived here before I was married."

"What's around the corner?"

"A nightclub: a couple of restaurants. It was the nightclub dil'Sorden came out of. He'd come in earlier, alone. Had a snack and a few drinks, listened to the jazz combo that was playing there last night, paid his bill, and left."

"He didn't meet anybody?"

"Not according to the club owner."

"Did he go there often?"

"The owner said he saw him occasionally. Not a regular, but he would drop in for something to eat after working late. The place has a rep for its ribs."

Lee nodded. "Jim, he was already running as he came around the corner. Whoever shot him came around after him, fast. He had to have been waiting for dil'Sorden in one of the doorways that face onto Wilshire: I'm going to have another look at that later. Here's how it went—"

She and Blessington went up to the corner, and Lee reenacted for Blessington what she had seen. At the end of it all they stood there again over the tarp, looking down at the spot where dil'Sorden had fallen.

"Contract job?" Blessington said at last.

"I can't see why, but then I only had time to skim his pro-file on the way over," Lee said. "There seemed to be some urgency 'Upstairs.' "

Blessington made that sour face again. "Which smells weird to me to start with," he said, "but then I'm just a de-tective." The delivery was ironic but not hostile: Lee smiled slightly. "Speaking of smells," Blessington said, and gri-maced. "Bensen, what the hell are you guys up to?"

He listened for a moment, face immobile. "How about that," he said. "Yeah, bring it back. Be careful about how you wrap it; it might have been handled two or three times before it got there, and maybe after."

Blessington looked over at Lee. "He's good," he said. "He found the murder weapon three blocks over and two blocks up, in somebody's front yard, two feet deep in pachysandra."

"You owe him one, then," Lee said. "Think how many manpower-hours he saved you."

"He'll remind me of it, I'm sure," Blessington said.

Down the street, Gelert and the two uniforms were com-ing around the corner again: one of them, Echevarria, was carrying an antistatic evidence bag, glancing back smoky silver reflections in the hot sun as they approached. Gelert was trotting along with his tongue hanging out, looking to Lee's eyes unusually pleased with himself. As the officers stowed the shotgun in the car, Gelert sat down beside Lee and Blessington.

"The murderer caught a bus," Gelert said. "About twenty minutes after the killing: one of the night buses down Mel-rose."

"Stupid," Blessington said. "Too many witnesses."

"He seemed willing to take the risk," Gelert said. "Foren-sically it was smart: his lifetrace got tangled up with a lot of others, fresh and stale. And by the time we pull that bus out of service so that I can go over it, there'll be more overlay still. But it won't help him, because I should still be able to tell when he got off, and once we plot the times against the bus schedule, that'll tell us where."

"Assuming it ran on time," Lee said, with understandable skepticism. No Ellay native ever really believed public transit would do anything so unusual.

"Night buses usually do," Gelert said. "Especially the automated ones, and I think this route went auto some time back." He looked up at Lee. "Did you see the other Alfen?"

"I did," she said.

"Where'd he come from?"

"Around the corner. He went back that way. I'm going to work on him on the second pass. But I think we need to go up to Parker first to talk to physical forensics and take a little more time to go over the victim's profile. Oh, and Jim? I'm going to ask the club to stay closed until this evening, so Gelert and I can go over the ground."

"Right," Blessington said. "Tell them to call me if they need authorization. Meanwhile, we need to get this weapon to Parker. Bensen will stay with the site here. Meet you afterward?"

"Sure, Jim."

Blessington and Echevarria got into one of the black-and-whites and drove off: Gelert sat panting for a moment, watching them go. "That didn't take you long," Lee said.

"The trace was pretty strong," Gelert said. "What I found odd was the way it dropped off as the guy who'd used the gun got to the bus stop. Normally it gets stronger when you stand in one place for a few minutes." He was starting to frown.

Lee looked down toward Melrose. "You thinking that someone was helping him hide his trace somehow?"

"I'm thinking about that second Alfen," Gelert said.

"So am I. Bensen?" Lee called. "Have you got any more site tape in the car?"

"Miles of it. Want some?"

"Please." Lee went over to the black-and-white, and Bensen handed her out roll after roll. "Three be enough, ma'am?"

"Should be. I'm going to block off the sidewalk from the corner to the club dil'Sorden was in: it looks as if our perp came out that way."

"Right. I'll keep an eye on it."

Lee headed for the corner, and Gelert got up and came with her. "So what are you thinking of?" she said softly, as they came up to the corner of the side street with Melrose, and Lee fastened the tape to the street sign there. "How do you fade out a lifetrace?"

"No way that I know," Gelert said, "unless the person himself is dying. Not having seen the news today, maybe our murderer did die on a bus last night, but frankly, I doubt it. Something else happened. I want to know what. At the very least, I'm going to get a paper out of it."

Lee smiled slightly. "I thought you were through with your post-doctorate publication cycle."

"One more never hurts."

"Yeah, right. Research junkie." Lee stopped opposite the door of the club. LA VIDA LOCA, said the cold dark neon sign attached to the blind white stucco of the building's frontage. No window: solid brown wood door. One of those "we keep it dark in here for a reason" places: intimate, or secretive, depending on the crowd that used it. "You want to go on with this?" she said to Gelert, holding out the roll of tape she'd just finished looping around the parking meter opposite the club's door. "Take it on down another couple of shops, say to the dry cleaner's there."

"Right," Gelert said, taking the tape in his teeth and backing down the street with it. Lee went to the club door, pushed it open.

After the brightness of the street it took a moment or so for her eyes to get used to the dimness, even though the lights inside the place were on full. The décor was modern enough, but very dark, all reds and hardwoods: if the furnishings had been less well kept, it would have struck Lee as the kind of place where married men went to have dinner with the women they weren't married to. "Can I help you?" a male voice said.

Lee turned. A man stood there in white T-shirt and jeans; the first glance gave her an impression of longish, unruly gray hair, wide-set dark eyes, big shoulders, big hands, polishing a glass with a glass cloth. "Yes," Lee said, bringing out her professional ID and showing it to him. "My name is Lee Enfield: I'm a 'mancer working with the LAPD, investigating the murder that happened around the corner last night."

"Mike Ibanez," the man said.

"What time would you normally be opening tonight, Mr. Ibanez?"

"Six," Ibanez said.

"All right. Mr. Ibanez, my partner *Madra* Gelert and I are going to need to do a psychoforensic sweep through here later today: probably early this afternoon, though we'll come sooner if we can. Until the first sweep is done, we'll need you to keep the premises locked, and not open them again until we clear them. You can stay inside, that's all right, but no one else should come in: no deliveries, that kind of thing. The County will compensate you for your downtime and any employee overtime or reimbursement that the closure entails. I'll bring the paperwork for you when we come back. Is that all right?"

"Sure," Ibanez said.

"Thank you," Lee said. "My partner and I may have some questions for you afterward."

"Sure, no problem."

Lee wondered whether he was always going to be this voluble. *Of course, he may just be freaked out. It's hard to remember that other people don't see murders every other day . . .* "Thank you," Lee said. "Will you lock the front door behind me? We're taping off the front sidewalk, but all the same we don't want anyone slipping in and contaminating the scene before we've had a chance to examine it."

He nodded and accompanied Lee to the door: as she stepped out, she heard it lock behind her. Lee made her way down the sidewalk toward the middle of the block, staying close to the wall, and out past the dry cleaner's where Gelert had fastened the tape.

"Talkative guy," she said to him, as he held the tape up to her and they started to walk back. "We'll see what we find out later on. You want to drive? I wouldn't mind a few minutes to look over the profile Hagen sent us."

"Go ahead."

Their company hov was a Skoda Palacia with the flex-species package. Gelert nosed the driver's side door open, and the hov recognized his touch on the lock and reconfigured the driver's seat as the forward-facing flat contour pallet that Gelert preferred. He jumped in, lay down, and let the guidance sleeves and safety webbing connect up around his limbs and hook into his implant, while Lee got in on the passenger side and kept the hov from belting her up until she could reach into the backseat for the printed report that Mass had handed them as they left the office.

She started paging through it as Gelert pulled out into traffic. Omren dil'Sorden had just turned thirty-two years old. He had been working in ExTel's network development department for eight years: his official title there was "senior research assistant." The personnel-department files appended to his CV explained that his work mostly had to do with building and enhancing telecommunications network structures at the point where they interfaced with intraworld gating facilities—both commercial gates like those at Kennedy and LAX, and "electrons-only" minicollider exchanges such as were maintained by many public and private companies. It was specialized work—Lee understood the general concept, but she had the sinking feeling that she was going to get to know it a lot better in the coming days. For the moment, she gathered that dil'Sorden had been mostly busy with improving present solid and wireless telecom networks in the LA area, and designing the new ones that would replace them—nets specifically structured to integrate with the new intercontinual comms gateways being installed at LAX over the next couple of years. *Not exactly a job that makes people want to kill you, most of the time,* Lee thought. *At least you wouldn't think so.*

She read down the list of projects dil'Sorden was involved in, one after another, and found herself shaking her head. *When did he sleep?* Lee thought. The terminology was bewildering: when she ran into a description of a "packet-shunt squirt pipeline array," she stopped, able to get no impression of anything but some kind of giant lawn sprinkler. Whatever the technical details of the systems he was designing, Omren dil'Sorden was plainly a busy guy.

Lee flipped forward through the profile to the personal evaluation pages. There were a lot of them. There was no way to work for a big company these days without having their psych and sentient-dynamics people all over you, monitoring your personality and mental health and assessing how they stacked up in relation to the corporate persona. Lee had never particularly liked the idea of this, which was one reason why she had originally risked low pay and an uncertain lifestyle to go into business "on the small" with Gelert. However, at times like this, the psych profiles and all the rest of the bean-counting had their uses, if only to give you a place to start asking your own questions. *Intelligence levels border-high/high,* Lee read in one of the summaries. *Good cooperation coefficient. Good intuition/data ratio. Good initiative/teamwork-integration compromises. Acceptable attendance and tardiness record. No visible or expressed bigotries. Negative vice/antisocial coefficient. Coworker attitudes toward subject generally good, with the usual offset.*

"Now what does that mean?" she said softly.

"What?" Gelert looked over her shoulder.

Lee pointed to the phrase on the page. Gelert looked, then snorted down his nose. "It's corporate code for the fact that he's Alfen, and they know that most people hate Alfen."

"Oh, come on. 'Hate' is kind of a strong word, wouldn't you say?"

"Well, maybe it is. After all, the Elves are all spiffy dressers, they all drive Porsches or better, their parties never run out of ice; when not merely rich, they're fabulously wealthy, and they're all stunningly beautiful, immortal, and eternally young: what's *not* to like?"

Lee gave him an ironic look, dropping the report in her lap as they merged off the Wilshire on-ramp onto the Hollywood Slideway, and the Skoda locked itself into the traffic flow at 100 kph. "Seriously, Gel. Why would anybody come after this poor guy with a shotgun?" Lee said. "He was just some kind of hardware maven. No family in this universe, as far as I can tell from this—there are holes in it."

"I know. I'll go digging and add in some background when we get back to the office."

"No relationships—that, if anything, would have turned up in a corporate detailing."

"Assuming it had been kept updated in a timely manner."

"I bet this one is as updated as it can be. We'll find out. But if it is, then that means there goes your *crime passionelle*. Your broker buddies are going to have to make do with something else: dil'Sorden wasn't even dating." Lee looked out the window for a moment, watching the green, dusty, upsloping ground cover beside the slideway rush by. "Unless this guy stole someone else's project and made them mad enough to kill him because of it. Work is all he seems to have had time for, to judge by this."

"Could have been. Don't worry . . . motivation will out." Gelert looked grim. "Just give it time. No murder is motiveless, any more than anything else in sentient behavior is."

"Just sometimes the motive is buried deeper than usual," Lee said. "Not too deep for us to dig up, I hope . . ."

The hov progressed as far as Fourth and took itself off the slideway: Gel took over the driving again and ran the hov down through the traffic toward Parker Center. The parking lots for the center were all underground, and access to them was backed up as always, so Lee had another fifteen minutes to pore over dil'Sorden's personnel report between the time Gelert surrendered the hov to the local traffic management system and the time it deposited them in a slot at the back of beyond, six levels down and easily half a mile from the main complex.

They hiked through the catacombs to the nearest elevator/escalator stack and made their up through the levels to the sun and the air again. Ten minutes or so later they broke out into the windy central plaza. Lee glanced over at the main court building with a slight smile of triumph as she and Gelert made their way over to the LAPD's HQ building, identical to the other porticoed white edifices around the plaza except for the department's shield.

Inside the building was huge, open, and airy, a rebellion

against the claustrophobic facilities of earlier years, all too conducive to making the people inside it think they were a fortress against a prying world that had no right to know what they were doing. In its latest incarnation, the LAPD headquarters looked more like a Silicon Lakeshore facility than anything else: the central atrium let the diffuse sunlight in everywhere, the colors were pale and cool, and voices murmured on all sides, individual words lost in the rush of the four slender waterfalls that poured down from the roof level into the central basin five floors up. Lee and Gelert took the escalators up around the sides of the basin to the fourth floor, where Forensics was located, and went hunting across the right side of the big open-plan space for the team of analysts working on the dil'Sorden case.

Four or five rows of cubicles in they found the team assigned to the case, or at least three of its members. One set of four cubicles, arranged in a square, was notable amongst its neighbors for having a truly disreputable-looking ficus in the middle of it, its every skinny, straggly branch decorated with paper ornaments and less identifiable objects hung by strings: crayoned Christmas balls, foil dreydels, cellophane Jul fires, crumbling Day-of-the-Dead bone cookies, and here and there the occasional stranded paper plane. Under the spreading Whatsit Tree, in one of the cubicles, a young, short, round, dark-haired, dark-skinned man sat staring at the high-res vision plate set into the cubicle wall, with his hands in midair before him, seemingly twiddling with nothing. On the plate was an image of what seemed like a piece of thick rope.

Lee came up softly behind him and stood still, looking at the "rope," as the seated man worked with the virtual glove box program. "Silk," the man said, without turning to look at them. "Hi, Lee. Hi, Gelert."

"Hi, Telly," Gelert said. Lee said nothing as she watched

Telinu Umivera manipulate the fiber under the scanner—definitely something worth watching, as he was possibly one of the best materials people in the department.

"Alfen silk?" Lee said.

"Yup," Telinu said. "Look at the bump ratio." The definition on the scanner's enlargement changed, so that the "rope" filled the view. A pattern of shallow semi-hemispherical bumps became visible all across the view area. "It's a dead giveaway: Earth-sourced silk fibers don't bump that way. I teased this out of a thread someone left on the back of dil'Sorden's jacket. Fifty-fifty blend, Alfen silk, Earth-New Zealand merino wool. Spun in Auckland, woven in Singapore."

"But not from dil'Sorden's suit?" Gelert said.

Telinu shook his head. "Wrong color, wrong age, wrong everything else. Someone he'd seen within the last . . ."

"Could have been a week," said a voice from the other side of the cubicle. A head looked over the cubicle wall—blond, green downturned eyes, fluffy short hair: Stella de la Roux. "This guy wasn't real good at taking care of his clothes," she said in her soft breathy little voice. "I don't think he even brushed the suit down when it got stuff on it—just shook it off."

"Sounds like a gold mine for you, Stella," Gelert said.

"More like a mudhole," she said, and vanished behind the partition again. "It's going to take hours and hours to classify it all."

Telinu pushed his chair back a little from his desk, stretched his arms above his head. "You have a chance to look at our raw findings yet?" Lee said.

Telinu shook his head. "I had a look ten, fifteen minutes ago, but the system hadn't processed them through. Things are running slow today."

"Well, there was definitely another Alfen at the murder

scene," Lee said. "I saw him, and Gel smelled him . . . at least a witness, if not otherwise involved. This might possibly have come from his suit."

"Let me know if the interviewing makes it sound that way," Telinu said. "I'd be glad of whatever psych corroboration we can get, because there is simply too much physical evidence on this body. Stelladella wasn't kidding about his coat: half the county's plastered over it. Mikki is having to macro some of my custom search routines so that the system can start sorting and flagging some of the eight million samples the guys in the clean room have pulled off it already . . ."

"Alfen fiber, Tierran fiber, Earth fiber, Alfen hair, Alfen fur . . ." came a voice from the third cubicle.

Lee and Gelert walked around that way. "Fur?" Gelert said to the long lean silver-haired man who was sprawled in that cubicle's seat, watching line after line after line of code scroll up the display plate in front of him.

"Somebody's cat," Mikki Uiviinen said, looking over his shoulder at Gelert. "God only knows where he picked it up, and the problem is that *we're* going to have to figure it out."

"Did you know we found the murder weapon?" Gelert said.

"Yes indeed," Mikki said idly. "Good boy."

Gelert stepped forward, leaned his head over sideways, and took Mikki's upper arm gently between his jaws. "I invite you to restate that," he said, grinning around the arm.

"You bite me, I'll bleed on you, I swear," Mikki said, not moving. "Okay. Good *'mancer.*"

"Woof woof," Gelert said dryly, and let him go.

"How come *his* report gets up here before mine does?" Lee said, slightly aggrieved.

"Because the weapon did," Telinu said. "The eternal victory of the material over the immaterial, Lee. Sorry. Three sets of prints so far, they say in the clean room. One is Alfen: the characteristic double whorls and 'barred spirals' are clearly present. Ballistics is standing in line behind the dusters to get its hands on the weapon for barrel and muzzle work. Metallurgy has already pulled a sample for the registration."

"Okay," Lee said, breathing out. "Good."

"So this isn't just some mugging, you think," Mikki said.

"No," Lee and Gelert said in unison.

"Robbery?"

"No one touched the body after it fell," Gelert said. "The assailant took off down the street, ran a few blocks down, a few blocks over, ditched the gun, ran some more, then caught a bus."

"He wait long?"

"Not too long," Gelert said. "It suggests that the murderer may have known the timing of the bus . . ."

"It also suggests that someone else might have been operating to make sure that dil'Sorden was in the right place at around the right time," Lee said.

The others looked at her. She shook her head. "Conjecture," she said. "I have interviewing to do yet. We'll see if the facts support the theory."

"Revenge? Retaliation for something going wrong?" said Mikki.

"Nonpayment for drugs?" Stella said. "Or a gambling debt?"

"Not enough data," Gelert said. "We're a ways off motivation yet. But I'm glad there's at least some physical evidence supporting the idea that this was a joint Alfen-human job. Perceptual evidence may stand on its own in court these days, but it stands a whole lot taller with physical evidence to support it."

"Well, we'll stay on it," Telinu said, turning his attention back to the strand of silk. "This one's gonna take a lot of figuring out."

"Not that we mind," Stella said. "It's certainly interesting enough. Been a while since I've dealt with an Alfen murder."

Lee nodded . . . and then stopped. "Really?" she said. "A long while?"

Stella nodded. Telinu stopped a moment, thinking. "Yeah," he said. "There was that case, what, three years ago? That rape and murder. But nothing since."

Mikki looked over at him. "Not that you see them as perps all that often either," he said. "But they usually seem to be on the other side of the gun, or knife, or whatever."

Lee stood still and frowned at that for a moment. "Mikki," Lee said, "seemings aside . . . exactly how often *are* Elves murdered? It's statistics I'd be interested in. Worlds-wide, if possible."

Mikki looked at her with a somewhat bemused expression. "Lee," he said, "is it possible that you notice any news story in which you're *not* mentioned?"

"Self-promotion is nine-tenths of a career," Gelert said. "You heard it here first."

Lee gave Mikki a look, though she knew he was teasing. "This is a poor moment to descend into personalities," she said.

"I'm not kidding," Mikki said. "All right, maybe I am, you've been busy. But the Five-Interpol interspecies crime study is finally, finally about to be made public. After five, maybe six postponements. It was beginning to stink to high heaven; I think they just couldn't find any way to postpone it anymore after the UN &' ME started breathing down their necks. I would have thought you'd heard; it's been all over the news."

"The case we just finished really has been taking a lot of

my time," Lee said, "and I've had less time for the news than usual. *Mea culpa.* So can you get me a copy?"

"Not the slightest chance," Mikki said. And winked.

Lee had little time for the winking. "Mikki, are you trying to suggest that the report suggests the distribution of such crimes is *not* standard statistical distribution for a population in a given universe? Maybe not even Monte Carlo! Is that what you're trying to tell me?"

"I couldn't say," Mikki said, acquiring an expression of unusual innocence, even for him.

"That look of naked greed suggests that he could if the price was right," Gelert said. "But he's trying to maintain some poor semblance of innocence. He's going to take it out of you in cookies, Lee."

Mikki gave Gelert an annoyed look. "If word gets out," he said, "nobody will feed me this stuff anymore, Lee. That would be unfortunate. It's occasionally useful to be able to pick up bits and pieces of information this way . . ."

"It's the gingerbread you're after, isn't it," Lee said, resigned. "All right. Two dozen."

"Three. With the gilding."

"Don't ask me for cute shapes."

"I wasn't going to. But service has to be paid for in kind, Lee, you know that. Especially when you think it's going to make a difference to your case."

She let out a breath. "Mikki, I'd be lying if I said I knew *how* it was going to make a difference. But I have a feeling it's going to matter. If it's too much trouble, forget it."

"Not at all," Mikki said. "Three dozen, gilt, no cute designs. I'll have a word with my source." He cracked his knuckles and looked at his screen again, where the code continued to pour by.

"When will you be done with the findings on dil'Sorden?" Gelert said.

"At this rate," Stella said, "no sooner than the day after tomorrow. We'll call if anything surprising comes up."

Lee and Gelert said their good-byes and made their way downstairs again. "You having another of your famous hunches?" Gelert said, as they came down the last escalator.

"You always tell me to trust them . . ."

"So I do," Gelert said as he padded out ahead of Lee, into the blazing sun. "So. Lunch first? Then we'll go check out that nightclub."

"Right," Lee said. As they headed across the plaza, she kept losing the brilliance of the day in that image of the dark body-shape falling past her; and as she turned to look over her shoulder, the still, slim shadow stood there by the corner of the building, watched another Alfen go down with his life running out of him, and slowly, unmoved, pulled back out of sight.

The man with the gun we'll track down soon enough, Lee thought, not understanding her own anger, half-afraid to try. *But* you *I am going to find with extreme prejudice . . . and after that, watch out.*

Three

Inside the nightclub it was dim, and dimmer still from the observer's point of view. Here and there shapes were hunched over tables, pulled into themselves: but not many. A high wailing, like the keening for the dead, filled the air.

At a table near the front of the room, a shape sat by itself. A plate had been pushed off to one side, a crumpled paper napkin lying on it. A glass stood nearby, empty. The dark shape put some banknotes down on the table, some coins too, then got up slowly.

At the door he stood silent, hesitant, for a few moments. Then he pushed the door open. The orange light of the sodium-vapor streetlight outside threw his shadow against the wall near the door, sharp and distinct. He looked out the door, didn't move for several breaths: then eased out into the evening.

Inside the dark room, no one followed him: no one noticed the door closing again. The keening of the jazz band went on, muted as the song came to a bridging passage.

Outside, to a tracker with keener ears, the music seemed as loud as it had inside, and a waft or confluence of scents from within the club drifted out past the dark shape. The tracker, though, perceived the shape itself also as a tangle of scents and aromas; deathlessness, strangely melded with fear, concern, unease, now moved away from the door, looking down Melrose. A metallic scent as it looked over its shoulder, saw nothing, felt in its pockets for the source of the metal smell—

The second set of scents, present from the beginning but not at the forefront, stronger and coarser than the first set, now slipped out of a doorway farther down the street and presented itself fully to the night. The smell of gunpowder, blasting cap, barrel oil, pierced the dark air like a knife. The small grating sound of a footstep on the sidewalk alerted no one: but then sharp in the darkness, unmistakable, came the sound of the shotgun cocking. That sound lanced through the first tangle of scents like a missed heartbeat, made it turn, look behind, then break into a run, slide, go wide around the corner, vanish around it. The scents of gun and quiet enjoyment went after the smell of fear, fast, not afraid, anticipating. Then came the crash of the gun firing. And the second crash. Satisfaction, amusement, and the need to hurry, spread on the air. They faded away down Eighteenth Street, into darkness folding itself in on darkness, as scents of alarm, shock, surprise spread down the street after; and in the midst of them, in one spot, the smell of blood, of death, made itself all there was in that place, all there would be for a long time.

Then came the strange thing, the impossible thing: a scent that simply came from nowhere. The tracker always has a hint of every scent first—faint, then increasing until in full presence, then decreasing again to nothing. But this one drew itself as abruptly across the air as a trumpet note. Another scent of deathlessness stood at the corner, looking down Eighteenth Street at death. Its composure was not complete. Scorn lay on the air, and frustration. Yet it was pleased, for this was one more of several things that had needed to occur for some time. Soon the list would have been completed, and other things, even more final, could be brought about. Satisfaction filled the thinker, colder than that of the tangle of scents which had held the gun and pulled the trigger.

And abruptly as a trumpet note that does not fade, but simply ceases, the scent of satisfied deathlessness was gone.

Lee leaned back in her chair and let out a long breath. "That's the third time I've run through it," she said, turning her back on her commwall, "and I still don't understand it."

"You think I do?" Gelert said from his own office.

The wall between their offices was down. It was after seven in the evening. Mass had gone home for the day, and the two of them were going through the recordings of their "sniff" of the Vida Loca nightclub scene.

"Lee," Gelert said, "I'm telling you that that perception is of someone simply *vanishing*. Not going away, not walking off. Simply not being where they were anymore."

"And they do that how?" Lee said, getting up and starting to pace. It was her third outbreak of pacing for the evening, most unusual for her. "These are *Elves* we're talking about here, Gel, not the Tooth Fairy! They don't just fizzle out into nothing, any more than you or I do. The DA sees that attached to a prosecution case, he's going to throw it out. Or us, on the grounds that one or the other of us has taken leave of our senses."

"Or both," Gelert said. "You're going to have to review your own perception of that angle, and you don't like the idea much, do you?"

She didn't bother answering, because he was right. "Lee,

stop stonewalling," Gelert said. "If we both see it, then—somehow—it happened. Whether we like it or not! It's both our business to perceive the truth, and we're both good at it. So stop assuming I've had some kind of brain failure. Assume that I smelled what I smelled. How do we explain it?"

"I can't," Lee said.

"So for the moment let's concentrate on what we can explain, and leave the inexplicable to the DA: it'll be his problem anyway, once discovery is over. Let's take it all from the top."

Lee leaned back, and Gelert brought up the image of Omren dil'Sorden that appeared in his ExTel personnel file. "So here he is," Gelert said. "Born in the Alfen equivalent of Rio de Janeiro, birth date sometime in the 1970s if the computer is converting correctly between our dating systems. Standard educational history—taught at home until seven, fostered out to a relative on his mother's side in exchange for her own son, educated at what passes for a public elementary school and then a fast-track private secondary—"

Lee turned to her own commwall. Gelert had already brought the précis up on it, and the "long" version of the data was flowing by in a larger window to one side. A name stopped her. "Laurin—" She blinked. "Wait a minute. The *Elf-king* was on his school's board of governors?"

"Don't get excited. Apparently he's on all of them. There's some ceremonial connection—I think the Laurin is supposed to be 'patron of learning' for all Alfen children, directly or indirectly. Even private schools get a lot of funding from the central government, such as it is, in Aien Mhariseth—Geneva, as we would think of it. Except it's not Geneva; it's somewhere in the Dolomites instead. An imperfect congruence."

Lee nodded, went on to the other data. "University afterward," Gelert said, "at Mehisbon, which corresponds to our

Chicago. Another government-funded school, this one like the Sorbonne: strong on physical sciences and art."

"Interesting conjunction."

"Not for Elves: they don't see them as separate. Dil'Sorden took a joint degree in computer sciences and economics. Afterward he did some postgrad study in intrauniversal economics at their version of Columbia, which strangely enough is a religious school in Alfheim."

That made Lee blink. "What religion?"

"I wondered about that myself. It's some local sect that worships a deity called Alma Mater—a variant on Herself, to judge by the name. The mainstream Alfen faiths consider this one kind of flaky, I take it, but their schools are highly thought of. . . . Then dil'Sorden took an interim year—got a medium-access visa for Xaihon and planethopped in their space for a while, the usual ex-student stuff. When he got back, someone head-hunted him for ExTel. And there he's been ever since, working like crazy. Six promotions since he came."

Lee shook her head. She touched her desktop and brought up once again the list of dil'Sorden's projects at ExTel. "There's a thought," she said, as the characters flowed by under the surface of the desk. "Did he get promoted over someone's head? Does someone hold a grudge?"

"Worth looking into."

The project descriptions kept flowing by. Lee shook her head again. "I keep running into these references to fairy gold all through his proposals," she said. "FG network lattices, FG core bindings . . ."

"Why wouldn't you?" Gelert said. "Without a room-temperature superconductor, you've got no broadband comms, no high-speed computers. No interstellar travel, no intersystem spacing, no gating facilities. . . ."

That brought Lee's head around. "Oh, come on now, there was gating before there was fairy gold. How did our version of MacIlwain break through to his first alternate universe, otherwise?"

"By accident. And supercooling. Lady of the Hunts, Lee, imagine what it must have been like. Liquid nitrogen everywhere: it's a wonder the poor man didn't wind up as an ice cube. But you can't tune an accelerator ring predictably for interdimensional location without fairy gold for the inner winding on the dees. Without superconductor winding, there's no telling which world out of seven you'd wind up in once you walked through a patent gate locus. Think how long it took poor MacIlwain to duplicate his results! That was the first thing Earth secured through Huictilopochtli when the two worlds came into phase again: the tuning technology, and enough fairy gold to make one gate that could be counted on, in phase or out. The Alfen even donated it." Gelert grinned, a predator's look. "So altruistic of them. They knew they were getting yet another universe's worth of customers for their most expensive export . . ."

"I should do some more reading on this," Lee said, mournful. She had been hoping to avoid it.

"You should." Gelert grinned at her, shaking his ears until they flapped. "Instead of dancing around technology the way you dance around the tarantulas in my driveway. Sometimes I think your mother was frightened by a math textbook."

"Sometimes I think *your* mother was a—"

"Now, now."

"Sorry."

"No, you're not, so don't say you are. You've been bad-tempered for the last month or so, but you've had an excuse, and you'll get over it. It's not interfering with work, anyway, which is the important thing."

They were quiet for a few moments. Lee looked up at her commwall again and watched the list of dil'Sorden's next five years of planned projects go spilling by: work he would never now do. "You know what I keep coming back to?" Lee said.

"What?"

"Hagen," she said. "Why he's so antsy about this murder being 'cleared up'—I assume he means solved—in such a hurry. Though I understand your explanation about the markets perfectly well."

"I'm not sure you do," Gelert said. "Lee, I know it sounds dumb . . . but the markets always do overreact, and ExTel in particular has been waiting for this particular set of circumstances for a long time. Hagen's boss was offered any number of golden parachutes over the last few years, attached to fat offers from other companies, and he refused them. He was waiting for the antitrust case to end, waiting to be the president of the biggest multi-universal comms corporation in town. Now *this* happens. Naturally it feels like a thorn in his paw, and he wants it out. We're just the tool that's nearest to hand." He grinned at her. "Your fault for being so good on that job six months ago."

"Thanks so much," Lee muttered.

"So here's dil'Sorden," Gelert said. "By all accounts a team player, a nice guy, well liked by his fellow employees, good performance ratings. Up to his ears in profitable work, stock options—"

"Do we know that?"

"It's a commonplace at his level of employment. We should probably ask Hagen for access to dil'Sorden's workspace to confirm it."

"You think he'd give us that?" Lee said.

"If he's really so hot about wanting this case 'solved,' let's dangle the suggestion in front of him tomorrow," Gelert said. "The worst he can do is tell us to go chase our tails. . . . Anyway, dil'Sorden's not hurting. Nice apartment, nice car, all the perks. But when we see him for the first time ourselves—he's down. Upset, would you have said?"

Lee closed her eyes and replayed her recording of her "sniff" of the inside of the nightclub. "Yes," she said. "Depressed. Extremely anxious about something he suspected was about to happen. Not the murder: something else, in the near but not immediate future."

"I concur. He goes outside with his mind on that trouble ahead of him. Then turns around, sees the guy with the gun—"

"And thinks, 'I never thought they'd go *this* far.' "

"I concur again. That's certainly how I read it. But this is stuff that I don't think a jury is going to be able to hear with you from your recording. It goes by awful fast in mine. If you can catch it more clearly when you run the site one last time—"

"All I can do is try," Lee said. "Truth is out there. All we have to do is catch her."

"If possible. These impressions are very general at the moment: they don't lead anywhere specific." Gelert lay back on his pad and stretched, long legs waving in all directions before he came upright again and lay there looking like an oversize statue of an albino Anubis. "So. A human lies in wait for dil'Sorden, shoots him, and escapes. An Elf watches, and leaves. And dil'Sorden was half expecting it. Why? What has he done wrong? Or done right, after which he can't be allowed to live longer? What has he *not* done that he was supposed to do?"

They both sat with the thought for a while. "Too soon to know," Lee said. "But this was no accident: no mugging that went wrong. It was him they meant to kill. . . . And you're right about his computer workspace. I'll ask Hagen tomorrow morning, after I sniff the site again."

"How many more runs on it do you think we have?"

"One each," Lee said. "There won't be much left to read afterward. But I'm going to milk my last run for all it's worth." Once again she saw it, that shadow by the corner, watching, satisfied, gone.

"You always were stubborn," Gelert said, getting up and stretching again.

"It takes over where smart runs out," Lee said, "and sometimes it's worth more. Let's go get some supper."

⟨divider⟩

Lee was in early the next morning, earlier even than Mass, which she knew was going to cause some teasing: but she didn't care. She spoke to the alarm system, had it bring the lights and office services online, and went back to the coffee room to make herself a cup of something strong. The shadow by the corner building had kept her awake for a long time, and when she'd finally slept, she'd gotten no good out of it.

She had dreamed about Matt again last night: one of those intense dreams, one of those very physical ones that left her awake and swiftly mortified, amid soaking wet sheets. The mortification was shortly replaced by anger, for in the dream everything was as it had been when everything was fine—the intimacy, the profound sense of trust. It was as if her traitor brain was intent on pretending that that last terrible night had never happened, the night all the talk about looks not being such an important thing had been laid bare for what it was, just talk—the night she let herself into Matt's apartment to pick up some clothes she'd left there, and found Matt kissing a face with which Lee instantly knew she could never compete, embracing a body that made it plain why he had been so busy after hours for the past couple of weeks.

Lee stood there stirring sugar into her coffee and brooding. The dialogue from that night kept replaying itself, as if there were some way it could be corrected. *Lee, let me explain. No, I understand perfectly well. Why didn't you ask me to give you back the key to your apartment? I didn't want you to think—I was trying to find a way to break it to you. Well, it looks like you found a way.* She had collected those of her things that she could quickly lay hands on and taken herself away before she found herself looking again at that lovely face, and cursing it.

There were enough people in the DA's Office who knew what Matt had been up to and had said nothing. Lee found that this hurt her, though she could understand their own conflicts about the situation. He was their boss: though the way he had been acting embarrassed them, they were still loyal to him. Some of them defended him, while still trying not to hurt her. *You know how guys are, Lee. Well, I do now. No, seriously. It's not their fault, they're just wired up that way. A relationship gets old . . . or something else is going on, work is tough, they're under stress . . . and they see a pretty face, some new young thing, and they . . .*

Lee sighed, took a drink of her coffee, and made a face. There were three sugars in it, maybe four. Lee started to throw it out, then thought that her blood sugar could probably use that much help right now. She dumped some more milk in the coffee to make it at least marginally palatable, and took it back to her desk.

She actually found herself able to smile a little as she considered the situation. There, in a department theoretically devoted to making sure people took responsibility for their actions, just about everyone was earnestly exculpating

Matt for not having had the guts to simply tell her it was all over, and that he was ditching Lee in favor of a "trophy babe." None of them seemed to see the incongruity of it. Finally, Lee had let it be known that the subject was closed and that they all needed to get on with "business as usual": if indeed there would ever be such a thing for her again. The way she felt at the moment, Lee had her doubts, but work had to be done, and she was carrying on with it; she wasn't going to give Matt the satisfaction of thinking that his thoughtlessness had enough power to ruin her life.

She sat and gazed "out" the commwall, running as usual on its default view of Saturn rising over Titan's methane snow. *I guess what makes it seem so unfair is that there are some of us who just never will be able to compete . . . not that way. We have many other accomplishments and talents, successful careers, good friendships, brains and talent and humor . . . but no matter what we do, we will never have that, that classic beauty that everyone claims not to really care about . . . and secretly does.*

Out in the front office, the comm alert shrilled. Lee looked that way in surprise, then glanced down at the desk: the clock under the surface said 0716. *Who the hell's calling at* this *hour of the morning?* she thought, for if it had been Gel or Mass or anyone else directly associated with the office, the call would have routed straight through to her wall.

Lee reached out and touched the spot on her desk that routed control of the switchboard to her. "Reh'Mechren and Enfield, good morning," she said.

The wall came alive. It was Hagen. "Lee," he said. "Another early riser, I see. Good to see it. Have you got anything for me yet?"

She blinked. "We've got some very early indications, Mr. Hagen. We've seen the murderer, at least."

"You have?"

It wasn't just surprise in his voice. It was alarm. Lee kept her face as immobile as she knew how when answering. "That's not to say we have an ID as yet," she said. "The conditions made the envisioning indistinct: we're having to depend on physical forensics as well. Gelert did find the murder weapon, which appears to have been used by a human male."

"That's great," Hagen said, sounding more natural, more enthusiastic this time. "I told them it was a good idea to bring you two onto the case."

Why am I not mentioning the Alfen to him? Lee wondered. As she thought about it, the disinclination to mention it got even stronger. Definitely a hunch, if a negative one. *So follow up on it; take the initiative, don't let him run this conversation.*

"Mr. Hagen," Lee said, "I mentioned to you yesterday that we might need to call on you or someone at ExTel for some additional information—"

"Sure. Name it."

"It would help us if we could have access to Omren dil'-Sorden's computer workspace. I know it's unusual, but we need to—"

"No problem with that at all," Hagen said. "I'll have someone from network management port the whole thing over to you at the start of business. Sooner, if someone with the right access-level privileges is on-site at the moment."

"Thanks very much—we appreciate it."

"You're likely to run into proprietary information in there, Lee. I know you'll keep it confidential. Meanwhile, I appreciate what you and Gelert are doing. Keep up the good work. When do you think you'll have a suspect in custody?"

"That's going to depend on the DA's Office," Lee said. "Once we get them the data, it's up to them." *There you go,*

Matt. Let him warm up your *commlink a little.* Lee felt guilty, but only slightly.

"That's fine. I'll be in touch later. Best to Gelert."

He vanished, and the cold serenity of the methane snows and the crescent Saturn reasserted themselves. Lee carefully put down the coffee cup she had been holding with both hands and found that her hands were actually trembling slightly with the kind of reaction she got after having looked at something judicially. There was no chance of such a thing happening down a commlink, of course, but Lee knew that she had correctly heard and interpreted the alarm in Hagen's voice.

Why would our having seen the assailant frighten him? Supposedly it's what he wants.

The most obvious possible answer to the question was that Hagen knew more about the murder than he was saying.

Lee clenched her fists on the desk. *I wish Gelert had been here to hear that,* she thought. *I don't think the desk was recording. Unless the switchboard protocol's recording routine caught it—*

She brought up its control menus in the desktop, ran down them, and swore softly: the "record" function had been off, as it normally would have been for legal reasons. *It's not like I understand the comm. system perfectly . . . but then that's Mass's job, not mine. Well, I won't touch anything until he comes in: maybe he can do something to retrieve that call . . .*

But when Mass came in around eight-thirty he checked the system and just shook his head. "Sorry, boss-lady," he said, "but it defaults to 'off' when the initial configuration comes up. I have custom configs that I bring up afterward, but even in those you have to trigger the record function on purpose. Was it important?"

"No . . ." Lee sighed. *Yes!* the back of her brain shouted at her. But now there was no proof . . .

Gelert came in around nine. Lee asked Mass to hold all their calls, and when the two of them had locked the office space down in private mode, Lee told Gelert about Hagen's call. Gelert sat there in the middle of the floor and looked at her oddly.

"You don't believe me," Lee said.

"Did you miss your breakfast? You look terrible. Of course I believe you," Gelert said, as Lee opened her mouth to answer him. "What we have to do now is figure out what to do with the data."

He put his ears down flat. "Did he pick up anything from you, do you think? That you noticed his unease, I mean?"

"I don't think so."

"Then as far as he's concerned, we keep playing it as we have been. But I'm starting to agree with you now, Lee. He does seem awfully eager to see something happening fast: too fast. And now this . . ."

Gelert slowly lay down and gave one forepaw a few meditative licks. "All we can do is see how things develop, in light of what you noticed. It leaves us with questions, though. If he's somehow involved in this murder, or knows something about it that makes him nervous, why is he so damn eager to get it investigated at all? Is he grandstanding for someone's benefit? And whose?"

"Someone human?" Lee said. "Or someone Alfen?"

Gelert looked up at her. "I wonder," he said. "It's an interesting spoor to follow. But I'm not sure it goes anywhere . . . yet."

"I'm not so sure, Gel. I didn't mention our second figure."

"Oh?"

"No. A hunch. When all I mentioned was a human with a gun, Hagen sounded relieved."

Gelert thought about that for a moment. "All right. Let's take care of the day's business. I have to go chase down that bus this morning. Whereas you—"

The intercom link beeped softly. "Yes, Mass?" Lee said.

"Boss-lady, there's a *whole* lot of storage just come in for you."

"Who from?"

"Omren dil'Sorden . . ."

Gelert's ears pricked up. "I was expecting that," Lee said. "Have my own workspace encapsulate it, would you?"

"I'll take care of it now."

"Thanks." Lee looked back at Gelert. "You were going to say that I have to go down to the corner of Eighteenth and Melrose and see what I See," Lee said. "The Tooth Fairy . . . or something I can't explain either."

"Yes."

"Well, I may as well do it now," Lee said, getting up, "before it gets too hot out there. Do you want to put some search terms into my workspace and have it start going through dil'Sorden's material?"

"I'll do that," Gelert said.

Lee headed for the door.

"And Lee—"

She turned to look at him.

"It *will* be all right eventually," Gelert said quietly. "So go do your work."

Lee went.

~

Behind her, traffic roared up and down Melrose as it always did this time of morning: on the far side of the street, cars and buses and hovs came and went in the bright sun-shine, and the occasional pedestrian stared at the slender woman in jeans and a short, loose top who stood at the cor-ner, inside the yellow police tapes, looking down Eigh-teenth Street as if waiting for something: a ride, someone she was supposed to meet . . .

Eyes closed against the day, Lee said to the Source of her vision, *The psychoforensic field here has to be nearly de-pleted now. There'll be no other chances. For the sake of the murdered, let me see truly.*

She opened her eyes on hot still darkness. All the store-fronts on this side of the street were dark: only the blue neon that said LA VIDA LOCA flashed on and off, the light seeming to spatter and jitter rather than flashing evenly, the excited energy states of the atoms in the gas interacting oddly with the uncertainties of judicial vision and the Brownian motion of the night air. In the crazy stuttering lightning of the neon, Lee saw the door of the club pull open, and Omren dil'Sorden came partway out, and paused.

There was enough light that just this once she saw his face while still alive, despite the uncertainty-blurring. He looked haunted: he looked afraid. He moved, now, becom-ing a paint box blur against the stucco of the outside of the club. The door closed behind him. From farther behind him, to Lee's left, the shadow came out of the doorway, holding the shotgun.

It was the same short stocky shadow as before. But Lee turned away from it and looked at the corner instead. Dil'-Sorden looked behind him, saw the shape pursuing him, fled around the corner. The man with the shotgun went after.

A heartbeat passed. And suddenly, that dark figure was simply *there,* at the corner of the building, his back to Lee, leaning out to look down Eighteenth Street. The crack of the first shotgun blast bounced off the nearby buildings. Then came the second blast. The slim dark figure edged out a little farther . . . watched. Then pulled back. As Lee watched, he seemed to edge into the air itself, as if between two parted curtains: and then the air fell together again, like curtains, and the Alfen shadow was gone.

Lee let out a long breath, opened her eyes on common day again, closed down her implant's recording of what she had just Seen, "signed" and sealed it, and turned away. Off to her left, down Melrose a little from La Vida Loca, a black-and-white was parked: an officer she didn't know, a young Hispanic guy, sat in the driver's seat. Lee walked down to the cruiser, felt her recording route out of her as she came within range of the transponder and leaned down to the window. "If no one else needs the evidence tapes up," she said, "you can take them down now. This site's dry."

"That's fine, ma'am," the officer said; "we'll take care of it."

Lee walked on down Melrose to where she'd left the company hov parked, got in and started driving back toward the office. A few blocks down she hit a red light. "Call the office," she said to the hov.

"Yes, boss?" Mass said.

"Any calls?"

"One, repeated."

"Oh, no, not Hagen . . ."

"No. It was Mikki from LAPD Physical Forensics."

"Oh! Did they find the owner of the gun?"

"He didn't mention."

"He didn't? Weird."

"But you should call him back. Anything you need at this end?"

"No, I'll be back shortly. Is Gelert still there?"

"He was just going out."

"Before he goes, tell him I saw the Tooth Fairy."

There was a long pause. "Boss, did you miss your breakfast?"

The light changed. Lee laughed. "I'll talk to you later."

Ǝ⅃

It took her about three-quarters of an hour to get back through the pre-lunchtime traffic. The cool of the office was a relief. Mass looked up as she came in, and said, "Did you call Mikki?"

"Not yet."

"He just called again."

"Thanks . . . I'll take care of it." She went into her office, looked at her commwall, and stared, momentarily aghast.

Her normal window on cis-Saturn space had been replaced by a representation of a geometric space such as Picasso might have imagined: the "ground" was a huge Cartesian gridwork, even featuring a single barren tree in the foreground. Where a floppy watch should have lain over one of the tree limbs, though, Lee saw that someone had draped a representation of a file folder. And the whole background of the image was a series of piles of more file folders: thousands of them.

Lee walked over to her desktop and found that Gelert had left her a note under its surface. *I've left a scan running for a series of search terms*, the note said, streaming past in Palmerrand notation. *Don't interrupt it. It's going to take a while, as dil'Sorden's files amount to several terabytes of material. Articles, letters, and memos that fit the criteria are being placed in the file directory hanging off the tree. I hope you're a faster reader than I am.*

"Suuuzzz . . ." Lee swore, and sat down in her chair. "Oh

well . . ." She reached out to the desk, touched it, brought up the list of phone calls, and tapped Mikki's name.

The tree and the forest of files vanished: Mikki was looking at her, with the ornaments of the Whatsit Tree turning gently in the bright air behind him. "I was starting to think you'd left the planet," he said.

"Not today," Lee said. "What's up?"

"I have something for you. Or will have. A copy of the obscure object of your desire should pop out in the next day or so, if my connection is on time. She's having to be cautious: the press is hot to get its hands on these things before the embargo date, and the computers at Five-Interpol's PR department are being watched with some care."

"Okay. I'll start baking. As soon as you get it, day or night, send it to me here: it'll reach me wherever I am."

"To hear is to obey. But Lee, keep your head down about this release copy. There may be those who want to know how you got it before E-time if you're too obvious about how you use the info."

"I understand you. I doubt I'll have to use the data publicly anytime soon. What about that gun?"

"Stella says they're still tracking it through the usual several false registrations, and she'll let you know when there's something concrete."

"Tell her I said 'Sorry, mommy.' "

Mikki grinned. "Gotta go."

And he was gone. Lee sat back in her chair, looking once again at the field of Cartesian coordinates covered with file folders, sighed, and went off to get herself a sandwich before starting in to work.

When Gelert came in much later, the desktop was covered with the remains of several sandwiches and seven empty cans of green-tea soft drink, almost all other visible spots being obscured by Palmerrand notes Lee had scribbled to herself and sunk under the desk surface. "You find your bus?" she said, without looking up, as she scribbled another note.

"Yes," Gelert said, falling down on her floor, "and I don't care if I never smell chewing tobacco, bubble gum, or various other substances again. The *habits* of these people! It's no wonder no one wants to use public transport." He started washing the pads of one forepaw, wrinking his nose.

"You find the guy you were chasing?" Lee said.

"Impossible not to," Gelert said. "His scent is most distinctive. My guess is that he got off the bus about twenty minutes later, on the edge of a near-derelict area down by Rampart: one of the places where they're still doing quake clearance from '99." He put his ears down flat. "But at no time was his scent as strong as it should have been for someone who was in that bus all that while. It got weaker and weaker all the time . . . as if he were just fading away while he stood there."

He gave Lee a look. "And I saw someone just 'go away' in plain sight," Lee said. "Like pushing a curtain aside, and going behind it." She shook her head. "It's in the record now, Gel. What Matt and his boss will make of it, I have not the slightest idea. But we both perceived it, each in our own way . . . so if I'm crazy, at least it's *folie à deux*."

Gelert started washing the pads of the other forepaw. "The idea that Elves have secret powers that they've never told anybody about isn't going to wash terribly well as part of a prosecution case," Gelert said morosely. "Besides, the guy didn't do anything *but* vanish."

"We can't help that," Lee said, "and I refuse to worry

about it right now. My life seems at the moment to be narrowing to one subject: fairy gold."

"Wait a minute. Tell me what you haven't found before you start out on what you have."

"Oh, the negative side is the big one." Lee chucked her stylus to the desktop and stretched wearily, leaning back in her chair. "Taking more or less in order the scans you programmed in," she said, "there is no evidence of drug dealing, drug use, or anything of that sort. No gambling, legal or otherwise—"

"Even in the encrypted files?"

She nodded. "The network manager at ExTel sent along a backdoor key to the encryption."

"*Suuuz,* they were forthcoming!" Gelert said.

"Which is something else we may want to consider later on," Lee said. "*Why* were they? But anyway, no gambling, no vice, no sexual content even . . . nothing even remotely shady."

"You don't think ExTel purged these records before they came to you?"

"Of course they could have," Lee said, "and I'm not sure how we would tell they had, any more than I know how to tell they hadn't. But let's assume, for the moment and for the sake of our sanity, that they haven't, because there was very little time between my concrete request and Hagen's fulfillment of it. I know I mentioned the possibility of wanting more data to him yesterday, but if he really does want dil'Sorden's case 'cleaned up' in a hurry, I'm assuming he'd at least leave anything in that might lead us to a murderer. Yes?"

"I'll allow you that for the moment," Gelert said.

"So. Clean criminal record, nothing covert tucked away in the files, a lot of correspondence but all very innocent— mails to and from friends back in Alfheim, and other friends and work associates here and in Tierra and Huictilopochtli. Everything else has to do with work, or finances. And so much of his work is about fairy gold that—"

"Wait a minute," Gelert said. "Finances?"

Lee shrugged. "Bank statements, investment portfolios, brokerage stuff . . ."

Gelert got up. "Lee," he said, "you have no mathematics in your soul . . . it's your only major failing. You leave the banking information to me: I'll sort through it. Everything else you've looked at, though, has been clean?"

"Boringly so. I think we have here that true rarity, the complete geek. He really seems to have lived for his work."

"Leaving me to wonder whether perhaps for some reason, he died for it," Gelert muttered. "Because if he really wasn't doing anything else . . ." He trailed off. "Well, one thing at a time. You have any notes on the desk that might help me?"

"I'll copy them all to your desktop."

"Thanks."

"And in the meantime I'll go back to studying dil'Sorden's ExTel projects." She breathed out. "But what are we going to do about your 'guy who faded'?"

Gelert shrugged one ear. "Pass on the info to the DA's Office in the morning, with everything else. It's no worse than the Elf who 'vanished.' They don't like what we Saw? Let them go hire themselves some other 'mancers." He walked off to his office to examine the slab of glass in the middle of the floor that was his own "desk": and Lee sighed and turned back to her work.

They worked late. Soft drink cans and paper plates began to pile up again on Lee's desk, and Chinese food containers on the floor on Gelert's side.

"There's something here I'm not seeing," Lee said.

"The forest for the trees?" Gelert said.

"Go on, be that way," Lee said. "Meanwhile, explain to me why there are two transmission speeds for fairy gold."

"What?" Gelert got up from his desk and ambled in to look over her shoulder.

"Look at this." Lee snapped her fingers at the commwall, so that it showed Gelert the output from her desk, enlarged. She had been looking through the footnotes to the *Britannica*'s basic article on fairy gold. It was surprising how much you might think you knew about something so basic to the civilization of the worlds, and how little you found you knew about it when you started digging. Lee was now down into the sixth or seventh level of technical annotations, getting more confused and more fascinated all the time.

This last annotation showed two conduction speeds for fairy gold at $18°$ C: 3.063×10^{13}cm/s, 3.065×10^{14}cm/s: and next to the second one was a "dagger" pointing at a footnote that said only, *attributed.* "Attributed to what?" said Lee. "I've never seen anything but the first value, at least not since high school. It's supposed to be a constant, like the speed of light in normal space. But now here's this other one. Is it something you get in college physics? Because I admit right now, I wasn't paying attention in my first-year course. I had a crush on the instructor."

"Tall guy? Dark-haired?" Gelert said. "Blue eyes? Kind of a drawl—"

"I'd kill you," Lee said, "but I'd have to explain it to Nuala and the pups afterward, and that would pain me."

Gelert gave her a slightly penitent look. "All right, withdrawn. But as for this—" He stared at the wall, shook his head. "You're asking the wrong person. My usual intersection with FG is on the commodities markets, and as a fashion statement most other people don't notice."

"Yeah, I know," Lee muttered, pushing her chair back from the desk. "But seriously, you're always going on about your connections at UCLA. Isn't there someone there you could ask?"

Gelert sat down, looking thoughtful. "UC's a little short on the harder sciences these days, except for astronomy and medicine. Most of the multidimensional physics specialists are up at Stanford or over at Brookhaven or the University of Chicago these days: the schools that have 'history' with rings or colliders seem to attract most of the people interested in gating work. I'll see what I can find out in the morning, though."

"Okay. How're you doing over there?"

"Not too badly. Our guy's investment portfolio shows some interesting preferences."

"Oh?"

"Take a guess, Lee."

"Fairy gold?"

"He's bought a lot of contracts over the past few years," Gelert said thoughtfully. "Not necessarily strange: it's a standard commodities metal—better than most because the price per gram is so high and the market supply is steadier than most. Dil'Sorden would always sell again after a few months, make a small profit, nothing spectacular . . . Deal in what you know, I guess."

"I suppose that makes sense . . ."

The commlink went off in the front office. Lee reached over to her desk. "Reh'Mechren and Enfield, good evening . . ."

Mikki's face looked down at her from the commwall. "Sorry, am I interrupting something?"

"*No!*" Lee and Gelert said in unison, then both laughed. "What have you got for us?" Lee said.

"Official business first," Mikki said. "We had a breakthrough, and I thought you two should be the first to know. We tracked the gun back to the real owner. His name is Jok Castelain: he lives in Upper San Francisco, and he has multiple arrests and several convictions for armed robbery and assault with a deadly weapon. Kind of an errand boy, and it looks like he was doing someone's errand the night before last. At least one piece of clothing in his apartment matches at first assessment with some fibers we found yesterday in the doorway your assailant jumped out of. And at least one set of prints on the shotgun is his."

"All *right,*" Lee said softly.

"It gets better. He's under arrest in San Fran. They caught up with him as he was heading for SF Intercontinual."

Lee slumped back in her chair, grinning.

"So at least you have that much good news. San Fran are talking to LAPD right now: he'll be down here for questioning in due course."

"You guys are miracle workers," Gelert said.

"Couldn't have done much without you. So, as your reward . . . here we have the piece of resistance," Mikki said.

An icon representing a file appeared on Lee's desktop. In small clear letters, the "cover" of the file said, ANALYSIS OF INTERSPECIES HOMICIDE AND OTHER CRIMINAL MORTALITY IN THE SIX WORLDS, 1993–2003. "You should print this," Mikki said, "and then destroy the file, and then probably burn the printout when you're done with it. It's going to take you a while to get through it, but I had a quick skim, and there are two things

I want to draw your attention to. First, look at the chart here."

The icon popped open in her desktop, riffled through a number of virtual "pages," and stopped at one two-page spread, a graph of incidents plotted against time. "Check out this curve," Mikki said. "There's definitely been an increase in the number of murders of Elves in the last ten years. Look at the curve. It never goes down."

Lee looked at it, a steady sprinkling of plotted points, arcing slowly upward. Remembered voices spoke in her head. *It's code for the fact that the company knows he's Alfen, and everybody hates Elves.* And a "joke" she had heard once: *What do you call a thousand dead Alfen? A start.*

"Always up," she said, thinking out loud.

"It gets better, Lee," Mikki said.

"It can hardly get worse," she said softly.

"Wanna bet? Look at this." The report riffled its virtual pages again, and showed her a bar graph: one very small sampling in green, another large one, much larger, in red— a curve not so much heading upward, as trying to launch itself out the top of the page. "That's the last three years," Mikki said. "That's the number of murders across the worlds in which at least one other Alfen has been involved in the killing."

"As victim?"

"No. As the murderer."

It was bizarre. It made no sense. *Why now? Why all of a sudden?* "Could it be a statistical blip?" Lee said.

"If this were only one universe we were looking at, I'd be suspicious myself. But Lee, this is a master average. Five worlds: Midgarth's out of the sample, since if you include it, the difference in the time constant makes it throw a false negative or false positive. If I knew anything about numbers"—and Mikki's mouth drew into a tight line—"I'd think I was looking at some kind of conspiracy here. . . ."

Gelert, looking over her shoulder at the graph, turned to look at her with his ears straight up in alarm, his eyes grave.

Lee sat thinking of a shape standing by a building's corner, pulling the air aside, stepping into it, and began to think Mikki was right.

Four

The office transport-sharing rotation made it Lee's turn to take home the company hov. She drove home slowly, thinking, and found herself parked in front of the pink-stuccoed bungalow at the end of her little side street without any clear sense of how she'd gotten there. She got out of the hov, listening to it locking itself up as she glanced up and down the street in the predusk light. The sky was dimming down to peach-color at the horizon, as much of it as she could see through the downhanging green fringe of the peppertrees behind her property; the air was full of their spicy smell. The street was quiet, the gardens and front yards of her neighbors going twilight-shadowed, some of their lawn sprinklers spitting rhythmically along now that night was coming on. Faintly, from down nearer the Boulevard, came shouts and laughter of children from the Belleclaires' back yard, followed by a splash: a pool party running late.

Lee took a few long breaths and tried to recover some kind of feeling that this was the real world—that indeed most of the world was like this, at peace with itself, running not too badly, all things considered. It was too easy to forget the peace in the face of the work she did every day, where most of her attention was bent on the aftereffects of rage, cruelty, violence. Re-grounding herself in a world that wasn't all about the less positive side of the many humanities was never easy, but she had to make sure she did it every day, or at least tried.

Now Lee made her way slowly up her front walk, resolving yet again to do something about the lawn, which had been coming down with brown patches, and also to call somebody about the cracked third slab from the front porch, which someday would at least trip her, if not the milkman, thus causing her an unwanted expedition into accident/injury law. Lee paused by the porch steps to bend down and examine one of the two skinny, scrawny rosebushes that stood to either side of the end of the walk. One of them had a single, wizened pink rose on it, half-open. This was something of an event, for in spite of Lee spending recent months trying every kind of pruning, and every kind of fertilizer, until now the rosebushes had refused to do anything but produce leaves and an abundance of thorns.

"Hey, good for you," she said, touching the outermost petals of the opening flower. Several of the petals had already had a hole chewed in them by some kind of bug, but Lee still had to smile at this small triumph. She bent down, sniffed, found no fragrance there. "Never mind," she said, "you're just getting started . . ."

As she walked up the steps with Mikki's report under her arm, the house unlatched the front door for her. It was old, wood with three small glass windows, more trouble to take care of than a door made of one of the more modern armored laminates. But Lee liked it: it was of a piece with the rest of the bungalow, dating back to the middle of the last century—solid, a little clunky. The shades in the front and side windows rotated themselves into evening configuration as she stepped into the bookshelf-lined living room, and the lights came on for her, gleaming off the polished floorboards that had cost her so much time and sweat to strip, sand, and finish. Lee closed the door, slipped her jacket off and tossed it onto the brown leather sofa, and headed into the kitchen. There she paused for a moment, considering what she wanted for dinner. She briefly thought of making some pasta from scratch, *orecchielle* or something of the kind, but then dismissed the idea—it would take too much fiddly kneading for her present mood. Lee spoke open the sliding doors that led out onto the deck and started work on dinner.

She spread Mikki's report out on the breakfast bar between her kitchen and dining area, glancing down at its pages while moving back and forth between the cooker and the fridge. Outside, the warm colors of the western sky cooled down to evening blues as Lee sautéed some mushrooms in olive oil, fished ground beef out of the freezer, stuck it into the fridge's "active" compartment, and told the fridge to defrost it. She spent a while paging through the report, then went for the hamburger and crumbled it into the pan. While stirring it, Lee turned a page of the report, then went to get herself a glass of wine and came back to that page. It featured no graphs, but the word "recidivism" in a section heading caught her eye.

—numerous repeat offenses by Alfen individuals whom evidence indicates have committed similar offenses in other jurisdictions. Additionally some repeat offenders have been assisted in escaping custody by persons unknown and have reappeared in jurisdictions, especially in Xaihon, where extradition is either problematic or impossible due to lack of local planetary political recognition of such "umbrella" structures as the Five-Geneva Pact. The conclusion that organized crime is involved in such escapes is supported only by circumstantial evidence, but cannot be discarded . . .

Lee turned away and went looking for some garlic. *The*

same people, she thought, finding the garlic safe empty: she sighed and went rooting in the spice rack on the counter for some garlic powder. *But who are they?* She dosed the pan with the powdered garlic and stirred for a few moments more, then found a jar of spaghetti sauce, dumped it in with the meat, kept on stirring, and started paging back toward the appendices at the end of the report. It took another ten minutes or so, but by the time she was ready to put the spaghetti on, she had found the list of names of repeat offenders, ten or twelve people. Some of them didn't actually have names, just case numbers; their descriptions and DNA evidence left behind were their only identification. *That's some information I want to see,* Lee thought. *Assuming I can find a way to get my hands on it without revealing that I've seen this report. Probably Mikki can help.*

Lee filled a pot with hot water from the faucet and put it on to boil. *And finally, why?* she thought. *Who stands to gain when Elves kill Elves?* But then Lee shook her head and laughed out loud at her own witlessness. Who stood to gain when humans killed humans, for pity's sake? Five billion lives on just this world, five billion motivations: invariably when some of them intersected with others, there would be trouble. *And after that, it gets complex.*

She picked up her wineglass again and turned her attention back to the report. Among those suspects or convicts who had names, the details of their criminal histories varied; but there were a few congruences that Lee found peculiar. Three of them had at one time or another held government jobs—one an advisor of some kind in Midgarth's Mass Relocation Authority; one a minor official in the Alfen consulate to Upas, a planet in Xainese space; one a former private secretary to the Alfen ambassador to Tierra—a kidnap victim, everyone had thought, until eight months after he vanished, an Elf matching his description came out of the dark on the south side of Chicago Grande one night, and knifed another Elf in the back—

Lee frowned at that. *Something else I need more data on. And what about these two—* Two more suspects, with names rather than numbers: but both of them, before they killed and vanished, had been working for communications companies . . . as had their victims.

Now, is that *just a coincidence?* Lee thought. *All right, 'workplace murders,' just personal animosities boiling over . . . that's what some people would say. But do I buy it?*

The pot was boiling. Lee pulled a big handful of spaghetti from the glass jar where it lived, threw back about a quarter of what she'd removed because she always overestimated how much she was about to make, and put the spaghetti in the water, watching it start to slump down. *With dil'Sorden, that makes three. I wonder, has ExTel lost any other Alfen staff recently? And how do I find out without rousing Hagen's interest?*

Lee stirred the spaghetti a little and went back to the report again, paging first ahead and then back to see if there were any conclusions relating directly to this issue. There weren't, at least not in black-and-white—and it occurred to Lee that however this report might have been assembled, its compilers were still somewhat nervous about the reactions of those who would eventually read it. *Criminal organizations have in the past attempted to influence or infiltrate communications or interworld transport technology groups, with their invariable links to the Alfen allotropic gold industry, always attractive to such organizations because of the large profit margins possible in smuggling or clandestine trade operations. Further investigation should attempt to establish whether these murders are part of another such strategy. Coordination with the government of Alfheim must continue in order to promote such investigations . . .*

Lee turned back to the pot. *Which more or less tells us that 'such investigations' are either stalled or just not happening at all,* she thought. *And nobody wants to push the subject, because financially speaking, the Elves are just too damn powerful to annoy. So we all shrug and say, If their people are killing each other, who cares? It's their problem. All us non-immortals will just look the other way and pretend nothing's happening . . . officially.*

Lee went rummaging under the sink for the colander, found it, put it in the sink, and dumped the spaghetti into it: shook it around until it was drained, then dumped it into the pan with the spaghetti sauce and stirred it all around. In her mind she suddenly found herself once again looking at the sidewalk around the corner from La Vida Loca, the red-brown seepage in the cracks of it, hard now, and beside her, slowly, in the dark, only partly seen, the body falling. Echoes of dil'Sorden's last feelings from her sweep inside the club still haunted her: his fear of the bad thing that was probably going to happen, that was coming after him; his inability to escape from it; and finally his horror that it had, after all, happened so soon. He'd thought he'd have at least a few more days of life . . . and was blasted into the darkness barely a few breaths later.

Lee breathed out, flipped the report closed, got herself down a plate from the cupboard, and served out some of the spaghetti. *Let them look away,* she thought. *I'm not going to.*

She sat down at the table, gazing out across the deck into her dark backyard, and ate her dinner, working out what to do next.

Lee found when she got in the next morning that her plans were going to have to wait, at least for a while. Jok

Castelain, the suspect, had been brought down from San Francisco overnight, and the processing people at Parker were attending to the formalities of booking him. "Which means," Gelert said to Lee not more than a breath after she walked in the door, "that we'd better get on the road. They're going to want us there to look him over when he makes his formal statement."

"Who's taking it?"

"Matt."

"Oh no," Lee said.

Gelert grinned at her. "Looks like Hagen has been warming up the DA's phone," he said.

"Oh no!" Lee said.

"Lee, why should you care?! Let him suffer." Gelert sat there with his tail thumping against the ground, looking ready to enjoy the show.

"I'm above that kind of thing," Lee said. *I desperately hope!* "Meanwhile, I had a long look at that report last night. I want you to look at it, too—I made some notes."

Gelert twitched one ear forward and back. "Lee, you're working too hard again. When are you going to take an evening off?"

"When we're not busy," Lee said, looking ruefully down at her desk: under the surface of it were swimming about twenty notes in various colors, all calls Mass had taken since coming in that morning. "Which I see happening sometime in the next decade."

"Come on, Lee. Nuala's been complaining that you haven't seen the little ones in ages: they'll be at university before you see them next, at the rate you're going."

"Gel, I really shouldn't. And I don't want to put her to any trouble . . ."

"You're not . . . don't be an idiot. Come on home with me tonight, we'll have dinner and get caught up."

Lee opened her mouth, and saw Gelert give her one of those looks meant to suggest that she was wasting her time. "All right," she said. "But let's get down to Parker and take a look at our suspect. Then I have some thoughts about those other murders that I want to run past you."

∿

Parker was as busy as ever as they made their way "up-stream" past the waterfalls to Six, where the detention blocks were located. The two of them made their way among the desk carrels and glassed-off office blocks to the west side of the building. There, in one of the booking-and-assessment "pens," a little complex of cubicles with metal and frosted-glass walls, they turned into the outer reception office and found the receptionist, a broad dark lady called Magda, waiting for them with a pad. "Good morning, lanthanomancers," she said. It was one of the reasons everyone remembered Magda: she never unbent her formality for anyone. "The assistant DA will be with you shortly, he's on a call. Here's the detainee you're evaluating." She handed them a pad.

Lee took it and examined the booking "mug shot." The image she saw was a good match for the shadowy one from her Seeing—a blocky man in his mid-forties, crewcut, big-shouldered, fairly muscular: but there was a slope to the shoulders, too, and the face was blunt, pained, pinched, with weary eyes spaced wide, a big nose, a wide mouth, a thick neck. Gel leaned over to look at it, flicked his ears at her in preliminary agreement.

Lee looked at the arrest time on the docket.

"They really did catch him awfully quick, didn't they?" Lee said.

"The file says they had a tip-off," said Magda.

"Really?"

"From the confidential tip line. Word gets around fast, I guess," said Magda, producing an expression of profound cynicism, and headed out of the front cubicle.

Lee looked at Gelert, raised her eyebrows. A moment later Matt came through one of the office's side doors, nodded to them both. He looked cheerful. "Lee, Gelert," he said. "I think we've got your boy. You ready to look him over?"

"All set," Gelert said. "You have time to run through our sweeps yet?"

"Right after this," Matt said. "Sorry, but yesterday got busier than I expected."

Lee exchanged a look with Gelert as Matt led them over to a frosted-glass and steel door to one side, touched a code into it, let them in. On the far side of the door was another long narrow room, empty, its only features a window that was half-silvered on the side away from them and frosted on the inside, with two vents high up on either side of the window. "Let me know when you're ready," he whispered.

Lee took a couple of long breaths, brought her implant online, glanced at Gelert. He flicked an ear at her.

"Go ahead," Lee said softly.

Matt touched the wall, and the glass went unfrosted. Sitting on a chair in the middle of the room, wearing a prisoner's orange coverall, was the blocky man with the crewcut. As Lee looked at him, the man raised his face and looked straight at the window. Possibly he had heard them coming in; or possibly he felt her regard—occasionally a suspect did. Lee simply looked at the man, and the Seeing settled itself down around her, around him. Within seconds Lee caught the same tang of mind as she had at the murder scene, and Saw the same shadow of self trembling about this man as had etched itself on the night outside the club. The shadows of his earlier anger, and a certain cold resolve, were still there: but so was sadness, and weariness, and fear. *Too bad,* Lee thought; *he should have considered the likely consequences of his actions a whole lot earlier.* For hard behind the image of this man came that of Omren dil'Sorden falling past her, in shock, already dying before he even hit the ground. "I positively identify this man's psychospoor as identical to one I detected at the scene of the murder of Omren dil'Sorden," Lee said for the benefit of the recording that her implant was making. "I also confirm co-location of his psychospoor with that of the person who used the weapon that killed Omren dil'Sorden, and with traces of the same psychospoor associated with the murder weapon itself." She glanced at Gelert.

He sat there gazing at Castelain for a long moment, his nose working. *No question,* Gelert said at last. *The scent is identical.* "I positively identify this man's psychospoor as identical to one I scented at the scene of the murder of Omren dil'Sorden," he said aloud. "Further, I co-locate this man's psychospoor with the location of the weapon used in this murder and found at premises at 3850 Rampart Avenue, Los Angeles."

They both stood quiet for a moment, and Matt said nothing while they "signed" their depositions and closed their implants down. "If you'll wait a few minutes, we'll move him into the interview room," Matt said.

"Sure," Lee said. Matt went out, and Lee took a few long breaths to bring herself fully out of the judicial state.

"That's the saddest murderer I've smelled in a long while," Gelert said softly, as a uniformed officer came into the room and took Castelain out.

"Yes," Lee said. She still wasn't up to feeling much in the way of pity for him.

"Betrayed," Gelert said.

Lee threw a glance at him. That was something she'd

thought she detected as well, but the impression had been so fleeting that she'd thought she would have to review her own recording before she could be sure of it. "By whom?" she said softly.

"Whoever called the tip-off line, for starters," Gelert said. "But it may not stop there. I got a sense that he thought more than one person was involved."

Lee was just thinking how to respond to this when the door opened again, and Matt stuck his head in. "We're ready for you," he said.

They followed him out and around to the door of the interviewing room, another pane of frosted glass set in metal. Outside it was a large, round, smiling man in a charcoal one-piece suit; he was bald as an egg, and had the kind of broad-featured face that wouldn't have been out of place painted on an egg—round eyes, flat nose, a smile threatening to become a grin that would go right around that head and meet on the far side. Paul McGinity worked for the Public Advocacy Office, and Lee grinned at the sight of him. He always had that effect on her, which sometimes amused and sometimes annoyed her, depending on whether it looked like he was going to win a given case, or she was. "Advocate," she said.

"'Mancers," McGinity said. "Saw you on the news the other day."

"Fame," Gelert said. "It's such a nuisance."

"Not politically," McGinity said, giving Lee a jocular look. "Thinking of a job in the DA's Office?"

"Please," Lee muttered. "That's not at *all* high on my list."

McGinity smiled, a look of disbelief. "Well, maybe not for you. But Gelert could probably manage something like that if he wanted. The DA's never been happy with the percentage of nonhuman employees there."

"He'll just have to stay unhappy, I'm afraid," Gelert said, as the door opened before them. "Anything like real work would interfere with my social schedule. And as for what I would have to do every day to *keep* that job, such as sticking my nose up Big Jim's—" He paused, grinned a fangy grin, said no more.

Inside the interview room, Castelain was sitting at a small one-person table to one side of the room. On the far side of the room were two benches—one nearer the table where McGinity took his seat, one where Lee sat down, and Gelert sat beside her on the floor. A fourth table, opposite Castelain's, was for Matt, the interviewer. There were a few minutes spent dealing with pads, briefcases, and so forth, then Matt closed the door and touched it locked.

"Interview with suspect LARC227-99-847, Jacques Xavier Castelain," Matt said, sitting down at the separate table, "as per"—he glanced at his own pad—"case docket CA-RR8574.665. Suspect is charged with assault with first-degree murder under statute number Ellay-LP2533.1 of the civil code of the city and county of Los Angeles. Present, the accused: Matthew Carathen, solicitor, District Attorney's Office, LAPD; defense mantic, Paul McGinity, lanthanomancer, Holmes, McGinity and Oaxachitl, acting for the Ellay County Advocate's Office; prosecution mantics, Liayna Enfield and Gelert reh'Mechren, reh'Mechren and Enfield, acting for the Ellay County District Attorney's Office. Time is 1138."

He paused for a moment to let everyone settle fully into judicial sensorium, glancing down at the pad again. "Mr. Castelain, state and national law require me to ask you at the beginning of this interview whether you have been informed of your legal rights by the advocate assigned to you."

"Yes," Castelain said.

"You are Jacques Xavier Castelain?"

"Yes," Castelain said. "Look, I did it, all right? Let's get this over with."

No one moved or said anything for a moment. Paul McGinity's expression was not one of surprise, but there was a thoughtful quality to it, as if something was occurring to him that had not occurred before.

"Advocate?" Matt said.

"Mr. Castelain," McGinity said, "please don't say anything for a moment. I have to remind you that your defense will be endangered if you become any more specific, about *anything*. Please just answer the questions."

Castelain squirmed a little in his seat, said nothing.

Lee saw his anxiety, and Saw the reason behind it. *He wants to be in jail,* Lee thought. *Desperately.* She said as much to Gelert down their Palmerrand linkage.

It's nearly rolling off him like panther sweat, Gelert answered, intrigued. *He's terrified of even being offered the possibility of being released on bail.*

"All right," Matt said. "Let me start with the evening of June 16. Where were you that night?"

"Ellay," Castelain said.

"At around ten o'clock—"

"I was in a bar on Wilshire Boulevard," Castelain said, looking from one of them to the next. As his eyes lit on Lee, she clearly heard him thinking, *nice-looking broad, shame about the eyes, they'd give you the creeps if she looked at you like that normally, guess she doesn't, but how'd you tell until it was too late*— Then he was looking at Gelert again, and the thought ebbed in intensity and felt much more clinical, *one of them deathhounds, keep expecting him to howl and jump you any minute, those teeth are as bad as her eyes*— But there was something else going on there: something he was much more afraid of. Lee held her curiosity in check with some difficulty: "digging" in a suspect's sensorial display tended to produce false negatives. *Just relax and See: the truth will reveal itself, it wants nothing more—*

"I left around ten and caught the bus down Santa Monica to Eighteenth," Castelain said. "I walked up Eighteenth and went around the corner to the club. I got into the doorway by there and waited—"

"Mr. Castelain—" McGinity said, sounding much more concerned.

"Mr. Castelain," Matt said, "if you could just—"

"Mr. Carathen," McGinity said. "May I ask—"

"Look, I *told* you, I shot him," Castelain said, annoyed. "Don't you people listen? Guys from one of the gambling clubs down here, they called me, said he had a big debt for a long time and he wouldn't pay. Said they were done with him, he needed shooting or people would stop taking them seriously. So I did it. Price was right. Not a hard job, either. Guy walked out of the club like he was walking out of his living room, didn't look right or left. Drunk, whacked out, who knows? He heard me then, saw me, started to run. I followed him around the corner, blam, that was it." He paused. "Actually," he said, "two blams."

Matt and McGinity were looking at each other rather helplessly. Matt was bemused. McGinity passed a hand over his eyes. But Lee spared neither of them much attention, for right now her intent was mostly bent on Castelain. All over him, as Gelert had said, was the desire to be safely behind bars. It wasn't just that jail was someplace Castelain was most familiar with after many years' worth of ins and outs, a secure and structured environment where he knew how to behave. Much more to the forefront of his mind at the moment was the image of jail as somewhere where *that* one would not be able to get him. A tall, dark figure . . .

Lee bent her Sight against that shadowy background perception with all her force. It faded, as if it had stepped sideways into the air.

He thinks whoever tipped off the police will think he's trying to get out of the deal if he's released, Gelert said.

Yes. But there's more. Lee looked at Matt and willed him fiercely to ask the question that most needed asking.

If he was aware of Lee's gaze, he showed no sign of it. "Right," Matt said. "If you insist on being so forthcoming despite your advocate's advice, then tell me: was there anyone working with you?"

"No. I work alone."

Lee Saw clearly that Castelain was telling the truth. Her mouth went dry. Could it be that he'd genuinely been unaware of the Alfen figure watching him?

"You didn't see anybody else?" Gelert said.

"Nobody. You think I'm stupid?" Castelain gave Gelert one of the faintly irritated looks with which he'd favored Matt. "That's why I shot him. If there'd been anybody else around, I would've waited, got him the next night or something."

"Did you look behind you?" Gelert said.

"Huh? No. Why? Nobody coulda been there: I looked all around first. Then I went around the corner, I shot him, I made sure he was dead. Afterward I ran down the road and over a few blocks, and ditched the gun. Caught the bus afterward."

Lee looked at Castelain and Saw nothing but a man telling almost all the truth with a kind of awful relief to be doing so, certain that this was the only way he was going to stay alive. But one thing he *was* lying about: the figure he'd seen watching him after he shot dil'Sorden . . . the figure that had stepped sideways and vanished. Once again Lee bent her Sight against that memory, and Saw a glimpse of something else: the interior of the bus, fading around Castelain's point of view as the floor suddenly, bizarrely came close, bumped up against his face. Did he pass out? Or was he knocked out?—Then the point of view fading back in, a glimpse of dirt: Castelain pushing himself up to hands and knees, looking blurrily around him at waste ground somewhere. *Up north, probably—*

"Mr. Castelain," Matt said after a moment, "under the circumstances the law requires me to offer you the chance to make a fuller statement regarding this incident in writing. I am required to advise you that no clemency in your case is implied or in any way guaranteed by your agreeing to make such a written statement, and that you may ask the Advocate to assist you with the statement if you desire."

Castelain waved a hand in a dismissive gesture. "I can write just fine by myself," he said. "Thanks."

"All right. Interview closes at 1156," Matt said.

He went to the door, touched it unlocked, opened it, and looked out. A few moments later a uniformed officer came to take Castelain away.

Lee and Gelert and Paul McGinity sat there for a moment closing their various visions down and sealing off their recordings of what they had just perceived. When Matt came back in, Paul had stood up and was recovering his briefcase. "Sorry, Paul," he said. "Looks like a wasted trip."

"*Looks* like?" Paul said, dry. "Matt, I think that boy needs a psych evaluation: I'm going to order one."

"You're not implying duress, though."

McGinity didn't say anything immediately. "I think I'd like to rule out insanity first," he said, "especially considering some of the imagery I saw at the end, which makes no sense whatsoever. I'll give you a call later." He nodded to Lee and Gelert and headed out.

"I'll have a chance to look at your sweeps after lunch," Matt said to them, "as well as Paul's. The boss has been looking at them this morning: I'll have his notes later." He rubbed his face with one hand, still looking thoroughly bemused, and pleased in a cautious way. "For once a case is going the way the boss wants it to . . ."

Lee said nothing, strongly suspecting that this assessment had a life expectancy of no more than half a sandwich or so. "Call us after lunch," Gelert said. "We'll drop by."

It was actually around quarter to one when Mass relayed the first of Matt's messages to reach the office, and Lee was glad she'd restricted herself to a few pieces of sushi and some green tea: her stomach had begun to roil. When they got up to Matt's office, one of about ten glass cubicles grouped around the DA's office on the northwest corner of Parker's eighth floor, they found the glass frosted down around him. This was unusual for a man who, Lee knew, liked to watch everybody, trusting his evaluation of their expressions as completely as Lee trusted her own Seeing—and with some justification, for he was good at reading people as long as he didn't get too close to them. Lee had often thought Matt had some of the Gift, but he'd never had the patience to take it through assessment and training. The more physical and concrete side of law enforcement was his chief love, and expressed itself also in a certain distrust of the less concrete types of detection.

Gelert scratched at the door, and Matt spoke it open for them: they went in. His desk was covered with imagery as usual, some of it flat under the surface, some of it still playing in the air in front of him as they walked in. He slapped one of the hot spots on the desk, freezing the playback, and waved them to chairs.

"You finished looking at the sweeps, I take it," Lee said.

"Just about," Matt said, collapsing the projection hanging in the air. "But the DA says that after that interview with Castelain, we've got more than enough to go to trial with a realistic chance of conviction. We have the murder weapon, and we have both physical and psychic forensics that link the suspect to the time and place of the murder."

Lee really wished she didn't have to say what she was going to: but she had no choice. "Motivation is too weak," she said.

Matt gave her a look Lee had seen all too often and learned to dislike, though she had never really broached the issue. The expression suggested that Lee was out of her mind, but he would forgive her because he thought she was so cute. *Problem was, I always thought it was funny . . . until I found out that all of a sudden my "cute" had passed its sell-by date.* "Lee, you heard him tell us about the gambling debt. It's more than enough to put Castelain away while we work on whoever took out the contract on dil'Sorden, and why: because though he believed the story about the gambling debt, I'm not sure I do."

"I'd feel happier about it if there was any evidence at all of gambling debts in dil'Sorden's personal profiling," Lee said. "Including his private mails, his banking and investment information, or anywhere else. And he's in an Alfheim-based Fund, Matt, just like every other Elf alive! How likely is he to be unable to raise money to pay a debt that could get him killed if unpaid? The Funds routinely advance hundreds of thousands of talers to any given member for uses a lot less urgent, just based on their life expectancy data, without even referring to their credit line!"

Matt gave her an annoyed look. "So why *didn't* he apply for a loan?"

"I don't know," Lee said. "How about because there wasn't any gambling debt?"

"There may not have been," Matt said. "But it's going to be hard to prove that there wasn't, so for the moment it's the story we're likely to run with. Assuming it *is* true, maybe there was something wrong with dil'Sorden's rating with whichever Fund he's in. The point is, dil'Sorden's dead. End of story, at least insofar as we have a confession from the suspect to whom we were led by the forensics."

"End of story?" Lee said softly.

Matt sat pushing a piece of paper back and forth on his desk for a few moments. "So now we come to the problematic part of this case. This mysterious Alfen of yours."

"Not just mine," Lee said. "Someone else *was* present at the murder scene, Matt. Both of us saw him. In my case, I saw him from two different angles. And more to the point, Castelain saw him—though not as clearly as we did. Don't you think it might answer some unanswered questions about this investigation if we could find out who that was?" *And where the heck he went,* Lee thought, but refused to say out loud: *and where Castelain went later . . . and how.*

Her restraint did her no good: Matt's thoughts were already there. He glared at her. "The DA," he said, "is having a lot of trouble with your sweeps."

"I just bet he is," Gelert said, looking down along his nose at Matt. "How do you think *we* feel? But they're what we Saw, Matt. You can't cherrypick a psychoforensics sweep for what you like and what you don't. The trial judge won't stand for it, and neither will She; it's either all admissible as evidence, or none of it. And when the trial starts, if you're going to use the sweeps as the evidential link to the murder weapon, and also use the observation of the murder itself, then the defense team is going to use the 'vanishing' evidence as an excuse to discredit everything else. So maybe if everyone just gets to work on understanding the 'impossible' right now, and finding an answer that'll hold water, rather than trying to pretend it just didn't happen, the case won't go down the drain."

Matt said nothing. "Renselaar can't afford to be seen ducking a possible conviction right now just because some of the evidence is peculiar," Lee said. "He should just take the case forward and stonewall when the press starts making its usual noises. Then, when we chase down a logical explanation and he breaks the news and takes credit for it, he gets to look like the stalwart defender of Justice refusing to be distracted from Her service by the muckraking journalists intent on a quick fix. Or on making the future Mayor look stupid for the sake of a juicy headline."

Lee tried her best not to sound too snide while saying this, but had no sense of whether she was being successful; she was too busy holding Matt's eyes with hers, uncomfortable though it made her, and trying to make him see the rightness of what she was saying. She could get no sense, though, that he was seeing any such thing.

Which left her with one remaining piece of business. "I want to suggest one other thing to you," Lee said. "Magda tells me there was a tip-off that led the San Fran police to Castelain."

"Yeah, saw that."

"So where did that come from, Matt?" Lee said, possibly more sharply than she meant to. "Who knew we were looking for him?"

"Everybody knew. There was an all-points out for him."

"The timing raises questions, Matt," Gelert said. "The team here at Parker ID'd Castelain yesterday afternoon. The tip-off came through just barely after they got in touch with San Francisco. Somebody pushed him over the edge so that he would roll right down into our laps, just when we need him."

"So he had some enemies," Matt said. But he sounded uneasy now.

"You know it's not that simple. There's a leak here," Lee said. "And outside is somebody who wants us to take the suspect we have and be content with him. And even the poor guy himself is desperate to be in jail. Even *you* saw it: I saw the look on your face. Why are so many people so eager to see this case wound up in a hurry, Matt? And are you going to let them get away with it?"

"No one's going to get away with anything," Matt said.

"Unless you talk yourself into a mistrial by purposely ignoring the implications of evidence," Gelert said. "Justice will be served, Matt. And I'd sooner be on the right side of Her when it happens. The other side's no fun."

Matt said nothing for several moments. Finally, he got up and looked at them both, expressionless. "You have two days to finish your casework," he said. "The DA wants the completed case on his desk first thing Friday morning, so he can find a place to slot it into the calendar. Don't miss the deadline."

"When have we ever?" Lee said, but he didn't even look at her: he was already halfway out the door.

It closed slowly behind him, leaving Lee and Gelert sitting there for a few moments in rather shocked silence. "Yes," Gelert said, "he's feeling the heat, I'd say. Come on . . ."

They went out and made their way down past the waterfalls and out into the central plaza. The sky had started to cloud over, just mackerel sky against pale blue at the moment, but thickening: the Santa Ana wind had broken, a cooler wind from the west beginning to take its place. "I don't think I've ever seen him so abrupt in the line of work," Lee said. "No matter how bad things got . . ."

"He's having trouble understanding what he saw," Gelert

said. "He doesn't like it any better than you or I do. If he supports us with the DA, then his credibility as well as ours is on the line. And if the DA can't be convinced . . ."

"We all go down together," Lee said.

Gelert shrugged his backpack forward a little as they came out on the flat after coming up the flight of steps to the plaza. "Elections are coming," he said. "The DA moves up, all the people under him move up too . . . if they're doing their best work and keeping him happy. If he gets unhappy, they get demoted. And we lose our freelance work for the DA's Office, and look stupid, or ineffective, or negligent. Which affects all our other work."

"So we have two days to figure out exactly what we saw, and then convince Matt, but more importantly, his boss, to believe it."

"Sounds about right."

Lee sighed. "Let's get back to the office."

"Only long enough to tidy up loose ends. Lee, you promised to come home for dinner with us."

The last thing she felt like right now was being social. *But I promised* . . . "Nuala isn't making anything special, is she?"

"Oh, no. She suggested we might bring something home."

"I could bring some pasta dough, make something . . ."

"No, you'll get all caught up in rolling those little ear things again all night, and we won't get anything done. How about Xainese? The kids like Xainese."

". . . Okay. Let's go."

"So how *do* Elves disappear?" Lee said softly.

They were sitting in Gelert's living room some hours

later. It was the largest of several adjoining domes that
butted against one another on several different levels, a
rosette of hex windows at the top of each for letting in daylight. The condo was a sleek compromise between the den-
structures that *madrín* built for themselves, and an
apartment more suited to a bipedal species, with a sort of
Southwestern tribal-NorthAm look about it—the interior all
smooth plaster, graceful curves and (Gelert's tastes being involved) much holoprojected art. The stairs between levels
would relapse into ramps when human guests were gone,
but right now most of Gelert's and Nuala's pups were racing
around and practicing falling up and down the stairs in a
mood of general rejoicing.

The floor was comfortably cushioned to a meter or so up
the walls, and Lee in her jeans and T-shirt was leaning
against one wall, surrounded by writing pads, printouts, and
transpads hooked into her office commwall, and by a welter
of mostly empty Xainese food containers. In Lee's lap was
a six-month-old *madra* pup about a meter long—Fhionn,
she thought: even now she had trouble telling them apart,
since they were all still identically covered with undiffen-
tiated pinky-white, wiry fluff—lying on his back, legs pointing into the air in various directions, and snoring a tiny
snore. A couple of meters from her, Gelert lounged amid
similar clutter, and behind him lay his mate Nuala, a little
bigger and a little slenderer than Gelert, lying listening quietly to them, only her eyes shifting occasionally as she
watched the children run around.

"The answer, as you well know, is that they don't disappear," Gelert said. "They're hominid bipeds, just like you
and the Xainese and the Huictli and the Tierrans and the
Midgarthr. They have a small range of psychic and psi abil-
ities, just as other hominids native to the various other
Earths do, but teleportation is not one of them."

"But they're not *just* like the rest of us," Lee said. "Even in terms of what they're made of. Matter sourced from Alfheim sometimes has properties not common to artifacts from other universes. Specially some of the pure chemical elements, which behave differently from elements native to other universes. The most obvious example being allotropic gold." She glanced down at her pad, which was once again showing the *Britannica* precís on Au^{100+}.

"That's not the *only* way the Alfen are different from other humans, of course," Nuala said in her soft little voice.

"No," Lee said. She stretched, leaned back among the cushions. "Nuala, tell me something. How do they look to you?"

"Really?" Nuala said.

"Really."

Nuala gave Lee a look out of her big soulful eyes. "I don't want to offend . . ."

"You won't."

"They look to me the way humans should," Nuala said, sadly, as if in apology, "and don't."

Lee folded her arms and leaned back for a moment, considering. It struck her as a good explanation: for when she, at least, saw an Alfen, there was always a kind of backtaste on the experience: a sense of sadness that everyone couldn't look like that.

"But there's more to it than that, isn't there?" Nuala said after a moment. "One does want to keep looking at them, for some reason. I always feel a little foolish about it."

"You wouldn't be alone," Gelert said. "Everybody does it. Anyway, the differences between Alfen matter and matter in the rest of the Earths aren't going to be enough to let them do the Tooth Fairy number under their own power. What we perceived has to have been something technological."

Lee sighed. "I don't know if that's so wonderful, either.

Alfheim has a lot of history of keeping advanced technologies to itself until it feels like sharing them with other worlds. Usually when it can get the biggest political or financial return out of them."

Gelert got up, stretched, turned around a few times, and lay down again: Nuala settled her head once more on his back. "Well," Gelert said, "seeing how tightly the government of Alfheim controls access to its information, not to mention its territory, if they *do* have some new technology that lets people seem to vanish into nothing, we're not likely to find out anything about it between now and the dil'Sorden case going to trial." He gave Lee a morose look. "No matter how many favors I call in, there's only so much that even I can do in the way of research in such a short time."

Lee sighed, because he was, of course, right. A chorus of yelps descended the nearest flight of stairs, and out of the midst of the storm of legs and muzzles and white fur that ensued, another of the kids flung herself at Lee, more or less knocking Fhionn out of Lee's lap and taking his place. "*Han'hi* Hlee, *Han'hi* Hlee," said Luin, the youngest and still the smallest, "Huan fell down and then Faha fell on her and then I jumped on top of them and I bit Huan in the *m'hon!*"

Lee gave Luin a good ruffling-up and a hug. "Yes, you did, didn't you?" she said. "What a good girl! You just go do that again." She put the baby down on the floor, and she scampered away after Fhionn and her other brothers, who were now running up the stairs again.

"You're inciting my children to do what they want," Nuala said, with an amused expression. "Don't help me out or anything, Lee."

Lee grinned and leaned back against the wall again. "I don't know if I'm being much help to anybody at the moment," she said. "Gel, we really have to get to the bottom of this, or at least be seen swimming for it. How *do* people usually vanish? I don't mean Elves."

"There are some personal stealth technologies; light diversion and so on. . . ."

"Yeah, but Gel, I'd still See someone who was using something like that, just as you'd still Scent them. What I Saw just went away and genuinely wasn't there anymore. He wasn't hidden: he was *gone*."

Gelert rolled over on his other side, looking disgruntled. "And there's always a fade. Even when someone is dying it's a progression; that's how you tell it from a—"

He stopped. Then Gelert sat up, so abruptly that Nuala's head slid off his back. Gelert sat blinking at the opposite wall, as if he were seeing visions in it; and a second later he began to howl.

Lee stared at him. Nuala was sitting up, too, now, staring at him: and the pups came barking down the stairs from the den level, falling over each other again. "Gelerh't mehHrnhuuh," Nuala barked, "what's come over you?"

"Premature senility!" Gelert said between howls of laughter. Around him the pups bounced and barked and tried to lick his jaws, confused by what sounded like their sire's distress. Gelert wrestled a couple of them to the ground, still laughing out loud; and when they had forgotten what their distress was about and had run off again, he sat up once more and shook his head until his ears rattled. "Lee," he said, "*that's* when you vanish in the Scent, in the Sight. The *only* time. When you're in the act of worldgating! The cutoff is sharp: there's no fade. It's weird enough to be rare even in the literature: I ran across it just once, a long, long time ago in one of the forensics journals. Someone was investigating a murder that had happened in a gating facility, actually in a private matrix cluster. The field of perception is sliced by the rotation of local space out of orientation with the 'perceptual' space in the gating matrix; it just cuts off sharp—"

Lee stared at Gelert and had to try hard not to laugh. He was grasping at straws. "Uh . . . Gel. There's just one little problem with that. You can't *have* a worldgate without an accelerator ring. And there aren't any accelerator rings at Eighteenth and Wilshire!"

"I'll grant you that," Gelert said. "But Lee, at least there *is* a prototype for what I Scented, what you Saw. A rare one, a bizarre one, but a *documented* one. Now all we have to find out is, how do you worldgate to someplace, and away from someplace, where there isn't a gating matrix already in place?"

Lee frowned as the pups began to flop down around Gelert now that the noise had stopped. Nuala, relieved, got up and headed into the kitchen, her tail swinging in bemusement. "What do you mean, that's 'all' we have to find out?" Lee said. "You can't gate to someplace that doesn't have a gate matrix tuned to the originator gate, and in phase with it!"

"That's the way it is now," Gelert said. "But think. It wasn't *always* that way, Lee. Otherwise, how did the very first MacIlwain, the one in Huictilopochtli, open the first gateway out of his home universe into another one? There has to have been a time when there was only one accelerator, and no second one to tune to."

Lee searched her memory and came up empty. "If I ever knew that," she said, "I've forgotten it. The history of science wasn't something I went in for much after grammar school."

"We're going to go in for it now," Gelert said. "I'm going to pull an all-nighter on it." He was grinning. Lee had to grin as well, for this was her partner at his most relentlessly alive, baying on the track of data. "And I intend to have enough information to hang a theory on by lunchtime tomorrow. Because here's your question: what did the Alfen version of MacIlwain use?"

Lee thought about that and didn't have even the beginning of an idea. "I'll leave it with you, then." She leaned back against the wall again; the pups, slightly disturbed by her movement, got up, and some went after their mother into the kitchen, others up the stairs again. "Meantime . . . what was all this other stuff you wanted me to look at?"

"It's dil'Sorden's banking and investment data."

Lee reached over, found a spare cushion, and started punching it soft. "Wake me up when you're done."

"I don't think you're going to sleep through this," Gelert said. His grin was stretching wide. "Just bear with me."

Both their screens began showing echoes of Gelert's commwall back in the office; bank statements started flowing by. "This is the investment portfolio part of his banking information," Gelert said. "He had the usual ExTel package to start with—they have an employee share deal of the normal kind. Nothing unusual there: mostly he let the "smart" fund manager program handle it for him. And his banking records show regular contributions to a pension fund and so on, as well as his own contributions back to one of the Alfen shared-equity trusts."

Lee blinked at that. "I didn't know they had to contribute back. I thought those trusts were just for disbursing each Elf's share in Alfheim's profits from fairy gold sales. Like that yearly oil-resources payout for Alaskans in Tierra."

"No," Gelert said. "If they're working, they have to return a certain percentage of their own earnings to the trust; seems to be a cultural requirement. Anyway, his contributions were all in order—what he seems to have done is just roll over any profits the company investment fund made straight into the Alfen trust. And by and large, his investments were straightforward enough—pretty conservative, really. But one place he did swing out, a little. Take a big guess?"

"Fairy gold?"

"See, I told you you wouldn't go to sleep." Gelert nosed his infopad, and the view on it and on Lee's pad changed to show a series of electronic correspondences. "He bought and sold FG futures on the Chicago Mercantile and a couple of the other commodities markets. It makes sense; it was a big interest area for him. And bearing in mind that most of his work at ExTel surrounded this huge new infrastructure program he was working on, the price of fairy gold would have been something that he thought about more or less constantly. In fact it was the controlling factor in his ring expansion project getting off the ground at all— the price was going to have to drop enough for the company to sanction it. To judge by his letters to various colleagues at work, both in Ellay and elsewhere on the planet, he didn't think the go-ahead was imminent. But then the approval came through . . . a whole lot sooner than he was expecting. One or two e-messages to other people suggested he hadn't thought anything would happen much before 2011; they were expecting a 'cyclic' drop in the price around then."

Lee shook her head. "Seems like a long time to wait . . ."

"If you're going to live forever unless you get sick enough to die or someone kills you," Gelert said, "does it really? But dil'Sorden knew it was a massive project when he and his team proposed it, with a very long lag time between development and implementation. It involved, among other things, installing a third data-only ring underneath LAX . . . and billions of talers' worth of investment on just that. Not to mention three other new comms-and-data-only gateways for the Ellay and New San Fran areas."

"Suuz," Lee said.

"Exactly. So when the okay came through, it looks to me from his notes and mail as if Omren got very curious as to the timing. He started making some discreet inquiries. At first he didn't find out much of anything, and it looks like for a couple of weeks he gave up and just got on with work. But then there are several mails to people, about a month after he got the go-ahead, bringing up the issue again. And a friend of his in Accounting, whose anonymity has been carefully preserved in dil'Sorden's notes, tells him that he thinks the project got the green light because there's going to be a change in the price of fairy gold."

Gelert looked at Lee as if he expected some particular response. "Well, wouldn't that be kind of unusual?" she said, cautious. "You told me that one reason fairy gold was such a good commodities metal was because its price was so steady."

"Yeah, but Lee, think about it. Most of the time, a steady market implies tight control. Think of the oil cartels in Tierra and Huictilopochtli: it's the same principle. I don't think there's ever been any doubt that the Alfen influence the price of fairy gold by controlling the rate of supply. The only thing preventing a big outcry on the issue is that the Elves have never shown any sign of using that control to induce artificial scarcity and push the price up."

Lee leaned back and frowned. "*Why* haven't they?"

Gelert grinned at her. "Ah, the sixty-four-taler question. I doubt it's altruism, but no one really knows. The received wisdom is that it's just generally better for their business to keep the price steady—but as usual they're not forthcoming as to why that should be so: intra-Alfheim trade is pretty much a closed book to economists in other universes. Some people say there's nothing sinister about it—it's simply in line with the general conservatism of all their other inter-

universal trading policies." Gelert shrugged his ears. "Maybe. In any case, when the price fluctuates, it usually has to do with events in other universes, and the price gets inflated only on the so-called post-supply 'middleman' markets, where you don't have to wait for a scheduled release of the commodity—places where you can gamble on making a fast buck. But this isn't one of those."

Gelert leaned over and looked at the message on his pad. "And there's the line that makes me wonder, right there. 'Main T&A,' that's ExTel trading and acquisitions, 'has authorized a major bid buy for early 2005 that will make the infrastructure projects more feasible than they would have been.' And here's his note to that: 'Mal says off the record that thirty tons have been bid at $1435.'" Gelert stared at the glowing words in the floor.

"So his project wouldn't have any problem going ahead."

"No kidding." Gelert looked at Lee. "But that's where the problem lies. Fourteen hundred thirty-five dollars is just shy of half the present market price."

"Half?" Lee stared at him. "How could fairy gold possibly drop that much value on the markets by then?"

"How indeed," said Gelert.

"And how would they possibly *know* it would? We're talking nearly two years from now."

"Whereas most futures contracts cut off at six months, a year at most," Gelert said. He bared his teeth for a moment. "Well, insider info gets spread around no matter how governments legislate against it. Sounds like someone knows there's going to be a big change in Alfen government policy, doesn't it? Except that if there was going to be a policy-driven change, you'd expect it to drive the price *up,* not down."

Lee rubbed her head. "And you'd think that the news

about the prospective change would have leaked out by now."

"Of course it would have, if this bid had gone through any public brokerage. People would be screaming from the rooftops about it. I'm betting it went through a private one, though. There are lots of private brokers with links to Chicago Mercantile and Axquitl Modals who would accept a bid like this on the quiet. The understanding being that some of the profits would be spun off to them later, equally quietly, in some other form—stock options, what have you. The old 'I dig a second hole, you drop your spare bone in it' routine." Gelert's lip wrinkled back to show fangs.

Lee was beginning to shake a little, the nervous tremor she always got when feeling that she was close to something vital to a case's solution. "Gel . . . could *this* be why Omren dil'Sorden died? Was no one supposed to find out about the size of the bid, or its price—but he did, maybe even accidentally for all we know, and then someone got wind of it and had him killed to make sure the information went no further?"

Gelert took a long breath, let it out. "It could be so," he said. "And I'd take it a little further, and bet that it's the price of the bid, not the size, that's the issue. But proving it's going to be exciting business."

"Gel," Lee said, "this is why Jok Castelain was pushed out into our laps, isn't it. To keep the investigation from having to go any further . . . and uncovering this. The real reason why dil'Sorden was targeted."

"I think you might be right," Gelert said. "And if our investigation along these lines becomes anybody's knowledge, *we* become targets, too."

They looked at each other without saying anything for a good few moments. "You have a mate and pups to think about," Lee said.

"It says 'partnership' on our office door," Gelert said, "and I take that seriously, along with my oaths to the Lady with the Scales and Her Boss upstream. If you think I'm going to back away from this and let you take the heat just because—"

Lee waved him silent. For another few moments neither of them spoke.

"What do we do now?" she said at last.

"What we've been doing," Gelert said. "If only to keep from attracting attention to ourselves."

"That's going to mean finishing the casework and sending it to the DA," Lee said. "And meanwhile, making private copies of everything so we can keep working. Because if you're right, we're going to have to seem to be moving on to other things. Renselaar and Hagen are both determined to have a big announcement real soon now about how the murder's been solved: Matt isn't going to be able to buy us any more time. If he's even willing."

"There's something else he might be able to affect," Gelert said, "much as I dislike it. As soon as dil'Sorden's murder case goes to trial, our psychoforensics records are unsealed and become public. At which point the figure at the murder which you didn't mention to Hagen, the one he was scared you saw, becomes a matter of record . . . and *he* immediately realizes you lied to him, or withheld information, with an eye to getting hold of dil'Sorden's computer data. That means trouble for both of us no matter how you look at it."

Lee nodded. "If we can keep the case from going to trial for a while . . ." she said. "Gel, we're prosecuting. There are some procedural moves we can use to slow things down."

"But not for long," Gelert said. "It may just have to go ahead, finally. The worst that can happen is that they'll disbar us for use of confidential information outside of an official investigation, fine us everything we've got, and chuck us in the clink for forever and a day."

He sounded cheerful. Lee wasn't fooled, and could additionally think of many worse things that could happen. Yet none of them seemed as bad to her, somehow, as letting this case go to trial merely on its surface merits, stopping short of what her own oaths to Justice required—the *whole* truth, without which the people perish. Castelain might have Justice executed on him for his part in the murder, certainly: but Lee was sure there were other things yet to be unearthed about this case that Justice ought also to be allowed to deal with. *That won't happen if things stop here . . .*

And away on the edge of her Sight, as if perceived just outside the ambit of more normal vision, Lee sensed something else wrong—something that would cause a whole lot of perishing if it was allowed to progress unchecked. She had no idea what it was, and even less of an idea what to do about it. But turning her back on it would be wrong.

"Meanwhile," Gelert said, "I'm going to stay up tonight and have a look at that worldgating material . . . see if I can get a sense of just how you gate without a gate. If we can manage to convince Matt and the DA even partway that what we both perceived was something technologically based, then everything changes . . . at least insofar as it makes us, and incidentally them, look less like idiots."

"And it gives us more time to dig," Lee said. "Because there's still the problem of Castelain passing out on the bus, and waking up wherever . . . not to mention the fading psychospoor. We may be able to get a postponement just on the grounds that we need information on that gating technology from the Alfen. And if they try to stonewall—"

"When did they ever not?" Gelert said, and grinned. "It's

in their blood. To be Alfen is to be secret. The more resistance they put up, the more time we have to dig even deeper."

Lee stretched and leaned against the wall again, looking up the stairs, where one of the pups had flopped down on the topmost step and was hanging half over it, asleep. "And the more time the forces already interfering in this case have to find still other ways to interfere."

She looked over at Gelert. His eyes were resting on her, calm, but concerned. "I'd take a little more time over my personal security than usual if I were you," he said.

"If I were you," Lee said, "I'd do the same."

~~

There was nothing more they could do that evening. Lee got up and helped Gelert tidy the living room, then softly went up the stairs to avoid waking up any of the small white bodies littering the floors; made her goodbyes to Nuala, and headed back out to the hov. Lee walked around it once in the parking area, a well-lit place that suddenly seemed more threatening than usual. She let the Sight take her, and looked the hov over carefully for anything that seemed wrong: but the vehicle sat there, untampered-with, innocuous. Lee got in, started it up, and drove home.

The memory of the constant state of nerves that had followed the Eligieni multiple murder case was now imposing itself on her again; she started to see something she hadn't thought of for a couple of years now—images of that other parking lot where one of the two brothers involved had tried to shoot her. Lee was nervous all the way back, looking suspiciously at the roadsides, at any driver who passed her too fast; at everything. She hated this reaction—the upset caused by the first few moments in a given case when she realized that she was in danger, that someone might very well be willing to kill her to keep her from proceeding. Certainly nothing overt had happened yet. But Lee couldn't get rid of the feeling that there was going to be something overt: that Gelert was right. *Better to be prepared for it,* she thought as she pulled up in front of her house, calming down already.

She went up the front path, gazing into every shadow: in fact, doing everything she should have done except watch where she was going, so that she tripped on the cracked slab and nearly fell. "Damn, damn, damn," Lee said as she recovered herself. *What use is paranoia if it makes you break your own neck? Stop trying to look judicially at everything, and just watch where you're going . . . !* She stomped up the front steps and spoke the front door open. As it closed behind her she actually leaned back against it to feel it there, reassuring, a barrier against what presently felt like a very naughty world. "System," she said, "secure everything."

"Secured," the house system said to her implant. The blinds rotated themselves into closed mode; all the windows and doors double-bolted themselves.

"At least there's *something* I can depend on," Lee muttered, and went into the kitchen. Coffee was out of the question at the moment; her nerves were jangled enough. Xocolatl was more what she needed. She went to the sink to fill the electric kettle, set it in its stand and started it, then got down on her knees to open the bottom cupboard next to the sink and try to figure out where she'd hidden the xoco this time.

And all the lights went out.

The terror went right through Lee in a flash that seemed to start just above her kidneys and blast outward all through her. *Oh, wonderful! Someone's defeated your security system, and now you've locked them in here with you!*

The lights had been too bright when she came in; her vision would take too long to cope with this darkness. *My normal vision,* Lee thought, and closed her eyes.

She heard the *snick, snick* of someone's gun being cocked. She was not a great expert on firearms, but this one had a very big-gun sound to it; at the very least it was meant to sound big, and to scare her. "Okay," said the voice. Male, and processed: he was wearing a neolarynx of one kind or another. "Get up nice and slow, lady."

"Uh, yeah, right, look, just don't do anything, okay," Lee said, doing her best to sound scared out of her wits, and not having to work too hard at it. "If you want money, there's a safe in the back bedroom—"

"Never mind that. Get up slow."

I gave you a chance to pretend to be a burglar, Lee thought. *Too bad you wouldn't take it.* She kept her eyes closed, silently feeling her way along sideways via the cupboard under the sink, concentrating on Seeing. Without clear line of Sight, she had to depend on the directional sense, always a somewhat dicey business. But the gunman's sense of amusement and enjoyment of all this was palpable, easy enough to feel; it was coming from over by the patio doors, where he stood, confident, sure that she couldn't see him. *Probably wearing nightsighters, too. Well, it's not going to be enough.* She would know this man's psychospoor again anywhere, but the way things were going, she might not have to. "All right," she said, "I'm getting up. Don't do anything, okay?" Her voice broke most realistically. "I'm getting up—"

And perhaps the gunman then had reason to be surprised when Lee popped up from behind the breakfast bar and shot him in the chest, because not that many householders keep their gun safe under the sink.

He spun around sideways, staggered by the slug from

the big-caliber Sig. *Body armor. Dammit!* Lee dropped partway behind the breakfast bar again, braced, waiting. The man struggled to bring himself around to face her again, and the second he was face-on to her, Lee shot him again in the chest, twice, full on this time. The impact of the first bullet smashed him back into the glass of the patio door; the second one knocked him straight through it.

All the house alarms chose *this* moment to go off, screaming and hooting bloody murder, though the lights for some reason stayed off. Lee dropped down behind the breakfast bar again and put her head around the side of it, where as she braced the gun again she could clearly see through the patio doors, and could See the figure staggering to its feet, cursing at the broken glass—getting up, hesitating a moment, then turning, running, heading for the back wall. Five-foot-nine, Caucasian, light build, dark hair, plaid shirt, dark jacket, dark pants, black sneakers—she got a glimpse of the white soles as the gunman went over the back wall into the alley, and kept on running—and his psychospoor nicely recorded in her implant for the black-and-white to relay when the alarm system finished calling for armed response and went on to call the police.

Slowly and carefully Lee stood up. Behind her, the kettle boiled, and its switch popped up, *snick!*—and Lee whirled and very nearly shot it. Then she stood still and, after a few long moments, found it possible to laugh at herself.

The black-and-white seemed to take forever to arrive, though in reality it took no more than five minutes. Lee had had plenty of time to make that cup of xocolatl, which had possibly saved her life, and to call Gelert and tell him to have a look at his own security, before the armed response team rolled up at almost the same moment the cops did. She stood there on the doorstep with the cup, getting past the shock, heading along toward anger now as the security-system people came up to the front door. "Break-in?" one of them said to her.

Lee shook her head. "Hacked. I haven't touched the system box . . . go see what it has to tell you."

She left them to it and went down to the end of the walk to talk to the officers in the black-and-white. There were two of them, a dark woman with neatly cornrowed hair, a Hispanic man: the woman looked down at the datapad built into the dashboard, and said, "Ms. Enfield, is it? The system's got your load. You're going to press charges?"

"If you can catch him. He came pretty well prepared; armored, anyway. My money says he's been picked up, and he's halfway to San Diego by now. Over the back wall, into the alley—it runs into San Dimas at the north end and Willow at the south."

"We'll go around and look."

"Take me around with you?"

"Sure."

The officers in the black-and-white drove back down the street and around the corner, left and left again, into the alley, a long blind street lined only by garage doors and wheelie bins: today had been garbage day. Lee tsked. "Forgot to put my garbage out," she said.

"Did it a little late, maybe," said the female officer. Lee grinned. They got out of the hov just before Lee's property line, and Lee got out with the two officers, woke up her implant again, and looked at the wall and the road. "He went down that way," she said, pointing south toward Willow. "Turned west. That's all I can tell you from here."

"Okay," the male officer said. "We'll see if we can find anything, Ms. Enfield. But HQ notified the DA's Office about this . . . and they want you to have a security detail. We'll wait till the alarm people have restored your system and secured the back doors. There'll be plainclothes hovs in front and in back until Parker can assign you someone more permanent in the morning."

"Thanks, Officer. Want some xoco?"

They both grinned at her.

It took nearly another hour to get rid of everyone— though perhaps Lee was glad enough, for the moment, to see the dark car pull up out front as the uniformed officers left, and to know there was another one out in the alley. Gelert was on the comm again: it took longer to calm him down than it had taken Lee to calm herself. Finally, she told him to go to bed, because she was going to do that whether he did or not; and finally she sat down on the living room sofa with one more cup of xoco, staring at the soft shine of the dimmed lights on her hardwood floor, starting to feel both very angry, and also strangely satisfied. *We're on the right track,* Lee thought. *No question about it now. No one bothers to try killing you because you are getting it wrong.*

The comm went again. She sighed and spoke the living room entertainment screen on, switched it to comms and said, "Hello?"

The screen stayed black except for the area which would have shown the ID of the calling number or station, and which now simply said, SUPPRESSED.

Uh-oh, Lee thought. *Our little friend, calling back to threaten me?* "Hello?" she said again.

"Ms. Enfield," said a voice, another male voice, also certainly processed; but not the same as the last one.

"Who's calling?"

There was a pause, as much uncertainty on the other party's part, Lee thought, as anything to do with the processing software. "There are some parties who're interested in keeping you from progressing much further with your present investigations," the voice said.

A number of them, I'd say; which one do you *represent?*, Lee was tempted to say, and didn't. "Like your little friend just now," she said, "was *he* one of yours?"

The voiced paused. "What?"

"The man who suborned the alarm system in my house, closed it up after him, and waited for me in the dark, almost certainly with the intent to either put me in the hospital or kill me."

Genuine surprise. "I don't know what you mean."

"Then you may be good at getting comm numbers, but you're not real well informed otherwise." Lee was fuming, and also bemused. Possibly this person was *not* attached to the attempt on her life just now. So this was some different loony. *And why is he calling me here rather than at the office?* The answer suggested itself instantly: *Because there's no recording software on this line . . . and someone knows it. Boy, is* that *going to change in the next day or so!* Yet she still found herself getting a haunted feeling, with nothing to base it on, nothing that would ever stand up in court, something purely subjective. A tall, dark shape . . .

Ridiculous. That silhouette's been on your mind for days . . . that's all it is. But still she could hear Gelert saying, *Follow your hunches . . .*

"I'm sorry you've had trouble."

"I'm sure you are, but you still haven't identified yourself . . . so you have ten seconds to explain what you want."

"There are people who want to give you a hand."

Lee laughed. "Where were they this evening? I could have used them in the kitchen." *Okay, that sounded slightly hysterical. Fine. I have some hysterical coming.*

"Hagen isn't one of them."

Lee went quiet for the moment. "And? Five seconds."

"He knows what you know."

She had to laugh again. "Who was it," she said, "who

suggested that the perfect way to get someone to leave town was to send them a message that said, 'Flee, all is discovered'? What makes *you* think you know what I know? Any more than Hagen does?"

"There are more people than just ExTel," said the voice, "who know what was in Omren dil'Sorden's personnel records."

Alfen! Lee thought.

"Some of them are becoming nervous at what a thoughtful examination of those personnel records might reveal," the voice said. "Some of them are in quite high places . . . if not *the* highest. They'll be trying to have you removed from the case to prevent that."

The highest . . . ? Lee thought. Her thoughts abruptly went back to Le Chalet Perdu, to that beautiful, silent man sitting across the room, listening, impassive, taking everything in, revealing nothing. "I'd say someone's made a start on that already," Lee said. "What kind of help have you got in mind?"

"Advice. When an opportunity to leave town comes up," the voice said, "take it."

Lee smiled sardonically. "What career I have hasn't been built on running away."

"You won't be running away. It'll be pursuit. But it'll have the advantage of not looking like it."

Lee sat silent for a moment. "I'll think about it. Assuming anything of the kind happens."

"Don't just think about it. Your position is getting worse. You're likely to wind up in a situation where it'd take the roses of Aien Mhariseth themselves to get you off with your skin intact," the voice said. "Kind of a shame you don't have one of those in your pocket to start with. It'd save you a lot of trouble. Now, and later."

"It's not something I expect to find in my pocket anytime soon," Lee said. "Let's stick with the subject."

"But it's very much to the point," the voice said. "One could do all manner of things with such an instrumentality."

Oh, really? What are you leading up to here? "For whom, exactly?" Lee said. "Who stands to benefit?"

"The power of such an artifact, if imported without Alfen interference, would be considerable in this world," the voice said. "Its mere presence would render some Alfen technologies transparent . . . some ineffective. Insofar as this touches on those who vanish without the benefit of any technology known in Earth's universe, I'd think the effect would be of some interest to you."

Lee went first hot, then cold. "Accessing confidential material pertaining to an investigation in process is a serious crime," she said.

"So is conspiracy to commit murder," said the voice. "So is murder itself. And there are worse crimes that have no names as yet. But soon they may."

Lee held very still, experiencing more strongly than ever again that shadowy behind-the-back feeling that she was becoming more and more deeply involved in something that, if not stopped, would involve a lot of death. "It would help to be dealing with someone who could declare himself or herself," she said, "rather than someone too scared to come out in the open."

"Sometimes fear can be useful," that voice said. It sounded almost cheerful. "Goodbye."

The connection cleared itself. Lee sat there looking at the dark screen for a long time. Finally, she finished her xoco and made the rounds of the house one last time, irrationally, looking into every shadow, and spending a long few moments looking up at the now-boarded-up and bolted-over patio doors. They looked unusually vulnerable, despite the armor-laminate on the boarding, despite the steel strips, despite the thought of the unmarked out in the alley and the unmarked out in front.

Fear can be useful, the voice had said.

But to whom? Lee thought, and took that uneasy thought with her to bed.

Five

$\mathcal{M}$ikki was right, Lee," Gelert said down the comm. "They've gone public with the Five-Interpol homicide report."

She chuckled. "Well, certainly the juicy parts have finally started to make the news."

She had been up early, not anything to do with the report: rather her own shredded nerves, which were taking revenge on her the way they usually did . . . a stomach that felt like a bowl full of acid, a head that ached even after the aspirin. So the early news had caught her at a low ebb, and had (bizarrely) cheered her up. Mikki certainly had been right; the Five-Interpol report had been leaked as soon as it decently could have—no more than two days before the "official" publication date, if there was such a thing anymore—and every news agency that came across it was mining it for the kind of content that suited it best. Now she sat on the living room sofa, her legs curled under her, drinking xoco in a kind of amused acknowledgment of The Drink That Saved Her Life, wondering at the wide spectrum of response to the report. Even the newspeople at the local muckraking tabloid station had found as much material for scandal in the Five-

Interpol report as she had . . . though certainly not in the same places.

ARE ELVES THE WORLDS' BIGGEST RACISTS? was the question plastered all over that station's sister "paper," the one with the naked broads on page three. "The Pulchritude Paper," Gelert usually called it, having a strictly out-of-species take on human pulchritude ("Not nearly enough breasts," was his usual comment). But the typically ample charms of the lady on three were somewhat over-shadowed by the facing headline, which said, A MONOP-OLY REVEALED!

Only to your *mouth-breathing readers,* Lee thought un-charitably. To them, Their Paper apparently felt it would be big news that Alfheim strictly controlled rights of access to its universe, technological information native to it, and nearly everything else that made life worth living . . . and was therefore Inherently Evil, possibly even communist. The problem (for the Pulchritude Paper's lead writers, any-way) was that Alfheim also had a king, and therefore seemed unlikely to qualify as a communist domain. The Paper tried flinging some speculative mud at the Elf-King ("mysterious . . . secretive . . . extravagant, world-hopping lifestyle . . .") but was unable to make much of it stick: no one seemed able to find any evidence of murder, insanity, or even a romantic attraction in his history (much less a di-vorce), and they had been unsuccessful in getting any Alfen to reveal any scandalous secrets about him. To the Paper, of course, all of this was in itself evidence of a conspiracy. To be mysterious and secretive automatically meant that you had something to hide, and anyone who couldn't be bribed into revealing juicy secrets about a head of state must be under some kind of duress, possibly even going in fear of their lives.

"They don't bribe nearly high enough, that's their problem," Lee said under her breath, turning over the flexible display that she used to show her the papers. "Gelert, come on, I'm fine. I'm coming in."

"You stay right where you are," Gelert said from the office. "There's nothing happening here that you need to know about."

"I'd rather you'd let me be the judge of that."

"After your bodyguard arrives."

"Oh please," Lee said. "Someone else to drink my xoco. I really need this."

"After last night, I'd say you really do," Gelert said, "so don't give me trouble about it. It's only until we close this case out, Lee: just deal with it." He lay there in his office, looking casually over at his own commwall. "But what a day in the news. It's not a question of putting the cat among the pigeons: it's *tigers* out there."

She had to agree. Every news/info channel from the *Financial Times* down had gone through the Interpol report and found something "useful" for its readers. Of all the local news "papers," the *Times* was probably the most thoughtful . . . but only insofar as its analysis used words with more syllables. *Five-Interpol Report Suggests Wide-Ranging EAT Conspiracy Between Alfen, Multinationals,* the column-one headline said. The story had been passed, not to one of their investigative reporters, but to their leader writer; Lee suspected that some old scores were being paid off in the *Times*'s front office even as she read. "EAT" was "extra-'antitrust,'" the term used for an agreement which was suspected of having been constructed specifically to get around a given jurisdiction's antimonopoly legislation. She scanned down the article.

> . . . *the tip of an investigative iceberg that will probably be years in the excavation, considering Alfheim's traditional reporting restrictions and*

*equally restrictive attitudes toward legal "discovery"
and extradition . . .*

How do you excavate an iceberg? Lee thought, amused,
while agreeing with the article's thrust. She touched the control on the flat paper display in her lap to "turn" the page.

*. . . a veil of secrecy overtly justified by "world
sovereignty" needs which has also covertly assisted
Alfen-supported multinational entities, as well as
other ME's and "nonphysical sovereignties," in a
wide-flung network of (at least) collusion or (at best)
corruption, all aimed at keeping Alfen interests in
control of the price and supply of fairy gold.*

*The Five-Interpol report collates for the first time
evidence from police and security forces on Earth,
Tierra, Huichtilopochtli, Earth/Xaihon, and Midgarth.
This unusually large sampling, taken over five years
in the above sovereignties and "compound" sovereignties, suggests, that Alfen interests have been using
criminal means, even to the point of homicide, to influence and/or control the price of fairy gold and FG
futures on the major markets—a strategy that also finally acts to control which markets, and which firms
in which markets, have access to the single most important manufacturing and infrastructure commodity
in the Six Worlds. A disproportionate number of the
Alfen victims whose murders are detailed in the report
were involved either in industries intensively using
fairy gold, or in banking or other financial institutions
using FG or trading in it.*

*The report lends uncomfortable credence to a the-
ory some have long lacked facts to prove: an increasing tendency in Alfen governments to limit "expedited"
access to fairy gold to those countries or multina-*

tional entities that either agree with Alfen interior/exterior policy or are willing to carry it out.

Senior sources in the Alfen government have to date only said that they are carefully examining the report and will have no comment at this time. But interworld opinion is likely to force their hand, and some observers of Alfen affairs are already suggesting that the ramifications of the report are so far-reaching— possibly extending even to the Office of the Laurin himself—that the usual Alfen tactic of waiting quietly until the fuss dies down will be completely ineffective in this case. Among the final recommendations of the report is that the UN&ME should empanel an independent investigative committee to look for more concrete evidence of collusion or conspiracy, the overt purpose of such a committee being to lift the cloud of accusation as quickly as possible if no evidence can be found. If the UN&ME agrees with this assessment, the Elves will have little choice but to agree to so seemingly reasonable a request—and will also know that the other veto powers will not take it kindly if they use their own veto to derail the empanelment. In the face of what would seem like guilty behavior, intended to hide real evidence of Alfen conspiracy to restrict free trade and communications among the other five worlds, especially at so potentially unstable a time— when a new world has just been discovered—it would not take long for the mood in the UN&ME to shift toward sanctions should the Elves prove refractory . . .

Lee sat there thinking. *The very highest levels,* her faceless caller had said. "Gel," she said, "there's something I want to look up. I'll be back online later."

"Fine."

She waved the screen off; it reverted to its nonbusiness

appearance, a gaudy Miro print, and leaned back on the sofa. No one was going to call her up and give her covert offers of help without it being in some way to their own advantage; she owed it to herself to find out why someone thought she would be such a likely tool to use. If there was some advantage in it for Lee, of course, the picture would change somewhat. *I just have to keep my own curiosity from running away with me on this, that's all,* she thought.

She could just hear Gelert laughing at the very idea. She raised her eyebrows ironically and started to get up to get some more xoco.

The screen rang again. "Oh, *now* what," Lee muttered. "Answer . . ." she said to the comms system.

Lee found herself looking at Matt's face, and was horrified to feel the sudden wild affection that tore her at the sight of him, making her both want to weep and laugh, even though his expression was furious. *It's just reaction,* she thought. *Get a grip!*

"Matt," she said, and it was all she could manage.

"Well, you've done it again," he said.

"Done what?"

"You're all over the news. Prosecutor in Alfen murder case attacked, where was police protection, blah, blah, blah. If I didn't know better, I'd suspect that you'd cooked this whole thing up to make me look stupid."

You?? So many possible responses instantly presented themselves that Lee was spoiled for choice. "*Making* you look stupid? Why in the Worlds should we waste our time on *that* when God's done it already?" was the first one, closely followed by, "Oh, *I* planned my own assault and possible murder to do something, anything whatever, good or bad, to *your* reputation? Call *Webster's,* because 'self-centered' is going to have to be redefined!" . . . And several other possible retorts, far juicier, more unprofessional, and indeed more actionable, suggested themselves as well. Lee could do little but concentrate on her breathing until she was sure which part of her was in control of her mouth.

"Did you look at the sweep?" she finally said, as gently as she could.

"What?"

"The psychoforensic data I got off the guy while he was holding me at gunpoint, in the dark, in my kitchen," Lee said, "or thought he was; and when I shot him, and afterward, when he went over my back wall, and after that, out in the alley. Did you have a look at that?"

"Uh, no."

"Do," Lee said. "If he matches anything in the master database, let me know. I'll be happy to assist the Assistant DA in pressing charges. Meanwhile, my compliments to the DA: thank him for the security detail." Of course, the detail had almost certainly been Matt's immediate response after some busybody at HQ called him last night: but at the moment, Lee didn't care. "The casework he was inquiring about will be on his desk on Friday morning. Along with our invoice. Good morning, Mr. Assistant District Attorney." And she waved the comm off and stalked into the kitchen.

In the living room, the commlink instantly started ringing again. "System, who is it?" she said.

"Last caller."

"Refuse it. Redirect to the office."

"Refused. Redirected."

"Son of a bitch," Lee said, getting down on her knees again to get more xoco. It would stay in that cupboard, she vowed, until she felt a lot happier about life. "How dare you, you, you . . ." It was too much trouble even to feel around for a satisfying epithet.

"You," Lee muttered, frustrated. She got up off her knees with a couple of rediscovered filter bags of the real xoco, not the instant stuff but the organic Aztec Black, and went rummaging in the upper cupboard for the drip coffeemaker. Lee packed the beanbags into the upper chamber and reached for the kettle. "Poor baby," she said, dumping out what water remained from the instant xoco she'd made for the uniforms and the security people last night, and refilling the kettle. "I'm sorry I almost shot you . . ."

Which reminded her: she had secured the Sig back in its place in the gunsafe, but it still needed to be cleaned and reloaded. *Though maybe I shouldn't, they may want it later for forensics . . .*

Screw that. They don't need it to be dirty for ballistics. And if someone else comes in here . . . Lee opened the undersink cupboard, touched the gun safe open, removed the gun, and took it over to the kitchen table to disassemble it on the kitchen counter while the kettle boiled.

The roses of Aien Mhariseth . . .

The doorbell rang.

"Oh, great," she said, and went to answer it. "Peephole . . ." she said to the screen in the living room. It showed her the van from her security company parked outside, with a local glazier's van right behind it; the security-system guy and the glaziers were standing on the doorstep. "Open," Lee said, and the door swung wide. The three men walked in, and Lee was briefly surprised at the shocked look on their faces. "We weren't *that* late, lady," one of the glaziers said.

Lee stood puzzled for a moment, then realized they were all staring at the gun in her hand. "Oh. Sorry!" she said. "I was just going to clean it. Come on, the broken doors are back here."

She showed them into the kitchen, poured them xoco, poured some for herself, and put the gun away again: it would wait until later. Then she went back out to the living room. "Directional display," she said, sitting down on the sofa again, "and refuse everything except calls from the office until further notice."

The screen polarized itself. Lee had several ways to do anonymous research when she had to, and this seemed like a good time. She had her implant feed the commlink the encrypted password that routed the link through one of the public anonymizing facilities, then went into the *Britannica,* brought up its "search" facility, put a selection of search terms in, and waited to see what appeared. Meantime, it was much too quiet inside the house. "Sound system," she said. "Playback, classical, random."

"Starke scheite!" a woman began singing loudly to huge orchestral accompaniment; and Lee closed her eyes in brief annoyance . . . then had to laugh. Gelert had been playing around with her system's programming features when he'd been here last, and had dumped all her own settings in favor of what he considered a more "educational" menu. In Gelert's case, this naturally meant heavy doses of the most serious composers of the previous two centuries, or the loudest ones—Lee suspected that for him, the two were identical. Wagner therefore turned up high on his list, and the *Ring* cycle probably highest of all, with *Götterdammerung,* especially the last act, winning by sheer force of sound effects. Lee sat with it for a moment, reflecting, and then let it run; it effectively drowned out the sound of hammers and saws from the back of the house.

The screen started showing results to her research, a number of references; but they all seemed to be to fairy tales. *Once upon a time, a king married a dwarf woman,* one of them began.

Lee raised her eyebrows. *Mixed marriage . . . it'll never work.* She paged down. "Once upon a time . . ." "In a faraway land . . ." "Then the King stood up—"

"Expand that one," Lee said. The screen caught her

choice from her implant's connection to her optic nerve and showed her her full selection.

> *Then the king stood up*
> *and looked his last*
> *on his garden, storied in song:*
> *yet though he was chained,*
> *he lifted his hands*
> *to speak words that could not be imprisoned.*
> *You cannot trample my roses, he said;*
> *you cannot destroy my dreams!*
> *Neither by day*
> *nor yet by night*
> *will they ever again be seen;*
> *yet safe in the stone*
> *the dreams will sleep,*
> *safe from your thoughtless destruction!*
> *Stone the roses,*
> *stone my dreams,*
> *stone your mortal hearts! . . .*

Poetry, Lee thought, amused. *What am I doing wrong? Oh, wait a moment, I know.* She went back to the search form, removed the word "Elf" and added the term "Alfen."

The search ran itself again and still did not completely get rid of the fairy-tale references, though at least now she started to get historical ones as well. There were several references to occurrences of the terms "roses" and "Alfen" in Tierra, though there they took the form of some medieval myth tangled up with the history of the Ostrogoths, and with "Dietrich of Bern," who turned out to be actually the old Emperor Theodoric, and not from Bern at all, but Verona. There was a sentence down in the body of that article equating Elves with Alfen in a general sense, but nothing more concrete.

Lee raised her eyebrows and looked at the last entry, which at least seemed to have something to do with fact. . . . *the dolomite mountain range near Aien Mhariseth is famous in many old stories that tell of how the early Kings of the Elves kept gardens there of fabulous flowers, powerful for magic and inaccessible to lesser beings. These myths may be traced back to Laurin XXXVII, who founded what is now the modern city of Aien Mhariseth on the ruins of an older city of the 'Central European' Alfen, usually identified with the twentieth dynasty of the dil'Jhaira Hegemony, the site a near-cognate to Earth's Bozen and Tierra's Bolzano . . .*

"Yes, but what about the damn roses?" Lee muttered. She scrolled down several more pages, but could find no further references to anything but myths. *Great,* she thought. *Someone's sent us off to look for the Holy Grail.*

. . . possible confusion of the true rose, Rosa rosa, *with* Rhododendron ferrugineum, *a species of the* Ericaceae *popularly referred to in several languages as the "alpenrose." The plant which turns some mountainous regions red with its blooms in mid to late summer . . .*

Now botany, Lee thought. *Who needs this?*

But her curiosity really was beginning to itch now. *Are these things really just a myth . . . or do they actually exist, though very well concealed?* Certainly the Elves had the kind of clout to conceal something by misdirection or other means if they wanted to.

Look at you, she thought then in disgust. *You're getting as credulous as the Pulchritude Paper's readers . . . thinking that just because you can't find any information about something, someone must be hiding it.*

Still . . .

Lee sat there thinking. Her caller last night . . . what was the phrase he had used? "Imported without Alfen interference."

Stolen, Lee thought.

She shivered. The idea of the kind of trouble you could get into—getting caught stealing *anything* from Alfheim, let alone something that appeared to have some cultural significance . . .

But why am I being invited to do just that?

The doorbell rang. Lee sighed. "Peephole," she said.

The screen reverted to its security function. Standing on her doorstep she saw a man who could have been mistaken for some 'forties film star: big, rawboned, in a dark and retiring suit that fit him much too well, with open, kindly eyes in a chunky, honest face; an overall look that Lee had seen on enough suspects in her time to make her suspect him of white-collar crime. It was almost a disappointment when he held up a perfectly valid LAPD ident to the door. "Ms. Enfield?" he said, rather loudly.

Behind Lee, the sound system was reproducing the sound of the destruction of a neighboring universe by fire and a collapse of the local ethical system. "Just a moment," Lee shouted over the storm of brasses and thunder. "System, open," she said, getting up. "Then call Gelert at the office . . ."

The officer stepped in, looking around; Lee went over to him and shook his hand. "Larry Mitcheson," he said. "Division sent me to be with you until this cools off."

"Whatever 'this' is," Lee said, "and whenever that might be. Can I offer you something? Xoco?"

"Can't stand it," Larry said in an I'm-sorry tone of voice. "Got tea?"

"Just the bad strong kind made from warehouse sweepings."

"Thank you, ma'am," he said. "Mind if I look around?"

"Feel free," Lee said. "Don't mind the security people, they're replacing the patio doors."

"Armor glass?" Larry said.

"Doesn't seem like I have a choice," Lee said, resigned, as Larry went prowling off around her house *God knows what he's going to make of the closets,* Lee thought. *I knew I should have cleaned those out.* But that was probably like your mother's advice about wearing clean underwear, in case you should be in an accident; you obeyed it and didn't have an accident for twenty years, and then let it slip just once and got broadsided.

ON ANOTHER CALL: PLEASE HANG ON, said Gelert's personal herald. Lee sat down with a sigh and waited, while the sound system, having passed through the destruction of the ancient world without damage, began singing the rising of the waters of the Rhine and the motif of Redemption Through Love. Lee snorted softly; love had been singularly without redemption around here lately. But Gelert appeared a second later, lying in his office and looking through his mail on his commwall, and she let the wry face go.

"My bodyguard's here," Lee said softly to the commscreen. "And he looks like a crook. Or the mailman."

"Best kind, either way," Gelert said. "In the second case, the kind no one sees, let alone suspects. I'm glad you called, and I'm glad he turned up. You need to come in."

"Half an hour ago you were claiming I wasn't needed. What happened? Matt put a flea in your ear?"

Gelert twitched the ear. "Rather the other way around, I think. He wants to apologize to you. Yet again."

"Let him wait. Seriously, Gel, what is it?"

"Not over an open link, Lee," Gelert said. "Wait till you get into the office."

Indeed, Lee thought. "Search pan out?" she said.

"In spades."

"I'll be in as soon as the doors are fixed."

It took a little longer than that, for Larry the Bodyguard took a while to finish examining her house, her gun, her yard, and her perimeter wall, as well as carefully going over her alarm and security systems until he understood them. Then he gave the company hov the same treatment, until Lee was fairly dancing with impatience to get away. But Larry was methodical, and she supposed she couldn't argue the point: if more people were going to be coming after her, which seemed all too likely, better that he should know the territory as well as she did.

Finally, they locked up the house and headed for downtown. At least Larry let her drive, which was a relief to Lee: she hated to be driven by anyone but Gelert, who was monotonously safe. When they got to the office, though, Larry gave the place the same thorough going-over that he'd done with the house. Lee drew the line at her and Gelert's office, especially when Larry showed no sign of stepping outside so that Lee could talk to her partner.

"Look," Lee said, "this is *my office.* I am safe here. You do not have to sit in here with me! Look, we don't even have windows. Just commwalls. And confidential things go on in here which, forgive me, are none of your business even if you *are* here to keep me alive. It's all right for you to make yourself comfortable outside, all right? I promise I'll let you know if I'm going to go out. Believe me, I have no desire to go out *without* you at the moment. Besides, that's the only door out of here; I couldn't leave without you knowing. Now can you excuse us?"

With a reluctant smile, Larry went out and let the door slip shut behind him. "Mass," Lee said on the private channel, "give that nice man some tea and something to read. And warn us if he shows the slightest sign of coming in here."

Gotcha, boss.

Lee sat down in her chair with a sigh, looking at Saturn and the methane snow as if it had been months since she'd seen them last. In some ways, it felt like it. Gelert sat down by Lee and rested his head on her shoulder. "Now," he said. "Are you all right?"

"Yes. Well, no. As all right as I'm going to be. The only really good thing about this morning has been being nasty to Matt."

"He said he was the nasty one."

Lee raised her eyebrows. "He's having an unusually candid phase," she said. "Never mind. What was too sensitive for the commlink?"

"Well, now." Gelert walked in a couple of tight circles, then flopped down within gazing range of his "desk." "Remember that gating problem we were discussing?"

"How the first guy in Alfheim did it."

"Right. It turns out that the initial gating ring broke through to the next universe over partly by virtue of sheer brute power. It was a really big ring: apparently its builders had some concerns that it might actually create a local black hole, or cause the end of their universe."

"And they built it anyway?" Lee said. "Says something or other about their mind-set . . ."

"No argument. But then the MacIlwain in Tierra broke through much more easily by having the Huichtil gate to tune to. Each universe has followed the same pattern; once you don't have to build huge powerful rings, you stop doing it . . . especially once fairy gold gets into the equation, making fine-tuning much more accurate, and numerous, much smaller rings, viable."

And here Gelert grinned. "But here's the good part. The gating theorists say that the present technology means that small high-power rings, 'brute force' rings that can drive so-called 'free state' gates, can easily be built if anyone cares to. The point is, no one cares to, at least publicly, because they're really expensive. They need a *whole lot* of fairy gold for the multiplex core windings. And who has a whole lot of fairy gold . . . ?"

"Elves," Lee said.

Gelert grinned wider. "Better still, Lee, one of the tech journals I was looking at gives details of one specific kind of particle decay that can be detected in the neighborhood of such gatings. I bet you that our forensic sweeps can be rerun with an eye to looking for that decay. And if they can't, I'm willing to go to the corner of Eighteenth and Wilshire to-morrow night late and see if I can't wring just one last sweep out of the murder scene. Who knows what I might Scent?"

"Sounds like a great idea," Lee said. "There's only one problem. What's this 'I' thing?"

"Lee . . . come on. Take at least minimal precautions, all right?"

"I'll bring the bodyguard. Sorry. I'll bring Larry. He's a nice guy, you'll like him."

"I like him already, but that's not the point. The area's just too open."

"It says reh'Mechren *and* Enfield on the office door, Gel . . ."

"So it does, and I want to keep the glass looking the way it does at the moment, and not like your patio doors."

Lee frowned. Then something struck her. "Wait just a minute," she said. "You said that the Alfen 'MacIlwain' broke through *partly* by brute force."

"That's right." Gelert smiled. "And that leads us to the really interesting part. It seems that there are places where gating occurs spontaneously."

Lee sat still for a few moments and tried to wrap her brain around that concept, with very little success. It was like trying to believe that it was possible to receive commcalls on your fillings. "How in the worlds . . . ?" she said. "Gelert, the whole gating concept relies on the application of huge concentrations of forces that don't occur naturally."

"That's what you'd think, normally. But apparently, sometimes they do," Gelert said. "And no one knows why. Except possibly some people . . . who have been noticeable by their professed disinterest in the subject."

"The Alfen . . ." Lee said softly.

"The texts I was using for research were pretty general," Gelert said. "But it would seem there are places in Alfheim where gating phenomena occur naturally. Unpredictably, of course. But it seems like the very first MacIlwain—his name was de'Dilhath in Alfen, apparently it means about the same thing—was 'assisted' in his breakthrough by the fact that one of these gates was near the CERN-analogue where he was doing his research, a place called Ailathseneh. It had been notorious for centuries for disappearances and strange occurrences . . . rocks rolling uphill, strange lights, persistent lightning strikes. The best theory is that there may be some conditions under which a planet's surface naturally manifests cyclotron-like phenomena, as opposed to the atmosphere, which does that sometimes during sunspot highs. But the initial breakthrough from Alfheim to the first of the other worlds would never have happened without that 'strange place' being nearby."

Lee digested that.

"How many of these 'places' are there in Alfheim?" she said.

"No way to tell. Interesting, though; the implication in that very early theoretical work was that other worlds might have such places, too. But the whole concept seems to have been abandoned by the wayside very early on. Maybe with some reason. Once someone invents the commcaster, why keep inventing it? Or in this case, why bother hunting all over your planet for someplace that may occasionally behave as a worldgate, when with an accelerator ring and the right materials you can build one wherever you want it, one that behaves itself all the time?"

"And I bet I know who'll sell you the 'right materials,'" Lee said. She sat and thought for a little. "But, Gel, this still doesn't help us as regards the corner of Eighteenth and Wilshire. If 'cyclotron-like' phenomena happened at all often there, I would think we'd have heard about it by now."

"In that neighborhood," Gelert said dryly, "I'm not sure I can agree. Nonetheless, another sweep is in the cards, so I'll talk to our folks at LAPD and schedule it. Tonight if possible, because I'd love to put this data into the casework folder and send it off to the DA in the morning. Anyway, I've already put all the hard citations about these so-called free state gates in it. They're just what we needed, Lee: something concrete to hang our disappearing Alfen on. Take a little time to go over it and let me know if there's anything I missed. If there isn't, a sweep tonight to detect that decay is all we need to justify our ways to Big Jim."

"All right," she said. "But there's something else we need to discuss that I wouldn't have wanted to go down the link, either."

"I'm all ears."

"I've always said so."

Gelert laid them back and gave her a look. Lee ignored the look and told him about her unidentified caller.

"Alfen," Gelert said, when she was done.

"It seems likely, though I don't have any proof."

Gelert brooded for a few moments. "But with what axe to grind?" he said. "Alfen politics is as tangled as anybody's. There are people out to get the Elf-king, and people out to get his enemies, who are numerous—it looks like the Elves are no happier about being stuck in a hereditary monarchy than some people in the other worlds." He looked thoughtful. "And the thing with the roses . . . That's odd. No question that some Alfen artifacts are very powerful in other universes. Not that anyone knows why. But someone plainly wants us to be thinking about these. I wish I knew why."

"To get us in trouble?" Lee said. "To make us a target, somehow . . ."

"Because of the dil'Sorden case," Gelert said. "Because we've already found out too much about some things . . . and someone doesn't want us finding out any more."

"Simpler just to shoot us, I'd have thought," Lee said.

"Someone was certainly willing enough to try that," Gelert said. "But that was a strange line. 'You'll be offered an opportunity to leave town . . . Take it.' A threat?"

"I don't know why," Lee said, "but it didn't sound like one at the time."

"You have to follow your hunches . . ." Gelert said slowly. "Well. I'll do a little research on the roses myself. They may not be just flowers: the term could be code for something else."

Lee nodded. "I'll copy my research run to you," she said, "so we won't duplicate each other. Meanwhile, let's have a look at the casework folder."

It took rather more than "a little time." After Lee read through the accumulated casework and reviewed all their sweeps, she and Gelert spent most of the late afternoon and early evening on the fine points of their depositions, before Gelert went out to do the final sweep, with his implant enabled for detection of particle decay, around eight. Gelert did it alone, as he'd insisted, for Larry the Bodyguard agreed with him completely that the area around Eighteenth and Wilshire couldn't be secured well enough for Lee's safety. She tried arguing with him, but she was too new at it to be very effective yet, and additionally, she was unusually tired: the reaction from the previous night's excitement, Lee supposed, was setting in. The result was that she rode home with Larry in the passenger seat, he checked her house out most carefully, and then when she promised not to go out again, he left her inside, locked in, with the unmarked hovs still minding the front and back of the house.

Lee made dinner and fumed, waiting for Gelert's call. It didn't come until nearly eleven. But when she heard his voice, she grinned.

"Got it," he said.

"You got what you were looking for?"

"Exactly what I was looking for," Gelert said, and his grin matched hers. He was not going to be any more specific over the comm, she knew. "I'll patch it into the spot in the casework that's waiting for it, and then send this off to Big Jim's office."

"With our invoice!"

"I'd never forget. Mass has generated it . . . it's ready to go."

Lee sat there for a few moments and said nothing. "You look sad," Gelert said.

"Tired," Lee said. "I'm still dealing with yesterday, I guess. But, Gel, there's more to it than that. The DA will have enough to go to trial with . . . but we're still no closer to knowing for sure who sent Jok Castelain around with the gun: who's really responsible for dil'Sorden's death."

"I know what you mean," Gelert said. "No closure." He sighed. "Well, we've given them some good indications of where we should start to work when the trial phase begins. Meantime . . ." He looked at her thoughtfully. "You call Matt yet?"

Lee rubbed her eyes. "It's too late," she said. "Tomorrow."

"All right. Sign off on this, and Mass will send it in."

"Right. Listen, Gel . . . good work. Your nose has saved us again."

"Your nose isn't so bad either, Lee. Go get some sleep, and don't even think of showing up here before lunch."

"Right."

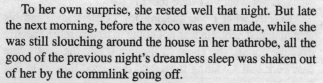

To her own surprise, she rested well that night. But late the next morning, before the xoco was even made, while she was still slouching around the house in her bathrobe, all the good of the previous night's dreamless sleep was shaken out of her by the commlink going off.

It was Gelert. "Are you watching the news?"

"Huh. No. Should I be?"

"Turn it on, fast. CTLA."

"System, split channel," Lee said. "Muckrakers.' "

The system kicked Gelert's image over to one side of the screen and displayed, on the other, what Lee instantly recognized as the front steps of Parker Center. It was a press conference. Indeed, it was a press conference with not only Big Jim Renselaar in the flesh, and there was a lot of it, but the Police Commissioner, a man not usually known for enjoying press conferences very much.

Renselaar was in full flight. "Too many rubber chicken dinners," Gelert said, "look at him!"

"Shhh!"

"—pioneering investigation of violence by Elves against Elves. The release of the Five-Interpol report makes it plain that the case we are presently investigating is merely the tip of the iceberg . . ."

"Icebergs," Lee moaned. "No more icebergs, please . . ."

"Look at that," Gelert said. "Just look at him taking credit for other people's work! Sheer genius. It's no wonder he's going to be our next Mayor."

Lee looked around for somewhere to be ill.

"And look at Matt standing there behind him, the loyal assistant DA. If things go as planned in some quarters, Matt's going to lose half his title . . ."

This was a thought that had occurred to Lee more than once lately. She refused to say anything; animus did not reflect well on the bearer. "Shh!"

"—obvious implications of the Five-Interpol report for the Ellay Alfen community. We take attacks on this community very seriously, as is demonstrated by our present investigation of the murder of Omren dil'Sorden, a heinous crime that I am pleased to announce will be going to court within the next two weeks—"

"My God, he read the casework *that* fast??"

"Ssh!"

"—one of our star prosecution teams, Liayna Enfield and Gelert reh'Mechren. However, the present situation suggests that their tremendous talents can be better used in an even wider investigative role than in the present investigation . . ."

"What the hell is he talking about?!" Lee whispered.

"—in light of the Federal Prosecutor's request this morning to the UN '&' ME to immediately organize an investigative panel, I am seconding Enfield and reh'Mechren to the FP's Office with a request that they be part of any panel. We are glad to lend the best and most expert aid we have to this wider investigation into the unacceptable face of intraspecies relations—"

"No," Lee murmured. "Oh, *no*."

"See that now, Lee," Gelert said. "How does it feel to be the biggest stepping-stone in the DA's mayoral campaign? Don't hide your feelings, now. Aren't you proud and yet also humbled?"

"He's fired us!"

"Not fired. 'Seconded.' Such a nice word. So rounded."

"The sonofabitch has thrown us right into the middle of it!" Lee said, lost between horror for herself and Gelert, and fury, well mixed with astonishment, at Big Jim. "Hasn't he thought of conflict of interest? Hasn't he thought of what happens when we go to trial?"

"No," Gelert said. "And I don't think he cares. It doesn't matter now if the dil'Sorden case *never* goes to trial. He's already being seen to do his part in the crusade against violence against other species, especially Elves. He's dumped us on the UN's doorstep, to his campaign's everlasting enhancement. Because how many of his electorate—how many of them who can *count*, anyway—are going to remember our names, or care about them, when Big Jim's mayoral campaign begins to roll?"

"Or where we've been buried," Lee said softly. "He's thrown us right in the laps of the other Elves, Gel. The Elves who don't want us to know why they're killing their own people. Who bought him? Who told him where to throw us?"

"Got a call in to Hagen, Lee?" Gelert said softly. "Somehow I think he may be a while getting back to us."

She looked at him in silence and could think of not a word to say.

Six

It took the better part of two weeks for the noise to reach
enough of a crescendo for the Alfen to respond: and the
noise that started them out of cover, finally, was the
UN&ME's Secretary General standing up in a Security
Council meeting to "guillotine" debate and call the vote on
the empanelment of the Special Investigative Committee.
The vote came down 10–6 in favor, Alfheim abstaining. The
Assembly then adopted a resolution requiring the Alfen authorities (specifically naming the Laurin) to allow more
transparency into Alfheim's relationships with other worlds,
and to immediately agree to a more detailed investigation.
To the applause of the delegates, at the end of the session the
Alfen ambassador walked out of the Assembly with her
lovely face looking unusually grim.

Lee watched all this happening with some concern,
when she had time to think about it. Mostly she was annoyed that nothing was happening, and apparently nothing
was going to happen, with the dil'Sorden case. Though a
trial date had been set, no magistrate had yet been assigned:
the reason Lee kept hearing from Matt's office was "man-
power shortages" caused by too many magistrates taking

their holidays at the same time. But she thought she knew better. Word was quietly about in the DA's Office: stall. And there were no more commcalls from Hagen.

"But it's hardly a surprise, Lee," Gelert said to her one afternoon in the office. "This is going to be the best way to make our discoveries go quietly away. The case itself won't be postponed . . . but its scheduling will, again and again. You know how the game goes; we've both seen it before. Meanwhile we'll have been packed off to Alfheim for Herself only knows how long, surrounded by lots of lovely bureaucracy, with our own communications curtailed, and almost certainly thoroughly snooped. We won't be able to do anything concrete about the dil'Sorden case while we're stuck there. And anything we do discover, we're going to have a hard time communicating privately."

"Assuming we actually ever *go*," Lee said. "There's been nothing from the FP's Office, or the UN, for ten days now."

"Oh, we'll be going, all right," Gelert said. He stretched, rolled over on his back. "It's just taking a while for the Alfen to blink. Sooner or later it's got to happen, though they're being slow about it . . . probably to look tough in front of their own people. The implication in the UN resolution was clear enough. If the Laurin doesn't cooperate now, then any leads that suggest he's involved in this conspiracy will be followed back to the source with vigor. And the Alfen don't like the idea of sanctions by the other worlds even to be mentioned."

"It's just saber rattling," Lee said. "No one's going to slap any kind of sanction on the Elves with an eye to isolating them. It can't be done! They're too tangled up in every part of interworld relationships." She pushed a can of green-tea drink across her desk, brooding. "What's going to happen is that after our committee makes its report, all the interests who think it's going to benefit their own agendas will start yelling for Alfheim to implement the findings, become more transparent, more accessible. And it won't stop there. Big money and big business all over the worlds are going to start pushing that little crack wider and wider, until finally they're demanding an open-door policy."

"The Alfen will never stand for it," Gelert said.

"Nope," Lee said. "But the other interests will all keep pushing. They'll call for the end of the monopoly, maybe an interworld/international body set up to administer the distribution of fairy gold."

"Enforced by an interworld armed force." Gelert said. "And just as any other world would, the Alfen will refuse. They'll say they have the right to sovereignty over their own world, and the right to control access. It's all right there in the Five-Geneva Pact."

"Which is not going to stop some people," Lee said. She swallowed. "They're going to perceive the monopoly as a tool that can be used to put a stranglehold on other worlds, whenever Alfheim gets an Elf-king who's prone to hold a grudge . . . or get territorial. Which means sooner or later, there's going to be a war."

"Probably sooner," Gelert said. "There's never been a war *between* worlds. It's going to be interesting."

Lee could hardly think of a bigger understatement. "We're thinking along the same lines," she said softly. "But Gel . . . here's what's bothering me. The Alfen are not a stupid species. Or a warlike one. They should have been able to defuse this particular problem a long time ago, but didn't. Why not? And why is this all coming to a head now?"

Gelert shook his head until his ears flapped. "No idea. But I wonder . . . is he having political problems of his own?"

"Who? The Laurin?" Lee raised her eyebrows. "If he was, how would we know?"

"Makes me wonder, though. How do you get a new Elf-king?"

"The old one dies, I think," Lee said.

"Takes a good long time for that," Gelert said, "at least from our point of view. I wonder if Alfen political usage includes a tradition of assassination? . . ."

"Not something I'm read up on," Lee said.

"It might be worth checking," said Gelert. "Not that they let other worlds know that much about their political systems to begin with. More secretiveness . . ."

"Why *are* they so secretive, I wonder?" Lee said, getting up to go over to their little cooler for another tea.

Gelert rolled right side up again and put his head down on his paws. "That's something we'll probably never find out," he said. "But then why are humans so aggressive in one universe and relatively pacifistic in another? Why has Midgarth never had a war bigger than the one that leads up to each Fimbulwinter—just little settlement-to-settlement raids—while the Huichtilopochtlin cultures seem to have wars every weekend, the way other species have football?"

"Ethical constants set differently in the different universes," Lee said. "Or so they told us in history class."

Gelert snorted softly. "It's a nice theory, but until I see an ethical constant running down the street, clearly enough to sink my teeth into it, I'll withhold judgment. . . . Anyway, we have other things to think about. When they finally *do* get the panel all chosen, and the Alfheim government finally blinks, we're going to have to make sure that our own agenda doesn't get buried under everybody else's."

"I've seen some of the names already," Lee said. "Not a bad group. Mellie Hopkins, you remember her. And guess who else? Sal Griffiths . . ."

"Really. Well, they're solid enough, I'll grant you that. But most of the rest of them are going to be strangers, and most of the rest of them will have their own axes to grind."

"It's not the humans I'm concerned about," Lee said. "It's the Alfen."

"Still thinking of your midnight caller . . ."

"Yes." She popped the top of her green tea, had a drink. "Gel, something bigger is going on."

"Bigger than the run-up to a war between worlds?" Gelert said, giving her an odd look. "What could be bigger than that?"

"I don't know," Lee said. "But you keep telling me to follow my hunches . . . And my hunch says something far worse than just a war is coming. Change. Or death. And we're going to be going into the middle of it, going into a world we don't know very well at all, into the midst of a people we don't really understand . . ."

Gelert's gaze rested on Lee for a little while. "If you get anything more concrete in the hunch department," he said, "let me know."

Lee nodded, wishing that this would happen as soon as possible . . . for the shadow brooding over her at the moment was making work increasingly difficult; a sense that what was coming was not merely death, not merely change, but something ineffably worse than either.

Lee shivered and turned back to her desk.

It was perhaps just as well that there wasn't much work to do in the office at the moment. She and Gelert had been concentrating on clearing away any remnants of earlier caseload in anticipation of the call from the Investigative Committee. That afternoon there had been no reason to hang around, and both of them had prepared to head home early. "Larry," Lee said, sticking her head out into the front office and looking over into the small corner niche he had made his own, "school's out for the day . . ."

"Right you are, Ms. Enfield." She could not break him of formal address, no matter how she tried.

She got her work bag, and they headed down to the hov together. "Going to be a quiet time for you when we head off," she said, as they got in.

"Not so quiet," Larry said. "They'll post me back to Homicide." He smiled slightly.

"Where your heart is, huh?"

"Yeah." Lee pulled out of the parking space and swung out into the main flow of traffic. "I guess the Alfen will be giving you one of their own people as a bodyguard when you go over . . ."

That was a thought that Lee didn't relish. Having either a male or female version of that difficult beauty around her for all her waking hours would not be terribly pleasant. She had managed to get used to Larry somewhat, but an Elf . . . "I don't know how they're going to manage it," she said. "They haven't even said yes to the committee yet . . ."

"But they will," Larry said as they got onto the freeway. Lee glanced sideways, a little surprised to see the frown settling onto Larry's face. "They're going to have to. And probably it's about time that they had to cooperate with something. There's always a feeling about them like they're better than you, somehow . . . and they know it . . . and they know *you* know it. And that, down deep, they really like it that way. Be kind of fun to see *them* having a hard time for a change."

Goodness, Lee thought, *my bodyguard is a bigot.* But then she thought, *Or is he? Any more than I am? . . .* For her thoughts went back to Nuala's line about Elves looking "the way people ought to, but didn't," and her own thought about how looking at and considering that beauty left her, at least, feeling sad. *If you dwell on that feeling for too long, how soon does it start to turn to a sense of unfairness?* And after that comes the anger that leads to the desire to do something about the other's unfair beauty. . . .

"I think I can see your point," Lee said, her patented neutral reply. They chatted about this and that on the way home, and in the house, Larry went carefully over everything before letting Lee settle in. "The unmarkeds are all set," Larry said. "If you want to go out anywhere, just call . . ."

"I will. Thanks, Larry."

She shut the door behind him and flopped down on the sofa, rejecting the idea of going anywhere at all; an afternoon off was something that lately she'd only have had time to dream about. There was some gardening she might do—what passed for her garden in the backyard, mostly summer succulents and the occasional sandpit cactus—needed to be raked. And there were various other tasks she'd been avoiding . . .

Lee sat there for a moment more, staring at the screen, and thought, *Right, let's get it over with.* "System," she said. "Call Matt . . ."

The screen flicked on and immediately showed Lee the "busy" herald. "Please hold," said the LAPD comm system's voice.

Lee went into the kitchen for some water, paused there a moment, looking out at the garden. *It really is a mess,* she thought. *Look at those leaves . . . And the grass is dying. I keep forgetting to tell the house to water it. I'm going to have to get the landscape guy out here . . .*

She walked into the living room and was surprised to see

Matt's face looking out of the screen, peering around. "Oh," she said, "sorry! I didn't hear the hold go away."

"I thought maybe it was a message of some kind," Matt said.

Lee sat down on the sofa. "Uh, no," she said, "I try to be a little more direct about my messages than that."

"Yes, I noticed," Matt said. "Lee . . ."

"I know, you're sorry."

"You won't even let me apologize, will you?"

Maybe she was doing him a disservice; but at the moment Lee really didn't care. "I don't know that I can stop you," she said, "if you really set your mind to it."

Matt simply looked at her for a moment, then let a breath out. "All right," he said. "Never mind. But I'm glad you called: I needed to talk to you."

"About what?"

"Dil'Sorden."

"Ah, our famous non-case," Lee said. "I wish Big Jim would just make up his mind to either throw it out or prosecute it."

"This is about that."

"Oh, really?"

"Yes. He wants you to continue your investigation when you go over to Alfheim."

" 'If,' I would have thought. 'When' is still up in the air."

"Not for long," Matt said. "Lee, there are still a lot of unanswered questions in that case. You know it yourself. Yet your casework up till now has been very, very sharp . . . maybe too sharp. The DA wants you to just quietly keep looking into it, while you're over there. In particular, he's interested in what possible political connections or ramifications there might be regarding this murder in Alfheim itself. Not as part of the bigger picture, necessarily; as an individual case in its own right. As it seems that there's an unusual amount of interest in it over there . . ."

Lee sat quite still and pondered, just for a second, whether to tell Matt about her midnight caller.

"You're the obvious choice," Matt said then. "You must be getting something right . . . since no one has tried to kill anyone else involved in this investigation."

"Thank you so much," Lee said. "So you're going to push me a little farther out on the limb, are you? Where would I be without my friends?"

Matt was silent. Maybe the bitterness of the words exceeded what Lee had intended. She didn't care.

"Seriously," Lee said, disgusted, "I'm beginning to think everybody involved in this case has a scheme but me."

"Even Gelert?"

She grinned sourly. "Oh, almost certainly. Gelert *always* has a scheme. But in his case at least I know which side he's scheming on. Whereas you—" She glared at Matt. "Forget it. Go find yourself some other girl."

He winced. *Gee, did I have to phrase it just that way?* Lee thought. *And to think I did that without even trying. Maybe I really am a bitch. And maybe I have reason to be.*

"Lee," Matt said. And then paused. "Look," he said, "I'm not going to get into the whole thing with us right now. I grant you, you have no reason to want to listen to anything I'm suggesting. But this is different. *Yes,* Big Jim has been wheeling and dealing as always. The man can no more avoid politicking than he can avoid breathing."

"Shame about that," Lee said. "He used to be worth something as a prosecutor before his priorities shifted."

Matt winced again. *Good,* Lee thought. *See that fate coming toward you, too? So do other people, and it's best you know it.* "That's not the point," Matt said. "Lee, this time the politicking has been to some purpose. Jim's managed to put you right where you'll be in a position to find out things that are going to make a difference to your case. And he's made it look as if it was *just* politics that did it. With you seconded away to this fact-finding mission, you'll be able to get a look at things and people that simply haven't been accessible to investigators from our world before—"

"I am not going to be a party to some random fishing expedition," Lee said, starting to get angrier and doing her best to keep it from showing. "Do you seriously believe that the Elves are going to allow me to get within screaming distance of anything that's going to break this case open the way it *could* be broken open, if our suspicions are correct? They're not stupid, Matt!"

"They have no choice but to cooperate now, Lee," Matt said. "There is a very narrow window of opportunity here, one it *would* be stupid to ignore. Just in the wider sense! Elves *have* been killing Elves, all over the worlds, in larger than usual numbers. You just happen to be involved in one such case right now. Under no circumstances at any other time would an investigator of such a case have been allowed into Alfheim to do casework. You've seen the report, you've seen the way these requests are always refused as 'not in Alfheim's interest,' 'prejudicial to world sovereignty,' all the other legal fast-talk. But just this once, they can't do it. And you want to walk away? I would have thought better of you."

Lee opened her mouth, closed it again. *He sounds committed.*

He sounded committed before, too. To you. And you saw where that *went.*

"Come on, Lee. You're too much of a professional, too much devoted to serving Justice, to turn your back on this. You know it's true."

Bastard, Lee thought. *Tell me the truth about myself . . . or what I really want to believe about myself. What a nasty trick.*

"And yes, I know what you're thinking. Forget it for a moment, Lee! Think about those remaining holes in your prosecution case. They're smaller than they were . . . but they're still there. This whole 'free state gating' thing is very nebulous as yet, very technical. But now you have a chance to just walk around inside Alfheim, perfectly innocently, with your eyes open for anything that will substantiate the line of investigation you most want to run down—most especially this clandestine worldgating thing. If you can find any kind of concrete evidence on the ground in Alfheim that supports your theory, anything at *all* . . . then you've got a potential win. Right now the case might simply have to be shelved because a win with the present evidence is impossible. Too many unanswered questions about your sweeps. Big Jim has bought you some time to answer those questions . . . even to find plausible theories to underpin them. Something that'll lead you to dil'Sorden's real killer, not some poor schmuck of a triggerman."

He has me. Oh, dear sweet God, he has me, and what do I say? Matt, they are going to know exactly what I'm there for. They're not going to like it."

"It's not going to matter whether they like it or not. The UN & ME is going to be staring over their shoulders the whole time. No one would dare move against someone associated with the official investigation: not a chance. You're in the position of a lifetime."

She sat back on the sofa and looked at Matt hard. "I think you know perfectly well it's not just Alfen background figures that are going to be dragged out into the daylight if our own investigation really takes off," Lee said.

"It's people from Earth as well. It's sure not going to hurt Big Jim's position, *politically,* when they're dragged kicking and screaming into the spotlight, is it, Matt?"

He twitched. It was a squirm, stopped halfway through. *Aha,* Lee thought. *Now we get to the meat of it. Let's see how he reacts to* this.

"Besides," Lee said, "the Alfen have come a little way out of the woodwork of late. I've had overtures from them. Did I mention?"

Matt's brief silence, and the sudden alert look in his eyes told her all she needed to know. "What did they want?"

"They were being cagey. But the roses of Aien Mhariseth were mentioned, Matt. The Elf-king's roses. Someone was suggesting they might be useful. Someone was suggesting that we should try to . . . acquire some, as something that might be useful in our case."

Matt took another long breath. "Go for it, then," he said.

"Are you out of your *mind?*" Lee shouted. "Go for it *how,* exactly? You'd have as much luck waltzing into the Blue House's rose garden and taking some of theirs. More!—since the Secret Service is at least vaguely accountable to the Treasury Department when they shoot you, for the cost of the bullets if nothing else, and the Elf-king is accountable to no one but his own sweet self. Where *are* these roses? What do they do? How do you use them? Who keeps them, who guards them, who knows how you can get them out of Alfheim without being nabbed at the nearest gating facility by the Alfen Department of Agriculture?" She threw her hands in the air in disgust at his obtuseness.

"I'm just suggesting that you should seem amenable to the overtures they've made to you," Matt said. "But resist. Whoever was making the suggestion may come a little further out of their shell and give you some information that they can be traced by."

And that you or your boss can make political hay out of,
Lee thought. *It's all politics for you, isn't it. And this leaves
me and Gelert where?*

"Oh, yeah; right. And when *they* don't resist," Lee said,
"and we find ourselves on Alfen soil and actually having to
produce a result? Having to get out the secateurs and raid
someone's garden in some high-security compound? Assuming it actually *exists* as something besides a folktale?"

"It must exist," Matt said. "Otherwise, no one would be
asking for the roses."

Lee wanted to clutch her head at his naïveté. "The roses
may only exist as a way for us to prove that some Alfen leak
is leaking the way they want it to," she said, "or that they
don't. It's going to present problems for Gelert and me,
after the fact."

Matt said nothing for a moment. "Obviously going that
far out on a limb would warrant you some form of protection—"

"Oh, *some* form. And who exactly is going to protect
us?"

"The DA's Office will do everything it—"

"Bushwah! I want it in *writing,* Matt. I want a piece of
paper with the Bear Seal on it, saying 'This absolves you of
all blame.' I want a piece of paper that says 'What the
bearer did was done for the good of the State.' It's probably
not going to be good enough to keep us from being killed,
but it'll clear our poor tattered names after we're dead."

The silence surprised her. He genuinely had not considered the possibility that paper immunity might not be
enough. "The state Attorney General—"

"This would go straight to national level, Matt, if your
boss had either the inclination or the power to swing it. But
the state AG's Office will have to do as a start until he sees

where the political advantages lie." *And please Herself, he'll see it in a hurry, because if he doesn't—*

The silence stretched. Finally, Matt said, "I'll fake a copy of a draft agreement over to your office in the morning. I'm sure the DA will see it your way."

"Are you?" Lee said.

She let that silence stretch, too. Finally, she said, "I could say I'm sorry that you're the one that Big Jim has made the bearer of this particular bad news. But I won't, because I don't believe you refused the job very hard. You are getting a little too used to doing things for expediency's sake, Matt, and one day you're going to go looking for your soul and find that expediency is all that's left. Meantime, I'll be waiting for that paperwork . . . much good may it do us."

She waved the comm dead and sat hunched over in a state of the most profound annoyance.

He wants me to just trust him.

Hah. I did that once.

Lee let out a long breath. *But could it be . . .* the thought came up, *could it just possibly be that if I had turned a blind eye . . . the trophy babe would have gone away, and everything would have been the way it was between us, eventually?*

Was it my pride that killed this relationship? My refusal to be second best? Or seen as second best?

She entertained the thought for no more than a few seconds before pushing it away. It annoyed her, for this line of thinking had come up several times lately. *It has to be stress.*

Or desperation, said that annoying voice in the back of her head. *Or plain old loneliness.*

Lee cursed softly and got up to go into the kitchen; cleaning her gun was on her mind again. Matt's handsomeness, his kindness—early on, anyway—had lulled her into a sense that everything between them was all right, would always be all right. To find out how wrong she'd been was still an open wound. *I won't be trusting anyone else that way,* she thought, *not for a long time . . . if ever.*

She sighed, and went out back for another look at the garden.

The next morning Gelert called her, sounding both triumphant and alarmed. "They blinked," he said.

"So I see . . ."

The release of the news had been embargoed so as to make the morning live news services: the "papers" would be a little slower in getting it out, but Lee could imagine the headlines in the Pulchritude Paper and its ilk: ELVES SAY YES! . . . would probably be the politest of them. The local live news was running and rerunning the video of that morning's press conference by the Alfen Ambassador to the UN&ME. She stood there, fair, blond, radiant, dressed in formal black skintights with the typical short Alfen cloak-wrap over it all, and looking for all the world like this whole business had been entirely her government's idea, as she made the formal statement. She did it fluently, gracefully, without notes. *Just like an Elf,* Lee thought . . .

"—full cooperation with the desires of the UN&ME in light of the findings of the Five-Interpol report," Elen dil'Khelev was saying. "It is the judgment of our government, and of the Elf-king, that our people's long tradition of privacy in our dealings with the other Worlds, while necessary for the protection of our culture, should on some occasions be relaxed somewhat when good and sufficient reason is presented. We will therefore look forward to receiving the investigative committee empaneled by the UN&ME, at its earliest convenience, and will extend it every appropriate cooperation. That's the formal statement; and now I'll take some questions."

The reporter whom she chose jumped up said, "Ma'am, why has it taken the Alfen government so long to reach this decision?"

The Ambassador laughed gently. "I would instead say, isn't it unusual that it's taken so short a time!—which can only be an indicator of how eager we are to cooperate with our cousin worlds and organizations in the UN. None of you will be ignorant of our long history of protecting the privacy and cultural integrity of our people, or of the violation of that principle by citizens of other worlds in the earliest phases of 'tween-universe commerce, before the Five-Geneva Pact. Many priceless cultural artifacts were lost to us during that period, and the will of our people that Alfheim should be protected from any such further losses has always been one of our government's highest priorities. We were equally sensitive to the destabilization sometimes caused in other sovereignties by the very nature of some of the artifacts removed from Alfheim without proper protective measures first being taken . . . so that it's always seemed the better course to be overly cautious in allowing access to and egress from our world."

Lee sat there with a dry smile. The ambassador had successfully avoided using the words "treasure hunters," "smugglers," or any other term that would say in the open why people in those earlier times would go to Alfheim and try to smuggle artifacts out: because their inherent power, compared to matter in other universes, could in some cases bend the fabric of local reality awry into most unusual shapes. *As the roses apparently would* . . . "In this case, however," the Ambassador was saying, "we could only be genuinely grateful for the concern among other worlds for the figures concerning mortality among our people in the outworlds, and with some reservations we share their interest in determing the cause of this phenomenon . . ."

Lee turned to the side of the screen where Gelert was lounging in his living room, with pups scattered around him, sleeping. "So," she said. "Full cooperation . . ."

"Full 'appropriate' cooperation, whatever that is," Gelert said, amused. "For the sake of 'greater transparency.' 'A confidence-building measure.' I guess we'd better start packing. Have you heard any suggestions as to the date?"

"Nothing concrete yet. I think their people have to get together with the FP's Office and synchronize everybody's schedules. Plus we're probably all going to have background checks run on us first . . ."

"In our case, I suspect they've been run already," Lee said. "Have you looked over Matt's little note?"

"All fifty-three pages of it."

"Is it going to be enough?"

Gelert looked up from his pad. "Well, the language is fairly robust."

"It's going to have to be, if we're going to be successfully extradited after they chuck us in jail over there."

Gelert sighed. "That little reference to lost cultural artifacts . . ." he said. "Was that pointed at us, I wonder?"

"Hmm. Paranoia, Gel . . . ?"

"I wouldn't be so sure."

"It sounded more like general exculpation to me," Lee said. "A kindly way of saying, 'Some of you guys ran amuck in our universe two centuries ago and stole "magical" things from us, and they blew you up, remember? So don't be surprised that we're so sensitive. And don't get cute, because you still don't know how those things work, or how *we* don't get blown up by them. —Nyaah, nyaah."

Gelert chuckled.

"And it might have been aimed at us, too," Lee said, re-signed, "so don't ask *me*. I have no idea who my mystery caller might have spoken to, or who's behind him, or indeed who may right this minute be wringing him out in some exclusive clinic with whatever the Alfen use for babble juice, or even Sight."

"It's been giving me some concern," Gelert said. ". . . You scrambled?"

"Yes."

"The things we were discussing . . . if they exist, their affiliation with a certain entity would seem to indicate they're potentially far more powerful than other, more mundane objects," Gelert said. "I had a look at some of the reports on the artifacts removed from Alfheim during the Tierran raiders' 'acquisitive period.' Universal law itself, in Tierra anyway, was profoundly subverted in places when these items were brought in . . . gravity, lightspeed, other forces and powers that are usually well beyond human interference."

"Justice?" Lee said softly.

"Hard to tell," Gelert said. "I didn't see anything in the literature. But if that was true . . . if you knew what to do with it, maybe even if you didn't . . . such an object could alter how one perceived the truth, even with the Sight."

"Break a case open," Lee said, "or destroy it. Possibly pervert Justice Herself . . ."

Gelert shook his head. "Or maybe just blow a hole in the LA area the size of Lake Val San Fernando," Gelert said, "the way a little jade statuette about two inches high blew up the Tierran gating complex at Mexica."

Lee sat there for a moment. "'Hagen knows what you know,' said my caller." She mused. "'All is revealed . . .'

Probably it's smarter for us to act as if the Alfen on the other side know exactly what our caller told us, too."

"But do they know what we're going to do about it?" Gelert said.

"Right now," Lee said, glancing at the screen and wondering how secure the scrambling really was, "I'm going to forget about it. We have the dil'Sorden case to go over, with an eye to where we're going to be, what information is likely to be made available to us, and what we might be able to push them into releasing that they don't really want to."

"I've got a little list," Gelert said. Behind him, Gilbert and Sullivan started playing. One of the pups, Fhionn, Lee thought, woke up, twitched his ears, then sat up and started to howl along.

Lee smiled, sat back, and looked at the list Gelert showed her; and they started to make their plans.

Some hours later they were done, and Lee got up and went to make herself a sandwich. She had shut the screen down, but left the commlink active, feeding the linkage from her implant into it; and that link she was sure was secure . . . here, anyway.

So now we wait to see if our unknown friend comes out of the woodwork again to see what we're going to do, she said, watching the Palmerrand characters stream by along the bottom of her field of vision. *With an eye to finding out more of what this is all about. Because, by God, if we're going to be used as pawns by him or the people behind him, we're going to be* alert *pawns . . . ready to use whatever we find to our own advantage, and "take" anything that gets too close.*

And when we're over there, Gelert said, *we make damned sure we don't get caught with somebody's roses actually in our teeth. I'm none too confident in Matt's wonderful piece of paper, or even of the protection of the UN&ME.*

But if we look like we're looking . . . then we draw our mystery man out a little further.

Which I would like to do, Gelert said, *since I want to know why we're suddenly so attractive as tools. But in the meantime, all we can do is tidy up our work and be ready for the call.*

⌒

The official announcement by the Federal Prosecutor's Office of the Hemispheres Union came three days later. *Not too eager,* Lee thought, *but not too slow, either . . . in case someone was thinking about changing their mind.* The investigative committee was a group of twenty-five accountants, fiscal analysts, police, and Federal detective staff, and three "coordinators" whose function, Lee thought, was probably merely political. *Ruffled-feather smoothers . . .* But she and Gelert were the only ones in the group who were psychoforensically trained: a fact that both interested Lee and bothered her. They were all directed to meet their Alfen escort in two days' time at the gating complex at JFK to begin their work.

Lee and Gelert both spent the next two days at the office, dealing with loose ends. It was quite late, the night before their departure, when Lee stuck her head out into the front office: both Gelert and Mass had already left. "Larry? Ten minutes."

"Right, Ms. Enfield."

She shut the door, looked around to see if there was anything else she needed to pack from the office. Her travel "pad" already had all the casework for the dil'Sorden murder packed away in it, along with other relevant case law and a hundred other odds and ends of data she'd thought she might be able to use. There was nothing in there, though, that had anything to do with the various confidential information searches she and Gelert had been running of late. Better to keep that safe in her head . . . *as safe as even that is, anymore . . .*

The commlink rang. Lee stood still for a moment. *I was half expecting this . . .* she thought, glancing down at the desktop to make sure that the recording facility was working.

"Reh'Mechren and Enfield," she said, "good evening . . ."

This time there was at least a shape looking back at her from the commwall . . . but only a shadowy one, silhouetted but only indefinitely; a shape that might be human, might not, the way it wavered. "So what I predicted has happened," the voice said.

"Yes," Lee said. "Could this possibly be because you set it up?"

The subsequent silence actually managed to sound surprised. "Not sure how I would have managed that."

"Neither am I," Lee said, "but then I have no idea who or what you are."

Silence again. "And what are you going to do there?" the voice finally said.

"My job."

"Even if it may bring you into personal danger?"

"It's done that before. One of the little perks. I'll take my chances, I guess."

"And what about the roses?"

"What about them?"

"I see," the voice said. This time its tone was too even to betray anything of the user's thought.

"I doubt that," Lee said—but it was too late: the line had already gone dead.

She sat back down at her desk again, looking at the commwall, which had reverted to methane snow and Saturn, gibbous at the moment, the rings casting a knife-edge shadow on the swirls of vague golden cloud below. *What am I getting myself into,* she thought. *Or more accurately: what am I being set up for?*

There was no telling. Yet she couldn't back out. Even Matt, damn him, had been right. Lee was in with a chance to discover the truth about something important. *If I had more of a hint what it might be . . .*

But no such hints were going to be forthcoming. She was just going to have to go in there and See what she could see, and hope to get out of Alfheim again with information that would be of use in their case.

She touched the desk. "Save that," she said. "Flag it for Matt's attention: store it in 'safekeeping' and encrypt a copy for the 'double redundancy' file."

The desk flickered the commcall's file designator at her, then vanished it, confirming storage. Lee touched the desk down into standby mode, picked up her pad and her bag, and left.

Larry brought Lee back to the house, checked it one last time. "I'll see you tomorrow morning early, Ms. Enfield," Larry said. "Then the Alfen will be handling security for you after the gates, my boss says."

"Back to Homicide, huh?" Lee said.

Larry grinned. "For the immediate future."

"The happy hunting grounds. Have a good time, Larry . . ."

Lee locked up, and Larry drove off. *Time to pack,* she thought. She headed into the bedroom.

And what about the roses? the voice said, in memory. *What about the roses?*

She was still uncertain of the answer.

Seven

Gelert was waiting for her at the curb with his hoverpack, sitting there with his ears up and his coat bristling a little. "I know, I know," Lee said as she got out of the hov and went around to the trunk to help Larry with her bag. "I'm late, I'm sorry . . ."

"Good luck, Ms. Enfield," Larry said, shaking Lee's hand. "Good luck, *Madra* Gelert. Good hunting . . ."

"Thanks, Larry. Take care," Lee said. And he was gone.

"Off to Homicide," Lee said with a slight smile. "Body-guarding isn't the right work for him. I hope they don't re-assign the poor guy to me when I get back . . ."

"Well, he did a good job," Gelert said. "Meanwhile, what kept you?"

Lee guided her bag up onto the curb and started digging around for her travel slips.

"I overslept."

"*Today?* You have to be kidding me."

Lee shook her head, annoyed at herself. "I couldn't get to sleep," she said. "When I finally did, I'd turned the alarm off, because I didn't think I was going to sleep at all. . . ."

They walked into the terminal under its great dome, half

a mile across. The sun glittered off the dome's myriad Fuller joints as Lee and Gelert threaded their way among thousands of other passengers, heading for the target clusters at the core of the dome space. LAX was a breakaway from the basic "engagement ring" architecture popular worldwide for gating facilities. The FG-augmented magnets that served the new generation of accelerators had made it possible to bend the targeting path so acutely that gating clusters could be sited directly on top of the ring: and LAPort, taking advantage of this technology, had used it to consolidate under the one dome all the facilities that would normally have been strung out along miles of a ring's circumference at multiple fixed targets. "It's beautiful in weather like this," Lee said, "when the sun comes in . . ."

"You mean, it started to be beautiful once they got the air-conditioning problem handled."

"Well, that didn't take them so long. But I still hate all the walking . . ."

Gelert produced a grin. "You mean you wouldn't rather be stuck on a nice maglev for hours at a time?"

"Please," Lee said. They came up to the central ring of check-in desks, found the ones with the TransCon logo showing on the displays above them, and gave the attendant their SlipCases and ID. Lee yawned.

"Well, maybe I shouldn't give you trouble," Gelert said. "I didn't sleep all that well either."

Lee looked at him thoughtfully, unwilling to say too much more about what was concerning them—at least while they stood somewhere so public. "You all right?" she said.

Gelert shook himself, hard enough that his ears rattled. "It's nothing I won't get over," he said. "Anyway, we're early enough that we'll have a little layover time at Kennedy. I can have a nap there."

The attendant gave them back their documentation, and

Lee and Gelert headed in through the desk ring and toward the gate cluster. Lee glanced at the virtual travel slip now glowing under the surface of the SlipCase, checking the gating time, but also looking curiously and with some concern at the second line of the routing. TC 8665 LAX–JFK, said the first line: but the second one said XX 1024 JFK–AXX. Just a blanket identifier for their destination in Alfheim, nothing specific as regarded the location: and no "carrier" designator, nothing to say who was responsible for their travel, no one to make responsible if something should go wrong . . .

"Not overly forthcoming, are they?" Gelert said. He paused and turned to the gate attendant to let her wave her reader wand over the SlipCase in his pack.

"Not terribly." Lee held out her case to be waved, and they walked on through, making for the central array of hexagonal target rooms. Most of them were opaque at the moment: a few had vanished their front faces and were taking incoming passengers. Lee looked for the TransCon herald on the displays over the hexes as they walked. "You have the usual trouble packing?" Gelert said.

Lee laughed at him. "For once, no. Any other time, yeah, I'd be running around in circles trying to figure out how to pack for a universe I'd never been to before . . ."

Gelert looked sidewise at her. "You *are* nervous," he said. "You can't even pack for a different climate as a rule, let alone another universe."

Lee raised her eyebrows. She'd been determined to say nothing further about the night before. Yet if she was going to say anything further to Gelert about it, this was the time: it was a fair bet that nearly every communication between them from now until they got back from Alfheim would be insecure. The Elves would be eager to make sure that none of their guests were abusing their hospitality, and even more eager to hear what they were saying about the progress and business of the commission.

At last she shook her head. "It wasn't anything, really," Lee said. Gelert put his ears back in an expression of skepticism, but said nothing.

"What about you?" Lee said, as they came to a still-opaqued hex labeled TC 8665, and stood in front of it waiting with a few other passengers—a family from Xaihon, all in ornate, bright tabards, a Midgardner in a fur cloak that must have been killing him even with the air-conditioning, various humans, and some assorted aliens from the Xainese Pangemony—a pair of salamandrines, and someone who at first glance looked like a dinosaur in morning dress. "Did you talk to Nuala about things?"

She didn't say which things, or need to. Gelert sat down and looked up at the glowing sign, which said in several fonts and several different frequencies and colors of light, *5 minutes to pretransit.* "She doesn't like me to," Gelert said. "Her feeling is that the less she knows about some things, the happier she is. If I try to push her on it, it causes trouble later. I've learned better, over time."

Lee nodded, though still she thought, *Maybe it's just a cultural thing, but I'd find that hard. If you're going to live with someone, you should live* with *them, not around them.* Then she sighed. It wasn't going to be an issue for a while, if ever. After the business with Matt, it had become more obvious to Lee than ever that living with someone that closely wasn't something she needed to be thinking about: it wasn't going to happen.

The wall in front of them went transparent, and from behind them, one of the LAPort gate managers went into the gate hex with an activation pod. The sign on the still-opaque part of the hex changed to *Assembling,* and the automated annunciator system started calling the transit.

Lee and Gelert showed their slips to the attendant as they stepped in, made their way to the back of the hex, and turned to face the open wall. "I don't know why we do this," Gelert said, "when the odds of us actually being turned the right way on arrival are as poor as we both know they are."

"Social conventions," Lee said. "Habit. Torschlusspanik. What climate did you pack for?"

"What?"

"What climate did you pack for?"

"Not *that* what. Tor something??"

The door in front of them went opaque again: apparently the transit slot wasn't very full. "Transit in fifteen seconds, ladies and gentlemen and so forth," said the gate manager, glancing at his pod with sublime indifference.

"Torschlusspanik," Lee said. "Fear of being locked in somewhere."

"Fine. Explain to me what which way you face has to do with this wonderful new panic."

The world went *flick!* Lee knew from various articles she'd read that the bland plain surfaces of the hex booths were an attempt to minimize the visual side effects of transit, but it never worked for her: that sight of the world seeming to wobble under her as if in two big waves, a sort of visual hula, followed by a sensation as of her eyes wobbling in their sockets and taking some moments to steady down, was something she had decided she was just going to have to live with. No one else she knew seemed to get it as badly as she did. "Gglp," she said as the transit completed and the people around them started to move toward Lee and Gelert with the bored, look-elsewhere expressions of commuters everywhere.

"You all right?" Gelert said, as they turned and followed the small crowd out into the transit section of the ring at Kennedy.

"Fine."

"You always say that. And you're not. Maybe it's something chemical," Gelert said. "You should go to that doctor that Leslie told you about. Maybe it's just some inner-ear thing."

"I read an article that said it might just be a side effect of traveling in a straight line for the only time that anyone really does it," Lee said. "All the rest of the time it's curves of some kind or another."

"That's just what I'm saying. Maybe it's like when you've been on a merry-go-round for a while and then you get off and try to walk straight. But in reverse."

Lee shrugged. The two of them walked counterclockwise along the ring, with clusters of hexes on their left and the inner ring-rail system on their right, toward the next car stop, maybe an eighth of a mile away. Gelert looked with interest at the windows of some of the small shops between the hex clusters as they passed. "You didn't finish about the torschlussthing," Gelert said.

"And I'm not going to. You just can't let go, can you?"

Gelert grinned. "My people have a saying—"

"They usually have a saying."

"—'Bite till your teeth meet, and after that, keep your mouthful.'"

"Profound." They came to the ring-rail entrance and studied the display beside it, which claimed that the next transport would be along in five minutes. "It always says five minutes," Gelert said, sitting down again, "and it's never been right. Not once."

"If people didn't keep holding the thing's doors open past the time it's supposed to leave," Lee said, "it would be right."

"So in the middle of the night it may be on time occasionally," Gelert said, as the display started scrolling through lists of gates due for departure in the next hour. "A lot of good that does us. . . . There it is, though. XX 1024, cluster 015." He got up again, sighed. "Typical, it's right across the ring from us . . ."

Lee smiled just a little as she sighted the transport coming toward them along the ring. "You know," she said, "I'd swear you're going out of your way to sound blasé about this. Listen to you, grumbling about shuttlecars and coming out on the wrong side of the ring. It's *Alfheim* we're going to, Gel. We're not even having to pay for it! This is the dream run, the trip everyone wants to make and no one's allowed to."

The transport pulled up: the glass doors slid aside, inner and outer, and they got in as several people got out, including a Borastran of truly tremendous size. Again Lee had to remind herself not to stare as the person just managed to wedge itself between the doors when they were open at its widest. "*That's* why these are late," Gelert said, as they got into the now-empty transport, and the doors closed immediately. He nosed his hoverbag over to the side of the transport, out of the way, and watched idly as the Borastran went rolling away across the ring concourse behind them like a giant rogue green-leather jelly donut, various legs and other appendages waving as it went. "But you're right. Sometimes I wonder why they don't loosen up a little and let more tourism in."

"More? Let *some* tourism in, you mean. Rather than the minuscule amount that they presently clear through."

Gelert shrugged and turned to look forward, the way the transport was going. "Maybe things are going to start changing soon," he said. "I'm not even sure that it matters, in some ways, what the committee's findings are. The Alfen are going to have to loosen up some of the access restrictions a little. Or rather, they're going to have to be *seen* to loosen them up. A little creative PR could do a lot for them."

"While I understand your point about the commission's findings," Lee said, "I think the PR is necessary anyway. It's not like they're not an incredibly intelligent and successful people; it's not like they're not entitled to that success—but by and large, whenever the Alfen are in contact with the media, they don't seem to care if the contacts suggest that they could do just fine without us. That they don't particularly care what we think—or what anyone thinks."

"Maybe it's true," Gelert said, glancing at Lee.

"Maybe it is. But it's not smart to rub people's noses in it. Sooner or later it's going to come back to haunt them."

"It's doing that now, I think," Gelert said. "I think someone high up among the Elves has realized that they'd better look cooperative with the UN." He looked back the way they came again. "But I don't think that's necessarily going to mean they're going to enjoy the process. I imagine we can expect a little hostility along the way."

Lee nodded. The transport stopped to let on a number of passengers from some other gates that TransCon was using at the moment: humans from various universes, various salamandrines and a pair of Kewa, all spindly legs and spines, and a couple of Alfen. Lee didn't look straight at them, but she didn't have to do that to see the way other human passengers, even the other aliens, edged away from them a little while trying not to look like they were.

That made her wonder, as she turned away to look the way Gelert was looking, at the maglev track curving and curving away to the left in front of them. But it had often made her wonder before. Humans she could understand being intimidated by that perfect beauty. But why the aliens? Why should one species' sense of beauty, so different from humans', be affected by it? Even just on Earth, the definition of what made a human being attractive shifted wildly with climatic and cultural zones. *What is it a Kewa senses about an Alfen that makes them take a step back? . . .*

Unfortunately that was something no Kewa was likely to confide in Lee, since they were so protective about the languages in which they discussed personal matters. *But then even humans are reticent enough about it,* Lee thought, as they pulled into the next transport stop. *In fact, about most things . . .*

"This our stop?" Gelert asked, craning his neck a little to look out the window.

"Three more," Lee said. "This one's a local."

The doors opened, and the two Alfen, a dark-complected, ebon-eyed man, and a tall fair woman with streaming silver hair, strolled out, followed by their luggage. Lee watched them go, especially the woman, and wondered how someone in a T-shirt and jeans could manage to look so much like exiled royalty. It was more than just carriage, or bearing . . . there was something else going on. Lee glanced sideways and saw all her fellow passengers watching the Alfen, too, though they, like her, were trying not to be caught at it. Even the Kewa were covertly slanting their spines in that direction, like two brown brooms trying to peek around a corner.

Lee sat back as the maglev started up again, watching the curve of the tracks before them pour past. After a few more stops, the one they wanted came up, and Lee and Gelert got out, their luggage floating along behind them. "You see a display anywhere?" Gelert said, gazing up and down the ring.

"Over there . . ." They made their way to the tall stack of displays by a large hex cluster set aside for custom transits. The XX-designated gate wouldn't be patent for an hour yet, and there was as yet no sign of any other commission members. "Here's where you get your nap," Lee said.

Gelert heaved a sigh and looked around. There was a waiting lounge not far away, with a bar next to it. "No," he said. "I have some journals to read: I might as well get caught up. You want to go do some shopping?"

"Not today. Might take a walk, though."

"Right. I'll watch this for you." Gelert nosed Lee's luggage to activate the follow-me function, and wandered off toward the bar, the bags trundling obediently along behind him.

Lee walked around the ring a little ways, looking at stores and newsstands with no great interest, until she came to a facility map. The structure of Kennedy's ring facility was open to the sky, but not to either side—the signs hovering just below the glass ceiling were usually the only way to tell where you were. But the facility map confirmed for Lee what she'd expected: she was still on the landward side of the ring, and there was access to an observation platform not too far away.

She walked on a little farther and went up the escalator, then showed her SlipCase to the reader by the glass doors; they opened and let her out on the platform. Lee stepped out into the salt breeze, looking around. The square platform was glass brick underfoot, and surrounded by the stanchions of a general restraint field. To her back was salt marsh, and then the endless jumble of the roofs of Brooklyn and Queens. Before her was the rest of the ring, stretching away to either side, following the old lines of Sheepshead Bay and reaching out to complete the great glass-roofed circle in the waters of New York Inlet. Far off to her right was Manhattan, crowned with towers, glistening, bristly and brittle in the early sun.

She stood there for a few minutes, smelling seaweed and ocean, listening to the wind hissing in the marshgrass and the distance-attenuated sound of surf rolling up on the Rockaway beaches. Up here, the tension that had kept her up all night seemed unreal. But so did the shape that had appeared in her commwall, indistinct, its voice altered.

Why be so obvious about it? Lee thought. *Why not just assume a virtual seeming that has nothing whatsoever to do with his or her or its real shape?* Heaven only knew there were enough commwall utilities that would let you do something of the kind. *What's served by turning up in my office with I AM IN DISGUISE written all over you?*

It was puzzling enough. But more troubling was the idea that her visitor had put into her head. *Every now and then you hear some speculation about some weird or powerful Alfen artifact, something else that can affect its surroundings the way fairy gold does . . . the same kind of syncatalytic response. The roses, whenever they're mentioned, seem to be something like that. Though as far as I can tell, the Elves never comment past the basic insistence that there's 'no such thing.'*

Yet that's not what my visitor thought. It was sure they were real. And that they would have power here: that even a single one of them could be used somehow. And maybe not just as a way to reveal Alfen technology, render it inactive. Something that powerful, if you understood it, could very likely have applications as a weapon . . .

She wandered forward to lean on the neutral top of one of the stanchions, gazing out at the sun-glitter on the water, the cloud shadows that slid across it. Her concerns about who might be behind this, who might want such a tool, such a weapon . . . The Elves had made themselves more than enough enemies over time. And by and large, over time, they had also proved themselves invulnerable to any real damage. Anyone who really wanted to hurt Alfen interests had to get into Alfheim—but their controls were so tight that there was no way to do that. *Which leaves some people wanting to hurt them as best they can on the outside, in the other universes where they have influence, or significant holdings. Maybe even to use their own technologies, something Alfen, to do it—to rub some salt into the wound.*

What bothered Lee was her visitor's assumption that she would be willing to cooperate with such people, no matter what the reward might be. She was offended. But she was also fascinated—and she wanted to get to the bottom of why this offer was being made to her and Gelert now. *Obviously something to do with the dil'Sorden case. Obviously someone sees us as usable, one way or another. As independent investigators . . . or as pawns.*

Or else someone sees this as a way to find out just how independent we are. Whether we can be fooled into being useful to them, while at the same time setting ourselves up to be discredited and removed from the UN&ME investigation. Any sense that the commission had been seeded with people covertly hostile to Alfen interests, or in cahoots with such people, would give the Elves the edge they needed to have the whole thing called off.

She turned into the wind, running her hands through her hair to work out some of the tangles that the wind had already put there. *This is a very fine line we're going to be walking,* she thought. *Stray too far over it one way or the other and we're dead, in terms of business. The DA's Office will unload us on the spot, no matter how successful we've been for them, and we'll have trouble getting any work anywhere else.*

Not that that wouldn't please some people.

Lee sighed at the thought of Matt, and pushed him resolutely out of her mind again, in an exercise that had become all too common these last few weeks. *Am I ever going to feel any better about him?* she thought, feeling forlorn. *Is this sadness ever going to go away? Clinically speaking I*

*know it will . . . but right now I feel like I'm bleeding all the
time. And if the pain makes me careless, makes me make a
mistake . . .*

She took a moment to detangle her hair again. The wind
was picking up, making her eyes tear. *But I have to follow
this up,* Lee thought. *I have to know.* And in sudden memory
Matt's voice said, laughing that dark laugh of his, *You always have to know, don't you? No matter who it pisses off.
That curiosity of yours is going to get you killed someday.
But because it's what makes you good at your work, it'll be
the death you'd prefer.*

She'd had no answer for that at the time. Matt's genuine
humor was often so heavily flavored with irony that it was
easy to mistake it for hostility until you learned to read its
other accompanying signs. Lee pushed the thought aside
again. All she had to do now was work out some way to do
something that would help her find out what was really
going on, without seeming to be doing anything.

Her hair was about to become one big knot. Lee gri-
maced, cast one last look at the New York skyline, and went
back through the glass door. Once out of the wind she spent
a few minutes unknotting herself, then went back down the
escalator into the terminal and made her way back to the bar
where she'd left Gelert.

He wasn't alone. Standing there talking to him was a big,
bulky man, dressed in an incongruous combination of a
navy blue three-piece suit with a Midgarth-style daycloak
over it in gray; and all of it looked rumpled, as if he'd slept
in it. Lee grinned at the sight of him. Of all the other people
who'd been picked to participate in commission, Sal Griffiths was probably the one she knew the best, and certainly
the one she liked the best. He was out of the Manhattan DA's
Office, with years of experience in racketeering law and the
investigation of money laundering; it was Lee's opinion that

he could smell a quarter in your back pocket two blocks away, and tell you whether it was heads or tails. "Sal," she said, coming over with her hand out, "you're early."

"Always be early," Sal said, and pumped Lee's hand the way he always did, as if he was trying to jump-start her. "Gel here tells me you overslept this morning. Not your style."

"No," Lee said, giving Gelert a look intended to suggest that he should keep his muzzle shut. "My fault for taking work home with me. Sit down, Sal. You have trouble packing, too?"

He laughed at the look she was giving the daycloak. "No idea where we're going," he said, "so I'm more or less prepared for everything with this rig. Short of Antarctica. Are there Elves in Antarctica?"

"Probably there are," Gelert said. "And probably there are people who wish *all* the Elves were in Antarctica."

"Huh, Huh, Huh, Huh," said Sal. Lee restrained her own laughter: Sal's was nearly black with concentrated sarcasm, and until she'd gotten used to it, always sounded like he was in the early stages of an asthma attack.

"You and the audit team get all your prep work done?" Lee said.

"Everything we can do without seeing their books in their own computers," Sal said. Those little close-set eyes of his narrowed, a look that always made Lee think of a particularly intelligent and motivated rat getting ready to start gnawing through a door. "Of course, no way our work is going to be done when we've finished going through those. We have to find the pointers to the books they're not going to let us see. By which I don't mean the first extra set they release to us, privately and under great protest, when the pressure starts to go on." He smiled. "And we have to do it before they chuck us out of Alfheim, because getting in again to follow up the dirt, once we find it, is going to be damn near impossible."

"You're that sure about the dirt?" Gelert said, very quietly.

"There's always dirt," Sal said, nearly as softly. "Come on, Gel. They may be Elves, but they're human, or humanoid, anyway. They're no bunch of Kvei, who don't even know what a lie is, or Demesh, who'd immolate themselves rather than tell you one. Our psychologies are close enough for my understanding of the rules to work just fine over there, too. The initial figures they showed us already have some hints of things that don't work out. Broad hints, anyway. Some of them are broad enough that they look like they're meant to distract us from the fine detail. We'll allow ourselves to be distracted . . . at first." And there was that smile again. Sal loved his work, and Lee was glad of it.

Lee nodded. "Hey, here comes Doris," Sal said. "Doris!" He waved at the tall red-haired woman who stood across from them out in the concourse, looking at the cluster display.

That was the way it went for the next twenty minutes or so, as one by one members of the commission started to show up. The bar got full, and slightly noisy with the sound of people looking each other over, sizing each other up . . . and occasionally glancing over their shoulders to see if their Alfen escorts had shown up yet. Within maybe twenty minutes, everybody was there, the whole overqualified crowd, people from all over this planet and various others—Olafsson with his big blue eyes and wild blond hair, a bulky guy with a brain full of economics and a string of probably unnecessary but decorative degrees from UEU; Erlimi seTen, the Wasai political economist, tall and dark in plush tabby-patterned fur, with her mane tied up in an Hermès scarf, and her right forefang pierced and inlaid with ruby, like a drop of blood; Mellie Hopkins, like a little fierce tropical bird in her spiky red hair and her bright sari, and toting a briefcase stuffed with legal briefs and chocolate; leHeksat-urMekevet-Elte, sitting in a bucket chair and wreathing hir tentacles gently around hir while s/he discussed neoKeynsean finance theory with Mellie; Kei Yu Hwa, a small, dark, silent, watchful man who for no reason Lee could understand had left the fabulous wealth of his home and family at the heart of the Xainese space-travel empire for a job as a Frankfurt-based commodities broker.

There were various others Lee knew only slightly—both alien and human—but knew, because they were here, that they were the best in their various fields, possibly even irreplaceable. *If a bomb dropped on this room . . .* Lee thought, and then shied away from the thought. *Of course we're in no danger. Silly idea. The whole UN&ME is watching.*

But what about when they're not watching? said something in the back of Lee's head, as she spotted an Alfen walking toward them down the concourse.

Others saw her, too, and the ruckus at the bar began to quiet down a little. The approaching woman wore a sober charcoal business skirt suit, and what Lee at first took for a dark veil, it was so long and swirled so lightly around her. But as the woman got closer Lee saw that the darkness was waist-length hair, black as night on Midgarth in the middle of the Winter, almost invisible in its blackness. Suit or not, she looked about eighteen; but her eyes suggested a placid and wicked youth, somewhere in the high three figures. She paused near where the bar seating spilled out into the concourse, and the assembled members of the UN&ME Special Investigative Committee for Alfen-Intrauniversal Overview, silent now, looked at her as thoughtfully as she looked at them.

"Ladies and gentlemen," she said, "my name is Isif

dil'Hemrev. I've been assigned by the Elf-king's Office as one of the Committee's liaison officers, and I'll be assisting in escorting you to your various destinations in Alfheim. Would you follow me, please?"

Everybody picked up or poked or kicked their assorted luggage and went after her, slowly, as dil'Hemrev made her way over to the hex cluster that had been flagged for the Alfheim transit. It went transparent as she approached it, without any sign of her having used one of the usual activation keypads that port gating personnel usually carried. Lee gave Gelert a look; together they lined up behind Per Olafsson and a few others and began entering the hex.

A presence to her left and a sudden scent of bitter lime made Lee glance that way. "ExAff," Mellie Hopkins said under her breath, without looking at Lee.

"Sorry?"

"Alfen Bureau of External Affairs," Hopkins said softly, amid the rustle of footsteps and jostling luggage, as she stepped into the hex beside Lee and Gelert. "She's a spook."

Lee put her eyebrows up. She'd been of the opinion that pretty much everybody they'd see from this point on would have been a government operative of some kind or another. At least Hopkins shared it. "Pretty one, though," Lee said very softly.

Hopkins snorted. "Pretty is as pretty does, and her heart's as black as her hair," she said, almost inaudibly. "Ran into her on an antitrust case a few years ago. I'd like to feed her to a jesh, except it'd give the thing indigestion."

Lee made a wry expression but said nothing. "Is everybody in?" dil'Hemrev said. "Good, we'll transit right away then." The walls opaqued.

Lee swallowed and braced herself for the usual hula, but was surprised when suddenly the wall of the cubicle behind her vanished. *What happened? They forget somebody?* was her first thought. *What went wrong?* But dil'Hemrev was gesturing them out. "This way, everyone, if you please . . ."

Another layer of security? Lee thought, confused. But she followed dil'Hemrev out with the others, and quickly saw that wherever this was, it wasn't Kennedy anymore.

She and the others were standing under a dome more like that of LAX's main terminal than anything else: maybe only a quarter-mile or so across, but impressive enough in that it wasn't Fuller-braced, but used instead a more widely spaced bracing system more reminiscent of Gothic arches than anything else, the ribs as transparent as the glazing between them. Through the dome poured the cool, faint amber light of a sky shrouded in high haze: Lee was strongly reminded of an afternoon during her last visit to San Francisco. But another thought was more to the forefront at the moment. *I didn't feel anything! How did they do that?*

She followed the others out of the hex cluster, glancing back at it. It was in the center of that big space: there were no other clusters, just that single one of seven cells. *Somebody's private ring?* Lee wondered.

"Interesting," Gelert said under his breath as he padded along beside her. "No controls. None that we could see, anyway."

"Not as interesting as completely getting rid of the transit side effects," Lee said softly. "If they could bottle that and sell it, they'd make nearly as much as they do from FG futures."

Dil'Hemrev paused in the middle of the space, letting the commission members gather around her. They were all looking around them in slight confusion: there was no one else in all this big space but them. "Do we need to wait for transport?" Olafsson asked dil'Hemrev.

She shook her head, smiled, glanced up. Lee and the others followed her glance. Above them, the quality of the light coming through the dome changed suddenly, subtly, and it took the moment during which the first breeze reached Lee and ruffled her hair for her to understand that the glazing, whatever it was made of, had simply gone away. A second or so later the bracing that had supported that glazing began to slip away, running down the "surface" of where the dome ought to have been like rain running down a windowpane, contracting toward the shining white floor, vanishing. They were standing on a white island in the middle of a placid sea, and off to one side, the westering sun eased itself through fading veils of passing cloud and slowly came out in a splendor of tarnished gold.

"It's a nice day," dil'Hemrev said. "I thought we might put the top down."

Lee was both impressed and faintly annoyed at the staggeringly offhanded display of technology, for to her eye there was a message added: *Bet you don't have anything like this.* Seeing it, though, she had second thoughts about how few hex clusters stood under the dome. *They probably have a whole battery of matter-handlers in the floor, so that they can manifest clusters on demand, as many as they need.* But then that kind of matter handling, based on Bose-Einstein condensates, needed huge amounts of fairy gold. *Which they unquestionably have . . .*

There was the slightest shudder: the floor moved, settled. Everybody shuffled a little, balancing themselves. Dil'Hemrev turned, and most of the other commission members turned to look the way she was looking. There was some low cloud on the horizon: but the wind now ruffling all their hair and clothes was running through it, and it started to break and slip away.

"Suzanne H. Christ," Gelert said under his breath. "Will you look at that."

Lee looked at the near horizon, as the island on which

they all stood began slowly to move toward it, and thought of all the old stories about the city of Ys, Ys of the bells, which sank beneath the sea. *But which sea?* Lee thought. The old stories got so tangled over and through one another, even in the same universe—let alone with stories from other universes. Which world had had a king intent on building a city so splendid that all the men of his time would call it par-Ys, "like Ys" or equal to it?

Now, looking at that city's towers as they gazed down at themselves in a sea all brazen-blazing with afternoon, Lee thought that the poor king would have had his work cut out for him, if this was the city he meant. Described broadly, the place wouldn't have sounded all that special. A bay, the city following the line of the bay around, the spires of its greatest buildings centered on the center of the bay, dwindling in height as they spread around the crescent: handsomely designed, yes, the shapes of the towers sleek, varied and elegant, the colors and materials varied, too. It all looked planned, even studied. There was nothing haphazard or spontaneous about it, and it was unquestionably a work of art—nothing "extra" there, everything building necessary to the design, everything contributing to the effect as a whole.

Yet all your breath was taken away, not by the size of the buildings or the ambition of the design: nothing so heartless. Somehow this skyline said to you, not "I am great, I am powerful," but "I am fragile, I am temporary." Some immortal architect or planner, had looked on the passing things of the world and felt sorry for them—all the common, mortal, material elements of life, the things that crumble and fade and are outlived. That builder or designer had found a way to make the stone and the steel and glass themselves express that sorrow. And somehow the feeling came to you, across the water: it struck you about the heart, so that you gasped with the immediacy of it, and with the feeling that you and that city were kindred somehow.

"Welcome to Alfheim," dil'Hemrev said. "Welcome to Ys."

Lee blinked back the tears without being particularly concerned who might notice, for nearly everyone else in the commission party was either wiping their eyes furtively or looking for some way to turn to avoid having others see them doing it. One or two of them were actually crying on other commission members' shoulders, overcome, and plainly mortified by it.

Dil'Hemrev looked around at them, grave. "The . . . distress . . . will pass shortly," she said. "I apologize for not having mentioned it earlier, but some guests don't experience it, and we've found that mentioning the effect can actually induce it. The phenomenon seems to have something to do with the angle of orientation of the transit between our home universe and Earth's: it's much greater than usual. Please accept our apologies."

There was no immediate answer but some subdued snuffling. "The accelerator ring," Lee said after a moment to dil'Hemrev, for she gathered that it would be a few moments before any of the others were ready to speak, "it was right under us, wasn't it? It follows the arms of the bay around . . ."

Dil'Hemrev nodded. "It was installed under the seabed here, about forty years ago, around the same time the city was expanded and redesigned. It's not our biggest access ring, but probably the most powerful."

Lee nodded and gazed at the city again, and past it. Behind it, maybe fifty miles to the east, a range of massive, spiky, jagged peaks rose up and up behind it, matching the towers in symmetry, but rendered indistinct by distance and low cloud—an insubstantial barrier, half airbrushed-out in the pale gold of misty afternoon. They made the composition complete, for they were the permanence against which that fragility had to be balanced to make sense. Beautiful though they were, Lee found herself ever so slightly irked not to know what to call them. *It's amazing how little we know about this place,* she thought, *even though it's been part of the Five-Geneva Pact for ninety years. Most of their maps are classified, and even the ones that aren't have big empty spaces all over them. Paranoia? . . .*

Lee blinked again, starting to be annoyed at the irrational tears, and paused to fumble through her bag for a hanky. Still, even paranoiacs have real enemies. *They probably have their reasons. I just wish we knew more about them.*

The target platform kept on progressing across the water, heading for the city. Lee was surprised by how little it rocked as it went. *Either they've got really wonderful stabilizing systems on this thing,* she thought, *or it's absolutely massive.* It occurred to her that the ring's whole actuating apparatus could well be stowed away in this structure, making the gating complex even more secure. Moving it would be like removing the key from a door: without the gate targets and the actuator in place, the whole accelerator circle would be useless. *More paranoia? Or just clever design? Or both?*

Slowly they slid closer to the city, between the arms of the bay, and finally headed over toward its right-hand side, where there were some docks for boats—hovercraft and hydrofoils, as well as yachts of all sizes, and more mundane sailcraft, in about equal proportions, with the lower skyscrapers of the city towering over them all. "Looks like a millionaires' convention," Mellie muttered just behind Lee.

Lee nodded, feeling the whole platform slow as they approached what looked like a curving glass wall jutting out into the water. The circle of the platform slid ever so slowly up against it, then snugged, softly but very solidly, into something far below. Lee could feel several different sets of vibrations, each terminating in a gentle "closing" shock that came up through the floor. *This has to be the whole actuator array,* she thought. *If one of us has to leave here in a hurry for some reason, this isn't going to be the way to do it.*

The glass wall before them slipped down to ground level and vanished as the dome had done. "This way, please," dil'Hemrev said, leading them off the island and onto a long white marble jetty that joined what looked like a wide curved promenade paralleling the shoreline. The commission members followed her, gazing up and around at the buildings by the shore.

"We won't be needing ground transport," dil'Hemrev said; "all your accommodations are a few minutes' walk from here, and they back right up against the three buildings that make up Ys's 'financial district.' "

"Very convenient," Olafsson said. Lee could just hear him thinking what she was sure some of the others were thinking too: how convenient that we'll see as little as possible of the city without Alfen guides hanging around. She glanced at Gelert, who was innocently doing a good imitation of a tourist, gaping at everything: the look of witless wonder he threw her was as clear a comment as Lee needed.

After just a couple of minutes the group came up to a tall and graceful building with a café terrace in front of it. As dil'Hemrev led them up the walk that bisected the café and toward the main doors of the building, Lee began to twitch a little at the looks from the Alfen who sat in the café, drinking their wine, or eating their meals, and who now paused to stare, coolly, at the new arrivals. *The shoe's on the other foot now,* Lee thought. *Here we're the exotica . . . and we're not entirely welcome.*

The group made their way in through doors that vanished to admit them, and saw from the logo on the far wall of the entry hall that this was a hotel. "I didn't know Hilton operated here," Olafsson said to dil'Hemrev.

"We run it for them under license," said dil'Hemrev. "The same kind of arrangement they have with their properties in Midgarth. Come on over this way, we'll get you checked in."

Lee followed the others to the reception desk, meanwhile thinking that this kind of setup was "convenient" for the Alfen, too: it meant that only local people would be running the hotel. *I really have to watch this blanket paranoia . . .* she thought, as a smiling Alfen woman took Lee's SlipCase to wave it over the registration reader, then handed it back to her. "Suite 312," she said, taking the SlipCase that Gelert proffered her in his jaws, "enjoy your stay. Good afternoon, sir . . ."

Lee looked over the case, which was now showing her directions to the room and a thumbnail layout: the suite had a common living area and two bedrooms. Olafsson and several others who had already finished checking in had gathered around dil'Hemrev and were looking up from the reservations gallery into the center of the hotel atrium, in which a huge stylized fabric sculpture of some kind of winged creature hung, all done in flame-colors and seemingly caught in the act of soaring toward the roof and the starry stained-glass ceiling at the top of the atrium. Lee joined the others, looking up at it.

"Ystertve," dil'Hemrev was saying to Olafsson: "life reborn. It's a very old symbol, from a folktale. They say that this city was built on the foundations of another one that was drowned, millennia ago. The archaeologists have found signs of settlements that old some miles away, but no cities. None off the coast, either. Still, the story persists . . ."

"The Phoenix," Mellie Hopkins said, wiping her eyes again.

"That would be one of your versions of it, yes," dil'Hemrev said. More of the commission members were gathering around them: she looked around. "Ladies and gentlemen, I get the feeling you'll all have found the transit wearing. With that in mind, there's been nothing planned for the rest of the day: you're at leisure to rest or have a meal or tour around, as you please. We do ask that you respect our people's privacy: if you want to go out, get in touch with the front desk and someone will be glad to escort you around. As for business, that won't start until tomorrow. The elevators are over this way—"

Everyone began to head for the elevators. Lee and Gelert found themselves walking next to Sal Griffiths. "I hate this," he muttered, "but I feel like I've just changed about fifty time zones at once, and I've got to crash and burn."

"We're tired, too," Gelert said, before Lee could open her mouth. "A nice afternoon nap, that's what we need. . . ."

"Absolutely," Lee said. She smothered a not entirely sincere yawn.

They made their way up to their suite, waving to those they left behind them in the elevator: Sal and a few others got out on their floor, and headed off toward rooms on the other side of the elevator bank. Lee glanced at her SlipCase, which was now showing her a little arrow pointing down the hall to their room, as if it was necessary. She also noted the directory of commission members elsewhere in the hotel that had appeared. "We're all on these two floors, it looks like."

"Convenient," Gelert said. Ahead of them and to the right, their room door felt them coming and opened. Lee stepped in, looking around the big sitting area. Gelert came in behind her; the door closed, and Gelert nudged his luggage, telling it to set itself down. "Well, I feel a little better," he said, glancing around. "Not even the Elves can make a chain hotel surpassingly beautiful." He sighed. "But that's the only exception to the rule. Look at that view . . . !"

Lee was doing so, and having trouble managing the lump in her throat. The mist over that distant mountain range was lifting, and she was discovering that she had never before been so affected by a mere landscape. But there was nothing mere about this. Those mountains called to her.

With some difficulty she tore herself away and went over to the bedroom on the right-hand side. "Wow."

"Big bed?"

"No, this one's yours, it's got the padded floor and the custom bath. Look at the size of that plunge!"

Gelert wandered in behind her, looking at the bedroom and bathroom. "Don't get ideas, you probably have one this big. Did someone just knock?"

"Uh—" Lee went back into the sitting room, where someone had slipped a sheet of paper under their door from outside, and by the sound of it was now heading on down the corridor. Lee waited a moment, then went over to the sheet, picked it up, looked it over.

"The schedule for tomorrow," she said. "Morning meeting with the fiscal experts and the accountants and accounting team. The rest of us get an orientation tour."

"Sightseeing in Beautiful Ys," Gelert said, sounding unusually dry. "Probably even more boring than what we're going to be doing."

"Oh, I don't know . . . it really does look like such a gorgeous place: it'd be nice to see some more of it, especially considering that we're going to be inside hunched over computer terminals for most of our stay." Lee went to have a look at her own bedroom, and found inside it a bed that deserved to have its own zip code. She sat down on the silky bedspread and stroked it idly, looking around at the room, and at the windows that gave on that spectacular view.

Gelert looked in. "Nice," he said, glancing around. He was looking for listening and viewing devices, Lee knew: she also knew that it was probably useless, these days when you could hide a camera in a coin or a mike in a pinhead. "I guess I take back the line about chain hotels. Their furniture is nicer than usual."

Lee nodded, looking down from the view to the golden bedspread. She was surprised to find herself still stroking it, and indeed unable to keep her hands off it: the texture was ridiculously seductive. Annoyed, she stopped. *Damned if I'm going to be seduced by a bedspread.* She got up and walked back out to the lounge, gazing out at the view again. After a moment or so she rubbed her eyes.

"Allergies?" Gelert said.

"No. It's just—" She was going to say "I'm tired," but that wasn't exactly it. "I feel like I've been in court all day," Lee said. "Like I've been Seeing judicially—" Then she stopped again. "No. Like I've been *resisting* Seeing judicially."

"The same kind of worn-down feeling you get when the litigants are bogging a court down in procedural rigmarole, before you can get to the meat of the matter. . . ."

"That's right." She looked out at the mountains, away across the plain from the city. The clarity of the blue sky above those mountains seemed impossible to an LA native: but then Lee wondered if it wouldn't seem impossible to anyone. Nothing here looked ordinary, she realized. Everything looked preternaturally sharp, as if even though your vision was already perfect, someone had found a corrective lens that would make things seem clearer . . . and it was giving you a headache from looking through it. "Like someone had used image enhancement on reality . . ."

"What?"

"Just thinking." She got up and went over to investigate

the minibar. There were some soft drinks, some Alfen wine, both still and sparkling, some mineral water. She pulled out one of the mineral waters. "You thirsty?"

"Not right now," Gelert said, turning away from the window to pad around from sofa to chair to table, looking them over without trying to be too obvious about it. "Something else I noticed," Gelert said. "The way they have their gate access handled from the main gating facility. Very interesting."

"Scenic," Lee said. "Lovely view from out there." But the view wasn't what she had in mind, and Lee knew it wasn't what Gelert meant either. He meant there was no way to get in or out of Alfheim without the Elves' assistance. *We knew that before, of course. But only in an operational way. It hadn't occurred to me at the time that they might have also made it simply physically impossible.*

"I wasn't thinking of that specifically," Gelert said. "I was thinking that the arrangement would make the access very easy to service. But that view . . ." He was gazing out the window again. "Amazing how it affects you."

"Me, maybe," Lee said. "And everybody else. But you looked less troubled."

"My people don't have our tear ducts arranged the way you do," Gelert said. "It's not like I didn't want to sit down and have a good howl. But I have my dignity." He turned in a couple of circles and lay down on a big silken pillow on the floor.

"Your people also came from here, originally," Lee said.

Gelert was washing one paw. "A long time ago," he said. "You'd think that would make us immune."

"But you weren't."

"Not quite," Gelert said.

"Maybe you've been away for too long."

"Could be." Gelert put his head down on his paws, rolling his eyes.

"You tired?"

"A long day," Gelert said, rolling his eyes up in his head again, then closing them. Lee held still, carefully not looking at the light fixture above both their heads, which Gelert had indirectly been considering.

"I could probably use a bath myself," Lee said. She wandered into her own room, and the bathroom past it, taking a look at the fixtures and fittings. Not one, but two tubs, a long one and a round deep one. "Isn't this nice," she said, and started to fill the deep one. From the sitting room, she heard Gelert's tiny snore. That, at least, was genuine.

She took her time about preparing for the bath, bringing her jotter into the bathroom with her while considering which way one might sit in that round tub that would be the least likely to favor any viewing device. *If they've got signal snoopers in here, too, that's something to think about. But even so, they may have some problems with this . . .*

The tub filled. Lee swung the bathroom door shut, not entirely but enough to block the view of whatever might be up in that light fixture. Then she got undressed, put her hair up, turned to the tub, and put a hand in the water. *Ow! No point in making a lobster out of myself.* She ran some more cold water into the tub while pulling over a small table that held towels and so forth: she positioned it by the tub, dropping her jotter on it, then checked the water and found it acceptable. Lee climbed in very slowly and carefully, for the water was still really hot, at that point where moving too fast in the water actually stings. Slowly she got herself settled, leaned back and got comfortable, then reached over to the little table for her jotter. She thumbed a couple of the controls at the bottom and brought up a broadcast of "The Worlds

Today" that the jotter had picked up for her from Kennedy's wireless broadcast network as they passed through.

There Lee lay soaking idly for a good while, looking at the home news, then selecting worlds' news and spending a while listening to an analysis of the new Xainese trade initiative with the newly discovered Melekh systems. Under that display, though, where no inquisitive eye could see it, the Smalltalk program that she and Gelert used in the courtroom was running. It was a stepchild utility, fathered by the more modern wireless translation technologies on the old shorthand and stenography concepts, and cousin to the inbody neural broadcast translation technology that made it possible for Gelert's people, and other paravocal or nonvocal species, to produce words that speaking peoples could hear and understand. Some years back Lee had had a twin to one of Gelert's tiny implants installed just behind the cricoid cartilage in her throat, with one sensor connection running to the vocal cords and the other end neurilemma'd into the sixth cranial nerve. In open court, without anyone being the wiser, she could subvocalize and send silent-yet-"spoken" notes to her own pad, or to Gelert's, or even straight to his own implant if it was something urgent. Or, if there was any question of eavesdropping, she could do as she was doing now, and transcribe her subvocalizations directly to one of the steno languages like Palmerrand or Doorsill.

She didn't need to see readout at this point: the implant was giving her the little "feedback" echo which meant that what she was saying had been transcribed properly to Palmerrand. At the end of sentences she could hear the little in-system hiccup that meant her content was being saved for later transmission to Gelert's end of their paired system, either on Lee's command or Gelert's. Anybody using a character "sniffer" on her would get scrambled Palmerrand characters or an encrypted growl, not much else.

"I saw what you saw, I think," she said silently, and heard the machine transcribe the sentence. *"At least, about the room. First impressions..."* She spoke for a little about what she had seen, or thought she'd seen, on the way in. She was detailed about it: there was no telling what might turn out to be important later.

Finally, Lee noticed that the water was getting cold. She paused, listening: from the sitting room she heard more snoring. Dusk was falling, and no lights were turned on there, though she could see a dim orangy glow: probably a night-light or one of the other "finder" lights that a good hotel room might turn on in the dark. Lee smiled at the sound of the snores, scaling up. *No point in moving him: let him sleep.* She closed down her jotter, putting it aside, then let some water out of the tub and ran some more hot water into it.

A little while later, she got out, dripping, and wrapped a towel around her. It was almost dark out in the sitting room. Lee slipped in and scanned the walls, looking for the controls for the light switches. *Now where have they put them? And where's the night-light?* For the source of the deep reddish glow she'd seen wasn't in the room. *City light, I guess.* Lee turned toward the windows.

The mountains were afire. All the plain between the city and the peaks was drowned in twilight, with here and there the bright points of local streetlights showing in knots and tangles—little towns, villages, individual houses. But beyond them all, those mountains reared up glowing as if lit from inside, burning in the deepest imaginable carmine, a red hotter than any mere blood-color. They almost vibrated against the sky behind them, now a profound indigo in which the earliest stars were coming out. Lee stood there, gazing, hardly daring to breathe, as the Sight woke up in her and held her there, frozen, telling her that this mattered, this *meant* something. *But what? I just got here, I don't have enough information, I don't understand—*

Even as she watched, that light began to leak out of the mountains, irrevocably, as if someone with a dimmer switch was turning it down. Soon it was just the palest rose; then gone. Lee stood there a moment, shaking her head.

Then she got dressed as softly as she could, without bothering to look for the light switches. By the time she was done, the last embers of that light had dwindled to ash, and Lee spent a few moments more looking out the window, wondering at how pale the mountains looked even with the light gone from them. There was no moon up, and the city light diffusing up from street level shortly washed out any remaining sight of them.

Lee thought briefly of food, then realized how thirsty she was. She went to the minibar and pulled out another bottle of mineral water, then looked for ice: there wasn't any. She glanced briefly at Gelert, still snoring away, and smiled ruefully. *Their parties may never run out of ice, as he claims, but their hotels still need work . . .*

She rummaged around in the cupboards near the minibar, found the ice bucket, a plain square job, and then pocketed her SlipCase and went out, closing the door softly behind her. *Down at the end of the hall,* Lee thought. *As far away as possible. Inevitable, isn't it? . . .*

She went all the way down there, found nothing, and had to backtrack to find what she'd missed the first time, a door that looked exactly like all the others except for a minuscule sign that said SERVICE in Alfen, English, and Xainese. Lee pushed the door open and found a soft-drink vending machine, and an icemaker sitting and humming demurely to itself.

Lee put the bucket in place and pushed the button. The icemaker did what icemakers all over the six worlds did:

dropped cubes into the bucket from the greatest possible height and showered her with wet, cold chips and shards. Lee brushed herself off as well as she could, picked up the bucket, and pushed the door open.

"—not his problem at this point," someone was saying down the hall. What stopped Lee in her tracks was how loud the voice seemed: it sounded as if it was immediately to her right, down toward the end of the hall. Yet when she looked down there, she couldn't see anything.

"Yes, well, he isn't going to want it to be a problem later, either. And we should be able to do something about that."

Why are they as loud as if they're shouting, when they're not even in sight? Lee wondered. She paused, listening when they stopped speaking. There was a faint hum in her right ear.

Something wrong with the implant. Oh, that's just great! Why couldn't it have failed two hours ago, instead of—

"Let's not play games: I'm too tired for that right now. And you look worse than I do. What the Senator is going to want to know is exactly what kind of something."

"I wouldn't care to get too specific at the moment. Certainly not about anything as crass as figures. He doesn't need to, either. But we've been watching the way he's been voting on the bills that've come up over the last few months."

Lee held still for a moment. Then very, very slowly, to keep it from making any noise, she began letting the door close in front of her . . . but not all the way.

"Oh really. And your conclusions would be—"

"That the Senator is going to start needing some hefty contributions to his campaign war chest pretty soon, because the benighted apathetic electorate don't seem to be obliging him. Not even after that last tax cut. Ungrateful of them.

He'll never make it past the NY-Hampshire primary, the way he's going."

No voice spoke for a few seconds. Then the first one said, "And you were thinking of—what, exactly?"

"There's some business going on in Ellay at the moment that could use some quieting down, to make the situation easier for your man. The dil'Sorden thing. Just having them here isn't going to do much about it in the long run, I don't think. Additional measures may be needed. A word with some of the media . . . some kind of resolution. We can help with that."

Lee flushed first hot and then cold. *Them?*

"Where is this thing?" said the first voice. Faintly, Lee could hear a button being pushed, angrily, several times. After a pause the first voice spoke again. "Obviously these arrangements go both ways."

"Of course. Later on, when your man's where it matters, then we sort out the details. Open access is going to be an issue."

"Oh, to the candidate, certainly."

"No, afterward."

"He'd never want to be seen to do anything, you know, unethical."

"He wouldn't have to *do* anything. Not about this. Just refrain from—"

Ding! the elevator said, the fake electronic "chime" deafening in the implant. Lee clutched the right side of her head, cursing under her breath. "—until the issue's settled," said the second voice as the elevator doors slid open. "After that so many people are going to be grabbing for the goodies that any one political figure's—"

The elevator door closed. All Lee could hear was some faint muttering noises, lost in that electronic hum.

The Senator.

The dil'Sorden thing.

Having them *here.*

Her feet were cold. Lee looked down and saw that the ice bucket was dripping condensation on her shoes. But that had nothing to do with the way she suddenly found herself shivering.

Softly she pushed the door open again, listening hard. There was nothing to be heard but the same annoying hum from her implant. Lee came out into the hallway and walked back to the suite, let herself in, put the ice bucket down by the minibar, sat down in the dark, and thought as if her life depended on it . . . because possibly it did.

Eight

The next morning she found Gelert eating tidily from what appeared to be a Sèvres soup dish, glancing occasionally at the pad on the floor beside it. The pad was showing a news feed recorded the previous day and handed off to it by the local Alfen network. "What is that?" Lee said.

"The Worlds Today."

"I mean in the bowl."

"Best dog food I've ever had," Gelert said. "Either venison or buffalo. How're you feeling this morning?"

"Better."

"Me too . . ." Lee went over to the two-level table that had been rolled in by room service and uncovered some of the dishes on the top table. Mostly they contained fruit, some of which Lee didn't recognize, cereals, and breads and cheeses. "Nice," Lee said.

"Yeah. Not to my taste, but I thought you'd like the look of the stuff. What's that weird fruit with the ridges?" And silently, into her implant, Gelert said, *I read your notes. Our impressions coincide, pretty much. I left you some.*

"Uh, it looks like carambola. No, wait, it can't be, it has

lots more points." She paused as if to count. *I'll look at them later.* "Eleven. How about that . . ."

"Weird." *You want to check them on a regular basis after this,* Gelert said as he licked the bowl, *because I don't feel comfortable directing your attention to them openly. Our hosts can't read what we've got encrypted, but damned if I'm going to draw their attention to transmissions in progress. They might start looking for some way to crack them, and if they manage it and then overhear us, we're going to have problems.*

Okay. "You want some toast?"

"Is there marmalade?"

"You'll get it in your fur."

"Will you *stop* worrying about my fur! *I* can take care of my fur. And no, I don't need the toast. Eat your breakfast."

Lee smiled slightly and started assembling a plateful of bread and cheese and a few slices of the fruit. She poured a cup of coffee and took it to sit down at the table by the window, looking out at that astonishing view again. The gasping, slightly heartsick feeling caught her again, but this time it wasn't as strong. Lee picked up a slice of the greenish fruit, sniffed it, bit into it.

Her senses washed right out. Suddenly she was aware of Gelert sticking his face into hers, and looking at her most peculiarly. "Lee?"

"What?"

"That's the third time I've spoken to you. What's the matter?"

Lee stared at the fruit. "Wow," was all she could say for a moment. Then she held the slice out to Gelert. "I think," she said, "that this could be what Eve was supposed to have offered Adam. I think I understand the problem now."

Gelert gave her an odd look, then stood up and came over to her. "I'm not normally a veggie person," he said. "However—" Gelert took the slice of fruit in his mouth, swallowed it.

For a long moment he said nothing. The moment stretched into two, or three. Lee looked at Gelert curiously; his eyes were glazed. But finally he blinked.

"*Ouoowawa,*" he said.

"Yes."

Gelert sat down, looking bemused. "There always used to be those stories," Lee said, "about how it was dangerous to eat anything the Elves gave you. That the way time passed got strange: that a year might seem like a day . . ." She raised her eyebrows. "After this I'll stick to the bread."

"It's true," Gelert said. He looked at her with a slightly cockeyed expression. "I wonder why I didn't get anything like that with the meat?"

"We already know you're a little resistant."

"I'd be happier to understand why," Gelert said, shouldering under his saddlebags where they stood in their brace: the brace retracted itself and fastened around him. "Well, I should get going: the finance team is meeting downstairs in ten minutes."

"Yeah, the tour group's meeting downstairs about half an hour after that." Lee looked over at the breakfast cart again and decided to stick with the coffee. "See you later." *Good hunting, big guy.*

"Right. Have a good day." *Meanwhile, you know what you're here for . . .*

Yes. And so do they. But I'll get out there and see what I can See.

Gelert grinned, though not straight at her, as the door shut him out. *Keep your mouthful,* he said.

Lee stood there for a moment, then sat down and started shaking. The brain-blasting intensity of the fruit's flavor when it had been in her mouth, and the choiceless bliss of surrendering to it, scared her badly. And even so, she still wanted to go over to that cart and eat all that fruit, then go downstairs to the hotel's restaurant and demand all of it they had, and eat that, too, until there wasn't any more of it to eat, or until she burst. *This place is not safe,* she thought, shivering. *As far as that goes, the stories are true. We know* nothing *about these people . . . the dangers of them, the secrets they hold. But we've come blithely on in here, into the lion's den, to go digging around for the truth. What we dig up . . . will we survive finding it, I wonder?*

She sat there until she thought she was in control of the shaking, then got up and went to get her jotter. Lee spent perhaps ten minutes reading Gelert's notes, which were as unnerved as her own, if for different reasons. Then she got ready to go. At the door, she stopped, with a feeling of having forgotten something, and found herself staring at the breakfast cart, on the very point of going over to it again.

Lee shuddered and went out the door fast.

The guide for the tour group was waiting for them downstairs, and Lee was surprised and faintly concerned to find that it was Isif dil'Hemrev. "This is my home city," she said to the small group that gathered in the lobby—Lee and Mellie Hopkins and a few others that Lee didn't know so well. "So I thought I would walk you through a few of the highlights. It's not as famous or as historic a city as, say, Aien Mhariseth, but certainly it's pleasant enough . . ."

They headed out of the hotel into that bright morning. "We're lucky with the weather, so far," Mellie said, throwing Lee a thoughtful glance. She also had not missed the choice of tour guide. *She's a spook,* Mellie had said. Lee had always known in a general way that they would all be watched when they got here, but now she found it hard not to look at everyone they passed as if they were spies or informers.

Dil'Hemrev smiled that cool smile of hers with its faint edge of superiority, charming but very much there. "It's summer here at the moment," she said, as they headed out of the main street in front of the hotel; "we don't get a lot of wet weather until the fall. Even if we did, many of the streets we'll be going down this morning are arcaded. Come along this way . . ."

She led them down streets that grew steadily smaller in scale, compared to the taller towers that seemed to encircle the harbor proper. Lee looked around in some admiration as dil'Hemrev talked easily about the history of the Alfen who'd first settled here, the industries they practiced, the trade routes they established. The city itself, at least in its older buildings, had a look of both antiquity and calm prosperity, its architecture featuring both sharp and curved arches, and a great deal of what looked like a soft green sandstone, the delicate carvings pleasantly blunted by time.

Lee walked along behind the others and let dil'Hemrev's narration wash over her as she looked at the buildings—apartment houses and shops, rarely more than three or four stories high, with an odd tendency for windows and flights of steps to come in groups of eleven. *Something cultural?* she wondered. *Something to do with religion, or superstition?*

She resolved to ask dil'Hemrev about it later. But as they walked through the mild, pretty morning, passing various Alfen in the streets and being courteously saluted by them, something began to itch in the back of Lee's mind. The color of the sandstone started to look a little strange to her: watery, somehow. She would glance at a worn, charming old building that from the corner of her eye had seemed to waver slightly, as if submerged, only to find it perfectly steady when she looked at it. *I'm not trying to See . . .* she thought. Yet that was the effect she was getting . . . as if she was bringing judicial Sight to bear on something, and being resisted.

Or as if this whole place was under a glamour, Lee thought. Initially, the thought was laughable. There were ways to lay a deceptive seeming over physical objects for short periods—appearances generated by mind or by mechanical instrumentality—that could deceive people without the Sight easily, and those with it with more difficulty. But these required a considerable outlay of energy and couldn't be maintained long. If what she was perceiving here was indeed a glamour, it was one of a complexity and power Lee had never seen before. *And if it* is *a glamour . . . why are they doing it? Are we being shown a kind of Potemkin village?*

What for? . . .

Lee tried to keep herself from showing any unease and followed along behind their guide, who was talking again now about parts of the city that were said to have sunk under the sea. "There *is* an earthquake fault not far from here," dil'Hevren was saying. "Every thousand years or so it tends to slip; that may have happened in prehistory, and so the legend persists . . ."

She was refraining from using the Sight just now, if only because it tended to make her walk into things. But even as she and the group turned another corner into yet another tiny street, lined with small and cozy buildings, Lee began to wonder whether the innate "fragility" of Ys she had perceived yesterday was just that: perception, no more, well divorced from reality—or from any reality that mattered here and now. For a psychoforencisist it was always a question: were you doing physical reality a disservice by constantly prying around underneath it, trying to find out what it meant? And here more than usual, the physical reality was so arresting—

But that was the problem. Lee trailed her hand idly along a building's stonework as she passed, looking at it as she did: looking, just for a flash, judicially—though not very deep, and not long enough to be caught at it. And then she glanced away again, as casually, for what she'd seen was at odds with what she'd felt. The stone under her hand was stone, right enough: but it was being misrepresented by what Lee saw. It was not a small building, but a tall one, possibly even a skyscraper. She was certain of that, without even looking.

I'm being had, she thought. *We all are.*

And at all costs, I mustn't let them know that I know it.

Lee kept on walking along with the rest of the tour, and thought, looking casually at everything, trying not to be seen looking at any one thing terribly hard, storing away details for consideration later. In one of the main shopping streets into which dil'Hemrev led them, Lee spent some time playing the witless shopper, staring in store windows which were admittedly full of wonderful things, clothes and appliances and furnishings and art the likes of which she'd never seen. All her credit plates itched. It was the better part of an hour before she again dared to touch the corner of a building as the group and dil'Hemrev turned into a side street. But by then, Lee was ready for the difference between what she felt and what she saw. It was not a difference in anything so simple as texture. It was the attitude with which the building had been raised. It said, *I am the matter of eternity: I will last forever: I am permanence, hewn.* It said the exact opposite of what the skyline had said. There was no tug at the heartstrings, here. This was careless strength, unconcerned beauty spoken in the Alfen accent that Lee already knew quite well. These stones wore in spirit the same expression that Lee had seen on a dead Elf in the street, on Omren dil'-Sorden's face in the Ellay County Morgue, belying the fear of a few moments before.

So we're being shown the beauty that moves . . . but as a weapon. Or as something to put us off our guard, to keep us from seeing another truth. The question was, was that truth necessarily important? *Or does it just seem so to the Elves?* That was going to take a while to determine. But as far as Lee was concerned, she had had enough of having her heartstrings tugged. *What's behind the facades?* she thought.

They had been on their feet for nearly an hour and a half now. "We might sit down for a little while, if you like," dil'Hemrev said, again with the slight smile that suggested a touch of pity for humans, who tired, as compared with Alfen, who didn't, or at least not so easily. "There's a café near here with a nice view of the parklands behind the city . . ."

"Sounds like a good idea," Lee said, if only to break her own silence; she'd been quiet while the others had been oohing and aahing over the surroundings. "It'd be pleasant to sit and have a glass of something and look at the mountains, in such nice weather . . ."

Dil'Hemrev turned to look at Lee. The shocked, suspicious look sealed over almost instantly, leaving dil'Hemrev's face serene again; but seeing it, Lee knew immediately that she'd made a mistake, and she had to concentrate on keeping her own face innocent . . . for whatever good it did.

Oh, God, we're not supposed to see the mountains, either. But why?

Dil'Hemrev didn't deal with what Lee had said, and as she led them to the café, Lee did her best to concentrate on seeming harmless. There was no way to call the word back, no way to cover, and no way her guide was going to forget.

What else have I seen that I'm not supposed to? Lee wondered in near-panic. *This is going to mean trouble . . .*

Dil'Hemrev ordered drinks for the group, and they shared them uneventfully enough; and afterward their guide led them back to the hotel. But all the while, Lee could feel dil'Hemrev's attention on her, if not actually her gaze. The Alfen was playing it cool. Lee did her best to do the same, at least until they got back to the hotel.

She was somewhat surprised to find Gelert lounging around in the suite when she got back. "You finished early," she said.

"It's just that there weren't a lot of us still standing after yesterday's transit," Gelert said. "We'll have to do tomorrow a lot of what we thought we'd be doing today. But we got some preliminary work done."

"That's good," Lee said. She keyed her implant on, and said in Palmerrand, *I think their bug is active in here now . . .*

I heard it, Gelert said. *Those relays make a teeny, tiny noise when they shift states.* He flicked one ear back and forth. *E flat above C above high C, minus a quarter tone.*

Lee avoided giving him the amused look she would have at home. *The opera fan speaks.*

"So how was the architecture?"

"Extremely beautiful," Lee said. "There are some patterns that repeat . . ."

"The elevens thing?" Gelert said, sounding idle. "I noticed that in passing." *What's the matter with you? You look rattled.*

Partly that I heard more history from dil'Hemrev today than I think I've ever heard or read, Lee said silently, *and I'm still trying to digest what I remember of it. But there's another problem. I mentioned the mountains.*

He looked at her oddly. *What mountains?*

Lee's heart seized. *Have you looked out the window lately?*

First thing this morning. Lovely countryside, I thought. But no mountains.

Gelert looked at her strangely. *Lee, this is the flood plain of the Seine, or what would be the Seine if we were at home, which I'm really beginning to wish we were. Mountains are in short supply here. Or they should be.*

I'm not arguing. However, I am seeing mountains. And I don't think our hosts expected me to, or any of us, for that matter.

You think this is going to be a problem?

I think maybe it already is. But there's nothing I can do about it.

Gelert looked thoughtful. *And your implant's been working a little strangely since we got here. Picking up things it wouldn't, normally. Is it some effect on the machinery . . . or are our own sensitivities being sharpened by our presence here?*

It could be both. Something to watch out for . . . Lee said.

You mean, besides dil'Hemrev. Well, we'll see what comes of it.

There's still the problem of what I overheard last night.

I just wish the ice machines had been closer to the elevator, Gelert said. *What you got was tantalizing. And I have one easy guess which Senator he was discussing. Milelgua. He's widely known to be scraping the bottom of his campaign chest.*

What I want to know is what the 'goodies' were that they were discussing, Lee said.

Gelert let out a long breath and rolled over. *Not enough data . . .* he said. *Meanwhile, can you spare a few minutes? I'm chary of getting into long conversations inside the hotel,*

*and Sal wanted a word before we move on to our next loca-
tion.*

Already? Lee said.

Yes, Gelert said. *The records we're investigating, after
all, aren't physically located here. They're going to run us
up to Aien Mhariseth tomorrow. There's some weekly, or
ten-day-ly, meeting of the Alfen Grand Council tomorrow;
they want to bring us up there and give us the official seal of
approval. I don't know whether we'll be reconvening down
here again. But this is either a big honor, or an attempt to
keep us from getting comfortable in any one place.*

*If they try to take us over to their version of North Amer-
ica, I guess we'll know for sure,* Lee said. *Meanwhile . . . we
roll with the desires of our hosts, I suppose. Where's Sal
going to meet us?*

*He'll be down in the bar. We'll go for "a walk in the
park." They may have that bugged, but we can at least pick
the least buggable parts of it, and Sal's carrying a change-
able-frequency multispectrum surveillance-buster. We'll
find out soon enough if it works . . .*

Lee changed into something more casual than she'd been
wearing, a loose tunic and light pants suitable to the nearly
tropical weather, and wandered out with Gelert, for all the
world as if they had no plans. The people working behind
the desk looked at them curiously as they passed, but seeing
that they were heading straight across the main road into the
parkland by the lake, did nothing else.

Lee and Gelert went out across one of the paved paths
that led through the perfect lawn running to the perfect lake-
side. There they found a bench to sit down on, and did nothing for fifteen minutes or so but admire the perfect view out

across the water. "Would this be the Atlantic," Lee said at last, looking out into the rainbowed mist, "or the English Channel?"

"I have to confess that geography is not my highest priority in life," Gelert said. "Especially Alfen geography, which is half-classified anyway. But this should be central France, not the coast as it occurs in our own world . . . I think. The cognacy with Paris in our world is supposed to be fairly close."

Lee heard a step on the nearby walk, turned to see Sal coming. "Have you ever noticed," she said, "that Elves don't make any noise when they walk?"

"A whole lot less than humans of your type, anyway," Gelert said. "And a ton less than Sal. Hi, Sal . . ."

Sal lowered his considerable bulk to the bench beside Lee. "Gelert," he said, "you bad mouthing me again?"

"Somebody's got to do it."

"Yeah, well, you're not the skinny runt you used to be, either. It's those expense-account dinners. Look at the gut on you—"

"If you two could stop slagging each other ever so briefly," Lee said, "who knows how human knowledge might be increased."

"Huh," Sal said, a world's worth of doubt in the word.

"Your widget working?" Lee said softly.

Sal nodded just once. "Far as I know. Let's keep it fairly brief, though."

"So did your team have a good day?" Gelert said.

"Huh, huh, huh, huh," Sal said, laughing, and went on in that vein for so long that Lee became seriously concerned. That much laughter from this man usually indicated a disaster in the making.

She leaned back on the bench and waited, while Gelert lay down on the ground and rolled his eyes at the impossibly blue sky. Finally, Sal went quiet. "I take it," Lee said, "that your initial findings have been positive."

"Oh yes," Sal said. "Everything very much on the up-and-up. If you have about as much math, or networking expertise, as a high school graduate. I'd be really insulted, if I didn't find it all desperately funny."

"So they've showed you the 'not so public' version of their books," Gelert said, "as regards their mining records, and the data that suggests how much FG they release to the markets of the other worlds, and when, and in what amounts to which markets."

Sal nodded. "There are some holes in the numbers already," Sal said. "Nothing we can authenticate from the information they've let us see so far. But what really interests me is the details they've let fall about their accounting computers' connections to the worlds' computer networks ... which may present some possibilities for authentication from our side of things. Whether they like it or not."

Lee gave him a look. "I thought there *were* no direct connections between their home computers in Alfheim and the subsidiary computers in other universes," Lee said. "Privacy concerns, territorial 'information sovereignty,' and all that."

Sal sniffed. "That's what they want everybody to think," he said. "But it's operationally impossible. Oh, they go on in public about their secured data transfer, but it's just more obfuscation designed to direct attention elsewhere and make their own lives easy."

He leaned back and folded his hands over his ample stomach. "They have direct transfer, all right," Sol said. "They squeeze the data down to packets, and transmit it at unpredictable intervals using a randomization paradigm, using standard 'tween-universe protocols and comms channels. How better to cover their tracks than to blend in with all the other traffic between the worlds? And I can't believe they think we're so stupid as not to have seen the comms calls in some of their code. Yes, their cryptography is of a very high order. Not unbreakable; as usual, what the mind can devise, the mind can break. But in terms of anybody cracking their traffic in real time, which would be their main worry, they're safe enough."

Sal looked thoughtful. "What *does* seem to be very secure is access to *their* machines from *outside* their universe. They can get into our networks anytime they want to: but since they're the ones who control information flow, by controlling the 'ring time' that permits it in the first place, they make it almost impossible for anyone to get at their machines from outside."

Gelert's ears went up. " 'Almost' impossible?"

Sal got a dreamy look that Lee found most provocative. "When a data ring here gets in contact with one in one of the other worlds," he said, "they have to exchange authentication information first. Now, there are, oh, fifty different ring systems in our six worlds with which the Alfen rings at Ys and Aien Mhariseth communicate on a regular basis."

Gelert's eyes narrowed in sudden amusement. "But only two Alfen data rings."

"Three," Sal said. "There's a comms-only ring at Ayehmendeh, at the foot of Manhattan Mountain: their Brookhaven. Their first ring, I think—they keep it around for sentimental reasons. Or some other." He frowned, his usual look when he suspected an answer to a question hiding itself from him. "Anyway, each of their rings is programmed to generate a new ID herald each time they 'call up' another machine. But they can't change it *too* much: it's simpler and much more secure to change the cryptography in the message, rather than in the transmitter." Sal smiled. "But this allows us to compare all the log-in heralds from the small number of Alfen machines against the large number of heralds from the machines in the other five universes, and deduce . . . though very slowly . . . how to fake an Alfen herald that's likely to occur in a future cycle of communications. After that it's just a matter of sending it back to them, over and over, from all those other machines, for a long time. Sooner or later the Alfen machine at the other end of the linkage hears its own newly generated herald echoed back to it by the other machine, then goes on to the next step of the process, which is spilling its guts. Or at least, letting us capture the whole message it would have sent to that machine, without raising any warning flags."

"Have you been caught at this yet?" Lee said.

"Lee," said Sal, "is that a question you really want me to answer?"

"Uh, no."

Sal's smile got more ironic. "I trust the cardinal Virtues to know that I'm on their side," he said. "But I'd sooner not have to discover the truth about that in a courtroom. My goal is to make some other poor sonofabitch discover it. And with that goal in mind, I'll keep certain details in my own head until they need to get out in the fresh air."

"You'd need a lot of cooperation to do that kind of thing," Gelert said.

"Yup," said Sal. He smiled.

Mist was beginning gently to gather over the water as the shadows lengthened. Lee watched it creep in toward the shore. "So eventually you're going to be able to derive information, at home, to compare against the information you're being given here." Lee didn't have to say, "to see whether we're being lied to."

"Eventually?" Sal said. He smiled again.

Gelert rolled over on his side and fixed Sal with one eye. "I'm glad you're on our side," he said, "that's all."

"But these people are deep in deception, Gelert," Sal said

softly. "Deep. We are going to have to chase them right around the block, up hill and down dale, before we get what we really need to know out of them. The second 'set of books' looks tight enough . . . but the third set is going to look absolutely watertight, I'm sure. It's going to prove everything they've said to us about their balance of trade; it's going to confirm that they are on the straight and narrow, and all these other people are out to make them look bad. So you guys, and the other investigators, had better come up with the goods within a week or so, and give the rest of us a reason to stay around and dig deeper. Otherwise, this whole thing is going to turn into a PR exercise, for *them,* proving how hard-done-by the poor Alfen are. Played for a fool by naughty Interpol and the silly UN, so full of mere humans, so easily led astray. We need some nice solid excuses to hang around . . . and we need all the rest of the team, of which you two are part, to provide them to us. Otherwise, my data suggests they're going to turf us out of here in less than a week."

"We'll do what we can," Lee said, though she wasn't sure what that might be. "Gelert?"

"I could bury something and claim to forget where I left it," Gelert said.

Sal nudged Gelert with his foot. "Someone's reputation, probably," he said. "But somewhere here there's a smoking gun. We need to find it . . . and pronto."

Nine

The people gathered in the hotel lobby the next morning looked like an unusually worn-down tour group, standing around with their luggage and regarding the morning with bleary equanimity. Some of them looked much more bleary than others. Lee guessed that she was probably well into this second camp, for she hadn't slept well the previous night. She hadn't exactly been expecting to, anyway. But it had come as a shock to her to return to the suite and find a low mist lying over everything outside ... and when the mist rose, there had been no sign of the mountains.

That had shaken her badly enough to make Lee spend the whole night curled up on one of the couches in the suite's sitting room, looking out into the darkness, past the city lights. Morning began to gray out the black of the sky, little by little, and Lee sat there fixedly watching the horizon for the least sign of the jagged shapes she knew should be there. But they didn't come. And finally dawn slipped up over the far edge of the world to illuminate a broad and smiling plain, a beautiful green patchwork landscape of fields and forests, mostly flat until it melted away into gently rolling hills and the mist of distance away at the hinted-at horizon; but no mountains were to be seen anywhere.

Through her frustration and unease, Lee knew her own uncertainty was being used against her as a weapon. It was a potent one . . . and the only way to take it out of the hands of those using it against her was to admit that she had no idea what was going on here, and resign herself to apprehending what might present itself before her, rather than actively searching under appearances . . . for the moment. *If they think they've thrown me off the scent, as Gelert would put it, then they may get careless in some other way. So, fine: let them think I've learned my lesson. Or that I'm scared.*

I won't have to fake that very hard . . .

Exactly on time Isif dil'Hemrev turned up, looking what was to Lee almost intolerably beautiful, as if she had bathed in morning dew, that swirl of hair like night around her shimmering where the sun caught it as she escorted the group out to the pavement in front of the hotel. There Lee had a moment's irrational satisfaction as, ever so briefly, she saw dil'Hemrev look up and around at the sky and display annoyance. Her eyes went chilly, and a little straight deep frown line drove down from the middle of her forehead to the top of her nose, disfiguring that perfect face for just a few moments. Lee began to feel ashamed of herself for being so pleased to see the alabaster perfection marred. Then the shame gave way to puzzlement. *What's she so upset about? It's just a late bus or something . . .*

Beside Lee, Gelert looked up, his ears twitching. "Not bad," he said under his breath. Lee looked where he did, where dil'Hemrev was looking, and saw the transport angling in toward them in utter silence, the sun glinting on its long sleek shape through the still-fading morning mist as it landed with exactitude out in the center of the greensward near where she and Gelert and Sal had had their talk. She glanced over at dil'Hemrev and was bemused again to see her beautiful face get angrier still, before the look sealed over.

The craft was a big one, a forty-seater at least—a broad oval main body, with a slenderer oval of clearsteel or some similar substance mounted atop it. A door appeared in the craft's side as Dil'Hemrev led them out to it, and not until Lee was halfway there and waiting in line to go up the ramp the craft had extruded did she notice the symbol on its side near the nose—not the undifferentiated golden sun-disc of Alfheim, but an irregular green hexagon, wider than it was tall, pierced from below by an unfletched arrow or spear. Lee's eyes widened at that. *Oh, really?*, she said to Gelert via their Palmerrand link, for the sign was that of the Alfen *Miraha,* the executive body comprised of the Grand Council, the Survivor Lords, and the Elf-king.

Not what she was expecting, I take it, Gelert said. *Apparently the unexpected annoys her.*

Lee thought of the woman's expression yesterday. *That's not exactly news.* She was still worrying at the questions raised by dil'Hemrev's reaction yesterday. The Alfen had to know perfectly well that she was a Seeing psychoforensicist. So why should dil'Hemrev then have been surprised that she'd Seen the mountains? And since the mountains had been gone again, this morning, why should she now be trying to get Lee to admit that she'd Seen them?

. . . And again, if I wasn't meant to See those mountains, why were we given a suite on that side of the building, where I wouldn't have any choice to See them if I could?

Unless someone counted on me Seeing them. I was meant to See them. Meant to be noticed Seeing them.

By whom? . . .

They climbed up into the craft, found seats. Lee took a window seat behind Mellie Hopkins, but just as Gelert was about to slip into the same row and jump up on the seat beside her, dil'Hemrev sidestepped him and gracefully sat down there herself. Gelert flicked one ear at Lee, and went around to the next row behind. As the craft lifted, again in silence, dil'Hemrev turned to Lee, and said, "I'm sorry I didn't have a chance to talk to you after the group outing yesterday. We've been remiss, it seems."

Lee was uncertain just how to take this, but also intent on giving dil'Hemrev no leads to pursue. "I'm sure you've been very busy . . ."

The craft angled out over the sea, gaining altitude, then turned inland again, still gaining height and speed; Ys dropped away behind, more and more quickly, becoming indistinct under the scattered morning cloud. "Not so busy that we would willingly pay less than full attention to our guests' security," dil'Hemrev said, sounding apologetic. "We've had a rather angry communication from the LA Police Department this morning, wanting information on what personal protection we've assigned you. They're very concerned for your safety, and so naturally we are, too."

The second part of this, she had been expecting . . . but the first part took Lee by surprise. *Assuming it's true* . . . "It's certainly nothing I've asked them to act on," Lee said. "I'm convinced the break-in at my house was a one-off, and the extra security was probably unnecessary . . . certainly after the damage to the house was repaired, anyway. And as for security here, I very much doubt that common thieves or housebreakers are going to have managed to follow me into Alfheim." She smiled at dil'Hemrev. "I'm sure the security arrangements you have in place for the group as a whole will be more than adequate to keep me safe."

"All the same," dil'Hemrev said, "I'm not sure we would

feel comfortable with going against the express wishes of the organization which employs you. If we—"

"I'm sorry," Lee said gently, "but there's some misunderstanding here. I'll grant you the situation is complex; possibly there's no equivalent structure in Alfen law inducement. I'm not an employee of the LAPD: I'm an independent contractor. If anything, I employ *them,* from time to time, with an eye to the furtherance of Justice, Whom I serve. I understand their concern, on their own ground; but here it's almost certainly unnecessary."

"Ms. Enfield," dil'Hemrev said, "I'm sorry too, but I find myself in a position where I must insist—"

"I don't like to cause you trouble," Lee said, a flat lie for which she would have to make recompense later. "But if you do insist, then perhaps matters will be most simply handled if as soon as we set down, I make arrangements to be returned to Ellay. I'm sure the Security Council's oversight committee will understand when I explain the circumstances to them."

That produced a brief silence during which Lee concentrated on looking guileless and watching dil'Hemrev's face as mildly as if there was nothing unusual to be seen there at all. The Alfen woman did her best to keep her expression serene, but wasn't entirely successful. Lee knew what she was thinking: that any departure of a member of the investigative committee at this point would be looked upon most suspiciously, as possibly involving some kind of coercion . . . and Lee's side of the story, suggesting that the Alfen were trying to impose personal surveillance on her against her will, would only serve to reinforce that suspicion back home.

"I'll have to tell my superiors, then, that you've refused protection," dil'Hemrev said.

The alarm already growing in the back of Lee's mind

suddenly gathered itself into an entirely different shape. But she was not going to let that show. "I'd appreciate it if you'd do that," Lee said.

Dil'Hemrev got up with a smile and a nod, and headed away to sit down by Per Olafssen, beginning to chat with him as if nothing out of the ordinary had just happened. Lee spent the next few moments looking out the window as the craft ascended farther and farther above the clouds, beginning to shudder ever so slightly as it accelerated. The thought of dil'Hemrev's expression as this craft had landed was again on her mind. *Not at all what she was expecting* . . . And dil'Hemrev was ExAff, Mellie Hopkins had said.

There's a tendency for us to think of Alfen as if they all had the same agendas and all answered to the same authorities. And maybe it serves their purposes to have us think that. But Lee was now beginning to suspect what she should have realized long ago; that there were factions among them, and infighting, just as among any other kind of hominid. *And spotting the sigil of the* Miraha *on this ship threw her off-balance somehow. Was our group being covertly "sponsored" by one group, one governmental agency, for one set of purposes, until another one co-opted us? One higher up?* . . .

She felt the slight thump as someone sat down in the seat next to her, and across the bottom of her vision, the characters ran by: *That was a bluff that could have gone fairly wrong* . . .

She didn't turn to look at Gelert right away. *It didn't, though. Now all we have to worry about is who's going to attack me here, and how* . . .

She didn't actually threaten you, did she??

Oh, no, Lee said. *She was the one who felt threatened, if I'm any judge. But she does think something's going to hap-*

pen to us, or to me. They're trying to cover themselves. But at the same time, she thinks something's gone wrong—

They both started, then, as the craft shook with the characteristic double bang of a vessel going hypersonic; and Lee looked at Gelert, smiling slightly at his nervousness, and her own. But beyond that, she didn't feel much like smiling. *I think we're caught in the middle of some kind of obscure protocol fight*, Lee said. *If I'm reading the signs right, ExAff was supposed to be in charge of our group . . . until suddenly the* Miraha *took an interest.*

I would have thought the Miraha *would have been interested from the beginning*, Gelert said. *But what do I know? Meanwhile, there could be other possible readings, Lee. Herself only knows what the internal political situation here is like at the moment. The Alfen are pretty close-mouthed about their government departments' interrelationships . . .*

I suspect they're relying on our ignorance, Lee said. *Well, we'll see what we can do to remedy that over the next few days. And in the meantime, no matter what they may intend to try, I didn't want some Alfen version of Larry sleeping across our threshold.*

"Well, we've got half an hour or so before we get there, I believe," Gelert said. "Coffee?"

Lee turned to see one of the craft's Alfen staff standing by their seats with a tray, and noted in passing the *Miraha's* insignia on the man's one-piece uniform. "Xoco if you have it," Lee said.

"Certainly, Ms. Enfield. A moment. *Lhei'madra?*"

"Water would be fine. Still, please; at altitude the bubbles give me trouble."

The Alfen walked away. Lee looked at him idly as he went; he was as usual too handsome to be believed, as well as tall, radiantly blond, big-shouldered and narrow-waisted, though not too much so—a wrestler's build. *What I want to know is, where in that uniform could he be hiding a weapon?*

Gelert caught her look. "In the market for a 'professional boyfriend'?" he said, pulling his grin wider than usual.

Lee shook her head. *Not an Alfen one,* she said silently down their link.

"You sure? He might look decorative sleeping across the threshold . . ."

"Gelert . . ." Lee said.

Their drinks arrived. Lee took her xoco and tasted it cautiously; she had no confidence in the food here anymore, not after that piece of fruit back in the hotel, and she didn't want to be taken by surprise. "It would make Matt crazy," Gelert said, bending his head to the bowl that had been put on the side tray for him.

"Matt," Lee said under her breath. "Please don't mention him right now." She was wondering how she was going to find out anything useful at all if the Alfen kept hauling them from place to place before she had a chance to look hard at anything. *How did I let you inveigle me into this, Matt? I swear, when we get home, I'm going to take it out of your hide . . .*

The problem was, she knew she wouldn't. There were too many memories of him lying back against the pillows in the early morning, lazy, smiling tenderly at her . . .

Lee cursed herself inwardly and looked south out the window, ahead of them, toward the very slight curvature of the earth that concealed their destination.

The flight was as short as Gelert had predicted. They had hardly spent fifteen minutes cruising supersonic before the ship shook with subsonic re-insertion. It was still strange to do it in utter silence, except for the roar of air past the craft's hull, and even that was muted to a faint demure rushing sound like air-conditioning. *Another technology they've de-*

clined to share with the rest of us. I wonder, did they get it from the Xainese? . . . For Xaihon was as protective of its universe's monopoly on space travel and space technologies as Alfheim was of fairy gold. *Possibly these two cultures have better grounds for understanding each other than the rest of us know . . .*

They were dropping into a landscape of mountains tall enough to be snowcapped even at this time of year, in these latitudes; Alfheim's version of the Alps. Where in Lee's world those mountains were as full of the marks of civilizations as anyplace else, now she looked down out of the window and saw no sign of roads or habitations, nothing at all—a white waste lined here and there with green valleys, but the valleys were empty.

On the southern side of the great Alpine watershed, though, the picture began to change as their craft dropped lower. The character of the mountains changed, too; they became lower, the valleys wider and greener, and now signs of life began to appear—small handsome cities, valleys wide enough for cultivation, roads winding among the peaks. And then, without warning, the character of the mountains changed.

Before they had been more like the Rockies, granite or basalt, dark gray or almost black in places, an older, volcanic stone in stepped peaks and great massifs. Now, suddenly, as the craft descended, Lee found herself looking at a sharper, more dangerous landscape, a maze of upward-pointing daggers of white stone set against a cloudless blue sky. At the heart of one cluster of those daggers, almost as if set there for protection, a collection of sharp-pointed gems in greens and blues reached upward, glittering in the day: Aien Mhariseth, the Alfen's oldest settlement in Europe, and the ancient home and seat of power of the Elf-kings.

All their group were standing in the craft's aisles now to

look down at the view, or leaning against the windows. Lee felt no surprise to glance over her shoulder and see that dil'Hemrev was nearby again, looking at the staggering landscape with the gently amused expression of someone watching the reaction of tourists to a beauty she had herself long come to take for granted. Their eyes did not meet as Lee glanced back, but she knew that the Elf was waiting to discover what else Lee might see.

Standing behind dil'Hemrev, looking over her shoulder, Per Olafssen said, "These are the Italian pre-Alps, aren't they?"

"Close. But we're a little farther south, and a little farther west," dil'Hemrev said. "If the equivalencies were complete, it would be the area around Latemar, in your world—not too far from Bolzano, in the Italian Tyrol. But in our universe Bolzano, or Dalasthe as we call it, remained just a little settlement. Probably it's because the course of the Adige river runs a little differently here, farther east into what would be the Grödner Dolomites. With us, it was Aien Mhariseth that became the main trading center, because of the way the river and the pass road came together."

Lee filed the information away absently as the craft made a broad circle around the city, losing more altitude. Aien Mhariseth resembled Ys only in that some of the materials, metals and stone, looked like those used there. Otherwise, the building style was mostly different. The majority of the buildings were older, blunter, crouching down into the hollow under the mountain walls. In the center of the city, a double handful of towers reached up; newer buildings, Lee thought, meant to echo the natural surroundings in a more ordered architectural idiom. They were handsome enough. But to her eye the effect had failed, for those spires were effortlessly dominated and overshadowed by the spines and thorns of stone uprearing all around. The stone was pale, an

ancient coral-based limestone identical with that of the
Dolomites in Lee's own world. Once upon a time, all this
had lain beneath the warm waters of the prehistoric sea that
covered Europe. But the fires under the world had stirred,
and the planet's skin had heaved upward, shrugging the sea
away. The calcified coral of the seabed had cracked and
shattered, great layers of it tilting up onto their sides, as the
floor of that part of the world abruptly became its walls.
Millions of years' erosion had fretted slowly at those walls,
peeling them back and down along the now-vertical layers,
so that Aien Mhariseth was completely fenced about with
narrow peaks and pinnacles, jagged needles of stone like up-
thrust swords and spears, white or palest gray. Here and
there among them an occasional patch of green lay nestled
in some broad yoke or saddleback between the greater chain
of peaks; but elsewhere were only boulders in a hundred
sizes, gravel and rubble, and huge fans of gray scree scattered down the mountainsides.

But here and there, too, as they swung closer around the
great jagged wall that stood up directly behind Aien
Mhariseth, sheltering it to the north, Lee began to see the
patches of crimson clinging to the sheer stone. Only the
highest peaks were free of it just now. Elsewhere the color
became less of a patchwork, almost an unbroken blanket in
places, in purple or carmine or a dark dusky rose. At the
sight of the color, once again Lee felt that terrible disorient-
ing gripe of pain of the heart, as if she were suddenly remembering a loss she had suffered long ago, and had,
unconscionably, forgotten. But the feeling affected her less
strongly today, either because she had been here for a little
while now, or because she recognized it as possibly some
kind of weapon . . . in any case, as something more than just
the effect of transit between worlds. *And it's worse here,* Lee
thought. *Had we experienced this on our first day, it would*

have simply left us all nonfunctional. But why *is it stronger here?*

"Oh, isn't that beautiful," Mellie Hopkins was saying, and then she sniffed, and wiped a tear away. "It's all pink . . ."

Lee smiled. *As good a time as any to push the issue a little.* "The Elf-king's roses . . ." she said. "Or one variety of them, anyway."

"Yes, we had quite a display the other night, didn't we? The conditions were just right." Dil'Hemrev smiled, completely innocently. "I wish I could say we arranged it for you, but very few of us are quite that accomplished."

Lee didn't even dare glance at dil'Hemrev at that point. *Just what are you trying to pull?* she thought. *Why are you in such a rush all of a sudden to get me to incriminate myself? And who are you working for, really?* For she couldn't get rid of the sense that dil'Hemrev was feeling pressured in some way . . . and that there was more to it than just whatever orders dil'Hemrev might have from ExAff. *So do I take the bait?* Lee thought. It was tempting, but she had no idea how such a brazen betrayal of what she could see and couldn't might affect matters.

"What are you on about?" Mellie said. "Never knew you were a gardener, Lee."

"Believe me, I'm not," Lee said. "You should see *my* roses. It's just something from an old story that some central Europeans made up to explain the alpenglow. When you have sunset and . . ." Lee decided not to make life easy for dil'Hemrev by coming right out and saying "a mountain range." ". . . and high clouds in the right orientation to one another, sometimes it makes it look like the landscape is glowing internally. It lasts a while after local nightfall, because of the height of the clouds. People used to say those were the Elf-king's roses showing through from the next world . . ."

"That happen the night we came? It would have been lost on me," Mellie said. "I don't remember a thing after dropping my bags and checking where the plumbing was. I was wrecked." Mellie looked down again as the craft began to circle lower, toward a green spot at the edge of the city. "Those can't be real roses, though, can they. Not up here: it'd be too cold. This has to be a sub-alpine environment . . ."

"You're right, of course," dil'Hemrev said. "I wouldn't be an expert, but those are a little low shrubby kind of plant that blooms this time of year. A kind of giant heather, I think you would call them. They're very tough; they go right up past the snow line, and spend most of the year covered by snow, except for this little window of time when they bloom in a hurry. The name suggests that they got tangled up with the old legend somehow, probably when people found out that there weren't real roses up there in their own worlds. And of course there weren't any here in our world either; they couldn't have survived. Just a fairy tale . . ." Dil'Hemrev smiled indulgently.

Gelert had put his head over Lee's shoulder. *Pushing the issue, are we?*

Why not? Mellie gave me the opening.

No argument. Just you be careful . . . "It looks like nice walking country," Gelert said.

"It's very popular among those of our people who enjoy hiking," dil'Hemrev said. "I'd be glad to speak to someone and have them take you up there in your free time, if you like."

Lee thought she understood the message: *There's nothing there of any importance at all, and we want you to see that for yourself.* "Certainly," Lee said. "If there's some spare time in the next few days, I'd enjoy the opportunity. Gel?"

"Absolutely. I could use a good run in the park."

Dil'Hemrev nodded as if there was nothing unusual about this at all, and went farther back in the craft to talk to some others of the committee members. Lee didn't glance at Gelert, but via her implant she said: *If I was uncertain before, I'm not now. The way she came back to the question of any "real" roses being here tells me she knows about my caller. The only question is how. Which Alfen intelligence agency has the comms in my house bugged? Or have they already pulled my caller in and had ExAff wring him dry?*

For our sake, I hope not. They'd probably have enough cause under their jurisdictional laws to chuck us in the clink right now. But I don't think they'd like to do that . . . for the same reason your bluff worked just now.

Well, we'll see . . .

"The city looks like it's been here for a long time," Per said, sitting down across the aisle and a seat or two up from Lee and Gelert.

"Since our version of the Bronze Age," dil'Hemrev said, all polished tour guide again. "Our oldest fairy gold mines are here; not mined anymore, of course, since the area's now protected under cultural heritage statutes. And some of the buildings are very old indeed." She indicated one in particular, set actually into the huge wall of stone, high up on an inward-leaning spur of stone that stood perhaps fifty meters above the floor of the small valley that the peaks encircled. "Ealvien dil'Lavrinhad," she said, "the Laurins' House. Its oldest parts are now five thousand years old; it's the oldest continuously inhabited structure on the planet."

They all peered at it as the craft came down toward its landing site, in the shadow of what was a much more grand and impressive building, arched and porticoed like some-

thing out of ancient Greece, though the arches were more
Gothic than Hellenic. Lee's eyes, though, were still all for
that building up on its spur of stone, leaning against the
mountain behind it like someone very mindful of who might
come up from behind his back. What few towers the Laurins' House possessed had a grudging look to them, squared,
blunted like the oldest of the older buildings below. Only
one tower stood a little higher than the rest, sitting farthest
back in the structure and built partially into the spur as the
foundations of the building were. From it, a few cautious,
narrow-eyed windows looked down on the valley, giving an
impression of thoughtful watchfulness, a regard that trusted
no one and didn't sleep. *There's a message there,* she
thought, *if I could understand it* . . .

She lost sight of the building at last as the craft came
down on a paved area not far from the huge building with its
arched porticoes. "The *Miraha* are in morning session
there," dil'Hemrev said; "you've been invited to the afternoon session, which is formal . . . so you'll want to change.
We'll get you settled in the visitors' quarters and send someone around for you when it's time for the session. Then the
reception with the *Miraha* will be this evening."

"Is the Laurin likely to be in attendance?" Per said.

"I think not," said dil'Hemrev. "He's been traveling on
business for the last few weeks; we would have been informed if he'd returned. He'll be disappointed that he
missed you, of course."

"Of course," Per said.

The craft put its ramp out, and they all trooped down
after dil'Hemrev and followed her across the landing pad
and down a paved pathway to a great door in the bottom of
one of the nearest towers, a massive drum-shaped structure
with several smaller towers incorporated inside its outer
walls. Shortly thereafter, following a climb up several cir-

cles' worth of stairs, Lee and Gelert were ushered into their rooms by a young Alfen woman in the livery of the *Miraha*, and the massive steel-bound door closed behind them.

Neither of them could do much for the first few seconds except look around in astonishment. "It's a whole floor," Lee said, gazing around. From where they stood, a long straight stone-walled room at least fifty feet wide ran right across to the far side of the tower, and seemingly straight out onto an exterior balcony; there were no windows or doors there that Lee could see. Massive, dark wooden furniture, beautifully carved, stood here and there—tables, couches, almeries, and bookshelves ranged against the warm brown stone.

They walked in and looked through the big doors to right and left that opened from the main room. The one on the left was plainly meant for Gelert, at least half its great floor a single silken cushion, with heaps more silks lying here and there for warmth, and a door leading into a massive bath walled and floored in some dark sparkling stone that was warm to the touch. On Lee's side the bedroom was hung with darkly rich draperies and tapestries, floored with a beautiful old woven rug in designs the like of which Lee had never seen before. The bed had an ornately carved, curved headboard nearly two meters high, arching up and over the head of the bed into an outreaching canopy, as if the designer had been afraid it might start raining inside. The whole effect was lavish, but layered, an effect entirely different from the polished perfection of the hotel room in Ys. This place looked like people had lived in it.

My problem, Gelert said, *is that it looks like people have died in it.* He was examining some marks on the furniture in the common sitting area. *I'd swear that's a sword cut. Lee, does that look like a sword cut to you?*

She wandered idly past the chair in question, glanced at it. *No.*

I wish I could be so sure. Either way, no one's even polished it out. The maintenance around here leaves something to be desired.

Maybe it's something historic.

If it is, that just makes me more *nervous.*

Lee went back out into the central hall that led to the balcony, strolled down to its door, or where its door should have been, and stood gazing out. "Why can't I feel the wind from outside?" she said, and walked out onto the balcony. The few steps answered her question: the sensation as of a spiderweb brushing across her skin told her there was some kind of forcefield between the window and the room.

For a few moments she leaned there on the parapet, looking across the valley to the palace built into the cliff. After a little while Gelert came up behind her, got up on his hind legs, with his paws on the parapet, and looked over.

"I've never slept in a theme park before," Lee said, glancing up at the nearby towers, spired in silver and orichalc, clustered like candles in a stony candelabrum. "I feel like there should be somebody down in the bushes, wishing they were a glove upon my hand, like something out of Shakespeare."

Gelert sat down again and said nothing for a few moments. Finally, silently, he said, *You feel it too, don't you.*

Lee didn't nod, but inwardly she said, *There's a lot more here than shows at first glance.*

Or scent, Gelert said, *first or second.* He breathed the late-afternoon air, looking toward the mountains, closing his eyes to scent better. Lee followed his gaze. There was a claustrophobic quality to those mountains, a feeling as if they were not entirely a natural barrier, not an accident of geology, but a wall in truth, erected on purpose to keep something out . . . or in.

Something there that's not showing, Gelert said. *Can you feel it?*

Yes, Lee said. *Come on.*

The two of them stood there for ten minutes, twenty minutes, more. After that Lee stopped wondering how long, and simply stood, bending her Sight against those mountains, willing them with all her might to show her what they had to show. But they stood there, still as stone, mute as stone, and would not reveal anything at all. They were rock, just rock; nothing else. They had stood there for more than a million years, and had seen nothing worth seeing, and meant nothing in particular to anyone. The only secret they held in them was gold, clenched there inside them as if in a fist; but even that secret was an open one, no news to anybody.

Lee opened her eyes, let out a long breath of frustration. *Anything?* She said to Gelert.

Nothing at all. Which, as we both know, is wildly unlikely.

A glamour?

If it is one, as we understand it, I've never felt one so strong. It can't even be felt as such. Which means it's powerful enough to override our perception of reality—

Or our perception of reality is being interfered with.

Always a possibility. Lee thought again of the roses, of how a power like theirs might theoretically be enough, in some other universe, to subvert even the operation of a cardinal Virtue, of Justice herself.

If it is, Gelert said, *we're screwed. The whole reason for us coming has been derailed; we've effectively been neutralized.*

The other possibility, Lee said, *is that it's not a glamour as we understand it, but something else, some other kind of power being bent against us. That our judgment of what we're Seeing or Scenting is correct . . . and we need to keep on doing just what we're doing now.*

Gelert sighed. *We're going to have to play it that way for the time being,* he said. *But I smell trouble on the air that I can't pin down any more specifically than that. Something here is* wrong. *The air says so, the water says so, the stones on the ground and the trees on the hill and the sky looking down all say it, too . . .*

The question is, are we going to be able to find out what before they send us home again?

Way back down at the end of the main room, someone knocked on the door. *Not right this minute,* Gelert said. "Oh my gosh, we should have been changed by now . . ." Lee said, for the benefit of whoever might be doing surveillance on them at the moment. "Come on . . ."

Lee had attended her share of governmental sessions in her time, everything from the UN&ME in general session to that recurring bout of tag-team wrestling otherwise known as the biweekly meeting of the Ellay City Council. In content, the *Miraha's* "guest assembly" was probably no different from most of these, insofar as it involved a great many people, usually of advanced years, standing up and making long leisurely speeches in indecipherable language. *The only difference here,* Lee said silently, *is that even in the Senate, the average age isn't anywhere near as advanced as these people's . . . and the Senate don't speak Alfen.*

We should count ourselves lucky they can speak at all, Gelert said. *These people may not be speaking any language we can understand, but at least they dress better than the Senate.*

Lee was inclined to agree, but wondered if perhaps they

were doing it in self-defense. The building itself came of a period in Alfen architecture that had favored not only huge arched and domed spaces, but a luxury in materials and execution that would have made some parts of the Vatican, or for that matter the palace of the Dragon Emperor of Xaihon, look like a thatched hut by comparison. Elaborate frescoes and hangings adorned every wall of the long hallway that brought them under the central dome where the *Miraha* sat; delicate and impossibly complex mosaics and enamel-inlaid tilings covered the floors; detailings, carvings, and ornamentation in fairy gold were everywhere. Whole pillars made of semiprecious stone, especially a blue agate lined with green, had been inlaid with tiny gems that winked and glittered in the torchlight as one walked by—for the committee had actually been led into the vast space by Alfen women dressed all in black, wearing crowns and collars of black gems and bearing genuine torches. Gelert had muttered down his implant about not knowing whether they were destined for a barbecue or an *auto-da-fé,* and Lee had to restrain herself from poking him.

In the central hall they had been conducted into the middle of the *Miraha,* under the great painted dome, and nearly blinded by the shifting glitter of still more fairy gold and jewels on the lawmakers gathered there, either woven into their ceremonial garb—the Alfen short-cloak and trews or half-gown here augmented with dagged and slashed sleeves, and quilted or cross-gartered with even more fairy gold, in tissue—or worn as great chains of office, massive, many-linked. Lee had felt positively underdressed in her plain lanthanomancer's black and the simple chain of her rank.

But at least we get to sit down, she had thought. Chairs had been placed for the committee in the very center of the space. The eighty members of the *Miraha* did not sit, but stood. There was only one chair, off to one side, of plain black wood and very simply design, uncushioned, with a tall back on which was carved a more ornate version of the *Miraha's* sigil, the hexagon and the spear.

Gelert, sitting down beside Lee, had looked around with amusement at the standing arrangements. *Maybe this is intended to keep the speeches shorter,* he said. But the hope had proved vain. The speeches—when a given speaker deigned to speak in English—said a great deal about mutual respect, and the necessity for peoples to listen to one another, and much else. But looking at the faces of the speakers, and not even trying particularly hard to See, Lee thought she had never heard so much lying in her life. The atmosphere of resentment was overwhelming.

Gelert's nose nearly never stopped twitching. *They hate our guts,* he said. *Someone up high, and I'm betting it's the Elf-king, told them to have us here and like it. And they've managed the first part . . . but not the second.*

And we have to go to a party with these people later? Lee said. *That sounds like all kinds of fun . . .*

Protocol, Lee.

I'd rather work, she said. Here in the midst of all this privilege and power, the heart of Alfheim's wealth and influence, and amid all these people who despite their young faces had the eyes of old and wicked politicians, every one—she could not stop seeing the face of Omren dil'Sorden, dead too young without even really knowing why.

You're doing your work, Gelert said. *You're getting up their noses, by being a human at the heart of their world. And tomorrow you'll have your chance to get farther up their noses still . . . so just hang on.*

She didn't answer; she knew he was right. Eventually it was all over, and first Per and then the rest of the committee greeted the *Miraha's* speaker, a solemn man with the dignity of some ancient Roman statue and the perfect face of a supermodel, high-cheekboned, dark-eyed, lean, and graceful. Lee smiled at him and spoke to him courteously, and moved on a trifle more quickly than she might have in other circumstances . . . even at an Ellay City Council meeting. *I'm beginning to lose it,* she said to Gelert, as their group was led out once more, back to the residence tower, by the women in black with the torches. *I'm starting to really dislike these people, and I can't afford to do that.*

It's your blood sugar, Gelert said. *It's been a long time since breakfast.*

I hope you're right. Otherwise, I'm not going to do poor Omren dil'Sorden any good. Or anyone else . . .

That evening they were feted as royally as they had not been on their arrival in Alfheim. *That by itself was an issue that interested me,* Gelert said as he got himself ready for the gathering. *I was wondering when they were going to start treating us more like official guests of the government and less like a cut-rate package tour.*

Lee nodded idly. She was feeling much better—the cold collation and wine that the staff had brought up for them after the *Miraha* session had taken care of her hunger and her somewhat frayed temper—and now she was brushing down her dress for the reception. It was at least the third time on this trip that she'd had to brush it down, since even though she might be worlds away from them, somehow everything black Lee owned managed to pick up white fur from Gelert's kids. *Not sure how you mean,* she said, picking off some of the more resistant fluff between her fingers.

Think about it. One day they import us from JFK and dump us in a Hilton, and we don't see anybody higher-ranking than a few accountants and the fragrant dil'Hemrev from Alfen External Affairs. Then something happens, somebody in the Miraha *sends a shuttle for us, and now all the upper-ups are coming out of the woodwork to make nice on us. Has there been a 'palace coup' of some kind? Does ExAff have a new boss all of a sudden, one who's more kindly disposed to us? Or, regardless of what dil'Hemrev told us, did the Elf-king perhaps get back from some trip, decide the high-profile UN committee isn't getting high-profile-enough treatment, and kick some of the civil servants' butts upstairs, or down?*

Lee thought about that for a moment. It seemed as possible as anything else. Then, *"Fragrant"?* Lee said.

Gelert blinked at her, then grinned. *Irony. Probably I should have said "redolent," as in "she stinks."*

Not literally, Lee said. *At least not that I noticed . . .*

It's not just her perfume, Gelert said. *That woman's up to something.*

There we're in agreement. I just wish I knew what. This protection thing . . . I can't tell whether she's for or against the idea of someone sneaking up on us some night and putting a knife in me. But she seems eager not to have LAPD blame the Alfen for it.

Well, we'll find out, Gelert said. *Especially since an acreage like this is going to be difficult to secure at night. And our magic balcony door there . . . is it any better at keeping people out than it is at keeping us in?*

Another happy thought, Lee said. *Thank you so much.*

Gelert looked at Lee with some amusement as she slipped the dress on over her head. "You missed some fur on the back . . ."

Lee groaned and slipped it off again. "Why didn't you say so before?"

"You've got hours yet to get it clean," Gelert said. Then, naturally, came the knock on the door. "Oops, I tell a lie."

"They keep doing that!" Lee muttered. "Are all their clocks running fast? I haven't finished my makeup yet!"

She dashed into her own bathroom. *Though I don't know why I bother,* she thought, dealing with her makeup at the highest speed consonant with keeping it in the right places on her face. *The way all of them look, I could go in and have everything about me redone but my sensibilities, and it still wouldn't matter in the slightest; by comparison, I'd still look like an unmade bed.* She sighed. *Still, you have to let people see that you're trying . . .*

Five minutes or so later Lee was in order, and she and Gelert met their escort at the door again. When they got downstairs to the entrance of the residence tower, this time there were no women with torches, but just Isif dil'Hemrev again, much more formally dressed than they'd seen her so far, in a long deep-cut gown of a truly striking blue that exactly caught both the color of her eyes and of the sapphires wound into her hair.

Chatting casually with Per and the others, dil'Hemrev led them about a five minutes' walk from the residence tower to a smaller building that stood in the shadow of the *Miraha's* great hall. "The Laurin's banqueting hall," dil'Hemrev said, and stood aside to let the committee members walk in past her through great bronze doors laid open.

They came into a space far more humane and intimate than the *Miraha's* hall, though this one wasn't precisely small either. It was a long room with a barrel-vaulted ceiling some thirty meters high, all painted with the clouds of a sky at sunset. Tall windows ran down either side of the room, letting in the afternoon light, and a single great table ran right down the room's length, big enough to seat at least a hundred for a formal banquet. It was set as a buffet, though, and positively groaned with food and drink. At the sight of it, Gelert's stomach made an alarming noise.

Lee couldn't help but smile slightly. "I thought you just ate," she said.

"My stomach is having second thoughts," Gelert said. "Look at that salmon!"

There were already perhaps fifty Alfen in the room, but for the moment they were all hanging back as if waiting for something. Lee found out what when, from behind them, someone came whose approach made the small crowd part to right and left. Through the space they made came a small Alfen woman, silver-haired, slight-boned and delicate—something of a surprise at first glance, for Lee had gotten used to Alfen being on the tall side.

Whatever soft talk had been going on among the Alfen until now ceased completely. "Our guests," the woman said, "I welcome you to Alfheim, and to Aien Mhariseth, the Laurin's city. My name is Dierrich dil'Estenv. I am the mrin-Lauvrin, the Laurin's chief deputy; some people might call me the Elf-king's grand vizier."

There were some chuckles about that. "The Laurin is not presently in residence," dil'Estenv said, "being abroad on business; but I'm glad to do service for him in his place. I welcome you all to our hearth; may your own service to your own peoples prosper!"

The committee applauded her politely enough, and Per then made, apparently extemporaneously, a very gracious thank-you speech that confirmed to Lee why he'd been sent along on this mission—not just as a former law inducement officer and a present-day politician, but one of those who makes the work of diplomacy look easy even at uncomfortable times. At the end of it, dil'Estenv took Per's hand, much to his surprise, and bowed over it; then led him up to the nearest table, poured them both a glass of white wine out of a glass ewer that stood there, and pledged him. They both drank.

This seemed to be a signal for the Alfen equivalent of the catering staff to start making their rounds, and the Alfen who had been invited, members of the *Miraha* and of other government agencies, began to mingle. Shortly Lee found herself standing with a cup of wine in one hand and the third or fourth of several choice finger-food dainties in the other, talking art history to a red-haired Alfen "senator" who had commented in passing on the carved design of the cup.

Lee was rather astonished at how different the tone of the proceedings was from the session in the *Miraha*. *It's almost as if someone told them to cut it out*... And she was even more astonished when, as she and the senator, Lasme, had just gotten into some of the juicier details about recent discoveries in Earth pre-Columbian art, she saw someone come up beside her, turned to see who it was, and saw dil'Estenv there.

"Don't stop for me!" the mrinLauvrin said, amused; and Lasme laughed and went on about the differences between Aztec and Huichtilopochtlin terra-cotta for some minutes more, before realizing that his glass was empty and going to get a refill.

"I had no idea you were interested in art history, madam," Lee said.

"Art, perhaps less," dil'Estenv said. "History . . . rather more." She looked at Lee with an expression that had some regret in it. "We've been dealing with the fruits of that for some days, now, in ways that none of us might have expected even a few months ago. Our history with humans, with others . . ." That regret gathered to itself just an edge of a smile. "But maybe it's been delayed too long."

"To do something about that history now," Lee said, "especially about the histories of the Alfen who've been murdered in the past few years, too many of them . . . that's what matters now, madam."

"Dierrich, please," dil'Estenv said. "No one uses titles or house-names over wine. In that house over there"—she gestured with her head toward the *Miraha*—"things may be different . . ."

"They certainly felt that way today," Gelert said.

Dil'Estenv shook her head slightly. "Alfen can be very conservative," she said softly, "and for those of us who're a little less so—like my master—that place can be a difficult one to work. But one has to take it at its own value, and work through channels, slowly. When you live as long as my people do, there's no use getting the lawmakers angry; they stay that way for such a very long time . . ."

Her look was wry. Lee couldn't help but smile. "As for your specific investigation," dil'Estenv said, "my master has expressly required that you be given whatever you ask for in terms of data regarding outworld homicides. All of that would normally be held by the Bureau of External Affairs, which, as you might imagine, is most eager to keep the information right where it is. But they must obey the Laurin no less than I . . . so if they give you any trouble, let me know."

"And has there been trouble, madam—Dierrich?" Gelert said, noting her expression, jocularly warning.

Dierrich allowed herself only the slightest smile. "When has an intelligence organization ever wholeheartedly cooperated with orders to give up its hard-won data?" she said. "Oh, there've been some small ructions, disagreements over protocol and precedence . . . but nothing that should now interfere with your work. If there is any further interference, contact my office. Our interest is in having your work here go smoothly and with speed."

They talked for a little while more before Dierrich moved on, making her rounds of the committee. Lee found herself impressed by the woman. She was no less beautiful than any of the rest of the Alfen, but in her case that beauty was tempered by something else—a sense of mind, of thoughtfulness, and of power contained; and small as she was, the way she bore herself made her seem taller than those around her. Lee was reminded strongly of what she had almost-Seen in the Elf-king, that night in the restaurant, and found herself suddenly able to understand why this woman would have risen to the post of his second-in-command. There was a kinship of their styles of power; a weapon, but one kept in reserve.

Lee looked after her when she finally moved off to go talk to Mellie Hopkins and a couple of the others. "A very nice lady," Gelert said. *Unusually so for an Alfen.*

That's not what I'm thinking about at the moment, Lee said. *That woman's the local equivalent of the Young Emperor of the Xainese, or the UN SecGen. I wonder where her security is?*

Where it doesn't show, most likely. Even our own people know how to be discreet at events like this.

Lee nodded. *I suppose . . .* she said. *It's just that our blue-eyed dil'Hemrev and her "concerns" about my safety are still on my mind. Just because ExAff seems to have had its wrist slapped doesn't relieve me entirely. And when we get up into the "rose garden" tomorrow, or whenever . . . that concerns me a little, too.*

Well, we'll be together, Gelert said. *For the garden, anyway. For the data, you don't need me; you can savage ExAff yourself, after what Madam Dierrich there says. And,* he said, grinning, as he turned away toward the buffet table, *you can find out whether she's really to be trusted . . .*

Ten

The next morning, after breakfast, the committee met informally for an hour or so to coordinate details about who they would be meeting for the next couple of days, and to discuss their findings so far. The scheduling part of the meeting went well enough, but as for the rest of it, Lee thought to herself as she and the others prepared to leave that she had never heard so much doubletalk and obfuscation in one place in her life. Everyone on the committee was certain that they were being even more closely watched and listened to than they had been in Ys, and everyone was intent on giving absolutely nothing away to the listeners. As she got up, Lee hoped it was as frustrating for them as it was for her.

Gelert was shouldering into his doggie pack as Lee glanced over at him. "So you finally get to do the Homicide end of things," he said. "I envy you, but I'm still stuck with the numbers team . . ."

Don't envy me too quickly, Lee said. *It remains to be seen if ExAff is going to be as cooperative as dil'Estenv thinks they are.*

Gelert grinned. *Should be interesting.*

"But don't worry," Lee said. "I'll be recording everything for analysis; you'll have plenty of time to look it all over later."

"Right. See you for lunch?"

"I don't know."

"Well, you have the commcode of the offices they've assigned us over at the Exchequer; call me there if you need a break."

"Right."

𝒪𝓋

ExAff's buildings turned out to be unusually beautiful ones, built more or less in the shadow of the Laurins' House, at the edge of the city closest to the bottom of the rising ground that led up to the cliffs. That whole area had been turned into a sort of vast, naturalized rockery, planted with rhododendron, hardy alpines, and other trees and plants native to the area. The effect produced was of a natural landscape that had laid itself out in an unusually ordered manner, masses and colors balanced, but not so balanced or arranged that an observer immediately assumed the hand of man rather than nature. Against this varied tapestry, the ExAff buildings reared up, a set of six smaller towers connected by a low wall, containing a formal garden surrounding a central plaza, and in the middle of the plaza, one sharp short tower, almost pyramidal, like the point of a spear thrusting up out of the green grass.

In one of the smaller towers, Lee was not surprised at all to be met by Isif dil'Hemrev, back in uniform again and sporting an attitude that even for an Alfen, Lee could only characterize as chastened. Dil'Hemrev greeted her most cordially, led Lee to a large airy office with a view down onto the central plaza, furnished with a commwall three times the size of Lee's own and a state-of-the-art WilNo data retrieval and storage system. "Obedient to the mrinLauvrin's desires," dil'Hemrev said—*and was that the slightest hint of gritted teeth?* Lee wondered, "we've given you our entire 'untoward mortality' database. If you have any questions about how the data's been sorted, or you have any desire to look at physical evidence supporting the individual cases, you have only to ask for me or for my assistant, Weilin; you can comm her, or her office is that third one down the corridor. She'll be holding herself ready for you all today should you need her."

"Thank you," Lee said. "I appreciate it very much."

Dil'Hemrev went off, and for a moment or so Lee just stood there in the middle of the room, looking at the commwall and savoring the moment. She actually grinned. *About this, at least, Matt was right,* she thought. *This was worth coming for.* She sat down at the desk, where even the chair was comfortable, and got to work.

Two hours or so later, though, Lee wasn't so happy anymore, and by lunchtime, she was less happy still. The database the Alfen had assembled for her contained literally hundreds of cases, dating back some twenty years, a huge mass of data Lee spent the initial hour or so sorting in various ways to examine the cases for any correlations that would spring out quickly. The problem, as she discovered fairly quickly, was that the forensics in all these cases were "dry"; they came without any analysis of the events, at least none that Lee could find. At first she thought perhaps this was simply because she hadn't dug deep enough, or had scanned the data using insufficiently specific concepts or keywords. But as hour added itself to hour, it became plain to Lee that if analysis had been done at all, it hadn't been included in the material she'd been given. What she had here was the equivalent of about twenty years' worth of "cold cases," some of them right down in the bottom of the deep freeze, as coldness went. And while the forensic data seemed complete enough on the surface, if Lee or anyone else had wanted to actually go to any of the scenes and look for further data, so much time had passed on nearly all of them that there was now next to no hope of finding anything else useful, no matter how skillful the physical or psychoforensicist might be.

So they've left me with a huge mass of information, but no conclusions drawn about it by their own people, Lee thought. *And the majority of the cases otherwise so old that, though bureaucratically they're "cold," the reality of it is that they're closed without resolution or even final assessment. This does not exactly strike me as 'cooperation.'* She leaned back in her chair and looked at the big commwall, on which the list of pertinent files, hundreds of them, stared back at her. *Unless I'm coming at this from the wrong direction and missing some kind of cultural difference that's obvious to them and not to me. After all, why would Alfen necessarily perceive the crime the same way we do? And we're not always perfect in the way we classify murder, either.* She thought briefly of one police force in a neighboring state, some years back, which without a second thought had for many years classified people murdered in its jurisdiction as "male victim," "female victim," and "prostitute." *Is it possible that Alfen who're murdered become "non-people" in some way?*

Or am I just giving them too much benefit of the doubt, and is this just straightforward obfuscation?

She made a wry face. *Too soon to tell. Let's break for lunch.*

Lee spent a little while working out how to direct the local computer system to dump all the murder files to her pad; and while it was doing that, said to the commwall,

"Call Gelert reh'Mechren, please; a temporary code at the Exchequer."

A few seconds later Gelert glanced up at her from a low table where his own pad and some printouts and other documentation were lying. "Thought I might hear from you around now," he said. "The tourist board left a message with me for you."

"The tourist board?" Lee said. "They actually *have* one? Must be the quietest office in town."

Gelert grinned, an expression that suggested he shared her opinion, but wasn't going to say so in the clear. "Tomorrow afternoon, if the weather's good, they'll send someone around to show us the way up to the 'Rose Garden.' Seems there are some nice rock formations up there. Did you bring hiking shoes?"

"I've got some cross-trainers that'll do all right."

"Fine. The guy will stop by the residence tower at fourteen or so. Ready for lunch now?"

"Extremely. I'll see you back there shortly."

The wall flicked back to the file view. Lee killed her pad's connection to it, packed it up, and spent a few moments looking, not at the commwall, but at the view of the mountain wall behind the building. She'd spent the whole morning with her back turned to it on purpose, for even viewed sidelong, the rugged splendor of it drew her to spend minutes on end gazing at it. It was as if it had a message for her, one it was being prevented from communicating. Now, just for a few minutes, she bent her attention on the mountain and called for the Sight.

It wouldn't come.

Lee nodded, just slightly. Something was specifically blocking her. *All right,* she thought as she got up and headed for the door. *Fine. We'll see what happens tomorrow . . .*

She spent the rest of that afternoon, and all the morning of the next day, right through noontime, sifting through the Alfen homicidal mortality data for any sign that she was missing something obvious. If she was going to go knocking on Dierrich dil'Estenv's door with accusations of continued non-cooperation by ExAff, she wanted to be very sure she was in the right before she did it. But all her work left her exactly where she'd been the previous day—still lacking any trace in the record of any local analysis of the murders. *It's as if they wanted to ignore them,* she thought, pushing back from her desk around thirteen. *Is the very con-* cept *that an Elf can be murdered somehow embarrassing to them, I wonder? If it is, maybe dil'Estenv can suggest another tack I might take to get what I need.*

She headed back to the residence tower under a perfectly cloudless sky. The weather here seemed to get settled, the way it did at home in LA, and stay fair and surprisingly warm for prolonged periods in the summer; the way it had been behaving, it was hard to believe that this was still an alpine landscape, and would be deep in snow come January, *But I have a feeling we're unlikely to see ski season here,* she thought as she climbed the tower stairs toward her and Gelert's room. *Or the far side of next week, for that matter.* She'd managed a few quiet words with Sal in the midst of the clatter and stir of the group's buffet breakfast that morning—just long enough for him to tell her what she'd been afraid of: "Their new books are clean, Lee. We're going to have to go home empty-handed, unless . . ."

Unless. She went in and had a quick lunch with Gelert, and it was just as well it was quick, for she'd hardly had time to change and finish the hasty sandwich she'd thrown together at the sideboard before someone knocked at the door. Gelert went to speak it open.

There stood a tall, fair, freckled, somewhat sunburnt Alfen in casual climbing clothes, shorts, and a short-sleeved tunic and jacket, and high socks and climbing boots. He looked like any weekend hiker—except that the weekend hikers with whom Lee was acquainted rarely looked so much as if Michelangelo had carved them. "I'm Earmen dil'Undevhain," the Alfen said. "I am told you are interested in climbing up to Istelin'ru Semivh this afternoon?"

He doesn't even have knobby knees, Lee thought. *It's just not fair.* "That's right," Lee said.

"We should get started, then," dil'Undevhain said. "It is somewhat late already; but we have just enough time to get up there and back before dark."

"Two minutes," Lee said, and went to get her jacket. *Interesting,* she said privately to Gelert. *This is the first Alfen I've heard since we got here, except in the* Miraha, *who isn't perfectly fluent in English. Can it be that for a change we're meeting someone who isn't associated with one of the Alfen security services . . . ?*

It'd make an interesting change, Gelert said. *Meanwhile at least we get a nice afternoon out in the air. But Lee—*

Hmm?

Stay away from the edges of cliffs. You never can tell . . .

The walk up to Istelin'ru Semivh—if it could be called that, when it was eighty percent a climb up a thirty-percent incline—took nearly two hours. Dil'Undevhain was a pleasant enough guide, talking with apparent pleasure about the terrain, the plant and animal life, and the views. But he set a pace that Lee had some trouble matching, even though she often enough went hiking in the Angeles National Forest in her spare time. *Damned if I'm going to let him see that I'm having trouble, though,* she thought.

Their path took them eastward around the foot of the mountain wall that loomed behind Aien Mhariseth, over a small rubble-strewn yoke between it and a lesser peak farther east, then diagonally up the mountain's southern face. "Not a tall mountain," dil'Undevhain said; "only eight hundred meters. But the view near the summit is quite wonderful."

It had better be, Gelert said silently. *My paws are going to be in shreds after this.* Lee felt for him, for the scree that had tumbled down the mountain to define most of the paths they used when not climbing on or over raw rock was all that harsh dolomite limestone, white or pale gray, sharp-edged, and abrasive as sandpaper. The path wound back and forth across the mountain's south face a few times, sheltered from the sheer drop by huge scatters of boulders or up-standing, incompletely eroded piers of limestone, like sta-lagmites. There was little to see here but pale, shattered stone, in chunks of every size, and occasional gnarled, stunted arolla pines or small patches of the local alpines, mostly in flower at this season. Over everything, the steepled towers of the mountain reared up, hard and white against the afternoon blue, the forced perspective of the view from the path making them look even more forbidding than they were to start with.

There was one last switchback where the path gained nearly twenty meters in a final steep climb. Lee had to go from handhold to handhold up it, and was privately surprised that no one had sunk in pitons or a helping rail in such a difficult spot. *But maybe Alfen have rules against it or something, if this is a conservation area,* she thought, going up the last couple of meters as fast as she could, to avoid slipping down out of control. She came out on top gasping a little, despite her best intentions; dil'Undevhain stood waiting there, seemingly without a hair on him mussed and not even slightly out of breath.

He waved a hand in front of him as Gelert came scrambling up behind Lee. "And this is it," he said. "Istelin'ru Semivh."

Lee looked around. The place where they had stopped was little more than a twenty-meter-wide terrace against the mountainside, all strewn with rubble like everything else. Some more of those strange piers of raw limestone stuck up here too, like fossilized Christmas trees, some cracked by the contrasts of heat and cold, or shattered by the fall of stone cracked away from the mountain wall above. Their feet were buried in gray-white gravel and scree; thin, light-colored scrubby grass stuck out here and there in tufts. "And this is all there is . . ." Lee said, looking around.

"But certainly this view is enough," dil'Undevhain said.

It was hard to argue with that. The southern view, reaching down toward what would have been the kingdoms of the Italies in her own world, was a thorny vista of major and minor peaks, snow-free at this time of year, but still blinding white in the full sun. Lee walked a little way down to the far end of the terrace, where the view looked more eastward. There the mountains gave way more quickly to a view of low gray granite hills, the shadows of the westering sun already drowning some of the valleys between and behind them. She stood there, breathing the air, feeling the edge of chill that was beginning to come to it already, though the afternoon still had a ways to go.

" 'Istelin'ru Semivh,' you said. What's the name mean?" Gelert said.

Dil'Undevhain looked somewhat perplexed at that. "I am not sure how to translate it," he said, looking downslope.

" 'Last stop? Last hope?' It is the only flat ground between here and the summit, the last place you can rest before the big climb. Or the only thing that will stop you between here and the valley, if you fall down from the traverse above."

Lee nodded. "Not much growing here," she said, walking toward the back of the terrace, where the gravel was piled feet deep against the upward-leaping wall of the mountain. There were some patches of alpenrose there, some rooted in the gravel, some actually rooted opportunistically in cracks in the vertical wall, their branches and pink-red flowers dangling down and moving slightly in the wind.

"No," dil'Undevhain said, "except in the stories. Indeed in your world—it is Earth, I think?—this mountain is actually called the Rose Garden in one or another of the local languages. But that story keeps appearing in all kinds of shapes in the outworlds. There's a king of the people who live in the mountains, or under the mountains, and he falls in love with a mortal woman—" Her guide laughed gently at the ridiculousness of it. *Mixed marriage,* Lee's memory said to her: *it'll never work.* At the time, she had meant it as a joke. Here and now, her Alfen guide did, too, but for entirely different reasons, ones Lee suspected she probably wouldn't like. "He steals her away, and makes a great house for her in the mountains, and rears a crystal dome above it all. Then around the house, to please her, the King plants the garden of wonderful roses, and forbids all mortals to come there."

"But they come anyway," Gelert said, "and destroy the garden. Then, powerful as he is, they take the mountain king prisoner and haul him off in chains."

Lee looked sideways at Gelert. *Don't rub it in or anything, Gel . . .*

I'm not sure I like his tone. And I don't care if he knows it.

His hostility took Lee slightly by surprise. Dil'Undevhain looked at Gelert with entirely uncaring amusement. "Fortunately," he said, "it *is* just a story."

"With a happy ending, as I remember," Lee said, trying to sound idle. "The trouble between the King and the humans ends, finally, and the princess agrees to marry him. And becomes immortal as well."

Dil'Undevhain laughed again, more softly this time; but the message behind the laughter was the same, a marginally courteous indulgence of another's absurd idea. Lee turned away and bent down to one of the scrubby little bushes growing up from the gravel, knelt down on one knee to see if the flowers had a fragrance. They did, but it was most understated, a slight, spicy, heathery smell, almost piny; the scent of a plant that has no leisure to spend more than a minimum of its energy on fragrance, trusting its color to be enough to entice the mountain bees and flies in so monochrome a landscape. "I suppose," Lee said, "there would be no way for anyone, realistically, to plant a rose garden up here . . ." For some reason, having to admit it saddened her a little.

"I'm afraid the climate is much too variable for that," said dil'Undevhain. "And the temperatures here drop much too low, even in the spring and fall. Snow can come any time between September and June."

"That wouldn't be good for roses," Lee said, "no. And the soil's not great, either . . ." She ran her hand over the scree under the alpenrose. No soil there at all; a harsh gravelly bedding, this, though some of the stones had been slightly rounded by many years' flow of water down the steep mountainside. Lee idly picked up one round, pale pebble, rubbing it in her fingers, feeling the weight of it.

Then she bit her lip to keep from exclaiming in pain, for what she held was not smooth. It was razory sharp to the touch, as if newly shattered from the limestone crags above. Lee dared the slightest sideways glance, saw that dil'Undevhain's back was turned. She got up, dusting her pants off with one hand, slipping the stone unseen into her pocket with the other.

Dil'Undevhain had been looking at the angle of the sun. Now he turned and said, "Probably we should start back, soon, if we're to return before dark."

"Of course," Lee said, and followed dil'Undevhain as he started toward the path again. For a moment she paused, looked up at the mountain, willed the Sight to come, just for a second.

Nothing . . . or at least, nothing in the usual mode. As if at the edges of perception, at some half-visible periphery, an aura of trouble hovered; old anguish, unresolved, lurking under the surface of things—a stain of pain, like a bruise. *But otherwise, I'm blocked,* Lee thought. *And why?*

There were no answers for that. *So why should I give any credence to* anything *I'm being told?* Lee thought. She couldn't get rid of the idea that she was being lied to; in words, and somehow, even in images. Witnesses and defendants lied to her all the time, at home; but usually she was competent to detect it. Here, though, the rules seemed to have been changed.

Seemed to . . .

Their guide was heading down the path. As he turned back to see if Lee and Gelert were following, Lee was ready, and she bent her vision on him with all possible intent, willing the judicial state to assert itself in full, in haste, like a dropped rock.

On him, ever so briefly, it worked, at least as far as communicating his uppermost thought. Dil'Undevhain's eyes said it clearly enough to hers as she met them: *There's nothing here for you to steal. Do you finally believe it now? Then go back to your people and be glad you're not dangerous enough to worry us.*

Lee kept her face as still as she would have in any interviewing room, and went after dil'Undevhain, gazing around at the landscape as she came, like any tourist inwardly saying farewell to a place she wouldn't see again. But her mind was busy with other matters. Dil'Undevhain's look was a lie, just one more of many. *He's ExAff after all,* Lee thought. And the Alfen *were* worried about her and Gelert, worried enough to try to "defuse" them by bringing them up here. *There's something they're afraid we'll find out, so much that they want us to discount it ourselves.* And as for the landscape around them . . . Lee thought of legends left over from the old days, before people actually began normalized travel between the worlds—stories of Elves giving people gold that turned to withered leaves, or turning one object into another with an ease that suggested that the matter and the physical reality of Earth were effortlessly malleable for them. *Could that ability to shift appearances, even to shift the genuine states of matter, actually be sourced in something they learned from being resident in this universe?* She thought again of the buildings in Ys, that looked one way and felt another; she thought of the mountains that had been there . . . until they weren't. She was still blocked . . . but not entirely. Something had changed.

Quietly she went down the path behind dil'Undevhain, trying to look like someone who'd had a long, tiring climb that had been a waste of her time . . . but not like someone who was busily laying plans.

The day had been tiring, but not so much so that Lee felt at all inclined to sleep, even when it got late; even when

Gelert turned in, yawning, around eleven. She made some concession to appearances by going around her side of the suite and the central sitting area and speaking out all the lights, except for one in her own bedroom; she left that door open, so that the faint light of the globe by the bed, dimmed right down, streamed out the door into the sitting area. There, in the near-dark, Lee sat in one of the massive chairs, with her back to the wall and her eye on the terrace "door" at the other end of the room. A cool summer wind was now coming in that door, stirring the thin curtains that hung to either side. From out in the city, very faint lights washed up onto the terrace, along with a much fainter, more silver light, the Moon coming up on the far side of the mountains to the east.

Lee glanced at her ring, saw that it was nearly one-thirty. Her other hand was in her pocket, where it had been for a long time, touching the stone that didn't feel the way it looked. It was immediate, concrete evidence of the glamour she'd suspected, one of unusual power—far stronger than the one they had been subjected to in Ys. *How are they powering it?* Lee thought, turning the little stone over in her pocket, feeling its sharp edges. She was afraid to bring it out, afraid of what seeing and listening devices might be planted here. But she didn't really need to take it out. She knew perfectly well what the contrast between vision and touch had shown her on the mountainside. And within seconds of her touching it, the glamourie had begun to fray.

Lee gave the terrace door one last mistrustful look . . . then sighed. It seemed to let outside air in, or not, as it pleased; possibly it was simply the local take on air-conditioning. *Or something else* . . . But there was no point in worrying about it; she had other things to do.

She settled herself comfortably in the chair, closed her eyes, and shut out everything around her. *Assuming that this whole room is full of surveillance devices,* she thought, *they may be able to see everything I do physically in here. But they can't see what I See.* She smiled slightly in the dark. *And that uncertainty drives them crazy. It accounts for dil'Hemrev's unusual interest, for the attempt to stick me with a bodyguard here... for dil'Undevhain's little performance today. Well, let's see if this little rock and I can give them one more thing to be uncertain about.*

Lee spent an indeterminate time in the setup meditation that she used when Seeing as much as possible in a short time was particularly crucial. *The stone makes a difference,* she thought, *though since I don't know why or how it does that, better not to count on it for too much...* When she thought she was ready, she said silently, *Lady whom I serve, help me See truly...* And she opened her eyes.

It took a little while to see anything at all; in judicial mode or not, acclimatizing the eyes to darkness took a little while. But almost immediately Lee realized that there was a lot less darkness around than she'd been counting on. Without moving her head, she looked sideways.

And she Saw that the tower walls were glass. Perhaps not physically glass, but nonetheless transparent to the several Alfen who sat or stood outside them, outside what should have been solid stone hung with tapestries, looking in. One of the Alfen, gazing through the "stone wall" to one side of the door to the suite, was looking straight at her. Lee dared not look directly at him at the moment; he would realize that she was Seeing him. *Play it blind,* Lee thought.

She got up, stretched, yawned, went into her bedroom. There, too, the "walls" were glass, and beyond them, more rooms stretched, many empty this time of night, but some few with Alfen sitting in them, looking at commwalls or other types of large display. The whole "residence tower" was an illusion, simply a space enclosed inside a larger building. *More of ExAff,* Lee wondered, *or some other organization? The Department of Major Violations of Privacy, perhaps?* . . . Idly she turned back the covers on the bed, then headed for the bathroom.

Its far wall was "glass" too, and as Lee spoke the light on and looked at herself in the mirror, sure enough, a male Alfen slipped into view on the far side of the nonexistent wall, watching. Lee didn't react by so much as a flicker. She took a glass from the shelves by the sink, ran some water, filled the glass and took it out into the bedroom with her, speaking the light off again. The far wall there, which should have been tapestries and stone, was now a series of small and large cubicles. Another Alfen was standing there, watching her. Lee looked at him and past him as if he wasn't there, and walked out of the room again, into the sitting area.

The stone on either side of the massive door that supposedly led to the stairway was also "glass," and another Alfen shortly appeared there, looking at Lee as she sat down in the big chair again. Lee sat there ignoring him, sipping the water, concentrating on not becoming furious, on not doing anything that would break her Sight. *I should have been able to see this earlier,* Lee thought. *With or without the meditation. But something's happened. It can't* all *be just this little rock! Has someone out there slipped, or relaxed the intensity with which they're holding the illusion?*

She sat there for a little while more, sipping the water occasionally, and finally got up again and strolled slowly down the length of the room. At Gelert's door, still open, she looked in, and Saw that his walls, too, were glass. Away on the far side of his suite, near his own bathroom door, a bored-looking Alfen sat watching him as well, glancing up as he saw Lee in the doorway. Lee smiled, as if at Gelert, and went on down toward the terrace.

She brushed past the forcefield there and stood out on the

terrace, as if looking at the "mountains." *They really were a wonderful illusion,* she thought, seeing that here the "glass" revealed yet more offices. They were empty, though. No one was watching the terrace, which was simply a space jutting into one of those offices. *And why would they be?* Lee thought suddenly. *Gelert's asleep: there's nothing to eavesdrop on. I doubt anyone thinks I'm going to stand here talking to myself. And as for any movements I might make, if all I see is the illusion, then what am I going to do, walk off the "terrace" and go straight down five stories?*

But they don't know that I can *see something else—*

The moment decided her. Lee leaned sideways against the terrace railing, glancing casually back down the length of the sitting area, as if contemplating coming back in; then turned her regard halfway outward again, as if in the direction of the mountains. She had just enough peripheral vision of the "glass" at the other end of the room to see the Alfen watching her give her a glance, evaluating, and then move away out of sight, not believing she was likely to do anything much at the moment.

Lee swung one leg over the terrace railing, feeling under her. *Floor. It's real, all right.* She swung the other leg over, and stood there on what should have been empty air, but was actually rather prosaic office carpeting, dull blue in color.

Now what? she thought.

Well . . . first, don't get caught! Lee brought her implant up, made sure it was recording, and turned right around once to take quick stock of her surroundings. The place might have been any open-plan office between here and LA—doors in the far wall, and between those and Lee, numerous partitions, much off-the-rack office furniture, various free-standing commwalls and in-desk displays. *Which tell me nothing in particular—*

The implant was starting to make the same annoying

buzzing it had made in the hotel in Ys. *Oh, not now, of all the times for it to start malfunctioning again—!* Lee moved to get herself out of direct line of sight of the terrace, moving over to her right and crouching behind a desk-carrel in case someone should come in from outside the room. The buzzing was scaling up, and behind it Lee could just catch a quiet mutter of voices. Her first thought was to hold still for a few minutes and run one of the in-system diagnostics on it. *But I may not have a few minutes, or even a few moments. If that Elf who saw me go out doesn't see me come in pretty soon, someone may look harder at that terrace, and find me gone. I need to move right now, and find out what I can.*

She looked out cautiously from behind the desk carrel. There was still no sign of anyone, but she could still hear voices down the implant. *And besides . . . am I so sure this is a malfunction? Or is Alfheim the problem? The implant hasn't behaved this way anywhere but here.*

Lee cautiously skirted rightwards around the edge of the room, going from desk to filestack to desk again, using the cover; but no one came. The room had two sets of opaque doors, and near the rightmost one she thought that perhaps the sound of voices was a little louder. *All right,* she thought.

She slipped along the wall, closer to it. The door slid silently open. Lee froze, just beyond where the door's slide-track stopped, and listened. The voices were slightly clearer, tantalizingly close to being understandable.

Slowly she leaned forward and around the door, looking through it. A hallway. Lee held still and listened for as long as she dared, as afraid of being too cautious as of not being cautious enough. But it was curiosity driving her more than fear, now. She put her head out into the hall, looked up and down. Nothing. Blue carpet, beige walls, concealed light fixtures casting a subdued late-night glow over everything. And the voices, definitely down the hall to the right.

Nowhere to hide if someone comes along, now, she thought. There were no doors between here and where this hallway ended, about twenty meters down to the right, in a T-junction.

Lee swallowed and went down the hall, softly but quickly, keeping to the right-hand wall. The voices got a little louder. Just shy of the T-junction, Lee stopped, closed her eyes, listened. *Which way's louder?*

"—the UN won't—" More muttering. "—committee, it's just terrible timing—"

"—won't help them anyway, and they were crazy to think it would. Everything's too well hidden—"

To the left, Lee thought. She went down the hall in that direction. It had few other doorways, and ended in another T-junction; but about twenty meters down to the left, she saw another corridor she could duck into in a hurry if she had to. *Even if I get caught right this minute,* Lee thought, *I've got something interesting to show the UN when I get home. That the investigative committee was told they were being placed in secure 'diplomatic' housing, and instead were shoved into the middle of an Alfen government building and kept under extremely invasive surveillance the whole time. That their hosts claimed to be cooperating and telling them the truth, while actually lying to them most comprehensively, at every level including that of mere physical reality—*

She went down the left side of the hallway, softly, but as quickly as she could, listening hard. "—matter to us," said one of the voices, male. "Their own intelligence services are in it as deep as the supranationals are. Not that they've been able to find out much that helps them. ExAff's been busy enough in that regard."

"Possibly the only good thing about this mess. It should

be a long time before any Alfen with half a brain agrees to become a double agent."

"It's the ones without brains that I'm concerned about. The 'loyal' ones; or the ones with what the ephemerals have brainwashed them into thinking is a social conscience—"

Something occurred to Lee forcefully enough to make her stand still for a second. *How is it I can understand these people?* she thought. *If they're Alfen, why are they speaking English?*

Suddenly the sound faded to a mutter again. *Did they move?* Lee thought, frustrated. *I want to hear!*

"—wasting their time at the moment," said the second voice, a lighter one. The clarity of sound continued to increase, as if Lee was turning up the volume on her commwall at home. *Will,* she thought. *Will is enough.*

But why *is it enough?*

"—though their presidential race is turning out to be a welcome complication. Milelgua has told ExTel he'll sit still and do nothing, come the 'revolution,' if they help him now."

"Assuming even an ephemeral electorate is stupid enough to give him the job."

"It seems likely. But it doesn't matter. ExTel has paid him off, just as they've paid off all the other candidates—not that poor Milelgua knows. For our part, now we know clearly where he stands as regards our world interest—so we can start investigating the best way to get rid of him if he's elected. And meantime, the multis and supras are doing what they like to do best—spending money to get their way and planning their 'hostile takeover' of the Land. If that distracts them from discovering how completely we've infiltrated their operations, so much the better. They won't have a hint of what's going on until it's much too late for them, their little pocket armies, and their shareholders. We'll have plenty of time to sabotage them if they actually start moving on their plans. But we have much worse problems elsewhere."

"Yes. Where is he?"

"Huichtilopochtli. He's not rushing back; he knows his orders have been obeyed for the moment."

"It must have been an annoyance for you . . ."

Lee started to feel that she'd been standing in one place too long. She began to head up toward the T-junction. "Oh, not one I can't weather," said the lighter voice, sounding a little closer, a little stronger. "I've waited a long time. I can wait a little longer."

"Assuming that he lets you. He's always been too unpredictable. That's what's caused all this trouble to begin with. If he were dead—"

There was a silence. "It's an attractive idea, but not one we can entertain right now. It's always disastrous when the *Lauvrnhad* passes without the appropriate formalities being observed—"

Lee came to the junction, looked cautiously left and right. This corridor was darker, and looked as if it might bridge a space between this building and an older one; down to the left, the end of the corridor was a stone wall instead of plasterboard, and its lighting looked different. "If he's not dealt with according to the rules," said the second voice, "all the planning we've done will come to nothing."

Lee turned left and began quietly to slip down toward the end of the corridor, where the light was dimmer. The voices continued to get stronger. "Are you sure you're not being too careful?" the first one said. "Everything we are will be lost if he manages the madness he's planning. The nukes and invading armies he's contemplating would damage us less than what *he* wants to let loose."

"The care is necessary, Kil. Here we do have to be careful; the world makes the rules."

"The rules! I'd have thought your sensibilities would have rebelled at what 'the rules,' *his* reading of them anyway, made you do the other evening."

Laughter rang down the hallway, beautiful, silken, and bitter, and seeming so close that Lee stopped short—the sound seemed to come from just a couple of doors down. "I won't have to do him many more services of that kind, or any other. Soon enough he won't be an issue. And after that I'll be too busy with work to care about my last fifty years in the 'wilderness.' We'll be able to move against the multinationals and the allied nations before they can mobilize any serious attack."

Satisfaction filled that voice as Lee started to move again, more cautiously now, approaching the end of the hall, which she could see was an L-shaped intersection with another corridor in the older building. "It'll be our purpose they serve, not their own, in the end."

Lee took a long breath, kept on walking toward the end of the hall. "They're dangerous tools . . ."

"Oh, Kil, please! They're just ephemerals, and they're way out of their depth, for all their armies and bombs. They don't understand what a weapon a world can be, inside its own boundaries. But when they try to move against us, they'll find out. After that there'll be a lot of noise in the UN, but the pragmatists there will shut it up soon enough. The ephemerals know what they need to keep their civilization running, they know where it comes from, and they know who they have to deal with to get it. Everything will once again be as it was . . . except that our dear young amateur gardener will be out of his misery, assuming that's the world's pleasure. Which seems likely."

Lee's eyebrows went up as she came to the end of the hall

and peered around the corner, rightwards, toward the source of the voices. They had to be very close now. "When does he come back?"

"Two days from now. No one else knows: he notified my office privately this morning. He's expecting to catch dil'Hereth and his crowd at ExAff by surprise. I've no problem with him doing that; it leaves our people one less thing to worry about, at no cost to us. But immediately afterward, he deals with *me*."

The other voice now sounded alarmed. "You'll wait until the committee's gone, surely!"

"Why should I? What can they see or hear that we don't allow? No, as I said, the timing's too good to throw away. It'll happen right over their heads, and they'll never know. And those two pathetic keyhole-peepers they smuggled onto the committee—whether they've noticed anything or not, they'll go when the others do."

"Good riddance to all of them," the other voice said. "I heard from Tiri this morning; she said the accounting team went off in an absolute fury, trying to be polite, and muttering about needing more time." He laughed.

Lee's eyes narrowed in anger. *Careful,* she thought then, and clenched her fist on the stone in her pocket, turning it over and over to give her something to do besides be annoyed. "Oh, they can have it," said the woman's voice. "A few days' worth, at the very least. But then, regretfully, we send them home when it becomes plain that the circumstances require it, when the change of leadership comes. The obvious need to recall and re-instruct our ambassador to the UN, to renegotiate all present agreements, we're so sorry but we're sure the Security Council will understand—" She chuckled too. "How I'll enjoy dismantling the fool's work he's been about."

Lee stood there trying to contain her anger, and turning

and kneading the stone in her fingers, the way she kneaded pasta when she made it from scratch, to give her something to do while she was considering a problem. *Do I go forward, or back? What I've got on the implant right now is enough to make a lot of trouble for these people. But if I—*

In her fingers, the stone went soft, and squished like dough.

Lee gasped in terror and astonishment, and would have dropped it right on the floor if it had been out of her pocket. Even now she had to force herself to hold on to the stone; the feeling of what it was doing in her hand was bizarre. It was moving a little, squirming against her hand as if it was alive. *I wish it would cut that out—!*

It stopped.

Lee's eyes widened a little at that. *It's not just illusion they're working with here.* Things *here can be changed.*

And not just by them!

Lee gripped the stone in her fist harder. "—but he doesn't have the support he needs in the *Miraha*," the male voice was saying; "they've never trusted him—"

No matter how solid this reality seems, Lee thought, *it's not* that *solid. Others plainly perceive this malleability, too, as a commonplace: a truth. And the truth that others can perceive, I can See, no matter where I am or how others try to prevent it . . .* She took a long breath, preparing for the next experiment.

Two things happened then. "They won't have to trust him much longer," said the female voice, getting louder by the second. "Kil, I'm for my couch. Comm me in the morning; we have some things to work out." Away down the hall, near a wide archway of stone, Lee saw Dierrich dil'Estenv come out of another doorway, and saw her, without any fuss, seem simply to draw the air aside, and vanish through it and behind it, as if behind a curtain.

The hair stood right up on the back of Lee's neck. Suddenly she was standing at the corner of Eighteenth Street again, watching Omren dil'Sorden fall slowly past her, gasping out one of his last breaths; and that dark shape behind him, some Alfen male, pulled the air aside and was gone.

Matt was right, she thought. *The sonofabitch, he was right . . .* But she had no more time to spend hating Matt's guts, or making any further sense of what she'd seen—because the other thing happened. About two meters in front of her, one of the doors on the right-hand side of the hall opened, and an Alfen came out, and looked straight at Lee in complete astonishment.

In one of those frozen moments, Lee saw his mouth open to say she had no idea what. She didn't wait around to discover. She took to her heels and ran back the way she'd come. Behind her, his shout echoed: "They're out, the ephemerals are out!" *As if we were in a kennel, or a hutch,* Lee thought, running like a miler down that long hall, her fists pumping up and down as she ran. *I could really begin to dislike these people if I didn't need a door more!*

The blind wall a little way ahead of her began to ripple. The stone in her fist stung her hand, sharp-edged, a reminder or a warning. Lee hardly dared to slow, but there was no mistaking a sudden transparency of the wall, a doorway curtained in rippling air, leading somewhere else, anywhere but this hall—

Worth a try, she thought, and threw herself through it. It brushed across her face and body like cobwebs that didn't stop at clothes or skin but went straight through her. Lee shuddered, and came down clumsily on a stone floor, the jar of the landing shocking up into her knees. She looked around her in uncertainty and terror. Another hallway, in the modern part of the building this time. She saw someone come out a door at the far end of the hallway and head right for her—

One more time! Lee said to the rock, looking at the nearest wall. *And not just anywhere, this time! Our suite—*

The rippling melted into being, the texture of the stone moving with it. Lee jumped through it, once more enduring the cobwebs trailing across and through her, though they made her shiver—

She was outside the door of the suite, which stood open. Lee stood there trembling for a moment, staring at it and finally understanding both the "fading" of Jok Chastelain's psychospoor from the bus, and his strange vision that had looked to him like passing out. Someone had snatched him out of that bus through a gating just like this last one.

But why's the door open? "Gel?" she said, and went in.

That was when the attacker hit her, slamming Lee against the wall to the right of the door.

At another time, in another place where she hadn't been so thrown by so many things at once, she might have done better. As it was, Lee went down under the weight of him, and wound up rolling around on the floor with him in an unseemly tangle of limbs, that being all she could do to avoid the knife. She didn't avoid it entirely: once it scored down her left arm, and she couldn't even get out a decent scream: he was weighing her down, pushing the breath out of her. All Lee could think was, *Was it ever supposed to go this far? Was this just supposed to scare me into leaving? Well, guys, look, it worked—I'm scared!*

She was having a harder time breathing every second. But something white came flying over her, and the weight on top of her screamed and rolled off her sideways. Lee managed to scramble to her feet again, gasping, and awarded her assailant at least one good kick in the kidney before he managed to shake loose of the white nightmare that had bitten him in the haunch and was now tearing at his legs. Grunting in pain, he stumbled out the door, a shape in dark clothes, down the stairs, gone.

Gelert started to go after him. "No!" Lee said. *Gel, we've got about a minute before they get here! If that long—*

"I can't leave you alone for a moment, can I?" Gelert said. "Where have you been?"

"Never mind." She was shaking, and the tremors got worse by the moment; but also growing in her, irrationally, was a sense of tremendous amusement, even excitement. *I'm the Tooth Fairy!* Lee thought. *I've myself reproduced the effect that I came here to investigate. I've even got it saved to the implant. The only problem is that by the time I'm scheduled to testify, I may be dead.* "I want a hug," Lee said.

"What?" Gelert looked at her as if she was mad, but he came over to her regardless and reared up on his hind legs. Lee hugged him, pulling his huge head close over her chest with one arm, and making sure that no one could possibly see what her concealed hand was sticking into his mouth with the other. *Gel,* she said, *they're going to send us home.*

Ow! Well, after this, I think we should go! This is the second time someone's gone after you, Lee. It's no accident.

You're damn right it isn't. Somebody wants me at least, if not both of us, out of the way of something else we're not supposed to See or Scent, because it'll make even bigger trouble for them than has already been caused by the presence of the UN committee here. But I don't care about the setup. Something more important's going on.

Than your life?

Much. And it's important to our case, too. Something happens here the day after tomorrow, Gel, and I'm not leaving.

Something happens? What happens?

Someone's going to try to kill the Elf-king.

What, an assassination?

Not exactly, Lee said. *It's some kind of duel.*

Gelert stared at her as if she were insane. *But the Elf-kings rule for hundreds or even thousands of years at a time. Why haven't we ever heard anything about this kind of thing before?*

Because we don't hear a tenth of a percent of anything about what goes on in this place! Lee said. *That's why we still don't know who's behind Omren dil'Sorden's murder. And if I leave now, we're not going to find out anything else. But these people who're after the Elf-king know something about the murders. If we can stop what they're planning—*

There was sound from down the stairs: their hosts were faking the use of the stairs in the "residence tower," for the benefit of the other residents. *Oh, come on, Lee!* How, exactly? You going to get between them and tell them it's not nice to fight? Why should we care what they do, one way or another?

I'm not sure, Lee said. *But I care! And I have to do something.*

Like what? Stay here and get yourself—

Someone's had two tries at me already, Lee said. *Sitting still anywhere, either here or at home, I'm just a target. Let's see how well they do if the target's moving around a little.*

You're completely crazy!

That's what you told me while on the Migrin case, Lee said, *and you saw how that turned out.*

The Migrin case was in our own universe, where we knew what the hell was going on, and where we could run for help if we needed it! Gelert shouted at her down his implant. *Whereas here we don't know who the hell we can trust, we don't know how to get in or out, we don't know whether even Justice is working the way She ought to—*

But we do *know how to get in and out,* Lee said, very softly.

Gelert stared.

Remember Eighteenth Street? Lee said. *Remember the Tooth Fairy?*

Gelert turned his head just a little to one side, giving Lee a sidewise look.

An Alfen did that, Lee said. *An Alfen did it from* here. *And I did it. Because here—if you know what to do—you don't need a gate complex. You don't need a particle accelerator, or a ring; at least not a built one.*

You did *it. Did you make a recording?*

Huh? It's in the implant, yes—

Dump it to me! Hurry!

She activated the implant, and did so. *I don't know if it's going to help . . .*

I'll take a look at it.

They came in the door, then, a group of male Alfen in one-piece uniforms, ExAff's livery. One of them went straight to Lee, holding a spray injector. "What's that?" Lee cried.

"It shouldn't hurt you," the man said, bland, as he pulled her sleeve up and injected her before she could pull away. "Our physiologies are like enough. But you won't be walking where you're not wanted for a while."

He let Lee go, and she stood there rubbing her arm, while one of the other Alfen produced a locking module. "Until we can find you adequate security to stop whoever's trying to hurt you," the ExAff officer said, "you'll need to stay here. Have a quiet night."

They closed the door, and Lee heard the lock solenoids activate. She glanced down toward the terrace, and saw that what had been an open doorway was now a solid wall.

Gelert gave Lee what was intended to be taken by their

watchers as an angry look. "I don't know what trouble you've gotten us into now," he said, "but I had a long day, and I want to go back to sleep. I'll talk to you in the morning." *After I've reviewed this.* He stalked off.

In the dimness, Lee sat down in the big chair again, her hands empty now, nothing left to fiddle with. All she could do now was close her eyes, and see what she could See—and wait for her time.

Eleven

Lee was up early that morning. She'd found it difficult to get any sleep for fear of the possible actions of whatever had been injected into her. It had certainly not been a soporific, but it had also certainly done what the Alfen who administered it had claimed. She quickly found that she couldn't any longer See anything of the building that surrounded them, and she couldn't make any of her surroundings change as she had forced the walls to do.

Gelert was up fairly early as well. He ate a good breakfast from the sideboard while holding a more-in-sorrow-than-in-anger conversation with Lee about the events of the night before. She held up her end of it, but it was a desultory business for both of them; the more important conversation was going on silently, encrypted, in Palmerrand.

That was some little jaunt you took, partner. One of these days your impulsiveness is going to get you killed.

If I'd stayed in last night, the same thing might have happened! There's no security around here, Gel, when these guys have the keys to all the locks.

Something which will amuse the UN when they see your recording. Meantime, I looked at the rest of it. Interesting.

What about the you-know-what? It seems to be the key. She was reluctant, even under encryption, to actually mention the stone by name.

Maybe, maybe not. But it's handled; put your mind at rest. Meanwhile, it's now plain that Alfheim is at least potentially a lot more porous than they've been letting anyone think. All the Alfen's noise, all these years, about their impenetrable security—

Propaganda. Make everyone think Alfheim's impenetrable, and sooner or later that becomes the perceived wisdom. And as for getting out—

Lee had been breaking a piece of bread, eating it in small bits, one at a time. *It seems at least possible that, if you know how, you can step out of Alfheim into another world, the way I saw Dierrich do last night, just from one place inside the world to another.*

That's a possibility I've been considering, too. But it leaves you with one big problem. If they can do that, why would they spend all that money to build something like that huge array at Ys?

For inbound traffic from other worlds. For data, too . . . and to eavesdrop on other people's data, the way Sal wants to eavesdrop on theirs. But mostly to keep the secret, Gel; to make sure no one would suspect what they can do!

Gelert thought about that. *Those so-called free-state rings . . .*

Maybe they exist elsewhere. Maybe even here. But here, they're not absolutely necessary. Something else makes these personal gatings work.

Something local to this space. Gelert flicked an ear forward. *Why not? This space has other special qualities that we've known about for years.*

The reminder-chime in Gelert's doggie pack went off.

"The financial committee meets in twenty minutes," he said aloud. "I'd better get set."

"I have some things to talk over with dil'Estenv as well," Lee said, and got up.

Assuming she'll still talk to you after what you were up to last night.

Probably she won't, but I have to try. Better to be proactive about this than sit around waiting for the axe to fall.

You're right. Meanwhile, when I get back, I'll see if I can build some kind of bridge between your visual sense of how to 'walk' and my Scent-based way of perceiving things. If I can do this, too—Gelert grinned. *Two sets of proof, and no magistrate on Earth would be able to decline the evidence.*

You're right, Lee said as she went into her bedroom to finish dressing. *I just wish we could get a clearer sense of who that Alfen was. I'm betting it was the person who commissioned the murder . . .*

Gelert sighed at that. *I doubt we're going to get any information about that in the time we have left. Come on; let's see what the day holds . . .*

Ten minutes or so later, when Gelert spoke the door open to leave, he and Lee found themselves looking at two large Alfen from ExAff standing outside the door. "You can go ahead, *madra*," one of them said. "But with regrets, Ms. Enfield, we've been instructed that you're to remain here today."

"I need to see Dierrich dil'Estenv," Lee said, putting a bold face on it.

"I suspect her schedule is very full at the moment," said one of the guards. "I'll pass your request to her; but I wouldn't set aside any other plans you might have." He didn't quite smirk.

"That seems to have been done for me," Lee said, being polite in spite of her private preferences. "Thank you anyway." She spoke the door closed again, and went off to sit in her chair again, brooding.

Lee spent all that day, and much of the early part of the evening, leaning her will against the fabric of things, pushing, straining, without result. *There's always the chance that they might have misjudged the dosage,* she thought; *that there's something about our physiology that they don't know.* But the hope was vain.

The door/window onto the terrace had cleared itself again, showing the "view" out to the mountains; but the forcefield had gone solid. Lee leaned against it for a while that afternoon, looking at the view as the sun swung westward, still trying to assert the power that had been taken from her, even just to the extent of being able to See what was really there; but she had no success. She thought of the fairy tales, how there had been numerous references to magic ointments or talismans that Elves could give humans, enabling them to see the things happening in the secret realms, and how that vision could be withdrawn instantly if they chose. *All very well. But my own Sight is a function of the perception of Truth, of the function of Justice Herself. That shouldn't be something they ought to be able to interfere with.*

Unless natural law here is different in other ways, too . . . Or unless they have other "instrumentalities" like the roses . . .

Finally, as day's light died outside, Lee got tired of trying. She had just sat down in the big chair again, exhausted and rather depressed, when Gelert returned, surprisingly late. "Well," he said, as he shouldered his doggie pack off inside the door as it closed behind him, "that's it."

"What's it?"

"The Alfen government has formally notified the UN&ME that the committee's time here is at an end. Sal had the timing judged practically to the minute."

It's because of me, Lee said.

Only partly, I think. I suspect you're right; there's something going on with the Elf-king, and these people want us out of here before it starts.

"That's depressing," Lee said. "When are we supposed to leave?"

"Tomorrow morning. It would have been today, except that Per stood up and was unusually eloquent, for him, in asking for a few hours extra to confer with the UN. They agreed, though they were reluctant." *But what I think he really wanted was time to make sure all the data we've gathered was sufficiently safely squirreled away for the Elves to be unable to sabotage or confiscate all of it before we leave.*

You really think they'd do something like that?

I think they might try. Our hosts were unusually antsy today, much more so than just your little hijinks last night should have made them. Something else is definitely going on. So everybody is carrying copies of the whole group's data, and your own files and mine, compressed and encrypted, have been dumped to all the others as well.

"So I guess I'd better start packing," Lee said, and then laughed. "I've hardly actually had time to *un*pack . . ."

"It'll take you less time, then."

"Humorist." She went in to start doing something about her luggage. *But what about the Elf-king, Gel? He at least was in favor of this increased 'transparency' and openness we've been experiencing. If they kill or depose him, it'll be all over—that much I could tell from Dierrich last night. And something much worse will follow . . .*

Lee, we're not going to have any choice. They're going to

*ship us out of here tomorrow. Our job now is to make sure
that, at the very least, we leave with as much as we can of
what we came for . . . data. What the UN will make of it is
out of our hands. And for our own part, we haven't done
badly; we've got the proof we need to make the dil'Sorden
case stand up in court, even with the unanswered questions.*

Lee went into the bathroom, where her toiletries kit was,
and started to reassemble it, staring into the mirror there, as
if at the Alfen she was sure was watching her, though she
couldn't see him. *This isn't how I see it ending, Gel,* she
said. *Not at all.*

How you see it, Gelert said, *or how you See it?* The remark was pointed, but made gently enough, as from one person to another who knew that opinion and Truth were only
rarely the same thing.

Lee just went on packing the kit, and didn't answer.

It went much as he had predicted. The next morning, another aircraft was waiting for the committee outside the residence tower: not one from the *Miraha,* this time, but some
more prosaic craft with the gold disk and nothing else. There
was no one to see them off but more of the guards who had
been outside Lee's and Gelert's room all night, and the committee members went up the ramp into the craft with the air
of people whose job wasn't done, and who wouldn't be at
liberty to express their frustration and anger for some time
yet.

Lee and Gelert were the first ones to board, their guards
having brought them out early. Lee sat there by one of the
windows in annoyance as the rest of the committee boarded,
bearing their glances. How much any of them knew about
what had happened to her, she wasn't going to inquire right

now: she was tired again, and not feeling well, after a night
of being awake, with a sense of time running out, and trying
again and again without success to bend the local world to
her will. Around three in the morning Lee had finally given
it up, but not happily. That sense of something bad coming
had been assailing her more strongly than it had at any time
since she'd first felt it in Ellay, and it hung over her now, unresolved and unresolvable.

The craft sealed itself up after a few final boarders—
more faceless uniformed ExAff staff, Alfen who plainly
wanted not even to speak a word to the departing visitors if
they could avoid it. Lee sat there and watched the ground
drop away, wondering what the reality was. No green space
outside a tower: then some helipad, possibly, on top of the
larger building she'd Seen? No telling, and she wasn't going
to get a chance to find out later.

The feeling of some massive opportunity being lost,
some imperative going unanswered, grew on her minute by
minute as they lifted away and turned north, gaining altitude. Gelert, sitting in the seat next to Lee with its back
down to give him more room, looked at her with some concern. "You didn't sleep a lot last night . . ."

"No," she said.

"And you didn't eat breakfast, either."

"No." She wished just for that moment that he would
stop talking to her: she had the most peculiar feeling that
someone was trying to tell her something, though she
couldn't figure out who.

"Blood sugar again," Gelert said.

Lee was ready to snap *It is not my goddamn blood sugar!*
at him, and then caught herself. *I feel a little weird,* she said
at last.

The drug, maybe.

Maybe. She leaned her head against the window of the

climbing craft, looking down at the ground. It was sunny there, with only the very occasional patch of cloud; fields and forested places rolled by, the hilly country between the pre-Alps and the sharper mountains surrounding Aien Mhariseth. Buildings were few. *Though there,* she thought, *there's one. Odd kind of structure, but you can't tell with Alfen architecture—*

Lee looked at it more closely as the craft started to pass over it. In the back of her mind, something writhed, struggled, as if against a closed fist; and she suddenly both realized what she was looking at, and Saw it. The structure was no building, but a ring of tall stones with their shadows short beneath them, a henge without lintels. Her Sight, though, showed her the energies reaching from stone to stone, and running under them, through the ground, in a ring: and in the back of her mind, at the sight and feel of it, the feeling of what she had done the other night suddenly stirred in sympathy, jumped, as if something had put a shock through it—

It's the drug, all right, Lee thought. *It's wearing off!*

She gulped, then gulped again. "You okay?" Gelert said, looking at her with concern.

"Uh, a little airsick, maybe." She got up, wondering if she looked pale enough to suit the part. She certainly felt pale, though not from any drug. "Back in a minute," Lee said, getting up and heading toward the back of the craft. *And try not to look so concerned—someone might come after me.*

What are you thinking of? Gelert said, suddenly alarmed.

Doing something proactive, Lee said.

She went back to the toilet and shut herself in. *Talers to crullers they've got this place bugged and spy-eyed as well,* Lee thought, *but whether they do or not, I'm not just going to sit here.* Then, scared as she was, she had to laugh. *Then again, maybe I should. Mom always told me to go before I*

*went anywhere. And if it puts them off watching me for a mo-
ment—*

Lee steeled herself to the idea that they might be watching and used the toilet for its intended purpose. Then, after
she had put herself right again, she washed her hands, taking her time about it, thinking about what she'd just seen
below. *This image, Gel,* she said down the Palmerrand link,
and showed it to him; the ring of stones, the ring of power
underlying it. *Save this and use it to find me.*

What? I've got it, but, Lee, what are you doing?—

She had to ignore him. The sharp, stinging sense of that
place on the ground was already starting to fade as the craft
passed it. Lee closed down the Palmerrand link, afraid to be
distracted, and turned to the wall beside her, bending her intention against it as she had bent her intention against the
world to hear the voices she couldn't possibly have been
hearing, to pass through the true walls behind the walls of illusion. The stone had shown her what to do, how to manipulate this world. And now, with the drug losing its strength
inside her, the feeling grew stronger and stronger that she
could "walk" without it—if her will was strong enough. *This
place is malleable,* she thought. *It desires to be shaped and
managed, desires to have the will of the controlling mind
laid upon it. That's truth; that I can See. And so—*

For a terrible long moment nothing happened. But then
the world started to give, just a little. There was still resistance—

Lee pushed for all she was worth, not certain how she
was doing what she was doing without the stone, but unwilling to stop for fear she might not be able to start again.
The sweat started out on her forehead, ran trickling down
her back and down between her breasts under her sweater.
She pushed.

The resistance persisted, persisted—then started to give.

In front of her, the wall rippled. Past it she could see nothing; it simply looked like someone had taken the laminate of the toilet wall and turned it into a curtain. *If I've made the wrong decision here,* she thought, *this first step is going to be a long one—*

Lee said a quick prayer to Herself, looked once more at the image of that ring of stones in her mind, and stepped through the curtain.

The cobwebs brushed across her, through her—and Lee fell. The first second was the worst, when she felt the bite of cold and knew herself to be falling. The next second was bad too, as the pain hit her in the knees again, as she came down crooked, twisted her ankle as she slammed down onto the hard ground in the center of the circle of stones.

She lay there gasping in the light for some moments. *Alive. I'm alive*—Though the sun was warm on her back, the grass she lay on was wet and chilly, with gray stones showing through it and digging into the front of her. Lee pushed herself up to her hands and knees, looked around her. The ring of stones had a clear area around it, with some grass and some bare patches of ground, as if some inhibiting influence was associated with the stones. Past the clear ground, brush began to grow, and some clumps of trees, wind-twisted and somewhat dwarfed, probably by the weather. Any view past them to the horizon was blocked off by surrounding low brush-covered hills.

Lee got up and found herself wobbly. Then she laughed as she staggered over to one of the huge gray lichen-speckled stones and leaned against it. *I've just walked out of a flying craft at God knows how many thousand feet and lived to tell the tale: I'm entitled to wobble!* She looked up and could see, bright in the sun, the thin silvery contrail, way up high, of the craft she had been in moments before. She wished there was a way to let Gelert know she was all right, but there was not the slightest chance that the implant-to-implant connection would work at this range.

She hoped no one had to use the toilet badly, as she had left the door locked from the inside. *But they have to have a way to deal with that,* Lee thought. *And when they discover that I'm not there—*

Lee laughed again. *What are they going to do? It's got to take at least a* little *while for them to find me. After all, even if they can figure out what I did, and how I did it, I still could be almost anywhere . . .*

At least she liked to think that. But for the meantime she had to consider what to do next. *The first question is . . . where the heck am I?*

To judge by the direction of the sun while they'd been flying, Lee thought she had to be north of the Dolomite chain which held Aien Mhariseth. *But how far?* Lee stood still for a moment and tried to think in terms of distances and kilometers per hour. The craft had only been aloft for fifteen minutes or so. It hadn't yet gone transonic. *Which means something less than nine hundred klicks per hour, but more than, say, two hundred. So if you take an average—*

She tried to do it in her head, and after several attempts wound up swearing. It was beginning to sound like one of the witless math problems she'd hated in grammar school, and there were too many imponderables. The closest Lee could come up with was that she was perhaps a hundred klicks northeast of Aien Mhariseth, assuming that the craft had been heading directly toward Ys when she left it.

She stood there in the summer sunshine, looking south-ward. She could just see the line of mountains there against the horizon, slightly hazed by distance, but the peaks she was looking for were far beyond those. At least several days' walk, for a good walker: possibly more. *Though what do I know about long-distance walking, anyway? I'm an*

Angelena: I don't even walk to the convenience store! And here I am with no food, no proper clothes, no idea where to find food or water, and no clear plan of what to do next. Is this possibly the stupidest thing I've done since agreeing to let Matt take me out to dinner?

Then she had to laugh at herself again. Certainly Gelert would laugh at her, if he ever caught up with her here—because she would bet anything that he'd try. *So my business for the moment, anyway, is to keep myself in good enough condition that he finds me and doesn't immediately have to dig a hole to bury me in.*

Meanwhile—Aien Mhariseth is the goal. She had gotten the feeling from Dierrich's conversation with Kil, whoever Kil was, that whatever was planned for the Elf-king would be happening there. *I have to get there, stay out of the way of the Alfen who're out to get him, and find a way to help him.*

She had to grin wryly at that. *Nothing to it,* she thought. *So let's get busy.*

Lee turned back to the circle of stones. She could See the power running among them, a thin, fine network of strands and lines of force stretching between them and under them. *It is something natural,* she thought, *but God knows how it works, and probably I shouldn't waste my time right now trying to figure it out.* It had served her as an anchor point, a place to transit to; could she also use the circle, somehow, to help her transit between points?

Lee stepped into the circle and felt the power there respond to her as it hadn't done when she simply dropped into it. Her first impulse was to imagine someplace in Aien Mhariseth to "walk" to. *The suite? Boy, would that be a dumb move. You turn up there right now, and they just break out another shuttle, hit you with an even bigger dose of anti-"walking" juice, and send you home after the others. Also—*

what's the point of getting there before the Elf-king does, tonight? It's when he arrives that—

—something said, not exactly in her ear, *that you're needed.*

Lee held very still at that.

All right, she thought, *needed.* She turned to look at the circle of stones, and beyond them, to see if there was somewhere she could find some cover to wait for a while. The immediate neighborhood was entirely too flat and open for her liking.

But then waiting might not be such a good idea either, Lee thought. *The Alfen knew what I was doing, the evening before last: they'll suspect I've done it again. The circle might occur to them as a logical possibility . . . which would mean it might be one of the first places they'd look. Whether I want to use it for transit or not, I need to get away from it right now.*

With that in mind, she tried to think of another place to which she could transit . . . somewhere that she wouldn't immediately run afoul of hundreds of Alfen. After a moment, *The other side of the mountain,* Lee thought. *Or better still, as a little less obvious, the path leading over the mountain toward it. There were a couple of places we stopped on our hike that I can remember clearly enough to 'walk' to.*

Lee put her back up against the nearest stone for support, closed her eyes, and worked to See that spot in her mind. The image of it was clear enough. She opened her eyes again, then, and looked at the empty air, leaning her will against it and waiting to see the shimmer and ripple of its response.

Nothing.

Come on—! Lee thought. She tried again, and then several times more, but got no result.

Maybe there's a time limit? she thought. *Maybe you have to have a little while to recover from that? Maybe the drug hasn't worn off completely yet?*

Or maybe you don't have the slightest idea what you're doing, and you're screwing it up somehow? Or else it was a one-off, and you're not going to be able to do it again.

Lee sighed. *That* was her blood sugar talking. *All right,* she said to herself, and looked south, to the line of the nearest hills. They looked like a long enough walk—but they were away from here, they might offer some possibilities for cover, and she might run into something to eat along the way. *Better than just standing here straining my brain,* she thought.

She started walking.

✑

The walking went on near enough to what felt like forever. Lee was thanking whatever gods were current here that she favored flat-soled shoes for everything but the most formal occasions. At least she wasn't having to negotiate the countryside in heels. But she wished again and again for her cross-trainers, for even the flats weren't meant for this kind of usage. Her feet were blistering. She was hungry, too: now she was regretting not having taken Gelert's eternal advice about breakfast. There was also the matter of water. *Food I can do without for a while,* she thought. *But water's going to be more of an issue, and pretty soon.* And on top of everything else, the day was leaning toward late afternoon, and it was already starting to get cool. By contrast to noontime, it was pleasant at the moment. But it wouldn't stay that way.

The most frustrating thing about the walking, though, was that the hills didn't seem to get any closer. Lee felt terribly exposed; she kept an eye on the sky for more contrails, but saw none. *Not that that's necessarily a guarantee of anything,* she thought. *All I can really do right now is keep moving.*

So she kept moving, as afternoon leaned toward evening, and it got cooler. Lee hugged herself, in her thin sweater, as she walked. She could only be grateful that she'd decided to wear jeans this morning instead of the summer skirt she'd been contemplating. The growling noises her stomach was making were infuriating, in that they reminded her about once every three minutes how hungry she was; and she needed no reminder of her thirst.

Lee stopped, at one point, and picked up a pebble to suck on—something she remembered from some survival text she'd read long before. It helped a little, but not nearly enough; she had to force herself not to think of water. She also stopped once every half hour or so to attempt to transit again, but still she couldn't manage it. Lee began to wonder whether there were other ways to keep someone from transiting besides sticking them full of the anti-walking drug. *Anyone who could lay a glamourie over tens of square miles, as the Alfen seemed able to do around Aien Mhariseth, might be able to do something like that.*

The problem is that I don't know what they can *do. But at least my Sight works.*

Twilight drew on, and night fell, which made Lee feel somewhat better in mood . . . though physically, she began to suffer. It got cold, and there was no cover. Gelert had always teased her about being a native LA girl, with orange juice in her veins instead of blood; a sun-worshipper, unable to cope with even minor variations in climate, such as anything below seventy degrees Fahrenheit. *And if he was here right now,* Lee thought, her teeth chattering as she walked along through the dark, *I'd tell him, "You're absolutely right," . . . and then I'd skin him and make a coat out of his pelt.* She was walking with her head down, being very careful of her footing. The landscape that was part grassy, part stony, had now given way to countryside that was almost completely stony, with little tussocks of long stringy grass appearing only here and there. It was bad to walk on, but at least the hills were appreciably closer now.

Lee walked on, shivering under the rising moon, sucking on her pebble, trying not to concentrate on her own troubles, but on the bigger issues that had brought her here. But it was surprisingly difficult to concentrate on Big Issues when you had an empty stomach, a raging thirst, blistered feet, and muscles that ached from a long day's walking.

Still, Lee considered that she was doing better than she'd ever thought she might under such circumstances. It wasn't that she was tougher than she thought. She kept getting the feeling that she had some kind of obscure help, from things themselves—stones that didn't turn under her feet when they might have, a wind that didn't blow as hard as it might: help from the world. *If the world pleases,* she remembered Dierrich having said, the other night. At the time she'd thought it just an odd turn of phrase.

But on second thought, perhaps it wasn't so weird. Worlds did have different ways they behaved, physically; everyone knew that. And there did seem to be "behavioral" differences between them of the kind Gelert had mentioned when they were discussing it last. *Could it be that the Alfen are more closely in touch with the reason their world has those kinds of differences?—possibly in touch with the world's "personality," somehow?*

She stopped one more time to see if perhaps she might be able to transit. The wind around her rose, and Lee shivered; but once again she leaned her will against the empty air, thinking of the place she and Gelert had passed on their way over the yoke that led to the back of the mountain, to Istelin'ru Semivh. There had been a little cave in the next hill over—or maybe hill was the wrong name for it. It had been another of those big spires of stone that stuck up out of the landscape like a thorn, jagged, gray-white, and the weathering had split and scored one side of it so that a narrow winding cave-crevice had opened in it on the side facing the mountain wall and stony spire where the Laurins' House reared up, looking down over the valley. In other circumstances, it was the kind of place that Lee would have hiked up to with a bottle of wine and a picnic lunch, to contemplate life and the universe, the way she often went up to the top of Topanga for the view over Queen of Angels Park and the rest of LA. But right now, in memory, that cave just looked like a good place to hide. Lee laid her will against the air, against the world, thinking, *open! Open!*

. . . Nothing.

Lee stood there and sighed, and listened to the wind rushing around her, and started to shiver harder than ever.

Then she realized it wasn't just wind that she heard. Somewhere here, making a thin, faint white-noise sound just at the edge of hearing, was water.

Oh, God, Lee thought. *Thank You!*

The sound was coming from ahead of her and over to her right. Slowly, trying not to hurry, she made her way in that direction. *No point in finding water, then falling down and breaking a leg or something,* Lee thought.

The actual time it took her to find the little brook that ran down from the higher ground to the south couldn't have been more than five minutes . . . but it felt longer than the whole day's walk. Lee got carefully down on her knees beside the quick-flowing water, and drank, and drank, and drank. The water was so cold it made her teeth hurt, but she didn't mind; she drank it until she gasped. Lee splashed it on her face, started to drink again . . .

. . . and then gasped once more at the sound from right behind her.

Slowly she straightened up where she knelt, looked over her shoulder. There was a tall, still shape in ExAff uniform standing there behind her, holding a pulserifle of some kind. As she looked back across the stream, two more, an Alfen man and a woman, materialized in front of her—literally materialized, slipping out of the air as she hadn't been able to do all day.

"It's just not fair," Lee said.

"What?" said the Alfen behind her, amused. "That we can placewalk, and you can't? But our mistress didn't want you doing that . . . so she moved to prevent it, until you could be located."

Slowly, Lee stood up and turned to face the one with the weapon. "And now I suppose we go back to Mhariseth, and I get shoved in a shuttle and sent home," she said, furious that it should end this way, after all the day's hopes and troubles.

The Alfen with the gun shook his head slowly. "For ephemerals found unescorted or without permission from the Laurin or the mrinLauvrin within the bounds of the Land," he said, "the penalty is execution of the Ban."

Lee swallowed. "You mean," she said, hoping that the way she had begun to shake didn't show too much, "execution, plain and simple. And you don't even care what the UN, or anyone else, will think."

"It doesn't matter what anyone thinks," the Alfen said. "You were caught trespassing, and so you'll have suffered the penalty of our law. Unfortunate, but—" He shrugged. "Other sovereignties have penalties just as rigorous, in places. If you—"

Lee wasn't going to sit still listening to further explanations. She scrambled to her feet and threw herself at the

Alfen, and he pulled the weapon away from her, but Lee's sights were set lower at the moment: she kicked him hard in the kneecap. He grunted with pain and went down hard on the other knee, but Lee's grab for the gun didn't work. Too quickly for her to see how it happened, one of the other Alfen had it, and then Lee was the one who got kicked, so that she went sprawling and gasping across the stones, nearly pitching face-forward into the brook. *Shot while trying to escape?* she thought. *Not without giving you a little present first!*—and came up with a fist-sized rock from the bed of the brook. She fired it at the second Alfen, and managed to hit him in the bicep, but her aim was poor: it wasn't the bicep holding the gun. That weapon came up, aimed at her. Lee's eyes went wide—

From behind him, the white shape came leaping out of the darkness, silent, fastened on the neck of the Alfen, and pulled him backwards and down. The gun fired over Lee's head as she ducked, and as the second Alfen went down, she threw herself at the gun, grabbed it, came down on the stones and, rolled away. More gunfire from an energy weapon stitched the ground where she'd been. Gelert bounced away from his first victim, leaped over the brook, and hit the second Alfen chest-high: she went down flat under him, wrestled briefly with him—then rolled away, wheezing horribly, writhed against the stones for a few seconds before she went limp. Lee got to her feet as fast as she could, ready to fire the pulser at the first legitimate target— but not before she saw the first Alfen get to his hands and knees and topple sideways into a place where the stones were rippling like a curtain seen sideways. He vanished through them; they went solid again.

Lee stood there panting, not aware of much of anything for a few moments until Gelert's head came to rest on her shoulder. She put an arm around it, hugged it tight. "That one dead, too?" she said.

"With not much regret, I have to say yes."

"What *kept* you?"

"Well, gee, Lee, I'm glad to see you, too."

She turned to hug him properly. "Of course I'm glad to see you, you idiot!" She hugged him hard. "Twice in twenty-four hours—Suz, Gel, this isn't a habit I want to get into!"

"My pleasure to be of assistance. But meanwhile, it's a good thing I had your recording of your little vanishing trick," Gelert said, "or I *still* wouldn't be here, and this little episode would've turned out differently. As it was, it took me all night after we got back to adapt the technique. Using Scent rather than Sight as the paradigm is a little tricky, but I found my way, finally." He sat down, panting a little, looking around him with satisfaction. "It's harder from Earth, Lee . . . but it can be done, if you believe it can, and if you have a clue to the technique, and are really, really motivated. And maybe it also helps if you have one of these. Here—" His jaws worked for a moment, and then into Lee's hand he spat out the stone.

"Oh, thank God," Lee said, drying it off against her sweater. "I was afraid maybe someone was going to search you at the gating complex and take it off you."

"They searched me all right," Gelert said. "But not terribly well. They didn't like getting their hands in my mouth. Maybe they just didn't want doggie drool all over them." He grinned, exhibiting twenty-six other possible reasons, all sharp. "Of course, the stone was well past my mouth at that point."

Lee looked at Gelert in shock. "Gel, that thing could have ripped you up inside!"

"That occurred to me. Fortunately, I have firsthand experience with the weird things my kids are constantly eating."

His expression was amused, and resigned. "Rocks that size and sometimes that sharp haven't killed them yet: I thought I had at least a chance. Recovering the thing was a little distasteful, but I put it through the dishwasher afterward." Gelert looked rueful. "You have no idea the grief Nuala gave me about that."

Lee burst out laughing and pocketed the stone again, buttoning the pocket. "You're better at this than I am," she said.

"I wouldn't know about that . . ."

"Might have something to do with your people coming from here, once upon a time."

"Might be. The place smelled strangely familiar the whole time I was here—did I mention? Maybe not, we were busy. But, Lee . . . this kind of transit is relatively easy. Easier than I would ever have thought, just going from there to here, though it takes a lot of preparation. The Alfen are going to have a lot of explaining to do as to why they haven't shared this information with everyone else. It could open up the worlds in a way no one has imagined . . ."

"Control," Lee said. All around her, she felt the world vibrate obscurely, thrumming like a plucked string. "But there's no time for it right now. Gel, we've got to go. It's starting."

"What's starting?"

"I don't know. But the world thinks the Elf-king's coming, and if I correctly assess Madam Dierrich's mood, she's going to go after him the moment he turns up. We have to be there."

"Aien Mhariseth?" Gelert said. "We can't just walk in there . . ."

"Remember where we were hiking, Gel? About an hour after we left. That funny cave—"

"Have you noticed something?" Gelert said.

"What?"

"It's clouding over."

Lee looked up. He was right. The sky was suddenly full of cloud: some of it was still silver with the moonlight from above, but much more was opaque to the light, darkening easily three-quarters of the sky. As she watched, she saw the light continue to fade, the night grow darker. "It's not natural . . ." she said softly.

"We lost one guy," Gelert said. "He went right back to warn Dierrich, I'll bet . . ."

Lee looked up at the darkening sky as the last scraps of moonlight faded away. Something cold touched her face: she shivered. And something touched her there again, and again. It was beginning to snow. "Gel, they had some kind of block in place that kept me from moving. But it doesn't seem to affect you. Let's get out of here before they widen the effect—"

"That pathway leading up to the cave . . ." Gelert said. He stood there for a moment, still, concentrating.

The air in front of him rippled. Lee didn't wait: three quick steps brought her to it, through it . . .

She gasped with the sudden cold and wind. Behind her, Gelert came out of nothing, landed hock-deep in snow. Lee was up to her knees in it, and it was falling fast. She started to shiver again, harder, for the air temperature here was far more bitter than it had been in the place they'd just come from.

"This can't all be meant for us," Lee said. "There hasn't been time—"

"Hard to tell," Gelert said. "But we've got to deal with it anyway. Where's that cave? I think I brought us out too far down."

Lee looked around her, trying to remember the way the path had gone from this part of the climb. The problem was that it was difficult to tell which part of the climb this was.

The snow was falling fine around them, but even the snow was hard to see in the heavy fog that also surrounded them. *Whiteout*—

Lee closed her eyes for a moment, summoned up her Sight, opened her eyes. Even through the fog and under the snow, she could still See the shapes of boulders that she recognized from the climb. "Up and to the left for about ten meters," she said. "Then about a thirty-degree angle to the right."

They struggled through the swiftly deepening snow and up the path, or where Lee thought the path was—for the Sight kept failing her. *Interference? Or is it just my own physical state?*—for an exhausting day without food, without enough water, and with fear and cold added, would quickly reduce any practitioner's effectiveness to a fraction of its normal level. There was nothing Lee could do, at last, but rely on memory to keep herself and Gelert on the path. Many times one or the other of them strayed off it, only to discover the fact by banging into the boulders that were half-buried under the snow, their shapes somewhat disguised by the drifts the wind was piling up. Lee was terrified that they were going to make one mistake too many, somewhere along here, and go over the edge—for there were places where the path had been perfectly flat until suddenly it dropped off, to the right or sometimes the left, fifty or a hundred meters straight down. In this visibility, like the inside of a lightbulb, it could happen before either of them could react—

Lee thought of dil'Hemrev's seemingly casual remark about the sunset on the mountains: *I'd like to say that we arranged it for you, but we're not all that adept.* Lee pushed her wet, snowy hair out of her eyes, where the bitter wind was constantly whipping it. *Meaning that some of them are?* she thought. If some Alfen could manipulate the space of their world the way Lee had seen they could, then it might well follow that the same talent could be used to shift weather fronts, cause local changes in temperature, pressure—

If they could do it, Lee thought, *could* we *do it?* "Gel," Lee said, "think about this snow going away—or stopping—"

"You think it'll help?" he gasped from behind her.

Her heart seized. She was so used to thinking of Gelert as stronger, more robust than she was; but here it looked as if he was suffering far more from the cold than she was. "It might. Think of it at least not falling on us."

She tried to do that herself as she kept moving, tried to think of them both as being surrounded by a bubble of clear air, no fog in it, no snow. *Just a few meters' worth of visibility, say ten meters, that would be plenty*—She leaned her will against the world. It resisted her, or something did. *Just a pause in this,* Lee thought, briefly angry, *a fighting chance, come on—!*

Maybe it was the anger that helped. The air abruptly cleared around them, as if they were in the reverse of a paperweight snowglobe, the whiteness briefly beating all around the outside of the globe but not coming in. Lee paused, still hugging herself against the wind, for whatever she'd managed had no effect against that. "Come on, Gel!" she said, and went up what little she could still make out of the trail, a stretch where the snow had been a little less deep because of the mountain wall right next to it. And just past there, the spire of grey stone sticking up out of the foot of the neighboring hill, the spire all white with snow on the south side, but still mostly bare on the north: and at the bottom of it, half full of drifted snow, the little cave—"There it is, come on!"

The two of them floundered toward it through the snow.

Seconds later their protection gave way, as they reached the opening of the cave, and the snow slammed stinging into them from behind, as if in revenge for the temporary frustration. Lee used her arms and the Alfen pulserifle to try to sweep the snow out of the opening, back toward the trail: a frustrating business, as the wind just blew it right back in at her. The cave was smaller than she remembered it, shallower, and wasn't going to provide much protection against that wind, to judge by the snow already drifted in; but it was the best they were going to get. "Come on, we've got to get rid of some of this!" she said to Gelert. "If it drifts in on top of us, it's insulation—"

Gelert didn't answer her, just started digging. Within a couple of minutes there was enough room for them both to crouch into the little space. Gelert collapsed to the floor and curled himself into as tight a ball as he could: Lee wrapped herself more or less around him, shivering, feeling the snow melting between them. "Not much help," he said faintly. "Sorry."

Outside, the wind rose to a scream, then a shriek, and the relentless snow began to pile in on top of them again. Lee got the pulserifle around in front of her, out of the snow, and had little strength to do anything else. The shivering was shaking Lee's whole body now, and the cold of the snow burned her, but there was no use in trying to shake it off; it simply flew up into her eyes again, blinding her, and continued piling up. Insulating it might be, but it was still wet, and the chill of it seeped into her, relentless.

"We're going to die here," Gelert said softly.

It was a thought that had occurred to Lee just before he said it; but she hadn't been willing to make it real by letting it out. Too late now.

"This is my fault," Lee said. "I'm sorry."

There was a long silence. Finally, Gelert cocked one eye up at her. "It's all right," he said. "Nuala knew."

"Knew—"

"She wouldn't let me be, last night. I had to tell her, finally—" A tremor of cold shook him. "Tell her how dangerous this was likely to be. She said she understood. She said I had to go."

The tears came to Lee's eyes. It was almost impossible to listen to this, under the circumstances, let alone respond to it. But at the same time, if they were going to be dead soon, she could at least deal with the difficult things.

It still took her a while. "I envied you that, you know?" she said at last.

"What?" Gelert said.

"What you two have," Lee said, hugging herself against the cold. "The understanding. How you always seemed able to be together without rubbing each other raw. It always seemed to come so naturally to you. The closeness . . ." Her eyes hurt her; she tried to blink them against the ferocious cold, and found that she was having trouble. Lee put her hands over her eyes, trying to protect them from the wind . . . or at least that was the excuse. But her hands were as cold as her face.

"Once I actually had to leave the room," she said, between spasms of her teeth chattering, "after I'd been watching you two for a while. It was just after everything blew up with Matt." Lee shook her head. "I just couldn't bear it, sitting there, seeing how close you two were, knowing that I had something like that with Matt, and now it was gone, and wasn't going to come back. She was lying there with her head on your back, the way she does . . ." Lee had to stop for a moment, her teeth chattering so hard she couldn't speak. "That sense of trusting another person, knowing you were safe with them, and that they were safe with you . . . It pierced me. I had to leave. I felt so stupid, and so self-ish . . ."

"We knew you were hurting," Gelert said. "But some-times—that idiom about being there for somebody, actually just means to *be* there. Doing anything, saying anything, sometimes you know it'll hurt them worse than just being quiet, and being close."

For a while neither of them said anything. Finally, look-ing out into the blinding whiteness, Lee said, "It'll never happen now. And I was just starting to believe it didn't mat-ter if it never happened. I thought, we'll go home from this job, and I'll get used to being by myself. That foolish time in my life is over. And now look at me. Now that I know—" she looked at Gelert, and still couldn't say "we're going to die." "Now suddenly it feels important again." She started to laugh, bitter laughter that would have gone on for a long time—but the cold was more bitter than her mood; when she drew breath it cut the inside of her throat like breathing bro-ken glass.

We can't last much longer. "You've always been a good partner," Lee said. "I wish it wasn't going to end here."

"You've been a better one. Harder working, more seri-ous . . ." Gelert shook his head and winced at the pain of his ears. They looked stiff, and their insides were the wrong shade of pink; they were starting to freeze.

Lee gathered his head into her chest and tried to shelter it enough from the wind to share a little warmth with it. "What do you mean I was harder working?" Lee said, and had to shake her head to whip the tears out of it before they froze her eyes shut again. "You were the one who always made all the money . . ."

He didn't answer. She could hear and feel his breathing coming harder now, wheezing. His people weren't meant for this kind of temperature; she might actually last longer than he would. She had to do something. *It's got to stop,* she thought. *I can't get him out of here. It's got to stop . . .*

She closed her eyes and tried leaning her will against the world one last time.

Briefly, to Lee's delight and growing hope, the snow began to drop off somewhat, the flakes getting bigger, their fall becoming slower; and the wind dropped off too, the shriek dying to a moan over their heads. . . . But again it didn't last. Within a couple of minutes, long enough for Lee to feel certain that the effect was due to something she was doing, the wind started to pick up again—and there was almost a message in it: *No. No matter what happens to me, you're not going to live through it.*

Dierrich, Lee thought. She set her teeth and strove harder in her mind to make the snow stop; at the very least to make the wind drop off, for at these temperatures, it was the wind that would suck the heat out of their bodies and kill them at last. But it wasn't working.

"Gelert—"

He didn't reply. Lee felt the warmth start creeping up on her, slowly. *No!* Lee thought, for she knew what that meant. She tried to start moving again, just enough to slap herself with her arms if nothing else, but her body just wouldn't obey her. In this short time that she hadn't been moving, all her limbs had gone stiff as iron.

She closed her eyes for one last effort. *Don't leave them that way too long, they'll really freeze shut, this time*—She clarified the image of what she wanted in her mind. The wind silent, the snow ceased, the air warming, the sky clearing up past the mountain wall—

As she considered the mountain, without warning something seized Lee's imagery and pulled it farther up the wall of stone, rushing her past the boundaries she had been considering. Her vision was caught up in a larger flow of power:

more certain, more direct, going straight to the heart of what was happening around them. The wind was dropping off, too . . . but she began to get the feeling that it wasn't her doing.

Lee blinked, trying to see clearly what was going on around her. But her Sight had for the moment been co-opted, swept fully into the ambit of that larger power. She couldn't see anything of the snowy darkness of the cave, or the brighter world outside. All she could See was the walls of the Laurins' House, somewhere high above them, built of the same gray-white stone, but hewn and polished; and high up on those walls, a broad terrace inside the parapet on the longest wall that looked north. A group of people were gathered there down at one end of the terrace, seemingly looking northward, too. Lee tried to turn her Sight away, but it was as if something here, perhaps the world itself, thought that this was more important, the most important thing perhaps, and was overriding all other vision—

Lee gulped, suddenly finding it hard to breathe, as if the air itself was holding its breath. And then the voice spoke, the one the world had been waiting for.

"Dierrich," it said. "I dislike seeing my prerogatives usurped. Exercise of mastery in this world, when the Laurin is here, is the Laurin's business. What are you doing?"

The tone of voice was light, but there was more menace underlying it than Lee ever thought she had heard in a human voice. *But he's not human* . . . And as he spoke, the wind stopped completely, as if someone had thrown a switch. Perhaps the snow had stopped, too; Lee couldn't tell—she was blind to everything except what was happening up there on the castle walls. Her slightly frostbitten face could feel the air temperature starting to rise; an unpleasant sensation, as if someone was waving a blowtorch in front of her.

"Gelert. Gel!" Blind as she was, Lee could still feel him. She started shaking him, rubbing him. "Gelert—!"

He was cold. She couldn't see him; but after a long, terrible moment, she heard him sneeze. *Now,* he said down the implant, *I bet you're sorry you said that big soulful goodbye.*

Oh, shut up! She would have kept on rubbing him, but her Sight was locked so tightly to that other view that she finally had to stop, unable to see anything else. Up there on the terrace that overlooked the city, a group of Alfen stood, surrounding one small radiant form in daycloak and robes, traditional Alfen wear; and set over against them near the other end of the terrace was a single shape, a man's shape, still, tall, arms folded, very dark, in a business suit and a tie.

For a moment Lee was distracted even from her astonishment at what was unfolding by a sudden memory, a sense of something familiar. Looking with her Sight at the group of Alfen standing about Dierrich, Lee abruptly made the connection. One of them, one of the Alfen up there, had a psychospoor that she would have recognized anywhere, she had spent so long contemplating it, running and rerunning her recording. The being associated with it had looked out of a shadow at the corner of Eighteenth and Wilshire, and been amused by the death of another Alfen, and had then parted the air and the darkness and stepped back into them. *That's him!*

The little silver-haired woman walked slowly out of the group of Alfen among whom she'd been standing, walked up to the Elf-king, considered him a moment—then struck him hard across the face. *"Traitor!"*

His voice, when he replied, was surprisingly unmoved. "I trusted you with all my plans and dreams," he said. "Bitter it is to discover that trust can be so utterly misplaced."

Lee's heart seized. Above, Dierrich's beautiful, grave, calm face contorted with rage. "When a madman trusts those around him to humor his madness," Dierrich said, "he'd better *expect* to be disappointed. We don't want you for our lord anymore, 'King of all the Elves!' Our people waited patiently, they watched a long time, to see if the exercise of power would eventually teach you sense. No one forgot how you came to rule, in your arrogance, so sure you knew everything just because your power was greatest! Half a millennium, we all thought, would teach you better. World-mastery's its own school, our forefathers always said; give it time to work. And for a while it looked as if you'd seen sense, and some of us became willing to stand with you. But then your vision went irrational again, and you went back to your paranoid babblings about the great war between the worlds that was coming. No one will ever manage such a thing—"

"The supranationals are managing it right now, Dierrich," the Elf-king said. "You've seen the preparations. You know the invasion they're planning as well as I do. Another six months, no more, and they'll be ready."

Dierrich's voice was scornful. "They don't have six months, and they don't even know it. We've been moving against them for the last five years . . . and *you* haven't even known it! We've been playing the ephemeral nations and worlds off against each other; our people have been killing their operatives, especially the Alfen double agents they've suborned, sending them the message. Alfheim is *ours;* no one plots against us and escapes, even though Alfen may be helping them. They in particular will pay the price of their treachery in full."

The Elf-king shook his head. "You still don't understand. Stop this attempt by the mortals, teach them the lesson you think you're teaching them, and they'll back down . . . for a few years, a decade or two. But they'll remember other things besides the lesson. They'll remember that we hold final power in our hands, and that they're powerless against it; that we exclude them in every way we know from any access to the true power at the heart of things. The resentment will build again. And in twenty years, or thirty years, or fifty, they'll come again; with much more terrible weapons, this time. Right now, armies, yes, nuclear weapons, yes, those we might be able to stop them from using . . . perhaps. Or even absorb such a blow, and rebuild. But in fifty years, when their weapons are more terrible than we can presently predict, when maybe all it'll take is one slip-up on our part, one day's relaxation of vigilance at our borders . . . and all life in our universe can be snuffed out in a week, or a day?" He shook his head. "This is our last chance, our best chance, to solve the problem—to cure the disease before it's too late."

Dierrich laughed, a great angry shout of laughter like the cry of a bird of prey. "You think the one thing that guarantees our survival as a people is a *disease,* something to be cured? You're even madder than I thought! If there's to be a war with the ephemerals, our immortality's the only thing that will ensure our victory!" Her voice went grim. "But it will never happen, because you won't be Laurin for much longer. *Rai'lauvrin het-suuriul,* worldmasterer that was and shall be no more, stand forth and end your reign!"

The feeling of gathering fury in the air, in the ground, gathering and growing, was difficult for Lee to bear. "I stand forth with my world in my hand," the Elf-king said, very softly, "but whether my reign shall end or not, the world itself decides."

The people among whom Dierrich had been standing now backed away from her. She stood there, proud and alone, fists clenched at her sides, holding herself like a weapon that has waited a long time to be unleashed, and is ready now. The Elf-king did not move at all.

The wind began to scale up to a scream again; just the wind, this time, no snow on it, howling among the parapets, battering the front of the castle. The Alfen watching her were pushed back by the force of it, against the inner wall of the castle. But the Elf-king didn't move. He let the wind rise, screaming, until first grit and then gravel and then even stones from the mountain above the castle began to be thrown through the air by it. Then he shook his head, and once again the wind fell away, silent in a breath's time.

Dierrich stood there, breathing hard. "All right," the Elf-king said. "Water next? Or fire?"

She didn't say anything, didn't move either.

Under them, the ground began to vibrate. A slow, low rumbling built, a sound like the deepest possible note on an organ, terrifying to feel, terrifying to hear. The stones of the mountain began to tumble again, down the jagged wall this time; great slabs and flakes of stone the size of vehicles, the size of houses, fell toward the castle, and the roots of the mountain shook. The Elf-king moved only so much as it took to glance up at the mountainside, an offhand look. The falling stones were aimed right at him; but as he glanced up, they fell to the left and right of the castle, as if hitting some high invisible barrier, and bounced away in a thunder of ruin, down the mountainside. At the same time, the clouds began to rush together above the castle, and rain began to fall from them, lightly at first, then harder, until the shower became a downpour, and the downpour a torrent.

In the cave, Lee could hear water splashing into the snow, and started to worry. *We could be flooded out of here,* she thought, *we could drown!* "Gelert—"

He was already scrabbling to his feet, wobbly as a foal. "Can you get up?" he said, but Lee was halfway up already, having kept hold of him as he stood. "Come on—"

She went with him, letting him lead, still unable to see except with the Sight, and unable to See anything with that but the terrace high above them on the mountainside. The Elf-king, who until now had moved not at all, now moved to the parapet of the castle and rested a hand on it, stroking the stone; under his touch the shuddering mountain slowly went quiet. Then he glanced up into the sky. He should have been wet, but the water storming down out of the sky never touched him. As he looked up, the clouds curdled, flattened, began slowly to stream away; and the rain stopped as they did so.

His face looked strained now, and Lee could see the sweat standing on his brow. But his expression was still composed, almost sad. "I don't think we need to go through the rest of the moves, Dierrich," the Elf-king said. "There's more to this than just weather . . . but you never understood that, no matter how often I told you. Mastery of a world means more than just making it do what you want. Mastery goes both ways, but you were never willing to accept the world's mastery of *you*. That's why you have no idea what it needs now . . . what it fears."

"And *you* do?" Dierrich shouted. "You're the one who wants to destroy our people's basic nature, make it over into something the world never intended! They'll have no choice in the matter if you have your way. But they'll find a way to kill you first, Laurin! If I fall here—"

"I am afraid," the Laurin said, "there's no 'if.' "

Over them, around them, a darkness began to gather. It was not the dark of night; this darkness excluded that, and was a different shade, of a different quality. It shut away the view of the clouds, the view of the city down at the mountain's foot. Dierrich looked up and around at this, and for the first time her face began to show fear. "It doesn't matter what you do to me, Laurin," Dierrich cried. "It doesn't mat-

ter if I die! The Alfen will still rise against you! Those of us
who know what you're planning will make sure that everyone else does—and afterward, no Alfen anywhere will refrain from trying to kill you, not even those who've been in
the pay of the UN and the supranationals all this while. You
think this whole business of transparency, of cooperation
with humans, will buy you the ephemerals' protection? It
won't be enough! Sooner or later, in mastery, or just with a
gun, one of us will take you out of Alfheim's history forever.
There's nowhere you can hide, now that your own people
fear you and the change you threaten, more even than they
ever feared being without a worldmasterer—"

"It's not change I threaten," the Elf-king said, as the
darkness gathered in the air around them. "It's something
that would frighten you much worse, frighten you the way it
frightens me, if you had the wit to understand it. But I guess
you never have. In the meantime, what mastery you possess
isn't nearly enough, though you do come of the line of the
old Elf-kings. For all that you grew up here, in the very heart
of the Land, in the shadow of Istelin'ru Semivh itself, you
still don't understand Alfheim." He was almost invisible
now in that darkness, and outside the cave, in air no colder
now than that of a normal summer night, Lee and Gelert
staggered into the lee of the spine of stone where they had
sheltered, both of them gasping with the sudden sense of
pressure in the air.

"Have you forgotten what this place once was?" the Elf-
king said. "I haven't. And *it* hasn't. But my memory for its
buried realities has always been longer than yours . . . even
though it's you who're supposedly old-world Alfen, supe-
rior to us outcasts, we 'foreigners' from the lesser realms
west over the Sea." His voice was suddenly amused . . .
though the amusement had something under it so dark that
Lee would have given anything to turn her Sight away. "It

makes you too uncomfortable, that oldest reality. Now comes the time when you pay for being unwilling to face that discomfort . . . and say your farewells."

The darkness gathered there about the castle became a solid thing, fathomless green depths that came real out of the night, and all remaining light wavered and went out in a sudden crushing night of water, a night half a mile deep. Lee couldn't close her eyes, couldn't stop seeing, as only one shape remained standing upright in all that darkness—and everywhere else around it, bodies flailed, bubbles rose in hectic streams until the lungs that gasped them out were crushed, and cries echoed bluntly through the massive weight of water until there were no cries left in it, and no more life. One last shape tried to stand, tried to fight, pushing the water away; but the sea knew its weight and its place, and nothing she did could dissuade it. Dierrich dil'Estenv crumpled to the stone of the parapet at last, the life crushed out of her; and when that was done, the waters ran slowly back into the past from which they had come, still leaving only that one form standing.

How long he would stay that way, Lee had her doubts, for she could see in his face the awful toll taken by what he'd just done. "I am the Laurin," the Elf-king said in a voice that itself sounded half-drowned, "and my world is in my hand; yet am I still its servant, until it needs me no more."

Then he fell.

The lock on her vision began to give. Had he held it there, Lee wondered, or was it again the world that was turning its attention elsewhere? From elsewhere in the castle, from a doorway on the terrace, other Alfen began to come running. The Elf-king turned, would have spoken to them— but before he could get more than a word or two out, he had fallen to his knees, then onto his face. They stood over him as the vision faded. Lee tried to keep it for a few seconds longer, could only manage to catch a few words.

"—put him somewhere secure—"

"Just kill him now! You see he can't do anything."

"Are you crazy?" The first voice was more frightened. "The World just said it wants him as Master. You kill him now, you could destroy everything even more certainly than he wants to do it. Lock him up, and then we'll get the other candidates for mastery and bring them here. Once the Land's accepted someone else, you can kill him all you like—"

They picked him up, hauled him away; and then the Sight was gone. Lee sagged against the stone of the rock-spur where she and Gelert had sheltered, shaking her head until something like regular sight returned. She and Gelert stood in the dark, in a rocky landscape where snow was melting fast, helped by rivers of water running fast enough down the trail past them to roll small rocks along.

It took her a few moments to tell Gelert what had happened. He shook his head, wincing at the pain from his ears. "And now," Gelert said, "we go rescue him, I suppose."

Lee looked up at the castle, in the darkness. She took a moment to test a theory, leaning her will against the world again. It gave, ever so slightly; all resistance, with Dierrich, was gone.

"I don't have anything else planned tonight," she said. "Let's go."

Twelve

It was like Lee's excursion into the building surrounding the "residence tower" all over again, except that the Laurin's House was much older, much more complex, and—instead of being middle-of-the-night quiet—alive with frightened, confused Alfen running in all directions. But this time Lee wasn't alone. This time an alert, angry Gelert was with her to help her sense what was going on around them; and this time both he and Lee had psychospoor to follow.

The Alfen presently in the Laurins' House were a mixed batch. Some, to gather from snatches of conversation Lee caught as they slipped from hiding place to hiding place in the ancient hallways, were loyal to Dierrich, and furious at her death; some were loyal to the Laurin; some wanted neither of them, but were stuck with the Laurin for the moment. It was in its way a perfect time to be attempting a rescue. Lee, though, was increasingly afraid that some ill-intentioned Elf was going to recover enough from the shock of the past half hour's occurrences simply to go to wherever the Laurin was being held and put a bullet or a forceblast through his head.

Are they gone yet? she said silently to Gelert.

Not yet. Hush up.

They were crouched together behind a door that led into a long, cold, dim stone corridor, somewhere in the depths of the castle. The room in which they were presently hiding was a wardrobe, full of Alfen ceremonial clothing, all very neatly hung up on clothes rack after clothes rack, the bags and carriers all tagged with numbers and notes written in the spidery Alfen diagonal cursive. The other rooms on this level seemed to be storerooms, as far as Lee could tell, not residential. They would normally have been of zero interest to Lee, except that her Sight and Gelert's Scent told them both that the Elf-king was in the room down at the end of the corridor. The problem at the moment was that there were at least four people standing in front of that door, all with guns, arguing with one another in Alfen.

Do you think that thing will fire? Gelert said to Lee, his nose working as he peered out through the crack of door opening that Lee was holding ajar.

Lee looked dubiously at the Alfen weapon she'd brought up from the cave. *After being snowed on, and rained on, and all the rest? God knows. It's not showing a charge light, and I don't know whether that's good or bad. Can't we just "walk" in there, using his spoor as an anchor? It's strong.*

Lee, it takes a lot out of you. I'd sooner save it for a larger distance. Ah—

Are they leaving?

Two of them. Gelert was silent for a moment. *No, three. They've left one guy outside the door.*

Armed?

Yes.

Damn!

It's not going to help him. I'm betting I can cover that distance before he can react.

Gelert—

Lee suddenly found she had no one to argue with: Gelert had slipped out the door in perfect silence and was running down the hall. She went out the door after him, leveling the weapon above Gelert's head-level at the Alfen standing in front of that metal-bound wooden door, feeling for the recessed trigger and praying that the thing would fire if it had to—

Gelert hit the Alfen chest-high and slammed him back against the stone wall by the door with terrible impact. The Elf with the weapon went down hard, the weapon practically leaping out of his hands. Lee wasn't in time to catch it before it fell to the stone floor, but it hit Gel first, and she caught it on the rebound, first glancing down at the unconscious Alfen, then at the short hallway they presently stood in. *Nowhere to hide him—*

Drag him back the way we came, around the corner there.

She did that while Gelert stood guard, then hurried back to the doorway the Elf had been guarding. It had a simple throw-bolt, not even keyed. Lee opened it; she and Gelert stepped inside, and she pulled the door to behind her and held it nearly closed.

It was another wardrobe, though this one had a single small translucent window, and only one or two racks of clothes, which to judge by the dust on the clothes bags hadn't been used in a while. The room was otherwise empty except for a business-suited form that had been dumped unceremoniously against the far wall.

He lay there lax, unmoving. Lee's stomach twisted inside her: *they've killed him already!* But then she saw his chest rise and fall. "Oh, thank God!" she said.

The Elf-king twitched, then. After a moment his eyes opened, and he looked at the ceiling.

He lay there a moment longer, then turned his head to

look around at his surroundings, and at Lee and Gelert. The look was uncomprehending.

Slowly he sat up, looking around him again. "It's a closet," the Elf-king said, sounding and looking at first bemused, then indignant. "They put me in a *closet!*"

"Probably because they thought you knew the way out of all the dungeons," Gelert said.

The Elf-king sat still a moment, as if considering this, and nodded. He got up then, slowly and with some difficulty, and brushed himself off. Finally, he came shakily over to Lee and Gelert, looking at them curiously, but with no surprise at all. He was as Lee remembered him, tall even for an Elf, dark-haired, dark-eyed, with a face like something the old Greeks would have sculpted as a god; except that not even the Greeks could have rendered sufficiently perfectly the perfection of the face Lee had first seen when curiosity at the sound of someone's voice made her look up from a fondue pot. And not all the processing in the Worlds could have kept Lee from recognizing his voice, now that she'd heard it not just twice but four times.

"I would ask what's kept you," said the King of All the Elves, "but that might sound ungrateful. Which I definitely am not."

Lee would probably simply have relapsed into staring at him again, for the effect of being close to him was very like that of her first view of Alfheim, and even more concentrated, for some reason; and the black eye and various cuts and scratches he had picked up since the battle on the terrace did nothing to lessen the effect. Lee wanted to weep, to turn away in shame at how little she looked like one of these people. Yet perhaps because she had been here for as long as she had, she was able to resist the urge. *Probably a good thing, because there's not a lot of time for standing around staring or crying right now,* she thought, and the thought was reinforced by a sound that raised the hair all over her: small-arms fire coming from somewhere nearby, perhaps the next hallway over.

"That's nice to hear," Gelert said. "Meantime, maybe it would make more sense if we all got ourselves out of here before the war zone gets any closer. . . ."

The Elf-king shook his head again as he looked at them, as if not quite sure yet that he believed in them. "How did you get in?"

"We 'walked,'" Lee said. "Maybe you have an idea as to the best way to get out? Seeing that you do live here."

"I'd walk you out myself, but I can't," he said. "They've given me a drug—"

"I know that drug," Lee said. "You have any idea how much they gave you?"

"There's a maximum dosage, which I haven't had, or I wouldn't be talking to you," the Elf-king said. "So it's less than that. They assume I won't be able to 'walk' unassisted for perhaps two days."

"Is there an antidote, by any chance?" Gelert said.

The Laurin shook his head. "It wears off—"

"It doesn't matter," Lee said. "They're not expecting anyone to help you get out. Let's go. Gel?"

"Where? Down into Aien Mhariseth?"

The Elf-king wobbled again, braced himself against a wall. "Not into the city!" he said. "They'd find us there in a minute. But if we can go around the mountain . . ."

"Where the rose garden isn't," Lee said. "I remember the way. Come on—"

He stared at Lee in utter shock. *What did you say?* Did you actually get there? Did you see it?"

"What?"

"The garden!"

It was Lee's turn to stare. "There's nothing up there but

stone and alpenrose," she said. "Nothing I could see, any-way." Then she added, "But there *should* have been some-thing. I could feel it, even if I couldn't see it."

"It was as I'd hoped," the Elf-king whispered. "I spoke to the World, told it to reveal the truth of itself to you, to help you every way it could. I didn't know how well it would work, if at all, for Dierrich's people were bringing all their power to bear on you, to keep you from Seeing." He rubbed his face. "You're lucky to have survived: if they'd thought you could See anything worth seeing, they'd have done their best to cause you to have an 'accident.' "

"They did. But then people we've met over the last few weeks who *don't* want us to have an accident seem to be in the minority," Gelert said. "Will we be safer where you want to go than we are here?"

"Marginally," the Laurin said. "But nowhere's going to be safe while you're with me."

"It's you we were trying to find," Lee said. "We'll take our chances. Come on!"

He took another step, staggered. Lee reached out and took him under one arm, and was briefly staggered herself by a sense of being abruptly out of circuit with her own body, forced into contact with a whole range of sensation that she didn't know how to understand—blurred and con-fused imageries, and a vast and looming presence that was watching her, watching—

Lee closed her eyes for a second, enforced control on herself as if during a Sight that had gotten out of hand, then opened her eyes again. The alien feelings receded, not com-pletely, but enough for her to get on with business. "I don't even know what to call you," she said. "Are you only 'the Laurin'?"

"That you'll know before the end. If we live that long . . ."

Lee gave him a look, wondering what that was supposed to mean. "Before we do anything else," she said, "I just want to say I'm sorry I stared at you in the restaurant."

"I'm not," the Elf-king said. "But let's wait to discuss it."

"Agreed," Lee said. "Gel?"

Gelert was standing by the door, his nose working, his eyes half-closed. "Three of them down the hall to the right," he said. "They're all armed. Getting ready to advance."

"No way we're going out the way we came in! Gel, the cave—"

"It'll do. Anything's better than going out in that hall," Gelert said. He paused, then said, "They're moving, Lee!"

Lee looked at the door and leaned her will against it, expecting to see the stony ground and the cave-spine in the midst of it, melting snow still piled in its lee. The image resisted her. Through her concentration, somewhat remotely, she could hear voices outside the door, getting closer, shouting in Alfen.

Come on, Lee said to the World, *this is important; cooperate!* She closed her eyes to See better, feeling the resistance begin to fray and weaken. Then it started dissolving much more quickly as Gelert once more found the key to the full shift before she did and augmented her vision with his. The changed world flowed around them, that brief chaosstage briefer than ever this time, barely more than a flicker of color before the darkness around them was overtaken by a lighter darkness—a sky still overcast, a landscape streaked with shadows cast from a fitful light above.

The three of them plunged forward, collapsed to the ground together. Lee caught the impact hard on her knees as she came down on them, and gasped with the pain of it. But the sound of gunfire, now farther up the mountainside, above and behind them, was extremely motivating. Lee managed to scramble upright again and got herself and the

Elf-king crouched down behind the stone spine that once more loomed in front of them. In its lee, amid the snow that still lay there unmelted, the three of them sheltered for a few breaths. Then Lee put her head a little way around the side of the spine, cautiously, not sure who might have seen them arrive and be targeting them.

Up on the walls of the Laurins' House, the gunfire continued, the energy weapons illuminating the space behind the parapets like localized lightning. "Nasty," Lee said softly. "Were you expecting a *coup d'état?*"

"For a century or so now," the Elf-king said. He was sitting with his back to the stone, still gasping with even the slight exertion that getting here had required.

Lee glanced at Gelert, concerned. *He's in bad shape, still. We're not going to be able to get out of here in much of a hurry if we have to . . .*

And we have to, Lee. As soon as someone who can sense psychospoor turns up there and works out what we've done, they're going to be right behind us.

"Poor timing on our part, I guess," Lee said. "Never mind. We've got to get you somewhere safer than this."

"I doubt anywhere—in this universe—will be very safe for long," said the Elf-king. "We need to leave. But I can't do it yet—"

"We can," Gelert said. "But it's going to take a little preparation. We're still beginners at this."

Lee nodded. "The only reason we've done so well this far is that the place is so malleable. . . ."

The look the Elf-king turned on Lee, then, was an odd one: both hopeful and frightened. "You understand," he said. "I was right. About this, if nothing else. I was *right . . .*"

"We'll congratulate ourselves later," Lee said. "We've got to move again. Where?"

"Lee!" Gelert barked, and threw himself away from the spine, straight at Lee and the Elf-king. The two of them tumbled over on the stones, feet away from the spine, Gelert coming down on top of them; and blaster fire from the silent craft that had come down on them now glanced off the spine and blew the top of it to chips and stinging splinters. The three of them scrabbled away in the direction from which the craft had come as it swung around for another pass. Lee stared at the ground beneath them, willing it to open and drop the three of them somewhere else, anywhere else: but as she reached out to grab the Elf-king's arm, pulling him after her, something caught her and held her still. He had pushed himself up on hands and knees, and was looking at the craft as it swung around, simply looking at it—

Every part of Lee prickled intolerably, and her eyes burned—and the lightning came streaking down out of the tattered sky to strike the craft full on. Deafened, blinded, she was thrown back rolling on the nearby slush-covered scree. Gasping, she lay there for some seconds before she could move. Lee got herself somehow onto hands and knees again, feeling scorched all over. It was some moments before her eyes cleared enough of the afterimage of the lightning to show her her surroundings again. Gelert was half-sitting, half-crouching, shaking his head; the Elf-king was laid out flat as a fish on the ground, unmoving.

"Gel!"

"I'm all right. What about him?"

Lee got up, scuttled over to him, trying to keep low. She was almost reluctant to touch the Elf-king again, after the last time, but she did it anyway. This time the rush of strangeness and the torrent of imagery was much less, though she wasn't sure whether that was a good thing. It occurred to her, as she took him and shook him gingerly by one shoulder, that she didn't even know how to address him. "Laurin—"

He groaned. Slowly he pushed himself up on his hands again. "Sorry," he said. "Sorry. Too close. My control—" He put one hand to his head. "It's not what it should be."

Gelert was up on his feet again, and came staggering over to them. "I can't smell a thing," he said. "Ozone . . ."

The stink of it was considerable. "We can't stay here," Lee said. "That last ship may have told someone where we were before they blew."

"Anyone already in the air, and a lot of others who aren't, will have seen that and realized what happened," the Elf-king said, using another boulder nearby to help him stand. "They won't be eager to come straight in and have the same thing happen to them. And they won't be sure that I can't do the same thing again, immediately . . . or that much worse isn't about to happen. Their uncertainty will buy us a few minutes. No more."

"Let's get downslope, anyway," Lee said. "Down shouldn't be hard."

"Not doing it all at once is the problem," Gelert said. He dodged off among some of the smaller boulders, finding something that would serve as a path to parallel the main one. Lee put her arm around the Elf-king again, but was surprised when he froze under the touch, then pushed her away, gently, but firmly. "No," he said. "Thank you. A bad idea, right now. I can manage."

She nodded, went after Gelert: the Elf-king followed them. For some minutes there were no more sounds than the grunts and soft curses of people banging their shins on half-seen rocks, recovering themselves, moving on in haste. For ten or fifteen more minutes they worked their way down the steep slope around the shoulder of the mountain, falling sometimes, sliding sometimes, while the terror sang in the back of Lee's brain, what if they come again without us knowing, without us seeing, the way they just did—But Gelert had spotted them; and as she turned to see how he was doing, the Elf behind her had his eye on the sky as well, grimacing with the pain of his injuries, but looking more alert every second.

Up ahead of them, indistinct in the darkness, was a little stand of arolla pine, several wind-twisted trees with a cluster of shattered boulders trapped among them. Here the three of them stopped again, briefly, kneeling or crouching on the downhill side of the trees to catch their breath. Lee looked up at the castle, scanned the sky, and could see no pursuit; not that she felt that much better because of this, or entirely trusted her perceptions. It was an uncomfortable feeling, especially at a time when their lives might depend on her Seeing truly.

Gelert was holding his nose up into the wind, Scenting. "Nothing new coming," he said. "You may have surprised them more completely than you thought." He let out a *huh* of laughter. "You sure surprised *me*. If more heads of state could do that kind of thing, politics would be a much more interesting field . . ."

"It's how kingship works here," the Elf-king said. "A ruler has to feed his people. Those of us who could understand the World well enough to make the weather do what the crops needed, lived to breed descendants who could make it do that even better. Those who were no good at it—" He shrugged. "The gift got strong in the families that fought it out to become the royal lines. These days we can do a lot more than just make it rain."

Lee shuddered, and sneezed, still smelling ozone. "So we saw."

"But if you did that to *them*," Gelert said, glancing back

up at the wreckage of the destroyed aircraft, "why don't you just do it to all the Alfen who're against you?"

"Because even I can't do it constantly," the Elf-king said, "and I certainly can't do it in my sleep. Besides, they're my people. I shouldn't be killing them. Normally I don't have to: normally they have some respect for my power. But right now it's drowned out by fear of what I may do if they leave me alive. Yet if I kill them, it's hard to convince them that they were wrong to be afraid of me." He glanced up into that dark sky, where the smoke of the crashed craft rose pale, fading against the night. "And if I can't convince them otherwise, there won't be much left here when the armies of the multinationals arrive to take control of the source of fairy gold . . ."

"You know about that," Gelert said.

"I've feared it for centuries," the Elf-king said. "I'd hoped perhaps it wouldn't come for another century yet. By then perhaps I'd have prepared my people for what had to happen to prevent it. But hope's failed; the time is now, and the world's not ready yet . . ." He looked down at the ground. "If in fact I haven't simply been deluding myself all this while."

Everything had been happening so quickly that Lee couldn't do much but sit back on her haunches and shake her head. Right now, all she could think of to say was, "And as for you and your midnight commcalls. You and your roses! Was there anything *more* dangerous you could have sent me here to snoop around?"

The Elf-king nodded. "Maybe not. I was sorry I couldn't have been more forthcoming with you, but my own comms were being monitored . . . and it causes talk if the King of all the Elves is seen too often to sneak out and use a public comm box. You were a last chance, and I couldn't even explain why—"

From behind them and above there came the sound of an explosion, somewhere inside the castle walls. The three of them looked up, startled; the Elf-king shook his head. "So much history, up there," he said softly. "And how it repeats. For every ten Elf-kings or Elf-queens who've been made up there, two or three have been destroyed. But in the old days the fights tended to be fair. Now my House is where knives are stuck into backs and plots are hatched in the dark, where the betrayals happen." He looked up at the castle walls, and laughed one harsh, bitter laugh. "Though they'd tell you I was pondering a betrayal worse than anything they could have thought of, and so I deserved to die."

Above, on the castle walls, lights ran to and fro, there were shouts, indistinct reports, the sounds of weapons being discharged. "Some of them must not even know you got away," Gelert said, looking over his shoulder at the light of energies tearing the night above them on the castle walls. "Or maybe some of them don't care . . ."

"Old rivalries are being sorted out," the Elf-king said, "too many of them. They're fighting in a burning building, and they don't even know it. Let's get away."

They kept on heading down the mountainside and across the lower face of it, half-sliding, half-stumbling in the dark. Once or twice they came across something that seemed like a path, but they were wary of taking it, and just kept on slipping and staggering down through dwarf oak and pine scrub and alpenrose, and the splintered limestone and scree of the cliff-face. Finally Lee came down on a ledge and glanced around her. The moon was still behind some of the tattered remnants of cloud, but her Sight was sufficient to confirm her sense of where they were. "Gel, we need to head upslope from here—"

"Five minutes to rest," Gelert said, scenting the wind again, and turning away, satisfied for the moment. "But we don't dare wait much longer than that. And we've got to decide what to do now. We can't just keep running this way."

They crouched in the lee of a nearby boulder. Lee glanced again at the Elf-king, having for the first time a few moments really to take him in—the torn suit, the bruises, the cuts, and the black eye. Yet the beauty was still there, overwhelming, almost frightening, something it felt dangerous to be near—for somehow, here on its home ground, it hinted at the lightning.

Lee shook her head. "She got you a good one there," she said.

"Dierrich?" The Elf-king's expression was too grim to be a smile. "She won't do it again."

There was no arguing that. Lee still couldn't stop looking at him, and glancing sideways at Gelert, she was somewhat surprised to see his gaze lingering on the Elf-king, too, with an expression that under more normal circumstances would have been unbelieving. "It wasn't an accident, that evening in the restaurant, was it?" Gelert said.

Laurin looked wry, like a man the victim of his own joke. "Do you mean, did I plan our meeting? No," he said. "But unfortunately, being the ruler of an entire universe doesn't always mean *you* get to say how things go. Often enough the universe itself makes its wishes known. The places I go, the things I do, are most often on Alfheim's business in the truest sense. When I went to Le Chalet Perdu that night, I had no idea why I'd agreed to attend that dinner . . . why I was sitting and being polite to people who bored me. Even when I saw you looking at me, and Alfheim spoke in my ear, and said 'That's the one whose help you need,' I still had no idea why."

"I'd be glad of any hints you might have on the subject now," Lee said.

"Hints I've got," Laurin said, "but answers are still

scarce. That you got me out of there seems to be proof that my World was right that I would need you. Yet how much further this will take us . . ." He looked around them.

"I don't want to hang around, Lee," Gelert said. "These people have at least some ability to sense psychospoor."

Lee looked over the top of the boulder, scanning in all directions for any sign of pursuit. "That was quite a stunt, up there at the castle," she said.

Just for a moment, as she turned back to it in the cloud-dimmed moonlight, that inhumanly handsome face was transformed by something that to Lee looked purely human: pride. "I'm my ancestors' son," the Elf-king said, "and no Alfen of this continent was ever able to match the mastery of *my* side of the family over our world. North American weather was always more of a challenge than this soft European stuff. And my own family learned to go deeper into mastery than others had . . . into give-and-take, rather than just forcing the world into submission. So when *my* people became rai'Laurinhen, we did it the old-fashioned way, by right of sheer power, not manipulation of the old Elves' network." The grin made the split lip bleed again. "They've never cared for that, some of these old-worlders. But the World knows its true master . . . eventually." The blood dripped; he felt the itch of it, wiped it away. "Whether that'll be enough to save me now, though, I don't know. I can't do such a work again for a while. I need some hours to recover my strength and take care of other matters. And if we try to stay here long enough for me to recover fully, they'll find us before it happens."

"We'll go for a nice long walk, then," Gelert said.

"Where, *madra?*"

"Where we came from, if we have to."

"Earth," Lee said. "Maybe even LA, if we can manage it.

At least we can get you to the authorities there . . . keep you
safe, until you can find a way to get back here again."

Just before the darkness that fell again as the moon went
behind a cloud, Lee caught an odd anticipatory glint in his
eye, a look of which she could make nothing. "On one side,"
he said, "I can't argue that we must move. Yet your Ellay on
Earth is one of the first places they'd look. Also, if I leave
here, there's a chance I won't be able to get back in again
and do what I have to—"

"But what do you have to do?" Lee said.

Inexplicably, she shivered; so did he, and all Lee could
tell was that it didn't look like his trouble was with the cold.

"Destroy Alfheim as we've known it," he said. "All my
people must become mortal, and our world must be
changed . . . or we'll all die, and so will everyone in all the
Worlds, everywhere."

Lee and Gelert stared at each other.

"You wouldn't be exaggerating a little, perhaps?" Gelert
said. "Stress can make people do that . . ."

"There's much to tell," the Elf-king said. "But not here.
We'll have to come back to Alfheim before too long, but for
the meantime we need to elude pursuit. Right now climbing
will do . . . and once we're up the mountain again, there are
other possibilities." He grinned, a slightly feral look. "Istelin'ru Semivh and I have considerable history. Once in
contact with its stones, even though I can't walk, I may be
able to surprise them—"

Lee raised her eyebrows at that. "This wouldn't be any
help to you, would it?" she said. She reached into her but-
toned pocket, unbuttoned it, and gave him the little stone
she'd picked up from under the alpenrose.

As it dropped into his hand, the Elf-king's face became
so torn between rage and delight that Lee had trouble look-

ing at him. He burst out in angry laughter. "What made you take this?"

"I don't know."

"I do," he said. "You did it because the World spoke to you; because it needed something from you." Even in the dimness, Lee could tell there was something else he wasn't saying. *And also because I needed something from you,* Lee Saw him thinking; *but then they're the same thing.*

The concept was peculiarly phrased, and Lee wasn't even sure she'd understood it correctly. "I do things for the same reason," he said, "and sometimes don't know why." He shook his head. "But I still can't believe that they took you up there on purpose. They can only have done it to taunt you . . . and through you, me. The arrogance of them! That place is *mine.*"

The fury blasted off him like a wave of heat. Lee almost felt inclined to shield her face from it.

"But the whole place is yours, I thought," Gelert said.

The Elf-king looked at Gelert in sudden surprise. Then he laughed. "Some parts of it more than others. That place, that side of the mountain . . . it has its own history. No matter what they told you, there *was* a garden . . . though few Alfen like to think about it; for my people's first great downfall happened there." He gave Lee a wry look. "It may have established an archetype. Anyway, let's get away first. There'll be a little time to tell you the tale: not much, for they've forced my hand."

"Do we still need to go all the way up there?"

"No," the Elf-king said, though as he looked up and over his shoulder, it was plain that he would have liked to. "The power of my ancestor is in this for me." He gripped the stone. "This was part of the old garden, where he invested so much of his strength . . . the right to which passes to me. With *this,* we can go from here, drug or no drug; and we'll go a way they won't think we'll go." He briefly looked concerned. "I saw what Dierrich did to the weather. I'm sorry to have to take you back into the cold, but it's a way they won't expect, and it'll buy us some time. Are you willing?"

Gelert looked up in the direction of the castle, around the shoulder of the mountain. Lee followed his glance, and saw the lights lifting into the sky. "Willing or not, we'd better go."

The Elf-king cupped both hands around the little stone, closed his eyes. The air off to one side rippled obscurely: not a big opening, not very steady-looking. "Go," he said.

Gelert wasted no time in going through the shimmer in the air. The Elf-king went after him, vanishing almost entirely, holding out a hand to Lee through the shimmer. She took it, and vanished after him—

—into the dark again. It was as well that she had been warned about the cold. Maybe it was the contrast with the warmer air on the mountainside, maybe it was her body's reaction to being so cold again after nearly dying of it earlier; but the bitter stillness of the air stung her all over, and burnt Lee's face like cold fire.

Gelert was shaking his head again, wincing with the pain in his ears. "I'm sorry," the Elf-king said. "We won't stay here a moment longer than we must: just long enough for our trail to go cold."

"*That* shouldn't take long," Lee said, hugging herself again, looking up and around her. They stood in a vast waste of snow, utterly still, utterly quiet. Just the little dry squeak made by Lee's shifting her stance on the snow seemed terribly loud. And the terror was a subtle thing, creeping up in the back of her mind, a sense that she shouldn't make sound,

shouldn't attract attention, for something, someone awful
was watching—

Gelert was looking up into that utterly black-and-crys-
talline sky at the stars there. The constellations were
strangely altered, and the aurora danced high in that sky,
great green-and-violet curtains, hissing softly. As they
started to walk, that hiss was the only sound besides the
squeak of their footsteps in the snow, and the strange small
tinkling sounds each exhalation made in the terrible cold of
the air. "Is this where I think it is?" Gelert said.

"Midgarth," the Elf-king said. "Yes." He looked around
him as if trying to find a landmark. Lee thought that would
be a good trick, in this landscape as bald as an egg.

"Over that way," he said softly. "I know what you're feeling. That sense of watching . . . But it's usually spurious.
We're not likely to attract any attention at the moment. The
Battle hasn't started yet, and when it does, it'll be far south
of here."

If Lee hadn't been shivering already, she would have
started then. This would be the middle of the Fimbulwinter . . . absolutely the last time any but the most foolhardy
tourist would want to visit Midgarth. All those of its normal
inhabitants who didn't desire to take their chances fighting
at the side of the Gods were elsewhere in the worlds now, on
work permits, or lying on the beaches of Huichtilopochtli or
Tierra, soaking up rays and giving thanks for worldgating
technology.

"We're probably lucky that all the worlds aren't like
this," the Elf-king said, beginning to walk. As he went, he
turned and looked over his shoulder, and saw Lee shivering,
and without breaking stride, took off his jacket and gave it
to her. "But something went wrong with Midgarth's entropy
patterning when the core of the sheaf rotated. So it keeps repeating and repeating this cycle . . ."

"While this may be the beginning of the story," Gelert said, "maybe it's a little too *far* toward the beginning . . . ?"

"Maybe it is. But then you know at least half the story already. I know you do because Hagen knew you did . . . and I have, or had, other operatives in his organization, tapping his comms and feeding me information about his doings, besides the one that Dierrich's people killed."

"Omren dil'Sorden," Lee said softly, as she slipped the Elf-king's jacket around her.

The Elf-king nodded. "No one bids for fairy gold at a price as low as that big contract he found out about," he said, "unless they know the price is about to fall. And the way that ExTel, and the various other multinationals and supranationals colluding with it, know that the price will fall, is that they have an invasion scheduled for eighteen months from now. They will enter Alfheim by force, and—" He broke off, rubbing his eyes briefly. "There are aspects of this I still find hard to discuss. They will at the very least overthrow our government and take control of fairy gold production themselves. But let that wait for a moment. Dierrich and her party knew about the multinationals' plan for a while, but they never took it seriously. Mostly they amused themselves with hunting down Alfen double agents working in the outworlds, or Alfen whose loyalties they find questionable, even doubtful. They've killed many innocents in this way— and drawn to themselves exactly the attention they were hoping to avoid."

"The Interpol report," Gelert said.

"Yes."

"So Hagen is involved with this invasion plan," Lee said, "and when it became plain that dil'Sorden had probably realized what that buy meant . . . Hagen had him killed."

"No, that wouldn't have been his idea. I think it more likely to have been Dierrich's order, and the Alfen who hired the triggerman, almost certainly, is Dierrich's deputy Mevel dil'Amarens."

"I think Gelert and I would like to interview this person," Lee said.

"I think you must achieve another state of existence to do so," the Elf-king said, "since he was among the fifteen or so of Dierrich's creatures whom I've just killed."

Lee and Gelert looked at each other, and Gelert nodded. "I scented him up there, too," Gelert said. "One more piece of information that the DA will be glad to have . . . but Lee, did you record that?"

Lee shook her head. "I don't suppose we could get you to testify at the trial?" she said.

The Elf-king gave her a thoughtful look, and nodded. "It will doubtless mean other disclosures," he said, "such as the names of my deep-cover people in the LAPD, who fed the information about your forensic sweeps to me. But if I live through the next few days—yes, I'll do that for you gladly."

If any of us live through the next few days, Lee Saw him think. She shivered again, feeling more strongly the effect of the darkness about her, and the horror. Lee had always had an idle idea that the largest periodic total migration from Midgrath, the periodic mass migration in the Worlds, except for the Hajj, probably had more to do with the weather than anything else. Now, though, she saw how very wrong she'd been. People in microcultures all over the Worlds dealt with the cold without too much trouble; some of them even liked it. But this leaden, deadly darkness, and the fear lurking away high in it, were something she hadn't reckoned with. Out there the forces of Night and Hatred were moving; for this little while, this world was their own, and what life or light they found, they would stamp out without mercy. Lee almost wished she didn't have to breathe out. She felt as if even that slight exhalation of warmth might attract the attention of something she emphatically did not want to see her. Glancing up at that black sky, for once she had no desire to See it any better. The stars up there were set in no friendly patterns. They were merely cold eyes for something that viewed her only with scorn, the pitiful devotee of a Power that had no power here, at least in this time—not until the Winter ended in devastation, and the rising of the new-made Sun over a world broken but reborn. But that wouldn't be for years yet, as this world reckoned time. Right now the dark Powers were in the full of their strength, and held this world in Their hands—

Enough time for our trail to go cold, the Elf-king had said. Lee wondered exactly how much longer that was going to take. The wind was beginning to rise, now, and it sounded like the howling of wolves; or of one wolf, huge, hungry, that waited to eat the Sun.

"We're close," the Elf-king said. "At any rate, Dierrich's party, and some other parties in Alfheim who would prefer some other Laurin, all think if they deal with the multinationals now, they'll be safe. But they're blind to the cause of the problem. Genuinely blind in some cases . . . willfully blind in others. Dierrich fell into that second category, and so was as dangerous to our world by herself as all the others put together. She really thought that if she derailed the plans that ExTel and their many friends in the outworlds had built so far, they wouldn't come back and try again. She thought they were just ephemerals, unable to hold a thought for more than a year at a time." His expression was grim. "But sooner or later, their corporate descendants would come back and try the same thing again; more violently, more conclusively. Because the symptom persists—the fact that will bring them back again and again. The transmission speed of fairy gold in Alfheim is many times what it is in the outworlds. What they don't realize is that this is because Alfheim is the heart of the sheaf."

Lee looked at him in the darkness. "You mentioned that before. What sheaf?"

"The sheaf of eleven universes of which Earth and all the others are part."

Gelert gave the Elf-king an incredulous look as he paced along beside him. "Excuse me. *Eleven?*"

"There are four more that you haven't found yet," the Laurin said. "This wasn't something we felt we needed to mention to the other universes, as it might have provoked awkward questions—such as, how did *we* know? The answers, however roundabout, would have led those in other universes to the realization that whoever controls the central universe of the sheaf exerts control over all the others. And that might have had unfortunate results."

Lee and Gelert could do nothing but stare at each other.

"There," the Elf-king said, and pointed. "Finally."

Just rearing itself above the snow line, now, Lee could see something jutting up: a ring of stones, far bigger than the one she'd seen in Alfheim. "A transit ring?" Gelert said.

"Not a mechanical one. No particle accelerators: or at least, none of the built kind. It'll serve our purpose, anyway. This gate swings only one way . . . and I can close it after us. Or jam it shut, which means that anyone trying to come after us will have to go the long way around through three other universes, the way they're aligned at the moment, to come at us."

He broke into a trot, and Lee went after him eagerly enough; it was a way to stay warm . . . and she was eager to get out of here. Gelert trotted alongside her, glancing from side to side as he went. "They say this is really nice in the summer," he said.

"I'll take your word for it," Lee said.

The cold was beginning to bite hard into Lee again, and she was glad to get to the ring of stones, she was delighted, though the evil look of them dismayed her. They were black, rough-hewn, ruinous; the way they leaned inward gave them a terrible look of silent threat, as if they wanted to fall and crush whatever walked among them. But the Elf-king walked into the circle as calmly as Lee might walk into her own living room, and stood there looking around him as casually. *When did I last think about my living room?* Lee thought, as she went in among the stones, glancing at them mistrustfully. Right now she would have given anything to be sitting there on the sofa, nice and warm, with her feet tucked up underneath her, watching something mindless . . . or even just the news. But that thought immediately brought up the image of yellow sodium-vapor lights illuminating black-and-whites, and a sheeted corpse lying near Eighteenth and Wilshire. *No,* she thought. *For his sake, I'll see this through—*

She went to stand beside the Laurin; Gelert joined her. The Elf-king had the stone from the "garden" in his fist again, and was standing there gazing down at the snow, a concentrating look. "I know a quiet spot where we're going," he said. "You don't have to move. Just stand still and let the effect pass—"

Lee set her teeth as the cold, dark world around her shimmered and wobbled, as the cobweb feeling swept over her body and rooted in her bones for a long time, too long. She felt as if she was being thrown in the air like a ball, while outside her the world tumbled and tore itself to pieces in a way of which her Sight could make nothing, a distortion more upsetting than any mere gate-complex hula she'd ever experienced. After a moment everything settled down, and she opened her eyes, which she'd shut in self-defense.

It was hot, incredibly hot; but that was probably only by

contrast with the place they'd just come from. And she and Gelert and the Elf-king were standing in a little triangular park with two streets running along either side of it. There were wheeled vehicles, some of them parked on either side of the little triangle of concrete and grass: others drove by on the ground, bright yellow. *Taxis?* Lee thought. *New York?*

It was New York. But it wasn't. Lee looked around her, trying to See the difference. The street signs on the pole at the nearest corner said AVENUE OF THE AMERICAS and 12TH STREET; but the feel of the street on which she stood was so alien and different from that of the New York where she and Gelert had been not three weeks ago that Lee felt like she might as well have been on Mars. "This isn't Earth," Lee said. "Or Tierra. This is the new world, isn't it—"

"Terra," the Elf-king said, and it was all he could say for some moments. He bent right over at the waist, holding his legs like a runner who's just finished a marathon, like someone bracing himself in a desperate attempt not to fall over.

"My God," Gelert said. "Except for the initial investigation team, we must be the first ones to visit here . . ."

"Oh, no," Laurin said, and gasped for another breath. "Not at all."

They waited rather nervously for him to recover himself, wondering who was going to come over to them and demand to know who they were and where they'd come from. But no one was nearby, and no one at any distance paid the slightest attention to them. The Elf-king managed to straighten up a little, glancing around him, and getting his breath back. "You'd think people appear out of nothing every day here," Lee said.

"Probably not," Laurin said, "but if they did, what would people do? Tell the police? I seem to remember you didn't have a lot of luck with that." He looked amused, though not at Lee specifically. "And your police are probably a lot more broad-minded about people appearing and disappearing than the police here are."

"I wouldn't bet money on that just yet," Gelert said. "Wait till we go to trial." He looked around him thoughtfully. "You say that the Alfen who're going to follow won't be able to do so right away?"

"I'd be surprised if they could."

"How much time do we have?"

"Some hours, at the very least."

Gelert sat down, then, panting, looking like he was very much enjoying the hot humid air. Lee certainly was: but she still didn't feel she felt entirely comfortable. "So your people knew about this place before the investigative team in Greenland did?" she said.

"Years before they did," the Elf-king said.

"And you never thought to tell anyone?"

"We thought about it. Or rather, I thought about it. But there were reasons against it."

"Well, it's nice of you to decide for us what we should know and what we shouldn't!" Lee said.

"Swiftly enough I wished *we* didn't know about it," Laurin said. "After that all we could do was try to contain it, and there was only one way to do that: silence." He frowned at the cityscape around him. "We were the first ones to come to grief here. So many of us . . ."

He shook his head. "Not right now. Are you all right?"

Lee twitched her shoulders a little as she handed him back his jacket. "I'm not sure," she said. "Things don't look right somehow."

"They're not," the Elf-king said. "Come on—we have someplace to find."

The three of them headed for the corner of Sixth and started walking downtown. "We started exploring here not long after I came to rule," Laurin said. "At first it was casual interest; there were peculiarities about this world's timeflow. And other details that made it interesting." For a moment his face went closed; Lee noted that for later reference. "Normally those who went to explore, or visit, or even settle here, lost interest eventually and came back to Alfheim. Partly because of those oddities in the timeflow: four or five hundred years here would feel like a thousand years of local time in a more normal universe, say Earth. Of course that made this world a little unpopular: for my people the sensation of an accelerated timeflow like that is similar to chronic tiredness. But that seemed the place's only drawback at first. Then, slowly, we noticed that our people who came here were beginning not to come back. It was hard to understand the causes."

Then the Elf-king sighed, and the face that had seemed to be holding on to its secrets suddenly looked completely open, and frustrated. "Or maybe I should say, it was hard to get anyone interested in understanding the causes. Except as regards business, which means the fairy gold import/export business, the upper levels of our governmental structure have for a long time resolved that our people should be left alone in their travels into other worlds. There's been a general sense that once an Elf willingly walks beyond the bounds and into the realms of the ephemerals, it's that Elf's business what happens to him."

It occurred to Lee that this would explain some of the Alfen indifference to their own outworld murder statistics. "You mean," Gelert said, "once he goes where he doesn't belong . . ."

The look Laurin gave him was not nearly as hostile as Lee had been expecting. "There are enough of our people who feel that our kind shouldn't have anything more to do with humans than absolutely necessary," he said.

"Except to sell them allotropic gold," Gelert said.

They paused to wait for traffic lights to change at the corner of Sixth Avenue and Ninth Street, and Laurin sighed. "This goes partway to the root of the reason. There came a point where we knew that there remained some tens of thousands of Alfen in Terra, many of whom had been in relatively frequent contact with home . . . but more and more of them dropped out of contact, until now none had been heard from, not one, for many months. I began expressing strong interest in these disappearances. But I met a great deal of resistance." His expression would have looked wry, were it not also so very bitter. "Unfortunately, being absolute ruler of a world doesn't always mean that you routinely get what you want. Those theoretically subject to you soon become expert in finding ways to pursue their own agendas—and to make your own work difficult, in subtle ways, if your agenda conflicts with theirs. Nonetheless, I pushed the *Miraha* to set up an investigation of what was happening to our people in Terra. They resisted, but when I made it plain that they were not going to 'wait me out' of this desire, finally they agreed."

They paused at the next block for another light. "So you sent your own team here," Lee said.

"Yes; and quite a well-equipped one." Laurin's expression now was wry, indeed ironic. "In fact, some of those whose paths we crossed mistook us for space aliens. That seemed funny at the time. But in retrospect I would have far preferred the commonplace kinds of alien strangeness one runs into in Xaihon's universe to the awful kind the investigators found. The group returned safely, but they were unanimous that we should do everything we could to lock Terra away from the other worlds forever."

"But *why?*" Gelert said.

"There are problems with natural law here," Laurin said. "Terrible problems. *Science* is broken. The set of principles defined by the grand unified theory itself is flawed; something's damaged it, so that particles which should exist don't, or decay in bizarre fashions unknown anywhere else. Whether this is causally attached to the problems with that universe's ethical constant, we still don't know. But Terra's constant seems 'set' terribly low—lower than the constant in any other world. There are crimes here—" He shook his head. "You can't imagine. How good survives here at all, I don't fully understand. But Terra's universe is . . . not exactly maimed: say rather it has birth defects, terrible ones. There seems to be no way to correct them. But what's more frightening is that they're potentially contagious."

Lee had been wondering about the strange edgy sensation she'd been having since they arrived here, expressing itself in Sight as a slight uncomfortable skewing of things viewed, as if things just didn't look right. Now she understood why, and she shivered. There had been nothing about this in the articles Lee had read at home about this world's discovery . . . but then the emphasis of most of those had been economic or political. *And possibly it would have taken much longer stays for people who weren't trained sensitives to feel this difference . . .*

Gelert had been listening with eyes half-closed as he stood waiting for the light. Now he glanced up. "Some of the people with whom *'we'* crossed paths?" he said.

"Not much gets by you, does it, *madra?*" the Elf-king said. He sounded faintly amused as the light changed and they crossed the street. "Yes, I went with the investigatory team, though my people tried to prevent it. They were terrified of what would happen to Alfheim if something happened to me, for the Laurin traditionally doesn't leave the Realm for long, or go too far out of the way. Some rai'Laurinhen have never left, have spent their whole lives in the one world—some never even leaving Aien Mhariseth, for fear that without them in their proper place at the center of the universe, that universe would fail."

He laughed very softly. "Well, that was never going to be my style, as I made plain at my accession. I knew my world was robust enough to be able to do without me for a while. Yet Alfheim's own fear was already creeping into my bones . . . and feeling the world's fear, I was already afraid enough myself to insist that something terrible was likely to happen if I *didn't* go. The *Miraha* fought me. But I have ways of fighting back."

"So we saw . . ." Lee said.

He nodded, looking rather grim. Lee found herself wondering, perhaps unjustly, how many members of the *Miraha* the Elf-king had had to replace after the fighting died down—and then she suddenly wondered about the title some of them bore, the "Survivor Lords."

"So off we went into Terra," the Elf-king said, "at least as blindly and in as much ignorance as your own team came just now into Alfheim." There was no rancor in the way he said it, just a kind of rueful acknowledgment. "We arrived in a time which would roughly have corresponded with the late 1940s in your own world. We were aiming for a later period, but the way time runs in this universe, what with local eddying and the complexity of other forces affecting the home planet, it's not always possible to come out where you intend. As it happens, it was good we came out where we did."

They stopped for one more traffic light, and Laurin's face twisted in a way that suggested "good" was a word he would not normally have chosen. "Our study of the local history soon showed why our people had been vanishing," Laurin said. "Where their differences were sensed at all by the humans in Terra, they were hunted down without mercy . . . sometimes imprisoned or tortured: usually killed. But that was just a symptom of a wider malaise. Terra's world-soul had been withering steadily over the previous decades, as technology enabled its creatures ever more freely to enact their fears and hatreds of one another, their darkest desires. And the more they were enacted, the darker the desires grew. Finally, they found their fullest flower. A great war broke out here, as it did in Tierra about that period. The whole planet was convulsed with that war. But one side hit on a novel idea. It told its people—mostly for purposes of political advantage—that one specific kind of humanity was responsible for its troubles. It would solve its problems by completely wiping them out."

Lee stared at him, uncomprehending. "What?"

"They even have a word for it in most of the major languages here," the Elf-king said. "They call it 'genocide.'"

She and Gelert stared at each other again. "You mean," Gelert said, "that everyone on both sides fights, and all the people on one side are killed—"

Laurin shook his head. "I mean that one side captures all of one kind of human—say, all the Anglos in Ellay, or all the Xainese in New York—or let's even say all the people of whatever kind in Brasil, or Belgium, for there were signs when I last looked in that the definition was widening to where people lived, from what kind of people they were—and simply puts them to death."

Lee stopped in the middle of the block and stared at him in utter disbelief. *"How can such a thing be permitted . . . ?"*

"It's as I said. Their universe's ethical constant is set too low for the world itself to prevent such a crime. Thousands of our people were caught up in the war and killed, as both fighters and victims. Others were devoured in the greater terror, the one the Terrans made other names for: the *shoah*, the Holocaust." For a long moment he stared at the ground. "Some of my people," Laurin said, hardly to be heard now, "their natures twisted by the nature of the world around them, may even have been ... involved in the species-killing. Drawn into it by the desire to wipe out those more mortal, less perfect than they ..."

Lee could think of nothing at all to say. The silence hung heavy and deadly for a long time.

"But the terror here is an indicator of what's coming toward us," Laurin said. He shook his head. "To a certain extent, we're protected from such things until we know they exist."

"Heisenberg ..." Gelert said.

"Yes," the Elf-king said. "The observed affects the observer. That's the problem. As soon as we have perceived such a thing and know it to be real, in one world ... then it can spread to other worlds as well. Perhaps now it can also become worse yet. Now that we know 'genocide' is possible ... what else, worse than that, may become possible as well?"

Lee looked at Gelert in apprehension and horror.

"I still have some control over what I think," Gelert said, "so I'll exercise it."

"But others have no desire to exercise such control," Laurin said. "There the danger lies. All the same, when our team came back, we devoted all our energies, every scrap of our knowledge about the local world-sheaf, to find a way to seal Terra away from the other worlds. Our control over worldgating in our own spaces ..." He trailed off suddenly.

Gelert looked at him. "It extends to control over worldgating in other spaces as well, doesn't it."

It took a few moments before Laurin would meet Gelert's eyes. "Our world's position at the heart of the sheaf ... gives us certain advantages. We did everything we could, manipulating space to close down 'rogue' gating accesses on Terra. It has an unusual number of free-state gates—far more than any of the other cognate worlds in the sheaf except our own. Every one of them was potentially a way for contagion to spread. We closed all of those gates that we could find, except for a few that were too powerful; and those we watch. We also manipulated our own space to make access from the other worlds in the sheaf to Terra as difficult as possible. That work was mostly mine, as rai'Laurin. Whenever I've traveled in recent years to another world in the sheaf, there may have been business or politics involved, but also there's always been a more covert purpose: to make sure the walls between the worlds are holding— holding Terra out."

"But they're not holding anymore," Gelert said.

The Elf-King shook his head. "It was never more than a stopgap measure. Terra is as much a part of the sheaf as we are, horrible thought though that might be. And even if some other world didn't find them, they were likely enough to find us, eventually. They've got their own MacIlwains, working in high-energy physics right this minute. Fortunately, most of their research in physics is crippled by penny-pinching governments who have no inkling of what it's good for." He looked grim. "But it doesn't matter now. Your own people, and then the Tierrans, found Terra. By doing so they've pulled open a door that we can no longer keep closed, though we did our best. Now that they know Terra exists, the leakage of conditions there has begun. It'll get much worse when actual commerce begins between Terra and the other worlds; a matter of no more than a couple of years now, I'd guess. This world's ways, and ideas, and maybe even its ethical constant, will start to seep into yours. Eventually it will seep into Alfheim, too. And what happens in our world—"

Laurin broke off, like a man trying to avoid making a vision real by not giving voice to it. "And you can see it starting already, the pattern . . . repeating, spreading and growing in violence since Terra was rediscovered. Our people are being killed in ever-increasing numbers . . . though there always seem to be other reasons behind the killings. Politics, always; our people are too political. Those who oppose me, those who support me, those who think they can do without me—they've been savaging one another, using Alfen abroad as their tools, killing each other's tools more and more often. The factions think they see their way clearly. . . ."

"But they're being played off against each other by those with another set of agendas," Lee said. "The multinationals. The national powers and supranationals in every world, who see that the Elves control all the fairy gold, and it costs them too much. At least that's their excuse; it's bad for business. But the truth is that they want that control for themselves. And it's easy to hate the Alfen. They're not really people, are they . . ." The joke began repeating itself in her head. *What do you call a thousand dead Alfen? Ten thousand? A hundred thousand? A start . . .*

Slowly, Laurin nodded. "They've seized on this idea as the perfect way to maximize their bottom lines," he said. "They have their private armies; they even have nuclear weapons. Those have never been used before . . . not like in poor Terra. But they will be now, as that possibility also occurs to the multinationals, who aren't territorial and have least to lose. They'll come to Alfheim, and my people—wealthy beyond the dreams of avarice, unwilling to compromise or empathize with ephemerals—will be wiped out without mercy. Humankind will take possession. But they won't know how to manage our world's centrality, or contain the damage they've done by killing us."

Another long silence followed. Lee gulped. "If Alfheim is so central that what happens there eventually happens to every other world . . ."

The Elf-king looked at Lee, and nodded. "Within decades or less, all our worlds will lie empty of everything but corpses. That's the nightmare that's chased me from universe to universe, these last three centuries, these last five years . . . and now it's starting to happen at last."

They walked in silence for a while. "Where are we heading, exactly?" Lee said.

"East, and a little farther downtown," the Elf-king said. "There's another potential 'rogue' access nearby; we can use it to get out of here, and slow down the pursuit a little more."

He waited until they came to the next corner, gazed up at the sign. "This is it," Laurin said. "East from here."

They crossed Sixth Avenue. "It's weird," Lee said absently, while her mind was turning over the awful things the Elf-king had told them. "Except for the vehicles, the place looks normal." She glanced down Sixth Avenue. "But where's the World Trade Center gone?"

Gelert glanced down the way she was looking, shrugged his ears, winced. "Other side of the island, maybe? This *is* an alternate universe . . ."

They went on down Ninth Street, past the brownstones, mostly ignored by passersby who saw nothing but a man, a woman and a very big white dog, possibly some kind of wolfhound. Lee, for her own part, was finding it increasingly difficult just to be in this space; it itched, burning on her skin, and she wondered how the people here bore it. This was not a world that was kind to life. Her lungs were burning, too, not just with smog. The air here was full of something unfriendlier still, the presence of a universe that didn't care anymore, if it ever had. *How do you make a universe stop paying attention to what happens in it? How badly do you have to hurt it that it turns its back on what's living in it, just lies there, passive, unwilling to get involved?* For she couldn't shake the feeling that this place hadn't always been this way; its ethical constant hadn't always been this low, couldn't have been. Something had to have happened.

Or you hope it did, the colder side of her mind answered her back. *What if it was always this way? What if this is a perfectly normal way for some universes to be? And what if, when our sheaf rotates again someday, more universes are created like this—or worse?*

That was a thought too awful to entertain. *It has to be possible to heal such places,* Lee thought, *or to keep them from happening. If there was any way, any way in the worlds—*

They went around the corner of Ninth Street and Fifth Avenue, Laurin leading the way at a steady pace, heading uptown again now, looking always to the left of the street. Every now and then he gazed up at one or another of the buildings he passed. Finally, in front of one, an apartment building, he stopped.

Lee and Gelert caught up with him. The Elf-king looked up at the façade of the building, a golden brick Beaux-Arts building shorn of most of its ornament over many years, then walked on again, toward the next corner. "This is the place," he said.

Lee glanced back at the building. "What place?"

"In New York," he said, "—the New York in Earth, any-way, this is where our embassy to the UN&ME is located."

"Doesn't do us a lot of good here," Gelert said.

"But it does," Laurin said. "The Alfen Embassy has a gat-ing ring in it."

Lee and Gelert exchanged glances. The three of them paused at the corner, looking back the way they'd come, while oblivious passersby avoided them. "That piece of real estate is accustomed to being used for transits between Alfheim and the other worlds many times each day," the Elf-king said. "Such concentrated use means that the immediate neighborhood acquires resonances to other congruent spots in the neighboring worlds. Like this one."

"You mean we can get out from here—"

The Elf-king looked down the street, back the way they'd come, a nervous glance. "We should have enough time. I can't manipulate this world as easily as I can my own, no matter how powerful the local congruences are, but it should still work, thanks to this—" He tossed the pebble in his hand, pocketed it again. "Come on," Lee said.

They headed back down the block, passing by the frontage of the building again, more slowly this time. The Elf-king gave the front of the building no more than a glance; the building's doorman, a burly man in a long uniform coat, was standing there, looking at them without any tremendous interest, but noticing them nonetheless. "It's your fault," Lee muttered under her breath to Gelert. "You stick out like a white elephant."

"I was hoping for a gateway," Laurin said, as they passed a few doors down. "One of those alleys they have beside these buildings, sometimes, for access to utilities . . . the place where you leave the garbage for pickup."

It had never occurred to Lee that the King of All the Elves would notice, one way or another, what humans did with their garbage. She smiled, and beside her, Gelert made a couple of the small huffing sounds he used for audible laughter. "Not on an avenue," Gelert said. "But around the corner, on a side street, maybe. Let's have a look."

They headed around the corner again, but that whole side of the street was another large apartment building, and the barred gateway beside it led visibly down a dead-end alley and nowhere else. "We'll have to go around the block," Gelert said. He trotted on down the street, and Lee and the Elf-king trotted after him as if in pursuit of some refugee from the local leash laws.

"Will you need help with this gating?" Lee said.

"Probably it's better you let me handle it," Laurin said. "It wouldn't do for this particular transit to become deranged."

"The problem with you," Lee said, "is that you're a control freak."

The Elf-king grinned, and it was as feral an expression, for just a flash, as anything Lee had ever seen on Gelert. "By definition," he said. "Control is all a Laurin's for. One who doesn't, is dead." He looked ahead. "Where did he go?"

"Right—"

They went right around the next corner, their pace flagging a little, but Gelert was still trotting strongly ahead of them. Lee saw a few concerned pedestrians shy away from him to either side of the sidewalk as he came running down toward them, tongue lolling out and big jaws wide, a frizzy-coated white shape ten hands high. "Sorry," Lee called to them as she and the Elf-king ran past, "he gets out like this every day . . ."

When he stopped at last, and they caught up with him, they were facing a blind black metal gate at least ten feet high that shut away the alley behind it from view. Gelert reared up against it with his forepaws, shaking the gate until it clanged. "Not locked," he said. "Bolted from the inside, though."

"Oh, great—" Lee said.

Gelert sat down. Lee gave him a look. "Gel—"

The spring took her completely by surprise. Gelert was tall enough to begin with, and the strength of those powerful haunches sent him a good six feet into the air: he threw his forelegs over the top of the gate like a high-jumper trying to clear the bar, hung there in a most undignified position for some moments as his hind feet scrabbled and scratched at the sheer front of the gate for purchase—then found it, tipped himself over the top, and fell to the concrete on the other side. There was a yelp.

"Gelert? Gel, are you all right?" Lee said.

There was a long pause, too long. "Uh," Gelert said after a moment. "I came down wrong. Might have broken a tooth."

"Oh, Gel!"

"Might break another one," Gelert's voice came from the other side of the gate. "Told you we shouldn't scrimp on our dental plan. Let's see what I can do about this bolt."

They waited. Not far away, horns honked, and all around them life went on; people passed and looked with some slight curiosity at a man and a woman hanging around an alley service door . . . but it was the man they looked at, and Lee knew all too well the expression that was beginning to grow on their faces. Some of the people passing paused, then moved on; but the pauses were getting longer. "Come on, we're getting obvious here," Lee said softly. "Don't just stand there looking the way you do."

The expression in Laurin's eyes as they flashed sidewise at her was edged. "What do you suggest?"

She reached out and took him by the arm and turned him toward the door, bent her head toward his. "The only reason people stop in the middle of the street like this," she said softly, "is if they're exchanging sweet nothings, or having a fight. So if you'll just—"

As he bowed his own head toward hers, Lee found herself looking into his eyes again. It was astonishing how very dark a brown they were, almost black; and how very old. And not just his own two thousand years were there, Lee thought, but something more alarming—a terrible arrested youth, in abeyance for who knew how long now, waiting for who knew what liberation; but never realistically expecting to find it. Here was a king who even though he had fought his way to more freedom than any of his predecessors, was still prisoner of his throne, trapped in a situation which often enough had left him wondering whether death might be preferable. But now he was faced with a challenge desperate enough to shake even that idle surmise to fragments. Now death might indeed be coming after him, but he would resist it to the last, if only for the chance of finding the answer, finding—

To see oneself in another's eyes can strike any human heart deep; but Lee Saw herself there, not in any way she had expected, and without warning. Pierced, not knowing what it meant, what *he* meant or wanted, she staggered, almost fell against him, but was startled out of it by a soft groan in front of her—

—as the bolt inside the gate popped out of its socket and ran back, and the gate swung open in front of them. There stood Gelert, licking his chops and looking both uncomfortable and satisfied. "Henry the Magic Dentist is going to be cross with me when I get home," he said.

Lee and the Elf-king went in past him. Gelert pushed the gate closed again and followed them. The space beyond them was narrow: four high walls, two of them blank, two of them with windows up high that belonged to the apartment building, and some lower ones and a couple of doors that were utility entrances. The ground was stained concrete, cracked in places. The Elf-king walked in a short arc across it, then paused.

"Well?" Gelert said.

"This is it," the Elf-king said. "Still open . . . but not for long." He stood still a moment, then started walking again, pacing out the bounds of the gating circle.

Lee twitched again, feeling the inimical quality of this world fraying at her composure. "Are you sure this is going to work?" she said.

"It has little choice," the Elf-king said absently, as he finished the circle he was making in the little concreted space. "All spaces are continually trying to become all the other spaces that were created at the same time the core of their sheaf rotated. The difficult thing isn't bringing them together, as a rule; it's keeping them apart . . ."

He stood up straight, then, with a grim look on his face. "Crude," the Elf-king said. "But it'll work. You saw the circle? Step in, and we'll go where my own power is centered."

"Where," Gelert said, "Aien Mhariseth?"

"Not at all. Ellay."

Lee blinked at that. "Or rather, the version of Ellay that lies in Alfheim," the Elf-king said.

"You have a house there, don't you," Lee said. "I remember reading about that somewhere."

"The gossip columnists are fascinated by it," Laurin said, looking faintly annoyed. "They're sure the place is full of fabulous treasures . . . but they wouldn't know the real ones if they sat on them." He let out a breath of laughter. "Never mind that. Come into the circle . . . we have work to do."

"What work?" Gelert said as he paced into the circle and sat down.

"As you do," said the Elf-king, "I have a case to make . . . and a job to do."

Lee went to stand beside Gelert, wondering what to make of this. "You said your people feared to kill you," Lee said, "but feared even more what you might do if they left you alive . . ."

"I told you," the Elf-king said. "They think I'm going to destroy my world."

Gelert flicked his ears back and forth, so incredulous he forgot to wince. "Are they crazy?"

"Not in the slightest," Laurin said. "I *will* destroy it.

That's why I came to Earth: looking for a way to do that." He glanced over at Lee. "And I think I've found it."

She found herself shaking. "It's not them that's crazy," she said. "It's you."

The Elf-king shook his head. "The problem is that I'm still not sure," he said. "There's a factor in the destruction that hasn't been fully resolved yet."

"What?"

"You."

Thirteen

They stepped out into heat even more fierce than midsummer in New York. "But at least it's *dry* heat," Lee said, as she looked around her, relieved, though still profoundly disturbed by what the Elf-king had been saying.

"What an Angelena you are," Gelert said, and gazed around him too. They were standing on a hillside that in their own Ellay would have been up on one of the hills behind Pasadena, with the view of Lake Val San Fernando stretching down in front of them towards the sea, and Ellay proper off to the left. But here there was no lake. Lee looked down at the San Fernando Valley as it had once existed hundreds of years before on Earth—a great basin of widely scattered sagebrush, piñon pine, and wild walnut trees, still a desert dappled in olive-green and gold, barren but beautiful. Beyond the Santa Monicas to the southeast, the Alfen version of Ellay rose: a smaller city, still a fairly substantial gridwork etched on the Ellay basin, with the shimmer of the Pacific beyond them.

The whole hill on which the three of them stood was part of a walled compound that stretched far down below them to a terrace scooped out of the hillside. On the level ground there, a big white-stucco house with many wings and many red-tiled roofs sat toward the back of it; in front of it, between the house and the view, were formal gardens, patios, and paved terraces, a swimming pool. "We won't have long at peace here," the Elf-king said, leading them down the hillside by a little path that switched back and forth along its face. "When they realize how we've fled, this will be one of the first places they'll think of coming. But it has certain protections around it. No one but I can come here by gating; flying craft are also inhibited for some miles in all directions. And to a lesser extent, the World also takes care of the place." He looked troubled.

"But you think it might not now," Lee said.

"Everything becomes uncertain now," the Elf-king said, and suddenly looked very tired. "All the imponderables come together here. But come on . . . I can at least give you something to eat and drink before the trouble starts."

Before I die, Lee Saw him think. Her sudden realization of how very hungry and thirsty she was, and how tired, was somewhat blunted by the realization that she did not normally See what people were thinking so clearly. *Is it Alfheim?* she wondered. *Or is it him?* . . . But then she'd been doing it in Terra, too—

They made their way up onto a patio behind the house, then up onto a deck that surrounded the house completely. The back wall of the house, looking onto the hillside, was one big wall of glass; the Elf-king led them over to a set of patio doors in the glass, spoke them open. Lee thought longingly of her own patio doors as they went in.

A huge living space opened out in front of them, down a few steps—painted tile, glass, massive pale-stained furniture, a huge dining table. The architecture was surprisingly Southwestern, in stucco and distressed-oak beaming, except that the characteristic Alfen buttressed "neo-Gothic" arch was repeated in the windows on the valley side. "Palatial," Gelert said. "But then I guess there's a certain expectation that you of all people might live in a palace. . . ."

Laurin laughed at that. "This isn't anything," he said. "You should have seen the style in which my ancestors lived. This would have been a rustic country lodge to them. In fact, it *was* a rustic country lodge. This house is built on the foundations of one my grandfather built when he came with the first Alfen who came here for the gold rush."

Lee looked around her, bemused. "It seems a lot older than that . . ."

"*Our* gold rush," the Elf-king said. "Around your year one hundred fifteen of the common era. This house has been remodeled many times—the last time would have been in the seventeen hundreds. Come on along this way—"

They followed him into a kitchen that opened off the living space. Lee immediately fell in love with anyone who could design a room so big, so useful, and so humane. The Elf-king went over to the fridge and looked inside, then made a face. "I knew I should have gone shopping last elevenday," he muttered. "Nothing but mayonnaise and *mneush*."

"What's *mneush*?" Gelert said, sticking his head into the fridge.

"An acquired taste, and I don't think you have time to acquire it today," Laurin said, going over to a nearby floor-to-ceiling cupboard and pulling it open.

"I'd have thought you could just snap your fingers and have things appear," Gelert said.

"I'm the king of the world, not a magician," the Elf-king said, rather irritably, though the irritation, Lee thought, was more for the cupboard than for Gelert. "Well, there's some bread here. Some wine, some sparkling water . . ."

He brought them out, with a board and a knife to cut the

bread. "I meant, you must be able to send servants out for that kind of thing," Gelert said.

"I don't have any servants here," Laurin said. "I keep this house as a retreat from all the roles my people try to push me into back in Aien Mhariseth. No scepter, no throne. The one aspect of royalty I keep here is the one they wish I didn't." He poured a glass of wine, a rich dark red, and held it out to Lee.

"I couldn't drink . . ." Lee said.

"You should. Our wine is very strengthening; this vintage comes from the slopes just to the south of Istelin'ru Semivh." He poured a small crystal bowl of it for Gelert; then he poured his own glass and held it to the afternoon light coming in the valleyward windows. "Welcome to my hearth," he said. "For however long it's mine . . ."

They drank. "Dierrich said that," Lee said. "And later I heard her imply she wasn't happy about it . . ."

"Nor will the rest of her followers have been, and I'm sure they're going to let us know about it when they get here shortly," the Elf-king said. "Unless we can present them with a *fait accompli*."

Lee drank a little more of the wine, trying to keep her composure in the face of the fear she now saw growing, from moment to moment, in the Elf-king's eyes. "What is it you intend us to accomplish? You said 'the destruction of your world' . . . but you had to be speaking figuratively."

Slowly he shook his head. "Lee," he said. "May I call you Lee?"

She nodded.

"My world has to change," he said. "It can't stay the way it is. With its connivance, in a way, my people have created a situation over the millennia that has caused the people of the other worlds to hate us. In other times, when we had little congress with other worlds, or when their technologies were insufficient to destroy us, or each other, wholesale, this would have made less difference. Now it has to become different . . . not just because the anger and greed of mortals can destroy us, but because it can destroy them, too. All of them—everything that is."

He drank his wine and looked down into the glass. "For many years I looked for a solution . . . then, after we discovered Terra, I looked much more urgently. Finally, it came to me, a decade or so ago. As *I* go," he said, "so go my people. So goes my world. If I could become mortal . . . then so would they. The danger would be defused."

Lee drank a sip more of her wine. "They would not," she said, "be very happy with that idea."

She watched him carefully. He lifted his gaze to meet hers, as if knowing what she wanted to See. "Not at all," Laurin said. "I knew that. So I was cautious, sharing the idea with no one for a long time. Then I erred grievously by sharing it with Dierrich. She wasn't anywhere near my level of mastery; she couldn't feel the ache at the heart of the world. Or its ambivalence, which may yet trip us up." He turned the glass in his hands, staring down into it again.

Gelert had finished his wine and was now lying near Lee, his nose working, as intent on the Elf-king as she was. "All universes," the Elf-king said, "share their most basic qualities with all the others, if only in the potential that those qualities might come to fruit in one world or another. All worlds have the seeds of our immortality in them, dormant . . . or errupting in certain special circumstances. So it stands to reason that we in Alfheim have, buried in ourselves, the seeds of mortality . . . for those who can See them."

He looked at Lee. "You Saw that in me," he said. "That night in Perdu; you saw dimly, and would have Seen clearly, exactly what someone needed to see, exactly what I had been seeking. At first I was horrified. I thought the change might happen right there, before I was prepared, when I was in the wrong place."

Lee opened her mouth and closed it again, uncertain of what to say. "Where's the right place?" Gelert said.

"The rose garden," the Elf-king said.

"What, back at Aien Mhariseth?" Gelert said.

"No. We'd never get near that one now; they're certainly guarding it. But some of those roses are preserved here. And since we're still in Alfheim, at the center of the worlds, your Sight of me as mortal, with my consent, becomes enactment—it would write mortality into Alfheim's structure; the change, experienced in my own body and soul, will change everything else." His smile was wry, and also frightened. "A certain irony there, that to save my universe I have to give up what gives me power over it. But I can't do that by myself. I need you."

"Oh, my God," Lee said, and sat there in shock.

"What would have happened if she'd finished Seeing you in New York?" Gelert said.

"Nothing useful," the Elf-king said. "Earth isn't a coreworld. I left there in fear—most of it Alfheim's: my world still fears this change, though it knows it needs it." He turned to Lee again. "After that I intended to approach you privately, broach the subject with you over time, give you time to get used to the concept. But events began to move too quickly, both in your world and mine; events forced my hand." His smile was grim. "Was Alfheim trying to sabotage my intentions, both in my own world and indirectly in yours? Could be. I did what I could to try to direct you toward enough power to protect you. My own people, my own world, resisted that. They couldn't keep you out of Alfheim, because I wanted you there. But you couldn't see the roses at Istelin'ru Semivh, no matter how much I wanted you to;

Dierrich and her party made common cause with all the others who fear what I had in mind, to prevent it."

"It wasn't just blocking Lee's Sight that they tried," Gelert said. "They got a little more personal than that. Twice."

"Yes. The first time, because they suspected Lee might be able to See what was going on . . . the second time, because they were certain she could." He turned to Lee. "By the second time, you'd already proved that you at least had a chance of being able to do what I had in mind; Seeing the reality beneath things native to Alfheim. When the second attempt failed, they decided the simplest thing to do was ship you back home and deal with me separately when I arrived."

"I'd say they underestimated you," Gelert said.

"They always have. But this time they won't. This time I've killed too many people who have too many powerful friends, others who think they could command mastery more to our people's advantage than I've been doing. Though Dierrich's gone, there's no point in trying to go back to Aien Mhariseth: it'll be too well guarded now. But we can force the issue here. If we have time. If you agree." He put the glass down, gazed into her eyes. "I ask you to look at me now, Lee, here where my power's strongest. See me as mortal, *now,* quickly. See it, and save my people!"

Lee gulped, and put her wineglass down. "If I *See* it incorrectly—or too strongly—you might die."

His gaze didn't waver. "That's a possibility I've been considering for a good long while," he said. "But one life for eleven universes? It doesn't seem like too bad a bargain."

The look in his eyes seized Lee by the heart, but possibly had the wrong effect. It made him the being Lee least wanted to see die in all eleven worlds, or however many more. *I won't do it. I won't be his executioner!*

And then she paused. *Is this Alfheim's ambivalence?* Lee thought. *Or mine?* . . .

A sudden faint sound from outside brought all their heads up.

"Gunfire," Gelert said. "They're here."

The Elf-king looked at Lee.

Her heart was hammering inside her.

I am just a tool to this creature, something said inside her. *A tool to be used to a purpose.*

The answer felt like it took an eternity coming back. *And if the purpose is worthwhile,* Lee thought, *what's so damned bad about being a tool—the right tool for the job? It's how Justice uses me, after all—*

She got up. "If the world's got to be changed," Lee said, "then we'd better get on with it. What do we do?"

"Outside," he said.

They hurried out the patio doors. The sound of small-arms fire was louder. "Someone's shooting at the gate," the Elf-king said. "It'll hold . . . at which time they'll try something more assertive. Come on—" He headed toward the hillside.

Lee and Gelert followed him. "Now," Lee said, "I'm not sorry I said a big soppy goodbye after all. See all the time I've saved?"

"Pragmatist," was all Gelert said. He looked back down past the house. "It's starting," he said.

Lee looked out into the thundery day. Past the mountains, Ellay now lay looking scratchy and scarred, a hatchmarked cicatrix on the dusty earth, livid in the threatening light. And the weather off to the west had started turning abruptly ugly. She'd seen it do this before, sometimes, when the Santa Ana was blowing against bad weather out on the sea. The clouds would roll up, piling against the resistant wind, higher and higher, like some insubstantial mountain range; and sooner or later the wind would blow itself out. Sooner or later those clouds would come rolling across the land with the lightning crashing amongst them, and unless the conditions were right for rain to follow fast, there would be brushfires in the hills.

Ahead of them, the Elf-king paused, looked westward, nodded. "Changing the world doesn't look to you the way it does to me, does it," he said. He sounded most unnerved. "I never thought you would find this so easy. As if you think it's something you should be doing all the time."

"For the better, yes!" Lee said.

"But the worse still happens—"

To a small extent Lee's Sight was on her now, unsummoned, and she knew better than to reject such insights as came to her now. "Laurin, listen to me. Alfheim's going to use you as it can to keep things the way they are. It's self-preservation, for a universe, the same way it is for a mind: to keep itself the way it is, to keep things running the way they are . . . even when that way is the *wrong* way—toxic, or doomed. Your world wants you to be the Devil it knows! You can't let it do that. You have to make a choice; who's running this place, really? Who's King here: the Elf, or Alfheim?"

He looked at her as if she'd struck him across the face—white, staggered. "So long we've believed, we've been taught, they were the same . . ."

"So long things have been going to Hell in a handbasket," Lee said. "We may have a few minutes yet to change that."

Laurin looked at Lee rather narrowly. "I hadn't seen your role in this as being quite so—proactive."

"You hadn't seen yourself as being quite so out of control, you mean," Lee said. "Sorry about that. But the moment's on us, and we don't have a lot of time now to argue roles. I See the way through. You have the power. Let's get busy. What do you need to do?"

He turned toward the hillside. From the far side of the gates, a faint hubbub of voices could be heard. The Elf-king turned away from them, looked up the hill.

"First," he said. "I'll see these again before I die, no matter what they do."

Lee watched him, uncomprehending.

There on the hillside, the sunset began to spread. Or rather, it was a light like a sunset's, for to the west the sky was all leaden, except where it was beginning to be lashed with lurid fire. There, though, the spaces between the paths now darkened as if with coast fog or cloud—an indistinct shadowiness at first, then something more solid; and in that darkness, which started to gather itself slowly together in shadowy leaf and branch like growing things, light began to flower, coming out gradually, like stars. Mostly it was a red light, growing thicker in every shrub of shadow, glowing, like coals breathed on, brighter where the Elf-king turned to look. But the coals burned peach and yellow and white as well, brighter every moment. Farther up, the effect was more like a blanket of light against the hill, a mist-veiled rosy brilliance massed and clustered. But here the points of radiance were close enough to be individual, red stars and golden ones and white ones, fierce-burning and distinct.

They drew Lee. They would have drawn any living thing. Lee stepped close to the nearest rosebush and held out her hand to one of the roses, felt the heat of it—the power of desire bound into the bloom, like blood blazing in the heart; turned to another and leaned down, with tears in her eyes from the scent and the blinding light, to bathe her face in the cool white fire of innocence. She stood upright again, looking around her, rubbing the pain out of her eyes to take it all in—this vast chorus of virtues, large and small, preserved here for how long?—all hidden in plain sight, burning in the hills above where her home would have been were it in this world, and never once suspected by the Alfen here . . . or by her own world, when sometimes, at twilight, the power of the roses burst the barriers between the worlds and shone briefly through.

Laurin was watching her, and the pain was in his eyes, too. "All the things," the Elf-king said, "everything that was worth keeping of what we were; all the things I would have preserved, if I could, through the change; all here." He looked around him. "It was wrong of me to do this. But I couldn't help it."

"And to think they told me it wasn't real . . ." Lee said.

"They always wished it wasn't," Laurin said. "But they couldn't stop my ancestor from making that first garden, either. He insisted on reminding them of what they were . . . and of where his power lay, in defining them as he defined himself. And they couldn't stop him from manifesting that power just as he pleased."

He saw her shocked look. "Yes, of course it was real once," he said. "Here and there, versions of the story persist, though they tried to wipe them out. Once upon a time, very long ago, some of us thought we might be able to coexist with humans. It was my direct ancestor, the one who first made that garden, who let humans into it; that place where my people's uniquenesses were cultivated, revealed, as these are. And the humans didn't care for what they saw. They destroyed that place." He looked around him in sorrow. "His successor, another of my ancestors, took the lesson and started the work of closing Alfheim off to mortals. It took a long while. Partly they used the rings, the 'made gates,' to reverse-engineer our space and stop every place from becoming a door to every place. Partly they used men's own mortality against them, as a tool to forgetfulness. Even in the space of one lifetime, humans forget things so quickly . . ."

He looked around at the roses. "But our own memory of those first disasters, where our species met and wounded one another most intimately, wouldn't go away; and what the Elf-kings remember, their world can't forget. The light of that first old garden still seeps through the gates of twilight and dawn, which my latter forefathers forgot to include in the curse." He shook his head, laughing helplessly. "Alfheim's memory is so powerful that sometimes the light seeps right through into other worlds. I've even seen it in Ellay. Plan how you may, every spell has loopholes.—But the stricture against planting another such garden in that place remains. The story says that should it happen, the humans would destroy not just that, but our whole world . . ."

"But you made this one anyway," Lee said, looking around her in wonder.

"One has to put one's love, one's power, somewhere," Laurin said. "Or it dies." The sorrow in his voice tore her. "That old Elf-king, who loved his people's virtues so, and the flowers he made of them—the King who was so sure of the virtues of humans—he was my direct ancestor, as I said. Most Alfen think he was a fool; deluded by too much kindliness, too much confidence in the good intentions of mere mortals. But I would always think about him, when I was younger. I would think, 'Maybe he wasn't so far wrong. How can it be bad to put your love somewhere that people can see it? How can it be bad to preserve what you love?' And when I became Elf-king, and took possession of the house here, I couldn't resist. These hills were so like the country around Aien Mhariseth—what I always longed for when I was young, and couldn't have. I thought, 'Just a small garden, in exile . . . in his memory, remembering how he tried to make it work between my people and the humans of the other worlds. How could that hurt?' "

He looked around him like a man who has been denying a fatal disease for a long time, but now is brought face to face with it. "I discovered how my ancestor had made the roses first. I made them again. My will kept them secret, even from my own people, for a long time. But they found out, and began to plot my overthrow. I never thought that re-creating the garden *here* would bring Alfheim's doom . . ."

Lee reached out to another of the flowers, felt the heat of it, and felt the blossom shivering with Laurin's fear. "What's happening to your people isn't because of you," she said. "It's their nature."

"The two are the same thing," the Elf-king said, "close enough. What I am, they become. That's what they've made of me, what our world has made of me, what I was bred to be, over all this time. As I go, they go. And I can't go where they need to go if they're going to survive . . ."

He looked at her. And Lee Saw his thought, the thing he couldn't say: *Not by myself, at least.*

The sound of something being smashed against the gates started to racket around in the space below the hillside. "Not much time, Lee," Gelert said: and his voice was shaking. The sound of it shocked her—not from its unfamiliarity, but because she felt the same way; as if everything was shifting under her feet, as if time was running out not just for them, but for everything else as well. This was what she had felt coming ever since she and Gelert turned poor dil'Sorden's casework in—the sense of something massive, catastrophic, coming closer and closer, ready to roll over them all like the clouds piling up out over the sea, leaden, towering, full of final threat. *We're going to die,* she thought. *They'll take their King and kill him; they'll kill us, too.*

But there was more to it than that. *Can a whole world be afraid?* she thought. *Can a universe have a soul, and feel terror? Or desire? Even if the world all around us isn't strictly his universe—*this *part of it is. All the parts are parts of all the whole; every spot is every other spot, no matter how they may have reverse-engineered this space . . .*

The congruencies made her mind whirl as she stood there among the roses that burned fierce in the growing darkness, defying the ban against their visibility this one last time, while the being who had planted and nurtured them with his will, and hidden them, and held them dear, stood there gazing into the darkness, waiting for the end.

Not just the fear of one universe, Lee thought. *They all touch, here. It's the fear of* all *of them. If this place is part of the most central of universes—because* he's *here—then where better for a universe's soul to be, its heart? And now it's afraid, they're all afraid, of what's about to happen.*

If he dies . . . then his people and his world die. As his people and world go . . . sooner or later, we go too, and our worlds with us. How can the rest of the worlds not react to something like that . . . feel the fear as he feels it, as we feel it? . . .

But there Lee stopped. It wasn't just feeling that was required of her: not just sharing that desperate desire for self-preservation. To do Laurin any good, she would have to see through the appearance to the reality, even here, at the heart of things, at the center of the universe most devoted to hiding its heart, to keep it from being hurt as it was hurt once before; on seeing through the Elves, right down to the individual realities; on seeing not just through the Elves, but through the Elf.

She looked down at her shaking hands, and saw something that shocked her; some of their wrinkles were fading. They looked younger than they had.

Lee put one hand to her face . . . and stopped, feeling the difference. *This is what this world offers you if you'll just back off now,* Lee thought. *The bribe. The same one it offered the Elves. And they took it, and got used to taking it . . . so used to it that the thought of giving it up looks like death to them. It's not this world's fault; it's too malleable to human desires. Who* wouldn't *want to be young and beautiful forever? You'd have to be crazy to walk away from something like that. And the Alfen didn't. So the world keeps them that way . . . and they keep* the world keeping them that way.

It would keep me that way too, if I stayed here . . .

But Lee pushed the thought away, with the help of the crashing noise coming from the gates down below. "Laurin," she said. "Will you give it up? All of it?"

"To save all this?" he said, almost too low to be heard. "To save everything? You know I'd die to do that."

"It may take more."

He looked at Lee, shocked, uncomprehending. "Dying is easy," she said. "Living, and being completely known, that's hard. That's what has to happen." She swallowed hard; she wasn't sure what was going to happen next. "The beauty," she said, "the immortality. They're what's going to kill your people. And what they'd rather die than lose."

"Yes," he said.

"But if you lose them—If you throw them away—"

"*How can I do that?* I don't know how—"

"It's not just my Sight you need," Lee said, "You have to see *yourself* as mortal, too. That's how it goes in court. I See . . . then you accept it as the truth. It's not something that's done to you. *You* choose."

He stared at her. Was it hope, or anger, starting now to rise in his eyes? In this light, as the roses dimmed with his fear, Lee couldn't clearly see. *But that's the problem. I can't rely on them for illumination now. It's my own Sight that's going to have to show me the way.*

"Well?" Lee said.

Standing there in the dimming fire of the roses, for just a moment he looked at her, and without warning Lee Saw him, Saw right to the heart of him—the heart of a man alone, afraid, and uncertain what to do; just a man, and mortal, the uncanny Alfen beauty at last irrelevant. Suddenly she realized that for him, at least, mortality lay not in death or the lack of it, but in not knowing what to do, not knowing what was going to happen afterward, when "afterward" was forever: the loss of control, not just for a lifetime, but for eternity. The concept of the surrender of that certainty was there, too . . . but could he manage it? As she looked at him, he actually covered his face with one hand, hiding his eyes. Part of him was resisting, even now. *He can't help it,* Lee thought. *This world has its own ideas about self-preservation . . . even if they're erroneous. It'll keep him the way it's kept him all these centuries, even though he dies of it; even though it dies of it . . .*

"Well?" she said again.

He had no answer for her; only, as he uncovered his eyes, a stricken, pleading look; a whole species looking through one entity's eyes, beauty and immortality pleading just to be left the way they were, left alone. But that look wasn't all Lee had to go on. Before he had covered his eyes, his will had looked out first.

"I'll take that as a yes," Lee said, and closed her eyes to See better.

"What?"

The crashing noise came up from the gates again, a big ruinous sound: explosives, perhaps. Lee ignored it. Equally the cry of anguish that went up from just a few feet away was meant to distract her; she refused to let it do so. Lee looked at this man with all the concentration her training had taught her, looked at him as fiercely as she had looked at dil'Sorden's dying soul, or at any human being that had ever stood in the dock before her. Under her gaze he writhed and cried out, at first just in his own pain, desperate against the beginning of a final fate more terrible than any mere sacrifice by death.

This was where we left off, she thought. *This is where it started: and now I finish it. Or it finishes me.*

The shouting got louder, started to turn into screaming. It wasn't just the Elf-king's pain, now, not just his fear or anguish, but that of all the others native to this world, shaped by it and by the needs they'd learned from it. Desperate, their universe was crying out to them in their own bodies and souls, warning them of the gift about to be withdrawn from them by the stranger, the attacking enemy. Once more they were being violated from outside their world, once more the things that made them uniquely themselves were about to be stolen from them by the ephemerals. *Look at them!* the song warned. *They are deedless and cripple, their life is the length of a dream; how little and valueless a thing is that life, laid by yours—ineffectual, small;—*

No! Lee cried inwardly, while in her the Sight fought with the writhing painful appearance that now began to flow over everything like early morning fog, twisting what it touched—twisting the man who fell to his knees not far from her, hiding his face, his head in his arms, unable to bear what he was beginning to see; twisting Gelert, so that he howled in pain and betrayal and crouched down among the cloudy dark shapes of the great rosebushes, in which the fire of the roses now began to be smothered in that twisting darkness like flame in the heart of smoke. It was reaching out to her now, that darkness, smothering, furious, intent on killing her vision. But, *Sorry,* Lee said inside her; *I answer to a higher authority. You may be a universe, but that's all you are; and the Worlds were made for us, not we for them!*

The darkness flowed all around her, but Lee turned her mind from it, refusing again to be distracted. There was other business. Somewhere here, not far away, a man on his knees had dropped to hands and knees, moaning in pain and fury, hands clenched full of dirt. Which one was the master now, him or his world, was in doubt, and in the balance. *But the Balance is Hers,* Lee thought. *And mine*— She groped toward the Elf-king through the smoky uncertainty, reminding herself that this one was no different in its way than the uncertainties she dealt with every day at a crime scene, the irrationalities of the physical universe trying to blur the path to the truth, but always destined to fail if the practitioner remembered What she worked for, and kept her intention.

Lee's surroundings, in contact with the heart of that crouching figure, were intent on her, too. The smoke began to give way to flame, slow now, but scorching. Soon the true brushfire would get loose, the illusion against which even Lee would have no defense for long. *No use playing the extinguisher at the top of the flame,* she thought; *go low, go to the source, or nowhere.* But she was going to have to do her work differently here. This world was not quite the largely insensate kind of universe the other worlds had become, malleable in the physical sense but passive in the moral one; certainly not as horribly passive as the newfound world had become. *Poor Terra!* Lee thought, though this was a new mode of thought for her, to be sorry for a whole world as if it was a drug addict or a kitten someone had tried to drown, damaged from the start and doomed to a sorry fate unless someone was kind to it. *If this is a trend, we have to stop it. Who'd want to* live *in a world like that?*

A long red line of ember ran along the hillcrest above her. *Which is going to prove more real, now?* she thought, watching it run down toward her from the crest of the hill, unnatural but alive, full of fury—his fury. *Or what's been buried in him for a long time, knowing this moment would come. Hell of one kind or another: but I've been through that already, this past week!*

The fire came plunging down the hillside like a rockfall. Lee watched it come, and Saw it to be unreal, the world's fear speaking through the Elf-king's power. Lee stood her ground, and her Sight into Laurin told her what to do. She looked up into the fire and it splashed away to either side of her, as the rocks had fallen away from the Elf-king when Dierrich tried to call the mountain down on top of him. Here, through him, she had access to the same power he had been using, the same certainty of mastery—and even more, because the roses were here, the fire of his irrational and un-conditional love for them burning fierce in them. *A lot of power here,* Lee thought, as she started to feel the earth rumble under her feet. *Huge amounts. But still not quite enough—*

The world was becoming really frightened. A sharp clattering heralded the rocks starting to fall down the hill, the world using the oldest weapon the Ellay basin afforded it. *No time for that now,* Lee thought, and laid herself fully open, not to Alfheim, but to something deeper, something stronger. *Justice here present,* she thought, *be in me now, see the truth I See, and make Truth manifest!*

Swift and terrible, here at the center of things, more powerful than in the outer universes, without hesitation, unmitigated, She came . . . not merely personified, and not alone. Lee held herself upright in the blast of light and imagery that followed—air that cut like swords, and was shadowed by something more central than mere Justice, mere Death; a transformed form of both, Entropy absorbed into Godhead, redeemed and invincible. That conjunct Power looked at the Elf-king through Lee . . . and hesitated.

In this moment, symbol was everything Lee reached out for one of the roses, plucked it from the bush, and clenched her fist on it until the white of its light was stained red with her blood.

Give him the gift he seeks!

And the Power descended on him, and did her bidding.

⁂

She saw, in that first instant, what *he* saw: saw it too intimately, because of her Sight . . . but she stayed with the vision, Saw it completely, as if from a god's point of view: so that she had to cry, with her own world's MacIlwain, in anguished acceptance, "I am become the Lady, the Creator of worlds . . . !"

And then she could only crouch down and wonder in terror, *what have I turned loose!*—as a darkness reared up above her, wavering, perhaps a man, perhaps not; and she thought of that commcall long ago, that moment echoing this one in essence if not in reality. *And what about the roses?* the voice had asked her, holding itself even because of its own fear, a flicker-vision of this moment, of terror at becoming the shadow that would someday drown everything in the final blackness and cold—

But the fire of the roses was still around them, and would not be drowned. Or rather, the darkness knew and loved them too well to allow it. All around them the immensities yawned, a rushing torrent of form dissolved in formlessness, a storm of potential with that towering shape at its heart—struggling with the torrent, thrusting against it, the sword's edge of power cleaving through. There was still something of human form about the one who wielded the sword of will, though how long he could keep that, Lee had no idea. Eleven worlds' worth of force battered at the shape and the will that reached out, reached inward to grapple with the heart of the heart of the worlds. Alfheim's core shrieked like a world dying as he gripped it, thrashed and tried to tear itself to shreds in rejection of the traitor Elf who had willingly made Death part of him. But in his own way, he *was* Alfheim's core, sensate as the world was not. It had always been subject to him; now, scream though it might, blacken its sun and kill its stars though it might, he was its ruler still. Lee could feel that terrible resolve gaining ground, unrelenting, unremitting, as he reached in and in to the power that even before he had possessed only in shadow, etiolated and incomplete. Now he was complete; everything else would follow.

. . . if he could only hang on! For the world kept fighting. Lee, staring into the chaos tumbling around them, could See—or hear, she hardly knew which—the desperate, wretched scream of Alfheim itself as it found voice. *I kept you immortal, I kept you beautiful, it would have lasted forever, why are you throwing it away?!* She covered her eyes, weeping for the world's pain; but that still couldn't stop the Sight.

Because it was never meant to stay that way, his answer came, as he kept reaching into the heart of the violent maelstrom, feeling for the very center, which was his very center as well. *Because this should have happened a long time ago, if something hadn't gone wrong, if the pain of the rotation hadn't made the world feel it was destroying itself. Because if it doesn't happen now,* everything *begins to die a death beyond anything mere entropy would have had in store. Because—*

—and he found and grasped the final core, the heart of the sheaf of worlds.

Lee felt him find it. Even through the paroxysm of despair and rage and terror that Alfheim was suffering, nothing could have kept her from feeling it. As his hand closed around the inmost heart of his world, Lee felt it close around hers; and along with Alfheim, and all the other worlds, and all the other lives in all the worlds, she bent double and clutched herself and screamed *No!*

But yes, he said. *At last, yes!*

And then he tore the core of the sheaf apart.

At least that was what it felt like. The pain was unbearable, so awful that the Worlds stopped screaming, and a silence of utter torment fell such as had not been heard for aeons. But Lee, transfixed by the agony equally with all the rest of creation, at least had some inkling of what was happening; and the pain didn't blind her. Indeed, she wondered if anything would ever be able to blind her after what she Saw now, what she could not in any way have prevented herself from Seeing.

It seemed to him as if he was working with his hands, and therefore Lee Saw it so—though what forces he was applying to the blazing core of light he held, she couldn't imagine. All eleven universes' energy, all eleven universes' matter, all grasped in one mind and concentrated in one place, was a concept incomprehensible enough to her. She understood even less why, as he concentrated his will upon it, the sheaf should lose that appearance of a billion billion suns crushed together, and suddenly become transparent, hardly there, a bubble iridescent not with light but with probability.

Until the bubble burst, burst outward, and became not one, but eleven, commingling, interpenetrating, all their surfaces swirling with urgent brilliance . . .

. . . and in a vast and deafening tumult that would have been a cry equally of terror and deliverance, each of those eleven became eleven more, and their surfaces swirled in turn, power ready to be unleashed—

Yes, he said. *Be.*

In a silent roar of light, they burst into darkness, and Lee, and everything else, went with them.

But still she was not blind: still she Saw. She saw the new outrush of stars in the worlds just made, matter and energy in their old embrace of fire. But much more of her attention was for the old worlds, the ones that had been created by the first rotation of the sheaf's core. Theoretically she was still on a planet inside one of them. *Yes, well, theoretically . . .* Lee thought; for though she could see a hundred other universes' events beginning to unfold, she had no idea where she was, or whether she still even had a body to be anywhere in. Stars in plenty she could see around her, but she couldn't see anything of herself.

"You're not looking," he said.

His voice seemed to come from very near, and it was localized again, rather than feeling like gravity or some other universal force that spoke from inside your bones, or your heart. Lee looked around for him, and slowly realized that it was possible to look around; that she had knees, and was kneeling on them . . . which was a good thing, since if she'd been standing, she would certainly have fallen down by now. Lee blinked, and once more saw the darkness behind her eyes, which she'd thought she would never see again. And the stars dimmed through the thickening smoke of re-established being, and were not stars, but just roses, burning in the twilight . . .

"Just roses," she said, and then had to laugh rather weakly. " 'Just' . . . Gel?"

Not far away she heard the rustling as he staggered to his feet. "I'm here," he said. "Wherever 'here' is."

"I rotated the core," the Elf-king said. "Or actually, I took away what was stopping it from rotating. It finished doing what it wanted to do, aeons and aeons ago . . ."

Gelert got to his feet, shook himself, prepared to wince . . . then didn't. "Huh," he said. "My ears are better—"

Someone pushed open the patio door from the living space of the house, came out onto the deck and stared up the hillside at the three of them.

The Elf-king smiled slightly. "Come up," he said.

That first Alfen came up, followed by about ten others, singly; Alfen in ExAff livery, others in street clothes. All of them were carrying weapons. All of them came partway up the hill, then stopped, looking in confusion at Laurin. Lee looked at them in some slight confusion herself, for they didn't look quite right somehow. They were all good-looking enough people to be sure, but—

"Lord . . ." said the one who had led them out. *"Rai'Laurin . . ."*

"Well," Laurin said, "what is it?"

There was one of those long silences, and the Alfen all looked at each other, holding their guns as if they were sticks, awkward, suddenly useless. "Lord," said another, "we came to kill you."

"So I gathered," the Elf-king said. "Or to destroy this." He glanced around him at the glory of the roses, and from their light the Alfen actually flinched a little, as if they thought it might do them harm. "Well, what will you do now? Do you know what happened?"

"Rai'Laurin," another one said, "you changed the world. The worlds . . ." Some of them fell to their knees, looking at him with foreboding and terror.

Laurin shook his head. "The world changed itself," he said, "as it's wanted to do for a long time. Nothing stopped it, all this while, but us. If I changed anything, it was my

own heart. Now if you don't still want to kill me, maybe
you'd like to get up, and go home, and see how matters go
in Aien Mhariseth; help may be needed there. I'll follow
shortly."

Obedient, they got up, those who had been kneeling, and
they all turned to go. "And we'll need another mrinLauvrin," the Elf-king said. "Tell the Survivor Lords we'll con-
vene to choose one when I return."

The Alfen left. Some minutes after they passed the gates,
a silent cordon of smallcraft leapt up into the evening sky
and headed upward and eastward.

Lee stood there, trying to recover herself, and looking out
across the valley, toward the mountains and the sea. "It's
still beautiful," Lee said, looking out across the mountains.
"But beautiful differently . . ." That painful squeeze of the
heart was gone now; the mind and heart could rest comfortably in this landscape, instead of flinching from them and
returning, again and again, in obsessive desire to let that
beauty somehow rub off, sink in.

"That was because the core never rotated completely the
first time, when we were the only world," the Elf-king said.
"We were in the way. We were stuck, all of us resisting the
change; so it gave us what we wanted, and kept us the way
we were, refusing what was supposed to come next . . ."

"Supposed? Who supposes?"

He shrugged. "I just read the handwriting on the walls of
the Worlds," he said. "I don't pretend to be able to analyze
it. But what happened is what's been trying to happen for a
long time; the same kind of thing that Midgarth kept doing
again and again, in a small way, being born and dying and
being reborn, cyclically. I don't think it's going to do that
anymore, though. Now that the whole sheaf has finally rotated properly, Midgarth can settle down. No more Fimbul-
winters. When that world's people come home from this last

migration, they may find the Gods' chessmen in the grass again, one last time: but this time the Gods will be able to sit down and finish the game, and start a new one without the whole world having to start over from scratch." He smiled.

Before, Lee would have had trouble looking at that smile without having to hide her eyes, as if indeed a God were smiling it, blinding. He was still handsome, but he no longer wore that terrible beauty as if it was armor, or a weapon. "You've changed," she said.

"I'm mortal," he said. "I couldn't have done that by myself: and you were right . . . it took living, not dying. That was your gift . . ."

Slowly he came toward her. Before, the slow approach would have filled Lee with unease. Now, she felt a small smile of her own stirring. "You've shifted the whole nature of your people," she said. "A whole species reborn . . ."

"Not just ours," he said. "But when I first heard the word 'genocide,' I knew it had to have an opposite. I couldn't imagine what that would be. It took you to teach me that." He stood before her, now, and took her hand.

"You took a big risk," Lee said, "that I'd have the slightest idea what to do . . ."

"You took a bigger one," Laurin said. "But the myths told me to trust you. There's always a mortal woman—always one who willingly chooses the impossible, the unthinkable, and becomes the bride of infinity and the mother of universes. It was just a matter of finding the one who would say 'yes,' and not regret the choice . . ."

Lee wanted to glance away, embarrassed; but he wouldn't let her. "A lot of your people may be angry with you . . ." she said at last.

"Maybe not as angry as they would have been before. For everything is different, now. They'll still live long, long lives: maybe even longer than before the shift, who knows?

The lives of other humans, too, will be far longer now . . . for the gift that we were keeping to ourselves is going to be a lot more widely distributed now. So will others," he said, and smiled a harder-edged smile. "The transmission speed of fairy gold is now identical in all the worlds. ExTel and its ilk can use their armies for something else . . . if indeed their executives aren't distracted more or less completely from their business plans by what's happened to *them*."

"I want to go there . . ." Lee said.

"You're there now," said the Elf-king.

She and Gelert turned . . . and found that he was right. The gating which had been a strenuous business was now the matter of a moment. With Gelert, Lee looked westward. Lake Val San Fernando and to the souteast was there again. Yet—

"Are you sure?" Lee said. The vista below her *looked* like Ellay. All the streets seemed to be in the same places. But there was something—Lee would have said, "something wrong about it"; except that, emphatically, that wasn't it. There was something *right* about it. Yet the air did not look any cleaner. The sea didn't look any bluer. Traffic on the San Diego Freeway looked as backed up as ever . . . or perhaps that was just astonished drivers, stopped in their tracks by what had just happened to their world, and now standing around in the road, staring at each other, and their city, trying to figure out what had happened.

The Elf-king smiled. "It's made new," he said. "Though people are going to have trouble describing what's happened for a while. What are they going to say?" And he laughed; the first time Lee had ever heard him laugh for sheer amuse-

ment, no irony or fear about it. "That one afternoon, everything was going along as usual, and the next moment, the
world had become Paradise?" Now his grin became ironic,
and tinged with some sadness. "I don't think it's going to be
quite *that* good."

"No," Lee said.

"But as for you and me," Laurin said, "all the possibilities shift as well . . . if we can let go of our own pain."

Lee turned to him, surprised. *How could you tell—*

Because the vision you had, you passed to me, he said.
*How else could I have seen what to do with the worlds, ex-
cept with the gift of Seeing truth, and implementing it?*

But it's not what it was, she said. *Everything you've
done—*

We've done, he said.

She had to accept it. *It's all a wonder. A wonder beyond
wonders. The world has started over. All the worlds are new.
And there are a hundred more to explore . . .*

And every one of them is the core of its own sheaf, Laurin said. *The possibilities will only keep on unfolding. Every
world that's born now has the chance to make itself over, to
make itself more perfect, as soon as it's ready . . .*

"And so can you," the Elf-king said.

She looked at him without comprehension. "In the
myth," Laurin said, "the Elf-king steals the princess from
her lover, and brings her to rule over his people beside him.
Though perhaps that's an archetype that needs to be re-
worked somewhat."

"In the myth," Lee said, "she stops her people and the Elf-
king's from fighting by *agreeing* to rule his realm beside
him. 'And there she lives under the mountain yet, and is
young forever, and can never die . . . '" She looked at him
gently, and with some regret. "I think the archetype is working matters out for itself in a different direction, something a

little less simplistic . . . for my people, and for yours; and for us too. Because . . . I couldn't—" She stopped, frustrated. "I can't explain in words," Lee said at last. "Look—"

Lee had to stop and think for a moment how to do it. This was no longer Alfheim, or Alfheim as it had been. But the space was still nearly as malleable, and so Lee bent her will against it and showed it the way she wanted it to part. "Just a step this way," she said, and took his hand.

He took that step as she did, so that together they suddenly stood amid the short, harsh, summer-parched grasses that grew at the edge of her favorite vantage point, the topmost ridge of Topanga Canyon, where the old road down bent westward just so. There it all lay, the late-afternoon vista she had driven up here a hundred times to see—everything rose-golden with haze or smog; the glitter of distant glass and steel all softened in the saffron light, movement on streets and around buildings becoming remote and sweetly obscure; freeways streaming and shining, winding slowly down warm hillsides and pouring themselves in and out of the long stripes of shadow cast by downtown's brave towers. The soft, crumpled hills drowsily embraced the city, leaning back against a sky blue only in the east; and off westward, the molten sea and haze-thickened sky reflected one another, blazing cinnamon-gold in the afternoon, while the honey sun poured down on Our Lady of the Harbor, where the statue of Her stood huge on that precipice above Malibu, gazing down in silence on Her city—

The man beside her stood silent. Lee looked down at it all, and breathed out in longing and irrational pain, looking down into the light.

"That," she said. "How could I ever leave that? I love it too much, and the people in it. It's where I do my work; it's *why* I do my work. Without the threat to that, to the people I serve there, I'd never have done for the worlds what I did.

That drove me . . . and I couldn't leave it now. It'll need me more than ever."

"I understand you," Laurin said. "I loved this, too." He looked over his shoulder through the still-patent gate at the garden, still lingering in the shadows behind them. "It was unique, endangered, as I was endangered . . . and I loved the roses even more because of that. But now they're safe. Now the garden can bloom again in Aien Mhariseth, without fear; now the curse is lifted, and twilight becomes just one more time when the roses burn. Maybe the sweetness of the danger is gone. That may take me a while to get used to. . . . and yes, that's sad. It's more of a price than I ever thought I'd have to pay." He breathed out. "But it's worth it!"

After a moment, Lee nodded. "Yes, of course it is."

His smile was sorrowful, but edged with humor. "But you knew that already . . . better than I did, probably. And if we can't stand a little sadness, a little suffering, then we're not worth much as gods."

Lee glanced over into the lengthening afternoon, where God stood all golden in the light, Her arms raised in astonishment and joy at what She had made. "She's not the jealous type," she said, "but I'd still be careful how I talked . . ."

The Elf-king laughed. "She won't mind if you hold Her place until She gets used to the new shape of things," he said. "And Justice will still have plenty of work that needs to be done . . . for there's going to be more than the usual amount of confusion in all the worlds for a good while."

"As long as we're not out of a job," Gelert said.

"Oh, no," Laurin said. "Why should a world reborn necessarily imply perfection? We're all in for interesting times." He rubbed his face in a gesture that was the same as that of the man on his knees in the garden, but not quite as hopeless.

" 'We' . . ."

"I can't speak for others," Laurin said, "but you and I will have more work to do together. We're standing *in loco parentis,* and it seems likely enough that there'll be 'teething pains' among these worlds, spots where things have gone wrong and we'll have to intervene. Physicality has changed. For all I know, some of the laws of science, some physical laws, have changed, too. We may have to go off and do some tinkering with that, here and there."

"I'm hardly an expert—"

"Lee, we officiated at this transformation together; it's not work I can do alone. Meantime, all we can do is go on living life at one second per second, and see how things unfold, in the new worlds and the old ones."

"New worlds to explore . . ." Lee said.

"Yes," Laurin said. "Not just planets. Humanity will be busy; all the humanities will, from here to Xaihon, and beyond. And as for the rest of it : . ."

"We'll see how it works out," she said. "There are going to be a lot of things to sort out. God knows what the LAPD is going to make of this . . ."

"You mean your murder case?"

Lee laughed out loud. "I mean a city that doesn't entirely resemble the way it looked last night! They're going to need some explanations; so will the city government . . ."

"So will the UN&ME, I would imagine," said the Elf-king. "And the committee, when it reports, will find it has answers to all the wrong questions. Or most of them . . ."

"Not all my questions are answered, either," Lee said. "Omren dil'Sorden is still dead."

"Yes," Laurin said. "But look what his death gave birth to; and look how many won't die, now, because he did . . ."

There was no arguing with that.

"We all need to get back to work now," Laurin said. "It's going to take a while for us to get used to the new order of things, and to help others get used to it. For myself, I've been alone for a long time. Many centuries, alone with the truth, and the burden, and the fear. Now, at last, the burden and the fear are gone . . . and I'm alone no longer."

Lee looked at him silently for some moments. "Neither am I," she said at last.

He smiled at her, understanding completely; understanding, Lee thought, as probably no one else in the universes could. "And for the first time," said the Elf-king, "*I* have a partner."

He looked over at Gelert. "Assuming you can spare her occasionally, *madra*."

Gelert merely grinned at him, and then at Lee. "You think we'll need more office space?" he said.

"We'll handle those problems as we come to them," Lee said. "But right now our universes are going to need separate attention."

The Elf-king nodded. "I'll call if I need your help," he said. "I have your number."

Lee gave him a wry look, then leaned over and kissed him on the cheek.

"Later," she said.

⌖

She went home via LAX: not because she had to, for she could for this little while go anywhere, but to confirm a suspicion she had. She and Gelert walked under that great dome, and saw more than a few Alfen coming and going about their business, graceful and fair. "Look," she said.

"There *is* a resemblance," Gelert said, "isn't there . . ." For he saw it as she did: the look which had been on the Elf-king's face, and on those of many others of his folk, though well mixed with confusion, and sometimes with fear. Lee knew the fear would pass. And in the meantime, perhaps for the first time, she enjoyed the sight of them—of creatures no longer immortal in the way they had been, aloof, untouchable, and unconcerned. There was something different about them now.

"As he goes, so go his people," Lee said. And then she smiled, for that was the key to it. *They look like people now.* They were still an astonishingly beautiful species, but now that beauty didn't repel. They looked like life and death mattered to them, and as a result, the casual observer would no longer have an irrational desire to kill them.

It was probably going to take everyone involved a little while to get used to that. Humans were not going to be quite perfect either, not for a good while yet if ever, and humans could be as stubborn about distrusting sudden change as Elves.

And the humans . . . Lee looked at her hands; the palms, the backs. There did seem to be fewer wrinkles there . . . though now she had to think, *Are there really less of them* . . . *or do they just matter less?* But the inhabitants of all the other worlds had now gained a share of the innate beauty that Alfheim wore as a result of being the core world of the sheaf. *We're all cores now,* he had said. *Oh, there'll be trouble too: who knows what kind? But life is now more worth living, if more unpredictable, than ever* . . .

"I know that look," Gelert said. "Take your time. I'll catch a cab to the office."

He nosed her in the neck, once, wetly, then trotted off toward the doors.

Lee spent perhaps another half hour there, watching the people come and go, starting to learn the change in them. Then she went out to find where Gelert had parked the hov, paid the parking fee at the gate, and drove back toward the office, slowly, looking at the changes in the streets and the buildings and the faces of the people as she went, until finally the mental cataloging simply got too tiring. It would be not just years, but lifetimes, before people learned the full meaning of what had happened to their lives, their worlds. Everything was new, and would be for a long, long time. *Not quite the definition of Heaven,* Lee thought. *But close enough.*

Not far from the office, she stopped the hov, parked it, and got out to look north and east. Sunset was easing along, golden. The peppertrees planted along in front of the suburban frame housing here hung their trailing green cool and shady over the sidewalk as if nothing had happened at all. Lee lifted her gaze toward the hills, where they stood silhouetted against the deepening creamy blue of an Ellay city sky. There, without having to See, she saw the burning, all carmine, crimson and blood-color, glowing on the hills— the burning of the roses, like a light from within, no longer hidden but now in plain sight for any mortal; the token of immortality visiting itself on the world, just a little alien, but so young and glad and splendid that no one would be afraid of it for long.

The curse is broken, Lee thought, *and the time for being afraid of each other is over at last. Now, finally, we get to work and find out what life in the Worlds is about . . .*

She walked to the office, in silence, musing. The silence was a short-lived thing. When Lee got in and pushed the glass door open, Mass looked over the desk at her, and said, "Eight million commcalls, boss! You're not gonna leave here for *days*."

"Order me a pizza," Lee said, and headed past him into her office. "Order me three. And no anchovies!"

Before she even looked, she could tell that the wall between her office and Gelert's was down, by the blast of sound that hit her. It was Wagner again, the end of *Götter-*

dammerung—the world of the old Gods, crashing in fire and orchestral ruin about their heads. Gelert was sitting in the middle of his office floor, talking hard to someone on the comm; he flashed Lee a grin as she came in, and then turned his attention back to business. *Giving interviews already,* Lee thought, with some amusement. *And he's probably already in the process of dickering with someone about the price of an option on the true story of the End of the World.*

She turned to her desk, sat down . . . and then could do nothing for a few moments but gaze at it with the beginnings of tears in her eyes. On the goldstone of the desk, in a pool of light of its own making, lay a single white rose; and the rose burned. Even from a meter away, the cool fragrance of it reached Lee—and latent in the light of it, even to someone without the Sight, were a million second chances, and all possibility.

Behind her, in the music, the Rhine rose and washed the old world away. Lee looked at the rose for a long, long moment. Then, "Mass?" she said.

"They'll be here in ten minutes, boss."

"Not that. Get Matt on the comm for me, will you?"

"Sure thing."

Lee reached out to the white rose, picked it up. Its cool light welled through the flesh of her hands, so that they glowed; and its thorns, when she tried one against her thumb, were blunt.

When Lee looked up again, Matt was looking at her from the commwall. His expression was haggard, guilty, even a little frightened. "Lee—" he said, and faltered into silence.

"We need to talk," she said.

"About the case—" Matt said.

Lee took the longest breath of a lifetime, and let it out again. "No. Not about the case," she said. "Got time for dinner? I know a place where they do great fondue . . ."

About the Author

Diane Duane has been writing science fiction and fantasy for more than twenty years, in an assortment of formats—books, short stories, comics, television (both live-action and animated) and computer games. With her husband and frequent collaborator, Belfast-born novelist and TV writer Peter Morwood, she lives in Ireland in a peaceful rural townland forty miles south of Dublin. There, acting as the Owl Springs Partnership (http://www.owlsprings.com), the two of them pursue total galactic domination in company with their cats Mr. Squeak, Goodman and Beemer; their computers Felix, George, Calanda and Ryoh-ohki, an ever-growing crowd of characters, and (at last count) six hundred and twenty-four cookbooks.

FROM ACCLAIMED AUTHOR IAN IRVINE

THE VIEW FROM THE MIRROR SERIES

"Once there were three worlds, each with its own human race.
Then, fleeing from out of the void came a fourth race, the
Charon. Desperate, on the edge of extinction, they changed the
balance between the worlds forever..."

Book I: A Shadow on the Glass
(0-446-60984-6)

Book II: Tower on the Rift
(0-446-60985-4)

Book III: Dark is the Moon
(0-446-60986-2)

Book IV: The Way Between the Worlds
(0-446-60987-0)

"Compelling . . . stands out as a world-building labor of love."
—*Locus*

"Complex, well written . . . a tremendous depth of description."
—*Midwest Book Review*

"A great find! . . . Refreshing, complicated, and compelling."
—Kate Elliott, author of *King's Dragon*